'As ever, James writes beautifully, maintaining the pace
with short, punchy chapters. But it's his firm grasp of
the moral issues surrounding designer babies that makes
Perfect People so satisfying – and so unsettling'
Guardian

'Peter James's clever page-turner *Perfect People* focuses
not on the past but risks for the future'
The Times

'Now, his first stand alone novel since the extraordinary,
though completely deserved, success of the Roy Grace series
features all James' strengths, including his ability to capture a
sense of real horror in a very real world . . . This is very much
a novel about the preciousness of life, the randomness
of survival and, ultimately, humanity as we've
always known it'
Mirror

'Police procedural expert Peter James has spread his wings
with this thought-provoking adventure . . . A gripping
tale from the not-so-distant future'
Sun

'A surreal journey of ethics, science, and religion . . . a
blindingly hot read set at the edges of our reality and
indicative that Peter James can carve a thriller as tortuous
as the DNA Double-Helix – in a word, remarkable'

PERFECT PEOPLE

Peter James was educated at Charterhouse, then at film school. He lived in North America for a number of years, working as a screenwriter and film producer before returning to England. His novels, including the *Sunday Times* number one best-selling Roy Grace series, have been translated into thirty-six languages, with world sales of fifteen million copies. Three novels have been filmed. All his books reflect his deep interest in the world of the police, with whom he does in-depth research, as well as his fascination with science, medicine and the paranormal. He has also produced numerous films, including *The Merchant of Venice*, starring Al Pacino, Jeremy Irons and Joseph Fiennes. He divides his time between his homes in Notting Hill, London and near Brighton in Sussex.

Visit his website at www.peterjames.com.
Or follow him on Twitter @peterjamesuk
Or Facebook: http://www.facebook.com/peterjames.roygrace

By Peter James

The Roy Grace Series

DEAD SIMPLE   LOOKING GOOD DEAD
NOT DEAD ENOUGH   DEAD MAN'S FOOTSTEPS
DEAD TOMORROW   DEAD LIKE YOU
DEAD MAN'S GRIP   NOT DEAD YET
DEAD MAN'S TIME   WANT YOU DEAD
YOU ARE DEAD

Other Novels

DEAD LETTER DROP   ATOM BOMB ANGEL
BILLIONAIRE   POSSESSION   DREAMER
SWEET HEART   TWILIGHT   PROPHECY
ALCHEMIST   HOST   THE TRUTH
DENIAL   FAITH   PERFECT PEOPLE

Short Stories

A TWIST OF THE KNIFE

Children's Novel

GETTING WIRED!

Novella

THE PERFECT MURDER

PERFECT PEOPLE

PETER JAMES

PAN BOOKS

First published 2011 by Macmillan

This edition published 2012 by Pan Books
an imprint of Pan Macmillan
20 New Wharf Road, London N1 9RR
Associated companies throughout the world
www.panmacmillan.com

ISBN 978-1-5098-2312-3

1 3 5 7 9 8 6 4 2

A CIP catalogue record for this book is available from
the British Library.

Typeset by SetSystems Ltd, Saffron Walden, Essex
Printed and bound by CPI Group (UK) Ltd, Croydon, CR0 4YY

FOR TONY MULLIKEN,

TO WHOM I OWE SO MUCH.

1

Late on an April afternoon, thirty nautical miles east of Cape Cod, a wind-blown young couple with luggage and worried faces are standing on the helicopter deck of a converted cruise liner, gripping the handrail.

Both of them know it is too late for doubts.

The *Serendipity Rose* is forty years old, her dents and cracks and rivets caked in paint like make-up on an old tart's face. As she ploughs through the freshening sea, a Panamanian flag of convenience crackling from her stern, her single yellow funnel trails a ribbon of smoke that is shredded in seconds by the wind. Making just sufficient way to keep the stabilizers working, she's not in any hurry, she's not heading towards any destination. She's just meandering around safely beyond the twelve-nautical-mile limit of the territorial waters of the United States. Safely beyond the reaches of US federal law.

John Klaesson, in a fleece-lined jacket, chinos and leather yachting shoes, is in his mid-thirties and has about him the rugged air of a mountaineer or an explorer, rather than the academic he is. Six feet tall, lean and strong with short blond hair and gentle blue eyes behind small oval glasses, he has a good-looking, serious face, with resolute Nordic features and a light Californian tan.

His wife, Naomi, concentrating to keep her balance, is huddled up in a long camel coat over a jumper, jeans and crêpe-soled black suede boots. Her fair hair is styled in a fashionable mid-length blowsy cut, the tangled strands batting over her attractive face accentuating the slight tomboy look she has about her, although her complexion is considerably paler at the moment than normal.

Yards above their heads the helicopter that has just delivered them hovers, haemorrhaging oily fumes into the mad air, dragging its shadow across the superstructure of the ship like some big empty sack. And that's how John's feeling right now; like he's been tipped out of a sack. Head bowed against the din and the maelstrom, he puts out an arm, steadies his wife, grips her slender frame beneath the softness of her camel coat, feeling close to her, desperately close and protective.

And responsible.

The wind is blowing so hard he has to breathe in snatched gulps, the salt misting his glasses, the fumes parching his mouth and throat already arid with nerves. Strands of Naomi's hair flail his face, hard as whipcords. The deck drops away beneath him, then a moment later is rising, pressing up on his feet like an elevator floor, heaving his stomach up against his rib cage.

Through the thrashing of the rotors above him he can hear a scuffing noise. This is the first time he's been in a helicopter and after an hour of pitching and yawing through an Atlantic depression he's not keen to repeat the experience; he's feeling the queasiness you get from a bad funfair ride that swivels your brain one way on its axis, and your internal organs another. The fumes aren't helping, either. Nor is the strong reek of paint and boat varnish, and the deck vibrating beneath his feet.

Naomi's arm curls around his waist, squeezing him through the thick lining of his leather jacket. He has a pretty good idea what's going through her mind, because it's sure as hell going through his. This uncomfortable feeling of finality. Up until now it has all been just an idea, something they could walk away from at any point. But not any more. Looking at her he thinks, *I love you so much, Naomi darling. You're so brave. I think sometimes you are a lot braver than I am.*

The chopper slips sideways, the roar of the engine increasing, belly light winking, then it angles steeply away and clatters across the water, climbing sharply, abandoning them. For some moments John watches it, then his eyes drop towards the foaming grey ocean hissing with sea-horses, stretching far off towards an indistinct horizon.

'OK? Follow me, please.'

Ahead of them, the polite, very serious-looking Filipino in a white jumpsuit who came out to greet them and to take their bags is holding a door open.

Stepping over the lip of the companionway, they follow him inside and the door slams shut on the elements behind them. In the sudden quiet they see a chart of the ocean in a frame on the wall, feel the sudden warmth, smell the reek of paint and varnish even stronger in here. The floor thrums beneath them. Naomi squeezes John's hand. She's a lousy sailor, always has been – she gets sick on boating ponds – and today she can take nothing for it. No pills, no medication, she's going to have to tough this one out. John squeezes back, trying to comfort her, and trying to comfort himself.

Are we doing the right thing?

It's a question he has asked himself a thousand times. He's going to go on asking it for many years. All he can do is keep convincing Naomi and himself that yes, it is the right thing. That's all. Doing the right thing.

Really we are.

2

In the sales brochure for this floating clinic, the cabin that was to be their home for the next month had been grandly described as a *stateroom*. It was furnished with a king-size bed, a tiny sofa, two equally small armchairs and a round table, on which sat a bowl of fruit, crammed into a space the size of a small hotel room. High up in one corner, a television with bad interference was showing CNN news. President Obama was talking, half his words distorted by static.

There was a marbled bathroom that, although cramped, felt distinctly luxurious – or at any rate would have done, Naomi thought, if it stopped heaving around and she could stand up in it without having to hang on to something. She knelt to scoop up the contents of John's wash-bag, which were rolling round on the floor, then stood up rapidly, feeling a dizzying bout of nausea.

'Do you need a hand?' John asked.

She shook her head. Then, unbalanced by a sudden lurch, she tottered across the floor and sat down sharply on the bed, narrowly missing his computer. 'I think I have about four minutes left to unpack before I become violently seasick.'

'I'm feeling queasy, too,' John said. He glanced at a safety notice. There was a layout of the muster stations and a diagram showing how to put on a life jacket.

'Why don't you take a seasick pill?' she said. 'You're allowed.'

'If you're not allowed one, I'm not taking one. I'll suffer with you.'

'Martyr!' She turned her head, leaned forward and kissed him on the cheek, comforted by his warm, rough skin, and by the heady, musky smell of his cologne. Comforted by the sheer mental and physical strength he exuded. Watching movies, as a teenager, she'd always been attracted to strong, quietly intelligent men – the kind of father she would have liked to have had. When she had first seen John, eight years ago in a ski lift queue in Jackson Hole, Wyoming, he'd struck her as having those same qualities of good looks and inner strength.

Then she kissed him again. 'I love you, John.'

Looking into her eyes, which were sometimes green, sometimes brown, always filled with a sparkle and with an incredible trust, his heart ached, suddenly, for her. 'And I adore you, Naomi. I adore you and I admire you.'

She smiled wistfully. 'I admire you, too. Sometimes you have no idea how much.'

There was a comfortable silence between them for some moments. It had taken a long time after the death of Halley for things to be good between them again, and there had been many times during those first two really dark years when Naomi had feared their marriage was over.

He'd been a strong kid. They'd named him after the comet because John had said he was special, that kids like him came along pretty rarely, maybe once every seventy-five years – and probably not even as often as that. Neither of them had known that he was born with a time bomb inside him.

Naomi still kept his photograph in her handbag. It showed a three-year-old boy in dungarees, with floppy blond hair all tangled up, as if he had just crawled out of a tumble dryer, teasing the camera with a big grin that showed two of his front teeth missing – knocked out when he fell off a swing.

For a long time after Halley's death John had been unwilling – or unable – to grieve or to talk about it, and had simply buried himself in his work, his chess and his photography, going out for hours on end and in all weather with his camera, taking photographs of absolutely anything he saw, obsessively and aimlessly.

She had tried to get back into work. Through a friend in Los Angeles she'd been given a good temporary position in a PR office, but she'd quit after a couple of weeks, unable to concentrate. Without Halley, everything had seemed to her to be shallow and pointless.

Eventually they had both gone into therapy, which they had ended only a few months ago.

John said, 'How do you feel about—'

'Being here?'

'Yes. Now that we are actually here.'

A tray on the dresser containing a bottle of mineral water and two glasses slid several inches across the surface, then stopped.

'It suddenly seems very real. I feel nervous as hell. You?'

He stroked her hair tenderly. 'If at any point, honey, you want to stop—'

They had taken a huge bank loan to fund this, and had had to borrow another hundred and fifty thousand dollars on top of that, which Naomi's mother and older sister, Harriet, in England, had insisted on lending them. The money, four hundred thousand dollars in total, had already been paid over, and it was non-refundable.

'We made our decision,' she said. 'We have to move on. We don't have to—'

They were interrupted by a rap on the door and a voice saying, 'Housekeeping!'

The door opened and a short, pleasant-looking Filipino maid, dressed in a white jumpsuit and plimsolls, smiled at them. 'Welcome aboard, Dr and Mrs Klaesson. I'm Leah, I'm going to be your cabin stewardess. Is there anything I can get you?'

'We're both feeling pretty queasy,' John said. 'Is there anything my wife is allowed to take?'

'Oh sure – I get you something right away.'

'There is?' he said, surprised. 'I thought there was no medication—'

The maid closed the door, then less than a minute later reappeared with two pairs of wrist bands and two tiny patches. Pulling her cuffs back, she revealed she was wearing similar bands, and then she showed them the patch behind her ear. 'You wear these and you won't get sick,' she said, and showed the correct position for them.

Whether it was psychological or they really did work, Naomi couldn't be sure, but within minutes of the maid leaving she felt a little better. At least well enough to carry on unpacking. She stood up and stared for a moment out of one of the twin portholes at the darkening ocean. Then she turned away, the sight of the waves bringing her queasiness straight back.

John turned his attention again to his laptop. They had a rule when they travelled together: Naomi unpacked and John kept out of the way. He was the world's worst packer and an even worse unpacker. Naomi stared despairingly at the contents of his suitcase strewn all around him after his search for the adaptor. Some of his clothes were on the counterpane, some were tossed over an armchair and some lay on the floor. John peered closely at his screen, oblivious to the chaos he had caused around him.

Naomi grinned, scooping up a cluster of his ties, and shook her head. There wasn't any point in getting angry.

John fiddled with his new wristbands and touched the patch that he had stuck behind his ear, not feeling any appreciable change in his nausea. Trying to ignore the motion of the ship, he focused on the chess game he was playing with a man called Gus Santiano, whom he'd met in a chess chatroom, and who lived in Brisbane, Australia.

He had been playing with this man for the past couple of years. They'd never met outside of cyberspace and John didn't even know what his opponent looked like. The Aussie played mean chess, but recently he'd been taking longer and longer between moves, prolonging a hopeless position from which there was no possible coming back, for no other reason than sheer cussedness, and John, getting bored, was starting to think about finding a new opponent. Now the man had made yet another pointless move.

'Sod you, Mr Santiano.'

John had the man in check – he was a queen, both bishops and a rook down, he didn't have a prayer – so why the hell not just resign and have done with it? He typed out an email suggesting this, then connected his cellphone to his computer to send it. But there was no carrier signal.

Too far out to sea, he realized. There was a phone by the bed that had a satellite link to the mainland, but at nine dollars a minute, according to the instruction tag, it was too expensive. Gus Santiano would just have to wait in suspense.

He closed the chess file, and opened his email inbox to start working through the dozens of messages he'd downloaded this morning but had not yet had a chance to read, feeling panicky about how he was going to send and receive mail if they were going to remain out of cellphone range for the next month. At the University of Southern California, where he was based and ran his research laboratory, he received an average of one hundred and fifty emails a day. Today's intake was closer to two hundred.

'This is amazing, darling! Do you remember reading this?'

John looked up and saw she had the brochure open. 'I was going to read it again in a minute.'

'They have only twenty private cabins for *clients*. That's a nice euphemism. Nice to know we're *clients*, not *patients*.' She read on. 'The ship used to take five hundred passengers, now the two main decks where the cabins were are completely taken up with computers. They have *five hundred* supercomputers on board! That's awesome! Why do they need so much computing power?'

'Genetics requires massive number crunching. That's part of what we're paying for. Let me see.'

She handed him the brochure. He looked at a photograph of a long, narrow bank of blue computer casings, with a solitary technician dressed in white, checking something on a monitor. Then he flicked to the start of the brochure, and stared at the photograph he recognized instantly from the scientist's website, from the interviews with him on television and from the numerous pictures of him that had appeared both in the scientific and the popular press. Then, although he knew most of it already, he scanned the scientist's biography.

Dr Leo Dettore had been a child prodigy. Graduating

9

magna cum laude in biology from MIT at sixteen, he then did a combined PhD MD at Stanford University, followed by biotechnology postdoctoral research at USC and then the Pasteur Institute in France, before identifying and patenting a modification of a crucial enzyme that allowed efficient high-fidelity replication of genes that made the polymerase chain reaction obsolete, and, which made him a billionaire, and for which he was made a MacArthur Fellow, and offered a Nobel Prize he would not accept, upsetting the scientific community by saying he believed all prizes were tarnished by politics.

The maverick geneticist had further upset the medical establishment by being one of the first people to start patenting human genes, and was actively battling the legislation that had subsequently reversed patents on them.

Leo Dettore was among the richest scientists in the world at this moment, and arguably the most controversial. Pilloried by religious leaders across the United States and many other countries, disbarred from practising medicine in the United States after he had publicly admitted to genetic experiments on embryos that had subsequently gone to term, he was unshakeable in his beliefs.

And he was knocking on their cabin door.

3

Naomi opened the door to be greeted by a tall man holding a manila envelope and wearing the white jumpsuit and plimsolls that seemed to be the ship's standard uniform. Recognizing him instantly, John stood up.

He was surprised at just how imposing the geneticist was in the flesh, far taller than he had imagined, a good head higher than himself, six-foot-six at least. He recognized the voice also, the disarming but assertive Southern Californian accent, from the phone conversations they had had in recent months.

'Dr Klaesson? Mrs Klaesson? I'm Leo Dettore. Hope I'm not disturbing you folks!'

The man to whom they had handed over just about every cent they had in the world, plus one hundred and fifty thousand dollars they didn't, gave Naomi's hand a firm, unhurried shake, fixing her eyes with his own, which were a soft grey colour, sharp and alert and sparkling with warmth. She mustered a smile back, shooting a fleeting, horrified glance at the mess of clothes all around John, desperately wishing she'd had a chance to tidy up. 'No, you're not disturbing us at all. Come in,' she said.

'Just wanted to swing by and introduce myself, and give you a bunch of stuff to read.' The geneticist had to duck his head as he entered the cabin. 'Great to meet you in person at last, Dr Klaesson.'

'And you too, Dr Dettore.'

Dettore's grip was strong, taking charge of the handshake the way he clearly took charge of everything else. John felt a moment of awkwardness between them. Dettore seemed to be signalling something in his smile, as if there was some secret pact between the two men. Perhaps an implied agreement between two scientists who understood a whole lot more about what this was than Naomi possibly could.

Except that was not the way John ever intended it should be. He and Naomi had made this decision together from day one, eyes wide open, equal partners. There was nothing he would hide from her and nothing he would twist or distort that he presented to her. Period.

Lean and tanned, with distinguished Latin looks, Leo Dettore exuded confidence and charm. His teeth were perfect, he had great hair, dark and luxuriant, swept immaculately back and tinged with elegant silver streaks at the temples. And although sixty-two years old, he could easily have passed for someone a good decade younger.

Naomi watched him carefully, looking for any chinks in his facade, trying to read this stranger to whom they were effectively entrusting their entire future, studying his face, his body language. Her instant impression was one of disappointment. He had that aura, she had noticed in her work in public relations, that only the very rich and very successful had; some almost indefinable quality that great wealth alone seemed able to buy. He looked too slick, too mediagenic, too much like a White House candidate purring for votes, too much like a captain of industry schmoozing a shareholders' meeting. But oddly, she found the more she looked at him, the more her confidence in him grew. Despite everything, there seemed something genuine about him, as well.

She noticed his hands. He had fine fingers. Not a politician's, nor a businessman's, but true surgeon's fingers, long, hairy, with immaculate nails. She liked his voice, also, finding it sincere and calming. And there was something reassuring about his sheer physical presence. Then she reminded herself, as she had done so often these past weeks, that only a couple of months ago, beneath a photograph of Leo Dettore's face, the front cover of *Time* magazine had borne the question, TWENTY-FIRST CEN-TURY FRANKENSTEIN?

'You know,' Dettore said, 'I'm actually really intrigued by your work, Dr Klaesson – maybe we can talk about it some time over the next few days. I read that paper you published in *Nature* a few months back – was it the February issue?'

'Yes, that's right.'

'The *virtual dog* genes. Fascinating work.'

'It was a big experiment,' John said. 'It took nearly four years.'

John had developed a computer simulation showing the evolution of a dog for one thousand generations into the future, using a set of selectors.

'And your conclusion was that they have become so linked with humans that as we evolve the dogs will evolve too. In effect they will grow smarter as man's domination of the planet increases. I liked that. I thought that was ingenious thinking.'

John was flattered that a scientist of Dettore's eminence should have read his work, let alone praise it. 'It was really the development of a few key algorithms devoted to how overcoming epistasis is the rate-limiting step in adaptation,' he replied, modestly.

'And you haven't yet run a simulation on how man will evolve over the next thousand generations?'

'That's a whole new set of parameters. Apart from the challenge of creating the program, there isn't that kind of computing power available for academic research at USC. I—'

Interrupting him, Dettore said, 'I think we should talk about that. I'd be interested in giving a donation, if that would drive it forward?'

'I'd be happy to talk about it,' John said, excited by the thought that funding from Dettore could make a difference to his research work, but not wanting to get sidetracked at this moment. On this ship it was Naomi who was important, not his work.

'Good. We'll have plenty of time over the next few weeks.' Then Dettore paused, looking first at John then at Naomi. 'I'm really sorry about what happened with your son.'

She shrugged, feeling the same twist of pain she always felt when she talked about it. 'Thanks,' she mouthed, emotion choking her voice.

'Tough call.' Fixing those grey eyes on her he said, 'Folks who've never experienced the death of a child can't even begin to understand.'

Naomi nodded.

Dettore, looking sad, suddenly, glanced at John as if to include him. 'My ex-wife and I lost two kids – one at a year old from an inherited genetic disease, and one at six from meningitis.'

'I – I didn't know that. I'm really sorry,' Naomi said, turning to John. 'You didn't tell me.'

'I didn't know either,' he said. 'I'm sorry.'

'You had no reason to, it's not something I go around broadcasting. We made a decision to keep that private. But—' The geneticist opened out the palms of his hands. 'It's a big part of why I'm here. There are certain things in life that happen which shouldn't happen – which don't need to happen – and which science can now prevent from happening. That essentially is what we're about at this clinic.'

'It's why we're here, too,' Naomi said.

Dettore smiled. 'Anyhow, so how was your journey? You caught the red-eye from LA last night?'

'We took a day flight and spent last night in New York – had dinner with some friends. We like eating out in New York,' said John.

Butting in, Naomi said, 'One of my husband's interests is food – except he treats each course like it's some scientific experiment. Everyone else has a great time, but there's always something not quite right with his.' She grinned at John affectionately.

John rocked his head defensively, smiling back. 'Cooking is science. I don't expect to pay for some chef's laboratory tests.'

'I'll be interested how you rate the food on board here,' Dettore said.

'The way I'm feeling,' Naomi said, 'I'm not going to be able to face any food.'

'A little seasick?'

'A little.'

'Forecast is bad for the next few hours, then it's clearing – should be a great day tomorrow.' He hesitated and there was a moment of awkwardness between the three of them. The ship lurched suddenly, and he put a hand against the cabin wall to steady himself.

'So, here's the plan. I just want you guys to relax tonight, have dinner in your cabin.' He held out the envelope. 'There's a medical history form I need you to fill out for me, Naomi, and there's a consent form I need you both to sign. The nurse will be along to take blood samples from you both shortly. We've already analysed the samples you had mailed to us and have had both your entire genomes mapped out; we'll start looking at them in the morning. We meet in my office at ten – meantime, is there anything I can do for you?'

Naomi had made a list of a million questions she wanted to ask, but at this moment with her whole insides spinning from motion sickness she had only one thought, which was trying to not throw up.

Dettore pulled a small container from his pocket and handed it to Naomi. 'I'd like you to take one of these, twice a day with food. We know they will help epigenetically modify the foetus right at the beginning of conception.' He smiled, then continued, 'If there's anything you think of you want to talk through, just pick up the phone and call my extension. See you in the morning. Have a good one.'

Then he was gone.

Naomi looked at John. 'Has he got great genes, or a great plastic surgeon and a great dentist?'

'What did you think of him?' John said. Then he looked at her in alarm; her face had turned grey and perspiration was rolling down her cheeks.

She dropped the container and lunged towards the bathroom.

4

Can barely write this. Thrown up twice now. It is three in the morning. My arm hurts from the third injection. Three lots of blood. What on earth did the nurse need three lots of blood for? She was v. sweet and apologetic, though. Everyone seems kind. John ordered a huge dinner then left it untouched, the smell of it making him sick – me too!

The cabin is vibrating because the ship's engines are running. The nurse – Yvonne – a pleasant black woman, said when it is calm they usually just drift or drop anchor at night, but when it's rough like now it's more stable if they run the engines and keep some forward motion.

Phoned Mum earlier – very brief call (at $9 per minute!) to say we were here. Then rang Harriet. She's really excited for us. Don't know when we are going to be able to afford to pay back the $150,000 they lent us. John is in with a chance on one or two science awards and he's putting together a book project for MIT press – although their advances aren't exactly huge.

Feel like a fugitive – which I suppose is what we are. Weighing everything up over and over. Trying to find that point where medical ethics, the acceptable boundaries of science, individual responsibility and plain common sense all meet. It is very elusive.

John's awake, unable to sleep, like me. We just had a long discussion about what we're doing and how we feel about it, going over the same old stuff. And of course how we would feel if it doesn't work – there's a fifty per cent chance of failure. We're both positive still. But the enormity does scare me. I guess I'm OK about it because it still hasn't happened yet, and although we wouldn't get our money back, there is still time to change our minds. We still have a couple of weeks in which we can do that.

But I don't think we will.

5

On the large flat screen mounted on the wall of Dr Dettore's stateroom office, directly facing the semi-circular leather sofa on which they were sitting, John and Naomi stared at the heading that had just appeared.

Klaesson, Naomi. Genetic defects. Disorders.
PAGE ONE OF 16 . . .

Dettore, sitting beside Naomi, dressed as before in his white jumpsuit and plimsolls, tapped the keypad on a console mounted on the low, brushed-steel table in front of them, and instantly the first page of the list appeared.

1. **Bipolar Mood Disorder**
2. **Attention Deficit Hyperactivity Disorder**
3. **Manic Depression**
4. **Anxiety**
5. **Glomerulosclerosis**
6. **Hypernasality**
7. **Premature Baldness/Alopecia**
8. **Cardiomyopathy**
9. **Optic Nerve Atrophy**
10. **Retinitis Pigmentosa**
11. **Al-antitrypsin Deficiency**
12. **Marfan Syndrome**
13. **Hypernephroma**
14. **Osteopetrosis**

15. **Diabetes Mellitus**
16. **Burkitt's Lymphoma**
17. **Crohn's Disease. Regional Ileitis**
(Cont . . . page 2)

'I have the genes for all these diseases?' Naomi said, shocked.

There was a tinge of humour in Dettore's voice. 'Yes, you have some genes that predispose you for all of them. I don't want to scare you, Mrs Klaesson, but there are another sixteen pages.'

'I've never heard of half of these.' She looked at John, who was staring expressionlessly at the screen. 'Do you know them?'

'Not all of them, no.'

Naomi stared down at the thick form that lay on the table in front of her and John. Pages and pages of little boxes that needed a tick or a cross.

'Believe me,' Dettore said, 'you absolutely do not want to pass any of these on to your kids.'

Naomi stared at the list on the screen again, finding it hard to concentrate. Nothing ever worked out the way you imagined it, she thought, her brain swilling around inside her head, fighting yet another bout of nausea. Her throat was parched and there was a vile taste in her mouth. She'd drunk one cup of tea and managed to force down just two mouthfuls of dry toast since arriving on the ship yesterday. The sea was calmer this morning, as Dr Dettore had forecast, but the motion of the ship did not seem to be a whole lot better.

'What is hypernephroma?' she asked.

'That's renal cell carcinoma – cancer of the kidney.'

'And osteopetrosis?'

20

'Actually, I'm quite excited to see that.'

She stared at him in horror. 'Excited? Why are you excited to see that?'

'It's an extremely rare congenital condition – it's known as Boyer's Ossification disease – that causes a thickening of the bones. There used to be a lot of argument about whether this is hereditary or not – now through genetics we can see that it is. Are you aware of anyone in your family having had it?'

She shook her head. 'Diabetes,' she said. 'I know we have that in my family. My grandfather was diabetic.'

Dr Dettore tapped a key and scrolled through the next page, then the next. The list was bewildering to her. When they reached the last page she said, 'I have ovarian cancer in my family – an aunt of mine died of it in her thirties. I didn't see that gene.'

Dettore scrolled back three pages, then pointed with his finger.

Gloomily she nodded as she saw it, too. 'That means I'm carrying it?'

'You're carrying everything you see.'

'How come I'm still alive?'

'There's a big element of lottery with genes,' the geneticist said. 'Dreyens-Schlemmer, which killed your son, can be carried by individuals like yourself and Dr Klaesson all your lives without harming you. It's only when you produce a child, and the child inherits the Dreyens-Schlemmer gene from both parents, that we see the disease. Other disease gene groups that you carry can be expressed by all kinds of factors, many of which we still don't understand. Age, smoking, environment, stress, shock, accidents – all of these can act as triggers for certain genes. It is quite possible you could carry everything you've seen on this list all your life and not be affected by any of the diseases they can create.'

'But I'll pass them on to any child I have?'

'Ordinarily you would pass some, absolutely. Probably around half. The other half of the baby's genes would be inherited from your husband – we're about to take a look at his list now.'

Naomi tried for a moment to take a step back, to distance herself and think objectively. Schizophrenia. Heart disease. Muscular dystrophy. Breast cancer. Ovarian cancer. 'Dr Dettore, you've identified all these disease genes I'm carrying, but are you able to do anything about them – I mean – OK, you can stop them being passed on to our child, but can you stop them affecting me – can you get rid of them from my genome?'

He shook his head. 'Not right now. We're working on it – the whole biotech industry is working on it. It might be possible to knock out some of them in a few years' time, but we could be talking many decades for others. I'm afraid you have your parents to thank. That's the one great thing you can do for your child: to have him or her born free of these.'

Naomi was silent for some moments. It seemed so totally bizarre, the three of them on this sofa, somewhere out in the Atlantic Ocean, about to start marking ticks in little boxes, as if they were entering a magazine quiz or answering a customer satisfaction survey.

There were eighty boxes per page, and thirty-five pages, nearly three thousand questions – or choices.

The words blurred and the little boxes blurred.

'Mrs Klaesson,' Dettore said gently, 'it's very important that you really are on top of this. The consequences of what you and John decide here on this ship will impact not just on yourselves, and not even just on your child, either. You have the chance to create a child that most parents can only dream about, a child who is going to be born free of life-threatening or debilitating diseases, and, subject to what you choose, who has other genetic adjustments that are going to give him or her every possible advantage in life.' He paused to let it sink in.

Naomi swallowed and nodded.

'None of what you are doing will mean anything if you don't love your child. And if you aren't comfortable with all the decisions you are making, you could have big problems later down the line, because you are going to have to live with those decisions. I've turned many parents down – sometimes refunded them their money right at the last minute – when I've realized either they're not going to be capable of rising to the standards their child will need – or that their motives are wrong.'

Naomi prised her hand free of John's, stood up and walked unsteadily towards a window.

'Honey, let's take a break. Dr Dettore is right.'

'I'm fine.' She smiled at him. 'I'll be fine, really. Just a couple of things I'm trying to get my head around.'

She had read every word of the hundreds of pages of literature from the Dettore Clinic over the past months, studied the website – and every other website covering the topic that she could find – and ploughed through several of his published papers although, like John's, they tended to be so technical she could only understand very small amounts. But her queasiness made it hard for her to focus her mind.

The nurse, Yvonne, told her the best thing to do if she

felt sick was to look at a fixed point. So she stared ahead now, then glanced up for a moment at a gull that seemed to be drifting through the air above them.

'Dr Dettore—'

'*Leo,*' he said. 'Please, call me Leo.'

'OK. Leo.' She hesitated for a moment, gathering her thoughts and her courage. 'Leo – why is it that you are so unpopular with the press and with so many of your fellow scientists? That recent piece in *Time* was pretty harsh, I thought.'

'Are you familiar with the teachings of Chuang Tze, Naomi?'

'No?'

'Chuang Tze wrote, *What the caterpillar calls the end of the world, the master calls the butterfly.*'

'We see the caterpillar's metamorphosis into a butterfly as a transition of great beauty, darling,' John said. 'But to the caterpillar it's a traumatic experience – it thinks it is dying.'

Dettore smiled. 'In the old days either politicians or the Pope threw scientists in jail if they didn't like what they were doing. A little pillorying from the press is OK, I can handle that. The question I haven't asked you both yet is: why are you doing this? I could just knock out the bad gene group for Dreyens-Schlemmer disease and your next child would be fine. Why do *you* folks want to take over from nature and design other advantages into your child?'

'We only want to have the bad stuff taken out,' Naomi said. 'As you will understand, the pain never goes away. We couldn't go through it again.'

'It is very simple,' John said. 'Naomi and I are not

wealthy; nor do we have high opinions of ourselves. We don't think we are *Dr and Mrs Beautiful* or *Dr and Mrs Genius*, we're people who feel we owe it to our child to do the best we can for him – or her.' He glanced at Naomi and after a moment's hesitation she nodded.

Looking back at Dettore, he continued, 'You are proof that the genie is out of the bottle. You're providing this service and there will soon be other clinics, too. We don't want our child developing cancer or diabetes or schizo-phrenia – or anything else Naomi and I have family histories of. We don't want him or her saying to us in forty years' time that I was a scientist, I knew what was possible, that we had the opportunity to give this child a really fabulous chance in life and we didn't take it because we were too mean to spend the money.'

Dettore smiled. 'I have a waiting list that's building up so fast, it's now running at three years. I can't give you any names, but several of the most influential people in America have been to this clinic. Some folks are jealous, some are scared because they don't understand. The world is changing and people don't like change. Not many people can even see too far ahead. A good chess player can see five, maybe ten moves ahead. But how far do most people's visions extend? We're not very good as a species at looking into the future. It's much easier to look back at the past. We can edit out the bits we don't like, reinvent ourselves. But there's nothing about the future we can edit or reinvent. Most people are prisoners of the future just as much as they are prisoners of their genes. Only the people who come to my clinic know they can change it.'

Naomi walked over to the sofa and sat back down, absorbing what he was saying. She felt a small pang of hunger, which was a good sign. Starting to feel better. 'This fifty per cent chance of rejection – if that happens, how soon before we can try again? Or if I miscarry later?'

'Six months – the body needs that length of time to get strong again after the drugs we've given.'

'And what we have paid – that allows us three attempts – three visits here? And beyond that we'd have to pay over again?'

'I'm sure it won't come to that.' Dettore smiled.

'One thing we haven't asked you about,' Naomi said, 'are any possible side effects for our child.'

Dettore frowned. 'Side effects?'

'There's always a trade-off in life,' she said. 'What you do with the genes – are there any negative effects as a result?'

He hesitated; the tiniest flicker of doubt seemed to cross his face, like the shadow of a passing bird. 'The only thing that's a negative, if you could call it that, is your child will have accelerated growth and maturity. He or she will grow up faster than other kids, mentally and physically.'

'A lot faster?'

Dettore shook his head. 'But it will be significant.'

'Can you tell me a little bit to set Naomi's – and my own mind – at rest about the legality of what we are doing?' John asked. 'We know that it's fine here, because this ship is not subject to United States federal law – but what about when we return?'

'The regulations are changing all the time, as different countries try to get their heads around the whole subject, and scientific and religious arguments about the ethics vary. That's why I'm running this offshore and will stay offshore until the dust settles. You are not breaking any law by being here and conceiving your child here.'

'And we can go back to the US freely?' Naomi asked.

'You can go anywhere in the world freely,' Dettore said. 'But my strong advice would be to keep quiet about it and avoid getting embroiled in controversy.'

'Thanks,' she said, looking up once more at the list of her bad genes on the screen on the wall. One tiny egg contained about twenty thousand genes but that only made up a very small part of the total DNA. The rest? It used to be called junk DNA but it was now known that most of it seemed to play a role in how these twenty thousand genes get expressed. Some of it might even make you the person that you are. Every human cell contained clusters of genes – for the colour of your eyes, for the length of your arms, for the speed at which you learned things, for diseases that would kill you.

And for the way that you behaved?

Smiling suddenly, feeling a need to lighten things up a little, she said, 'Tell me, Dr Dett— er, Leo,' she said. 'On this list, with all the boxes that you want us to read through' – and now she looked pointedly at John – 'is there a *tidiness* gene?'

6

Naomi's diary

I've only caught a glimpse of two other passengers, a man and a woman – he looks a bit like a younger George Clooney and she looks like Angelina Jolie – one of those naturally beautiful women who always make me feel so damned inferior; what is it about them? John asked Dr Dettore how many other couples – patients – are here on this ship, and he wouldn't say. Dr Dettore says he cannot talk about anyone else – total patient confidentiality. But I'm curious. So is John.

Apparently everyone is now on board this strange cruise, and we're heading south towards the Caribbean, to warm weather and a couple of nights alongside a quay in Cuba. Dr Dettore says Cuba isn't a signatory to any of the human embryo treaties, so it is not a problem to go there. He also says John will be able to get a good cellphone signal there. But we won't be able to go ashore, which is a shame. I'd like to have seen a little of Cuba.

Finally ate properly tonight, some salad and fish. John had urgent emails that couldn't wait, so he used the satellite phone – nine minutes – $81! I left him working on them and went for a walk up on deck – too blowy – then down below. Really eerie – just endless long, narrow, silent corridors with doors along them. It could be a ghost ship, sometimes. Just carrying us away. I needed the walk to try to clear my head. All the concentration today. All these *boxes, all these gene groups – clusters – you can have removed, or enhanced if you want – all you have to do is put a tick. The enormity of choices and decisions is making me realize what a lottery human life is. Poor little Halley got a shitty deal.*

It is going to be very different for the new baby. Our first choice is the sex. We've told Dr Dettore we want a boy, and it may sound silly at this stage, but John and I have been discussing names. Luke is our favourite. We haven't fully decided on that name, but John is keen and it's growing on me. Luke. Close to Luck.

He's going to be lucky for us.

7

'There is a whole science of how metabolism, energetics and sleep are all integrated by circadian rhythm, and this has a profound effect on children's success in life, Naomi,' Leo Dettore said. 'Have you ever wondered how, for example, company CEOs and senior politicians are only able to get through their workload because they can survive on less sleep than most of us? What we're looking at on the list now is the group of genes responsible for our circadian rhythms. We have the capability to reconfigure their architecture in what are called "pacemaker neurons" that keep the body as a whole in sync. By fine-tuning these genes, we can reduce the risk of heart disease, fat accumulation, inflammation, diabetes and even reduce the need for sleep to just two hours a night.'

Naomi looked down at the list. There were ticks in the boxes against twelve of the two hundred or so of the options they'd covered so far. This was their second morning on the ship, and their third session with Dr Dettore. The sea was calm and her seasickness had all but gone. Today she was able to concentrate better.

It was hot outside, but the air conditioning in this office seemed to be turned up higher than yesterday, and wearing just a light cotton top over her jeans today, Naomi felt cold. Her discomfort was increased by a steady dull ache in her right thigh where, earlier this morning, the nurse had given her the first of fifteen daily fertility-booster injections with a needle that looked like it had been designed to anaesthetize elephants.

'A baby who only sleeps two hours a night would be a nightmare,' she said. 'You've had children – surely you—?'

Dettore, beside her on the sofa, raised a hand. 'Absolutely! That would be a total nightmare, Naomi, I totally agree. But this would not be a problem you'd have to worry about as a parent. Your child would have normal sleep patterns until mid-teens, then it would be a gradual process from around fifteen years old until eighteen. His whole sleep system would start benefiting him at the crucial period of his studies, enabling him to hit the real world with maximum advantage over his peers.'

Naomi glanced around the stateroom for some moments, thinking, toying with her watch band. Ten to eleven. At the rate they were progressing it was going to take them months to work all the way through the list. 'Isn't it dangerous to tamper with people's sleeping rhythms? How can you be sure that you're not going to cause him psychological problems?' she asked.

'Sleep deprivation can lead to psychological problems, sure, Naomi. This is different – two hours' sleep for your son would be the equivalent of eight for anyone else. Now, if you do the calculations, say against someone who routinely needs eight hours' sleep, over a normal human lifespan you will effectively be gaining your son an extra fifteen years of conscious existence. That's quite a gift for a parent to give a child. Think how much more he would be able to read, learn, accomplish.'

Naomi glanced at John but was unable to glean anything from his expression. Then she turned back to the geneticist. 'Nothing we've ticked so far will make him a freak. We've taken decisions about his height in the hope he will be six foot tall like John, rather than a shortie like me, because for a man there are definite advantages in being tall. Other than that, all we've done is to try to eliminate the horrible disease genes. We're not interested in designing the shape of his nose or the colour of his eyes or his hair. We're happy to leave things like that to chance.'

John, making a note on his BlackBerry memo pad, nodded.

Dettore topped up his glass of mineral water. 'Park the sleep issue for now – we'll come back to it later. We'll move on to the next group on the list – these relate to the clusters of muscular, skeletal and neural genes that will affect his athletic abilities. We can redesign some of these groups to enhance your son's hand-eye coordination. That will help him at sports like tennis, squash, baseball and golf.'

John turned to Naomi. 'I think that's interesting. It's not something that could do him any harm.'

'No,' she said. 'I'm not comfortable about that at all. Why would you want to do that?'

'Neither of us are particularly good at sport,' John said. 'Why not give him a little help? It would be like coaching him before he's born.'

'Before he's conceived,' she corrected him, tartly. 'I'll tell you what my problem is: if we make him an absolute whizz at these sports, he could end up so much better than all his friends that he won't have anyone to play with. I'm not interested in creating some sporting superman – I just want my son to be healthy and normal.'

After some moments John conceded, 'You have a point, I hadn't seen it that way.'

She pressed her hands together partly for warmth and

partly from nerves. 'Now,' she said to the geneticist, 'the next group we come to does interest me – us. John and I read up on all the literature you gave us on this last night. All the genes relating to the body's energy levels?'

John said, 'You're able to enhance oxygen conversion efficiency, and to modify the metabolic pattern? What this means, if we're understanding it correctly, is that our son would be able to convert more energy from less food than normal people, and go longer on this food?'

'Essentially, yes,' Dettore said. 'Better maximization of the nutrients, more efficient conversion of starches, sugars, proteins, better storage and release mechanisms, more elegant insulin controls but without any additional appetite.'

Naomi nodded. 'These are good things – they're going to mean he stays in shape easily and he won't have weight problems.' She was silent for a moment and then she said, 'I'm comfortable about these in a way that I'm not about tampering with his sleep patterns.'

John leaned forward and poured himself some more coffee from the metal pot on the table, grinning. 'You sleep too much, darling.'

'Rubbish! I need my sleep.'

'Exactly my point. If you're not woken, you can easily sleep nine hours, even ten. Dr Dettore is right in one sense – it wastes so much of your life.'

'I like my sleep!'

'And if your genes were programmed so that you only needed two hours, darling, you'd like those hours of sleep just as much.'

'I don't think so.' Then she looked away, out of the window. There was a container ship in the distance, sitting high on the horizon, looking so elevated it might have been mounted on a plinth. 'You have to understand where I'm coming from in my own mind in all of this, Dr – er – Leo. I just want my child to be free of any risk of the disease that killed our son. It's great that you can also eliminate the other bad genes John and I are carrying, for prostate cancer, pancreatic cancer, depression, diabetes. I want to give our child advantages in life, sure, what parent wouldn't, but I don't want him to be too different from other human beings, do you understand that? I don't want him to be a freak.'

Dettore sat upright, folded his arms and rocked back and forward a few times, like a big child himself. 'Naomi, I hear what you're saying. You want your kid to be just a regular guy with corners of talent and occasional brilliance, right?'

'I – I suppose, yes. Exactly.'

'I'd go along with that, except there is one thing you have to take into account. You have to compare a model of the world today, with a model of what the world will be like when your son becomes an adult. You're twenty-eight years old, and the world is not substantially different to when you were a little girl. But, in twenty-eight years' time?' He opened his arms expansively. 'I'm telling you that in twenty-eight years' time the world *will* be different. There will be a genetic underclass that will create a divide bigger than you can imagine. You compare the knowledge, skills, advantages you have right now over some poor young woman your age brought up in the Third World, working on a paddy field in China, or maybe in the bush in Angola.'

Dettore stood up, went over to his desk and tapped his computer keyboard for some moments. A map of the world appeared on the large wall screen opposite them.

There were some pink blotches, but mostly the countries were in white.

'There are seven billion people in the world. Do you know how many of them can read or write?' He looked at John, then Naomi.

'No,' she said. 'I don't.'

'If I tell you that twenty-three per cent of adults in the United States, the most technologically advanced nation in the world, are illiterate, does that give you any clues? Forty-four million who cannot read in the *United States*, for heaven's sakes! It's less than a billion in the whole world who can. Less than twenty per cent. Just those pink areas on the map. The average rural dweller in the Third World receives less information in his or her entire lifetime than is contained in one issue of the *LA Times*.'

A phone rang; he glanced down at it, then ignored it and after a few moments it stopped. 'Naomi,' he said gently, 'you may not be comfortable with this fact, but you are already a member of a master-race. I don't think you'd want to go trade places with too many other people on this planet. I don't think you'd want your child to be brought up on the Russian steppes, or in a Himalayan tea plantation, or some settlement out in the Gobi Desert. Am I right?'

'Of course.'

'But you'd be prepared to take the risk that your son ends up in a kind of intellectual Third World?'

She looked at him and said nothing.

'These are early days,' Dettore said. 'In thirty years' time, all children from families or nations that can afford it are going to be genetically enhanced. You see the options you have on that list we're working through? At the moment they are just options, but when you start living in a world where every expectant mother is ticking her way through that same list, are you going to leave all the boxes blank? No way! Not unless you want to have a totally disadvantaged kid – one who won't be able to keep up or compete in the world.'

'I'll tell you what really worries me about this whole thing – and I know it worries John, too, because we've discussed this endlessly over the past months, since you accepted us, and it's this' – she shrugged – 'this whole *eugenics* thing. It has a bad history, bad associations.'

Dettore perched on the edge of his desk and leaned towards Naomi. 'If we human beings never try to improve the genes of our offspring because eighty years ago a madman called Mr Hitler tried to do it, then in my opinion we may have won the Second World War, but Mr Hitler will have won the peace that followed.' He looked very solemn. 'Edward Gibbon wrote, *All that is human must retrograde if it does not advance.* He was right. Any civilization, any generation that does not advance will eventually decline.'

'And didn't Einstein say that if he had known that the consequences of his work would have led to the atom bomb, he would have become a watchmaker instead?' Naomi said.

'Sure,' Dettore said. 'And if Einstein had become a watchmaker, we might today be living in a world where Hitler's eugenics was our future.'

'Instead of yours?' Naomi said. Instantly she regretted the remark. 'I'm sorry,' she said. 'I didn't mean—'

'I think what she's saying is that it's one perspective against another,' John butted in quickly.

'It's OK, it's a valid point,' Dettore said. 'Plenty of people have made the comparison. I've been called the Antichrist, a Neo-Nazi, Dr Frankenstein, you name it. I just hope I have more humanity than Mr Hitler did. And maybe a little more humility, too.'

He gave such a meek, disarming smile that Naomi felt sorry for offending him. 'I honestly didn't mean to make such a crass—'

The geneticist jumped to his feet, walked over, took her hand gently. 'Naomi, you must have been to hell and back losing Halley. Now you are going through another incredibly difficult time. These four weeks on this ship are going to be physically tough for you as well as mentally tough. It's very important you always say what you feel, and for you to recognize if you reach the point where you've changed your mind and want out. We have to be honest with each other, OK?'

'Thank you,' she said.

He released her hand but continued to hold her gaze. 'The world is changing, Naomi, that's why you and John are here. Because you are smart enough to realize that.'

There was a long silence. Naomi looked through the window at the vast expanse of flat blue water and at the container ship still visible on the horizon. She looked at her husband, then at the geneticist, then down at the form, thinking about Halley, remembering why they were here.

Dreyens-Schlemmer disease affects the body's immune system in a similar but far more aggressive way than lupus. It progressively induces a sustained innate immune response. It was as if it turned Halley's own first line of defence into a corrosive acid, literally eating away his own internal organs. He had died, after screaming non-stop for two days for the pain to cease, no drug able to help him, haemorrhaging blood through his mouth, nose, ears and rectum.

Dreyens-Schlemmer disease was identified in 1978 by two scientists at Heidelberg University in Germany. Because it was so rare, affecting fewer than one hundred children in the world at any one time, their discovery was of largely academic value only. Pharmaceutical companies are not interested because the costs of their research could never be recouped. The only way to defeat Dreyens-Schlemmer disease would be through a long, slow process of eliminating it by breeding it out of the human species.

Most people who carried the relatively rare gene for it had perfectly healthy children without any problem at all. It was only in the extreme circumstance when two unwitting carriers of the recessive gene produced a baby together that the problem could arise.

Neither John nor Naomi had any previous family history of Dreyens-Schlemmer – so far as they knew. But after Halley's birth – and by then too late – they had discovered they were both carriers of the gene. Which meant there was a one in four chance any child they had would be affected.

Naomi looked at Dettore again. 'You're wrong,' she said. 'The world might be changing, but I'm not smart enough to understand how. Maybe I don't even want to understand. It scares me.'

8

In the deserted gymnasium, John's shoes pounded on the treadmill of the running machine; it was ten to seven in the morning. Perspiration guttered down his face and down his body; beads of water streaked his glasses, making it hard to read the television monitor that was tuned to CNN business news and displaying lists of the previous day's closing NASDAQ prices.

From as far back into childhood as John could remember, he had been driven by a hunger for knowledge. He loved collecting tadpoles in the spring, watching them sprout legs, lose their tails, change into tiny frogs. He badgered his mother each school holiday to drive him from their home town of Örebro, in central Sweden, to Stockholm, to the Natural History Museum and the National Museum of Science and Technology. When he was eighteen he'd gone to London to a summer school to improve his English, and had spent almost the entire three months inside the Science, Natural History and British Museums.

John particularly admired the great scientists of past eras. People like Archimedes, Copernicus, Galileo, Newton, Pasteur, whose work, he considered, had shaped our modern world. And just as much, he admired the big men of physics and mathematics of the twentieth century, such as Einstein, Fermi, Oppenheimer, von Neumann, Feynman, Schrödinger, Turing, whose work, he believed, would shape our futures. All of them were people who had taken huge risks with their time and their reputations.

If John had been asked what his ambition was, he would have answered that he had no interest in becoming rich, but he would love to have his own name up there, one day, among the big men of science. Once, when he was ten, a few weeks after his father, a dreamer and failed businessman, had died in debt, he wrote down a list of what he wanted to achieve in life:

(a) To be a respected scientist.
(b) To leave the world a better place than when I was born.
(c) To extend human lifespan.
(d) To take care of Mamma.
(e) To stop pain in the world.
(f) To be a good father.

Whenever John felt low, he looked at the list. At some time during his teens he had transferred it from his little red notebook onto his computer, and subsequently from computer to computer. Reading it always made him smile; but it made him sad, too.

I'm thirty-six and haven't yet achieved one damned thing on that list.

He felt particularly bad about his neglect of his mother. As an only child he felt very responsible for her. She'd married again when he was eighteen, shortly before he'd gone to Uppsala University, to a widower, a schools inspector who had visited the *högstadiet* – senior school – where she taught mathematics. A quiet but decent man, he was the opposite of John's own father in just about every way. Five years later he died of a heart attack, and his mother had been on her own ever since, fiercely independent, despite the fact that she was losing her eyesight through macular degeneration.

As a child, John had been an avid science-fiction reader, his head full of theories and questions. Theories about why we existed, about how certain animals and insects had acquired their characteristics. Questions about why some creatures, like the common ant and the cockroach, had seemingly ceased evolving a million years ago – yet others, such as human beings, continued. Why had some animal brains stopped growing hundreds of thousands of years ago? Was it because having too smart a brain was a hindrance to survival rather than an asset? Would humans eventually destroy themselves precisely because evolution was making them too smart for their own good?

Or, as he explored in his work, did humans risk destroying themselves because they were developing technology at a faster pace than their brains were developing? And were they in need of a major evolutionary leap forward to catch up?

The ship lurched suddenly, unbalancing him, and he had to grab the handrail to stop himself falling sideways off the treadmill belt. Through the open door he could hear the water in the plunge pool sloshing. He hadn't felt as sick as Naomi had, but he still wasn't totally acclimatized yet to the motion.

Neither he nor Naomi had slept much again last night. The same questions were going through his mind now that they had discussed over and over. Yes, they both agreed that they wanted to give their son all the advantages they would have liked their own parents to have given them. But they didn't want him being *too* different and finding himself unable to relate or connect to people.

And that was the real problem. Dettore was pushing them all the time to go for more options, to enhance their son in ways that even John hadn't realized were already scientifically possible. And some of these options were tempting. My God, if they wanted, they could really make Luke into an incredible person!

But no thanks.

Luke wasn't going to be some kind of laboratory rat that they could just terminate humanely with a needle if he came out different to how they were expecting.

He did not want to gamble with his son's life. And yet what haunted him during the night was the knowledge that any child was just that, a gamble, a random throw of the genetic dice. What Dettore was offering was a way to reduce the odds, not increase them. In playing safe, would they be condemning their son to a life of mediocrity?

The machine beeped and the display flashed that another minute had passed. He was working out even harder on this ship than he did at home. Pushing himself into some kind of super-fit shape. Aware of his true reason for doing this, but having difficulty in admitting it to himself.

I want my kid to be proud of me. I want him to have a fit man for a dad, not some wheezing old fart.

It was totally deserted down here on G Deck, deep in the bowels of the ship.

His sole companion was his own reflection jigging up and down on all four mirrored walls, a reflection of a tall, slim man in a white T-shirt, blue running shorts, trainers. A tall, slim man with a tired, strained face and bags like black smudges beneath his eyes.

Young men see visions, old men dream dreams.

The damned line was going round and round in his head, in tune to the pounding of his feet, like a mantra. *I may have come here as a man with a vision*, he thought. *But now I feel more like a priest who is starting to question his faith.*

But if we do tone Luke right down, throwing away this chance to make him something really special, will I live to regret it? Will I end up as an old man dreaming of what might have been, if only I'd had the courage?

9

Naomi's Diary

If you haven't been through this you have no idea of the pain. This injection the nurse gives me every morning to boost my egg production feels like a spike being hammered into my thigh bone. I tried again to get Yvonne to talk about the other patients here, but she instantly clams up, as if she's scared to open her mouth.

John is being wonderful, very loving and putting no pressure at all on me. In fact, in terms of the openness between us, this is the best it has ever been since before poor Halley came along. I hug him in the nights, desperately wanting to make love to him, but that's forbidden – we were banned from making love for two weeks before we came here – and we're not going to be able to for weeks after, either. That's hard. We need that closeness.

I'm finding this place stranger by the day. The atmosphere on this ship is truly weird – we walk around, and there's not a soul apart from the occasional cleaner polishing a handrail. Where the hell is everyone? Are all the other patients so shy? How many are here? I'd love to talk to someone else, to one other couple, compare notes.

Four hundred thousand dollars! I think about all that money. Are we being selfish spending it on our unborn child? Should we have given it away to help children in need, or people in need, or medical research, rather than squandering it on bringing one new person into the world?

It's moments like this when I want to pray for guidance. But I gave up on God when he took Halley, and told him so.

How are you, Halley, darling? Are you OK? You're the one who should really give us the guidance, you were such a smart kid. The smartest kid I ever knew.

It's thinking about you that keeps me here. I'm thinking about your face when that needle goes in and I'm biting my handkerchief. All that suffering you went through. We want to have a son again now, one who will be smart enough, maybe, to do some real good in this world.

Luke.

We hope Luke's going to make great new scientific discoveries, we hope he will be smart enough to make some kind of a real difference. So that in the future, no child is ever going to have to die the way you died.

Today we dealt with the Housekeeping genes. Funny description! The Housekeeping group relate to things like the efficiency of each cell to replicate its DNA or synthesize proteins. Nothing too much to worry about there. Luke should heal faster and better from any injuries, which has to be a good thing.

But the cleverest work Dr Dettore is doing in this group is with adrenaline responses. He pointed out just how badly evolution has kept pace with modern life: adrenaline kicks in when we get nervous, giving us a boost of energy to help us run from an assailant. Fine in the days when a sabre-toothed tiger would appear in the mouth of your cave, he explained. But you definitely do not want to be breaking out in a sweat and shaking in a confrontation with the tax collector, or with anyone else in our modern world – you want to remain calm, feel relaxed, keeping your brain as clear as possible.

In other words, stay cool. That is an option I'm tempted by, because it makes so much sense. But we haven't agreed to it, not yet anyhow, because we're both worried about tinkering with such an important part of Luke's body's defence mechanism.

I'm already thinking of him as Luke now. At least that's one thing we're both agreed on. But now there's another issue – something that's really disturbing.

10

'Compassion,' John said.

Naomi, deep in thought, seated on a bench on the Promenade Deck writing her daily diary entry by hand into her iPhone, remained silent.

'Compassion,' John repeated, as if thinking out loud. '*Compassion.* How do you define it – how does anyone?'

They'd discussed the genes relating to compassion for over an hour in this morning's session with Dr Dettore and now, during their free time until the afternoon session, John and Naomi continued toying with the subject.

As the ship headed south the weather was improving noticeably. The air felt gloriously warm to Naomi, and the sea was the flattest she had seen so far. They would be alongside the quay in Havana, Cuba, at seven this evening, but Dettore did not want them to go ashore. It was a fuelling and provisioning stop only. It was crucial over the next month for Naomi to be as healthy as possible; there was no sense risking picking up a bug in a cab or a shop or a bar, he had already told them.

John stood up. 'Let's walk a little, darling, stretch our legs. The nurse said exercise would help ease the pain for you.'

'I'll try.' She slipped her phone into her handbag and stood up. 'What do you think Dettore meant that our child would grow up faster than ordinary children?'

'I guess he's implying because of the extra intelligence he'll have.'

'I don't think we should *guess* anything, John. We need to be sure about everything. He talked about *accelerated* growth and maturity. We don't want him being so different to other kids that he doesn't have friends.'

'We'll review everything before we finalize anything.'

'I'm going through those documents with a fine-tooth comb.'

With the breeze on their faces. they walked along the teak decking, past a muster station and an orange lifebelt printed with the ship's name. Naomi was limping, her leg aching badly from this morning's injection. She felt low today, and very vulnerable. Slipping her hand into John's, into his strong, reassuring grip, made her feel a little better. She squeezed and felt him squeeze back.

They walked past a row of portholes and she peered at each of them in turn, trying to see in. But the glass was mirrored like every other porthole on the ship, and all she could see was her own reflection, her pale face, her hair tangled by the wind.

'This secrecy thing is really getting to me,' she said.

'I guess if we were in any clinic on land, there'd be a lot of privacy. Also – it just feels as if it ought to be different because it's a ship.'

'I suppose. I just think it would be interesting to meet one or two of the other couples and compare notes.'

'It's a very private thing. Maybe other people don't want to talk – perhaps we'd find it difficult to talk, too, if we did meet anyone.'

So far the only people they'd met on the ship, other than Dettore, were a doctor called Tom Leu, a pleasant, good-looking Chinese-American in his mid-thirties, whom Dettore had introduced as his senior medical assistant; the nurse, Yvonne; their chambermaid; and a handful of Filipino staff.

There had been no sign of the captain or any of the other officers, other than a voice through the tannoy system at nine this morning giving advanced notice of a crew safety drill. All access doors and gates to the bridge and crew stations and quarters were permanently locked off. Apart from their fleeting sight of the handsome couple they had jokingly called George and Angelina, there had been no sign of any other clients.

Taking a stroll late afternoon yesterday they'd seen the helicopter come in, then leave a short while later. It had hovered for some moments after take-off and John had just been able to make out a woman's face through the darkened glass window. Taking a couple away who had changed their minds, they speculated.

'Do you want lunch?' Naomi asked.

John shook his head. He wasn't hungry, but it wasn't to do with the motion of the ship; it was the stress of worrying constantly about doing the right thing. Making the right decisions.

'Me neither. Why don't we sit out for a bit – it's warm enough to sunbathe,' Naomi said. 'And have a swim? And try to talk this compassion thing through?'

'Sure.'

A few minutes later, swathed in the clinic's white towelling dressing gowns and daubed in suntan lotion, they made their way back outside and around to the stern. Naomi gripped the handrail to walk down to the pool deck, then stopped suddenly and turned to John.

George and Angelina were lying on loungers by the otherwise deserted pool. Tanned and beautiful, in sharp swimsuits and cool sunglasses, they were both reading paperbacks.

Moments later Naomi heard a click. Her eyes shot back to John, who was surreptitiously jamming something into his dressing-gown pocket.

'You didn't take a photograph?'

He winked.

'That's bad. You shouldn't, you know the rules. We could get thrown off if you—'

'I shot from the hip. Nobody saw.'

'Please don't take any more.'

They walked over to a couple of loungers near them. 'Hi!' John boomed cheerily. 'Good afternoon!'

For some moments there was no reaction at all from either of them. Then, very slowly, the man they had nicknamed George lowered his paperback a few inches, then, equally slowly, he inclined his head a fraction, as if to confirm the source of the greeting. His expression did not change and he returned to his book, giving them no further acknowledgement. The woman did not move a muscle.

Naomi shrugged at John. He opened his mouth as if to say something further, then, appearing to think better of it, peeled off his dressing gown, went to the edge of the pool and dipped a foot in.

Naomi joined him. 'Friendly, aren't they?' she hissed.

'Maybe they're deaf.'

She sniggered. John climbed down into the water and began to swim.

'How's the water?' she asked.

'Like a sauna!'

Naomi tested it gingerly with her foot, remembering that John was used to freezing lakes in Sweden. His idea of warm was anything that didn't have ice floating in it.

Ten minutes later, when they emerged, George and Angelina had gone.

Naomi lay on her lounger, pushing her hair back and wringing out the water, letting the heat of the sun and the warm air dry her body. 'I think that was incredibly rude,' she said.

Towelling his head, John said, 'Maybe Dettore should insert a *politeness* gene into their child.' Then, sitting down on the edge of Naomi's chair, he said, 'OK, we need to get our heads around compassion – we have to get it resolved by three o'clock – that gives us an hour and a half.' He stroked her leg, then ducked his head down impulsively and kissed her shin. 'You haven't sucked my toes for a long time – remember you used to do that?'

'You used to suck mine, too,' she grinned.

'We're getting too middle-aged!'

Then, looking at him a little wistfully, she asked, 'Do you still fancy me as much as you used to?'

Caressing her navel suggestively, John said, 'More. It's the truth. I love the way you look, the way you smell, the way you feel when I'm holding you. When I'm apart from you, if I just think about you I get horny.'

She lifted his hand and kissed each of his fingers in turn. 'I feel the same about you, too. It just gets better with you all the time.'

'Let's concentrate,' he said. '*Compassion*.'

'And the *sensitivity* part as well,' she said. 'Look, I've just been thinking in the pool—'

'Uh-huh?'

Dettore had this morning presented them with modifications that could be made to the group of genes responsible for compassion and sensitivity. John saw compassion as a mathematical equation. You had to find the balance between where compassion was a crucial part of your humanity and where, through excess, it could threaten your survival. He told Dettore it was a danger-ous area to try to change. The geneticist had disagreed strongly.

Composing her thoughts carefully, Naomi said, 'If you and another soldier were travelling through a jungle, being pursued by an enemy, and your buddy was wounded suddenly, too badly to carry on walking, what would you do?'

'I'd carry him.'

'Right. But you wouldn't be able to carry him very far, so then what do you do? If you leave him, the enemy will capture him and kill him. If you stay with him the enemy will kill both of you.'

John craved a cigarette suddenly. He'd quit when Naomi quit, after she fell pregnant with Halley, then had taken it up again for a short time after Halley died. He hadn't had one now for eighteen months, but whenever he felt stressed, that was when he really wanted one.

'The Darwinian solution, I suppose, would be to leave my friend and continue,' he replied.

'Isn't the whole point of this, our whole reason for being here, to take charge of the future of our child ourselves – to not let him be a prisoner of haphazard random selection? If we did agree, God forbid, to messing around with his brain genes – as Dr Dettore keeps encour-aging us – and we succeeded in designing a *smarter* human being, wouldn't he be better at problem-solving than we are? Wouldn't he know the answer to this?'

'We're trying to make a healthier person who will have a few added advantages – that's all you and I can do,' John said. 'We can't make a better world.'

'And if you were going to mess with his brain, you would vote for ticking the box for the kind of genes that would have this advantaged person abandon his friend to the enemy and move on?'

'If we were serious about wanting him to be a high achiever, he would have to be able to make hard decisions like that and be able to live with them.'

Naomi touched his arm and looked up at him, searching his face. 'I think that's terrible.'

'So what's your solution?'

'If we were really going to reconfigure our child's mind, I'd want him to grow up with a value system that has much more honour than anything we are capable of understanding at present. Wouldn't that be a truly better person?'

John stared across the empty loungers towards the deck rail, and the ocean beyond. 'What would your better person do?'

'He'd stay with his friend and be comfortable with his decision – knowing that he could never have lived with himself if he'd gone on alone.'

'That's a nice way to think,' John said. 'But a child programmed like that would have no future out in the real world.'

'That's exactly why we're right not to tamper with the compassion and sensitivity genes at all. We should just let Luke inherit whatever ones we have, at random. We're both caring people – he can't go too far wrong having our genes for these things, can he?'

A deck hand walked past them, holding a toolbox, oil stains on his white jumpsuit. *Genetic underclass.* Dettore's words echoed in his mind. In Huxley's *Brave New World* they bred worker drones to do menial jobs. That's what children of the future were destined to become if their parents did not have the vision to alter their genes.

And the courage to take hard decisions when they did so.

11

Naomi's Diary

We sailed from Cuba tonight. John likes the occasional cigar and was miffed he wasn't allowed ashore to buy any. Dr Dettore, who I'm convinced would have made a great politician, invited us to dine with him tonight in his private dining room. Got the impression this is an honour all 'patients' get once. Serious schmoozing. John was impressed with the food and he doesn't impress easily.

Today, Dr Dettore asked John and I how we met. Actually, more than that, he asked how I felt about John when we first met. It was at Jackson Hole, Wyoming. I told him although I loved skiing, I had always been scared of heights, but, strangely, I hadn't been scared with John. We met in a ski-lift queue and shared a chair together. We just got on really well. Then the bloody chair stopped at the steepest point; halfway up a rock face with a two-thousand-foot sheer drop below us, and swaying crazily. If I had been on my own I would have been scared witless. But John made me laugh. He made me feel I could fly, that I could do anything.

I told Dr Dettore that. But I didn't tell him the rest.

I didn't tell him that it wasn't until Halley died that I realized for the first time that John had limitations, the same as all of us. That for a while I hated him. He'd made me believe he was a god, but when the chips were down he didn't have any miracle, just tears like you and me. Just the same damned helplessness we all have in common. Now I still love him, but in a different way. I still find him enormously attractive. I feel safe with him. I trust him. But he no longer makes me feel I can fly.

I wonder if all relationships that endure eventually reach this same point. A place where you are comfortable with each other. Where your dreams turn to reality, where you realize the secret of life is to know when it is good.

And that you are bloody lucky.

I have the feeling Dr Dettore is reaching for something more. That beneath all his charm there is a restlessness, a dissatisfaction. I'm normally very good at getting through to people, but although he is really affable, I find it hard to connect to him. Sometimes I have the sense he is contemptuous of ordinary human emotions. That he feels we should be above these and on some higher plane.

That he has some kind of hidden agenda.

12

Quite bizarre. We're surrounded on this ship by millions of dollars of technology. Yet today, poor John had to sit in a cubicle off one of the labs with a plastic jar, a box of Kleenex and an assortment of pornographic videotapes. I hope Luke never gets to see this diary, I'd like him to have some romantic notions about his beginnings. Nice for him to know that he was conceived on a cruise in the Caribbean. Not so nice to discover his father had been sitting with his pants around his ankles watching Busty Babes Meet Big Boy.

Dr D had a cute word for it. Harvesting. He told John, 'Just need to harvest a little of your semen.'

We're both committed to this thing. But I keep thinking that maybe we should forget about it, go home, perhaps try to find some other way around our problem. Adopt, or have a surrogate child of some kind, or get pregnant from donor sperm. Or forget about children altogether. Plenty of couples don't have children.

I think maybe Dr D is angry that we've taken so few of his options. No more than a few dozen ticks out of almost three thousand. All we have done is agree to the bad disease genes being taken out, ensure Luke will be six foot tall, and make some improvements to his metabolism, which will help him stay fit and healthy. If we'd let Dettore have his head, we'd have ended up agreeing to create some kind of a superman. No thanks!

But I'll say one thing for Dr D, he is good at explaining stuff. Although he has a technique even John didn't understand for separating high-quality sperm.

It was a real harvest today. John's semen and my eggs. Dr D was delighted with the crop – a total of twelve. He told me it had been worth all the pain of the injections (easy for him – he didn't have them).

He's now having the entire genetic code of each embryo analysed. Cells from the strongest one will be selected. As I understand it, some of the disease genes will be removed or disabled. Females have two X chromosomes. Males have one X and one Y. By separating the Y chromosome sperms from the X chromosome sperms, Dr D will ensure the baby is a boy.

Doesn't sound very romantic, does it?

In a fortnight, if it goes to plan, we'll be home. And I'll be pregnant.

I wonder how I'll feel.

13

Naomi had never been covetous of wealth. Sitting in John's ageing Volvo on the 405, heading home from the airport, she was wrapped in her thoughts. Her feet nestled in the mess of papers in the footwell; photocopied documents, pamphlets, a playbill, chewing-gum and chocolate-bar wrappers, petrol receipts, parking tickets; the interior of his car was part filing cabinet and part dustbin. John didn't seem to care about the mess. It was a tip; it looked like it might have recently been vacated by chickens.

As he drove he was talking on the hands-free speaker-phone to a work colleague. Beneath her the tyres rumbled over a section of corrugated road surface; she paid no attention to any of the other cars on the road; she didn't hanker after a Porsche or an open Mercedes or a custom Explorer. Cars were just transport to her. Yet, staring ahead towards the Hollywood Hills through the late-afternoon haze, she realized that seven years in Los Angeles had changed her in the way, she had noticed, it seemed to change most people who came here.

Los Angeles made you want money. You couldn't help yourself; you suddenly found yourself wanting things you'd never wanted before. And feeling emotions you'd never felt before. Such as envy.

She loved their modest little single-storey house south of Pico. It had a roof deck, and an orange tree in the back yard that once a year produced a crop of deliciously sweet fruit, and a light, airy feel inside. It was their home, their sanctuary. And yet, sometimes when she saw swanky homes high up in the Hollywood hills, or close to the ocean in Malibu, she couldn't help thinking that one of those would be a great place to raise a child.

She pressed a hand to her tummy. Luke was just a speck inside her, a mere two weeks old, who would be going to school in a few years' time. *To me you're a person now, Luke. How do you feel about that? Good? Me, too.*

After Halley was born, everyone had told her the best schools were in Beverly Hills, and they were the only schools a concerned parent could ever seriously consider – unless, of course, you particularly wanted your son to grow up as a pistol-toting crack dealer. But how would they ever be able to afford a home in Beverly Hills?

John's earnings were so limited. He was working on a book about his field, and sure, some impenetrable science books did become best-sellers, but his last book, although well reviewed in the academic press, had sold less than two thousand copies – and he had been pleased – he hadn't even expected to sell that many!

She would have to get her own career back into full gear, she decided. Since Halley's death she'd been free-lance, accepting occasional public relations work when she felt strong enough to cope. She had two months' work starting next week, on the promotion for a new Oliver Stone movie, but nothing beyond that. It was time to go job-hunting in earnest, to phone all her contacts at the studios, networks and independent companies, perhaps take a permanent position after Luke was born. Something with career-ladder opportunities, maybe Showtime or HBO or MTV or Comedy Central, where she had the chance to move up to producing, and start making serious money.

Enough money to move to Beverly Hills.

Some hope, in the thick of this recession.

It wasn't even certain, of course, that they would remain in LA. John was up for tenure at USC next year and he really didn't know whether he would get it. If he did, they would be committed to remaining in LA for a long time, probably the rest of his career, but if not, they might well have to move to another city, maybe even to another country. Although she liked the States, her dream was to live in England again one day, to be somewhere close to her mother and her older sister, Harriet.

It felt strange being back. Neither of them had spoken much on the plane; she'd tried to watch a film but had ended up channel surfing, unable to concentrate. Nor could she get into the book she had bought in the airport before getting on the plane, called *The Unborn Child – Caring For Your Foetus.*

They were both experiencing a reality check. After four weeks in the cocoon of the ship, they were coming back to be part of the normal world again. To nine months of pregnancy; to keeping absolutely quiet to their friends. To having to be careful with every penny. To a thousand things that needed doing and organizing.

Her pregnancy with Halley had been OK, but not especially great. Some of her friends seemed to sail through their terms; others had struggled. She had been up and down, with bad morning sickness, and she'd been very tired in the last months, which hadn't been helped by a freak heatwave that had lasted from early June through to August. She'd read in some magazine that the second baby was meant to be much easier. She hoped so.

John finished his call.

'Everything OK?' she asked.

'Yes, just about, I think. Some software glitch with my human evolution program no one can fix. I'll have to go in tomorrow.'

'It's Sunday,' she said. 'Do you need to?'

'Just for half an hour. And I have to get a load of stuff emailed off for Dettore. He seems pretty serious about coming up with funding – I mean, hell, his company spends billions on research – he could finance my whole department for the next thirty years out of petty cash.'

'I know your *half an hour*. That means you'll get home around midnight.'

John smiled, then placed a hand on her belly. 'How is he?'

'Fine so far. Good as gold.' She grinned and placed her hand on John's. 'I don't want to spend tomorrow on my own. I feel kind of flat, nervous about, you know—' She shrugged. 'Let's do something together. I understand you have to deal with your work, but can't we spend some of it together – go for a hike in the canyons, perhaps? And go visit Halley's grave – he'll need fresh flowers, it's been over a month.'

'Sure, we'll do that. And a hike sounds good. Nice to go and walk somewhere without the ground moving under us.'

'I can still feel the ship swaying,' Naomi said, pulling out of her handbag the printed booklet Dr Dettore had given her.

She opened it, but instantly her head swam. She closed her eyes and took a deep breath, fighting back a sudden, sharp bout of nausea, convinced for a moment that she was going to throw up. She glanced at John, but said nothing. Wondering. Fourteen days.

Was fourteen days too soon for morning sickness?

John's phone rang and he answered it. It was a young, eager postdoc fellow he had recently taken on called Sarah Neri. 'Sorry I was out when you rang earlier,' she said.

'No problem. Did you get any information?'

'Yes, there's a whole ton of stuff. It's a website connected to the Lloyd's Register, and the *Serendipity Rose* is on it. She has a sister ship operated by a cruise line, and all the information you requested is on the cruise company's website. I'll email it all to you.'

'Give me the beats of it now.'

Sarah Neri ran through the key points. Then after he had hung up, he began doing some calculations in his head.

The *Serendipity Rose* weighed twenty-five thousand tonnes. She had four six-thousand-horsepower engines.

Sarah had found out for him the price of the fuel. The ship was burning around seventeen thousand gallons a day of heavy fuel oil. He figured maintenance, insurance, harbour dues and the fuel costs of the helicopter. Then there was Dettore. Two junior doctors. Three nurses. Two lab technicians. Then all the staff running the ship. The total wage bill would have to be around two million dollars per annum, even assuming the Filipino crew were being paid poorly.

Twenty thousand dollars a day, bottom end, he calculated, and he could be way under in this estimate. The total charge to himself and Naomi had been four hundred thousand dollars. They were there for thirty days. Thirteen thousand, three hundred dollars a day. They had only seen one other couple on the ship, George and Angelina, and the couple who had left as they had arrived. For the first two weeks, Dettore had spent the major portion of each day with himself and Naomi. For the next fortnight, after

Naomi had been impregnated, they only saw him briefly once a day, for little more than a courtesy visit. A revolving cycle of three couples on the ship at any one time seemed probable.

Which would produce roughly thirty-nine thousand, nine hundred dollars a day. At these prices Dettore can't be covering his costs or making any profit.

Why not? If profit wasn't his agenda, what was?

'John!'

He glanced at Naomi, startled out of his thoughts by her voice. 'What?'

'You've driven past our turn-off.'

14

Ten weeks later, in his seventh-floor office at the Cedars-
Sinai hospital, the obstetrician was distracted. He was
talking to Naomi but his mind was altogether somewhere
else. Dressed in white scrubs and plimsolls that reminded
Naomi of Dettore on the ship, Dr Rosengarten was a small,
slender, camp man in his late forties, with a nasal voice,
wispy bleached hair and a tan with a slightly yellowish
hue that made Naomi suspect it came from a tube rather
than the Southern Californian sunshine.

She did not dislike him, but equally, he was too aloof
for her to warm to. And she found the ornately varnished
and gilded Louis XIV furniture, the tasselled drapes and
the displays of jade and onyx objets d'art slightly absurd
in such a modern setting as this building. It felt more like
a boudoir than a consulting room – which was exactly the
effect Dr Rosengarten intended, she presumed. No doubt
its faux-grandeur impressed some of his clientele.

To her surprise, after all the meticulous care and
planning on the ship, Dr Dettore had not offered any kind
of immediate follow-up. There was just his 'Post-Concep-
tion Guidelines' booklet, a suggested reading list of books
and websites about the unborn foetus, covering a range of
topics from nutrition to spiritual welfare, and a regime of
vitamin and mineral supplements. It seemed that once
they had climbed out of his helicopter at LaGuardia airport
they were out of his care – and out of his life. All he had
requested was notification when Luke was born, for his

records, and a further consultation to be arranged when Luke was three years old.

She wondered if Dettore's lack of interest was a reflection on how little of his package they had selected. Although he had kept up his charm towards them, she had sensed a hint of coolness and impatience creeping in towards the end.

It did surprise her that there was no obstetrician or paediatrician in Los Angeles whom he particularly recommended, and that he had simply told them to be guided by their own doctor. For the money they had spent, Naomi thought, she had been expecting some kind of well-planned after-care.

Their own doctor had suggested the same obstetrician, in Santa Monica, who had delivered Halley. But her best friend in LA, Lori Shapiro, had rejected him outright, and not because of the associations with Halley. Lori was married to a fabulously rich radiologist, Irwin, who knew all the medics in the area. Dr Rosengarten was the man to see. She'd had all three of her kids delivered by Dr Rosengarten, and both Irwin and Lori assured her and John that he was the best in the city – reeling off the names of all the A-list celebrities whose babies he had brought into the world.

Naomi and John had been pleased to go somewhere else. They were relieved at severing this tie with Halley and their past. And looking at the plush surroundings, John was grateful that one perk of being employed by the university was membership of their excellent professorial health insurance scheme.

Rosengarten's secretary opened the door, a willowy blonde Californian beauty, underweight and as friendly as ice, who mouthed something to the doctor.

'You'll have to forgive me,' he said. 'One of my clients is in labour three weeks early.' He raised a finger to his lips. 'She's like – I can't tell you her name, obviously, you'll read about in the papers tomorrow. Be right back!' He gave them a patronizing smile, and disappeared out of the door for the third time.

John felt like punching his lights out. Naomi lay on the examination bench in her open gown, a pool of gel on her abdomen, while his nurse explained, 'Dr Rosengarten is under a lot of pressure today.'

'Great,' said John, taking Naomi's hand, and staring at the swirly grey-and-white images on the monitor. 'Tell him how sorry I feel for him.'

The nurse, who appeared to have a sense of humour bypass said, 'Yes, I will tell him.'

After several long minutes the obstetrician returned. 'OK, right, now, I can confirm viability, Mrs Klaesson and – ah – Dr Klaesson. Everything looks normal, it's twelve weeks and the foetus is healthy, and the results of the nuchal thickness scan are good.' Dr Rosengarten let them absorb this for a moment then added, 'Would you like to know the sex?'

Naomi glanced at John, who gave her a conspiratorial grin. She smiled thinly back and looked away. She was feeling lousy, very queasy, as she had been for weeks, and had thrown up just before coming here. Taking her handkerchief out, she dabbed spittle from her lips; her mouth was constantly filling with it.

Through the double-glazing came the blattering, grinding howl of a drill down in the street, seven storeys below. She could see the grey concrete wall of the Beverly Center close by, through the pall of dust rising up from the roadworks, and made a mental note to go there at the weekend, to see if she could find some new bras and some looser outfits while the summer sale was on. She hadn't started gaining weight yet – although her breasts had got bigger, and incredibly painful – but from her memory with Halley, weight gain would start happening in another month or so.

John squeezed her hand. She looked again at the tiny silhouette on the fuzzy, swirly grey-and-white image on the monitor screen. She could see the arms, the legs and, when Dr Rosengarten indicated, she could even make out a foot.

'I didn't think you could tell the sex until at least sixteen weeks,' she said.

Rosengarten sounded pained. 'With *our* equipment, twelve weeks is fine.' He crossed his arms truculently, like a defiant child, and looked at his Oriental Barbie nurse. 'Text books,' he said dismissively. 'You probably read that nonsense about sixteen weeks in a text book. All text books are garbage, aren't they?'

The nurse nodded in agreement.

'If you've got questions, ask me,' Rosengarten said. 'Don't waste your time reading trashy text books.'

Naomi looked back at John. Despite everything, she was suddenly nervous as hell. John squeezed her hand again, just a tiny, gentle pressure. Like a pulse.

It was a strange feeling being pregnant again. There were moments in between the bouts of queasiness when she felt happy, but awed by a tremendous weight of responsibility. She knew that John was expecting a lot from Luke; she was, too.

Staring at the screen, she asked, 'Could I listen to the heartbeat again?'

'You may, certainly.' Dr Rosengarten placed the scanner on the gel he had smeared on her abdomen and moved it around until it picked up the sound, and Naomi lay still for some moments, entranced by the reassuring, rapid pop-pop-pop-pop bleeping. After a few moments, he glanced at his watch, removed the scanner, then said, 'OK, Mrs Klaesson, you can stand up now.'

The nurse stepped forward and wiped her.

As she stood up she felt a sudden feeling of panic.

What have we done? What if it has all gone wrong?

'The baby is normal?' she asked.

His bloody secretary was standing in the doorway yet again, signalling to him. He raised a finger in acknowledgement, then distractedly turned back to Naomi.

'Absolutely.'

'You're really sure?'

'In as much as we can tell at this stage, fit and healthy. You don't need to be worried. This severe sickness – this hyperemesis gravidarum – will pass soon. Just chill out, relax, enjoy your pregnancy – it's a great and wonderful time for you.'

The baby is healthy! she was thinking. My baby is fine, moving inside me. She closed her eyes for a moment, fighting off another wave of sickness. *I'm going to be a great mum to you, and John's going to be a great dad, I promise you. We're going to try really hard to give you a great life, to make the most of all the advantages Dr Dettore has given you. You're special, you know that? Just incredibly special. You're the most special baby in the world.*

'So,' John said, 'you didn't tell us.'

Dr Rosengarten flipped a glance at his watch. The session had clearly timed out. There was a hint of impatience in his voice, suddenly. 'Tell you what?'

'The sex?'

'You're sure you want to know?' He looked at them in turn.

'Yes,' Naomi said.

'We do,' John confirmed, smiling again at Naomi. 'Absolutely.'

'OK, good. Congratulations,' Dr Rosengarten said. 'You're going to have a girl.'

15

Naomi, belted in her seat, locked in her thoughts, was only dimly aware that they were travelling up a ramp, that John was driving, that they were stopping at a booth. It was hot inside the car; airless, stuffy, and the litter of paper in the footwell rustled and crunched as she moved her feet. John powered down his window and handed the car-park attendant the ticket. The man scrutinized the validation stickers with the rigour of an immigration officer studying a passport from a terrorism hotbed, then raised the barrier. John shut his window.

She was perspiring.

As they pulled out into the street, a fallen palm frond skimmed across in front of them, and moments later she sensed the car rock in a gust. High-rise walls rose sheer on either side of them, making it feel as if they had entered a canyon, and she peered up, feeling trapped suddenly. Above them, jet-black clouds jostled for space in the narrow corridor of sky. A spot of rain struck the windshield and trickled down.

They had been talking about the weather on television this morning, saying it was unseasonable for July. It seemed that for the entire seven years they had lived in Los Angeles, the weather had been unseasonable.

Global warming was to blame for the whole world's weather patterns being out of kilter – that was the considered opinion. Scientists messing with nature were to blame. Scientists were becoming the new heretics. First the bomb, then pollution, then GM food. And next? Designer babies?

Fear pounded inside her.

OK, good. Congratulations. You're going to have a girl.

If he couldn't get that right – Dettore, Dr Dettore (*call me Leo!*) – if he couldn't get that one absolute fundamental right, then . . . ?

Oh God, what have we done?

John drove the grimy grey Volvo out of the car park and made a left, followed by another left, then stopped in a queue at the lights of the junction with La Cienega. He indicated right. South.

Naomi pulled her iPhone out of her handbag and quickly glanced through her afternoon schedule. She'd gone straight from Oliver Stone's company to a six-week assignment for a company called Bright Spark Productions, which had made a documentary series about young filmmakers. The first show was going out on the Bravo channel in two weeks' time.

At two-thirty she had a meeting at UCLA film school. It was now twenty past twelve. Her car was at home, but she needed to go via the office to pick up some material. A twenty-five-minute drive, if the traffic wasn't too bad. She needed about half an hour there to put some stuff together. Then allow thirty minutes to the film school. Not much of a margin left; she hated to be late when she was working.

'What an asshole that guy is!' John said angrily, finally breaking the long silence between them since they had left Dr Rosengarten's office. 'What a total fucking asshole.'

Naomi said nothing. At five she was meant to be having a drink at the Four Seasons with a journalist friend who worked for *Variety*. She couldn't cancel, but how the hell was she going to get through the afternoon? She lowered her window. The gust of air, even laden with petrol fumes, felt good, better than the smell of the interior, of warm, old plastic. John inched forward. A tractor-trailer rumbled past them.

His cellphone rang. She was grateful that he killed the call. Moments later her own phone rang. She switched it off, with a tinge of guilt, knowing it was probably someone from the office but not able to deal with a work conversation at this moment.

'Are you thinking what I'm thinking?' she said, finally.

'He's wrong.' John tramped the gas pedal, making a more violent turn than he had intended, pulling out inches in front of a bus, which blasted its horn in anger.

'He *has* to be wrong,' she agreed.

'No one can know for sure at twelve weeks,' he said. 'It was dumb of him to claim he could.'

'He's arrogant. He doesn't care about us, we're little people. If you or I were A-list celebs, he wouldn't have made that mistake. He wouldn't have dared.'

The bus filled John's rear-view mirror as they crossed San Vincente and Wilshire. 'His mind wasn't on it.'

'We should get a second opinion.'

John negotiated the junction with Olympic in silence, then he said, 'We'll get one. He's an asshole, he's made a mistake. Sixteen weeks is the earliest you can tell, all the books say that. We'll go and see someone again when you are sixteen weeks.'

'I don't want to wait four weeks – I can't wait that long, John, I *have* to know. *We* have to know.'

'There's stuff on the net about a blood test called free

73

foetal DNA, but I'm not sure how reliable it is. It may not be possible – to be totally accurate – until sixteen weeks. I don't think we should panic.'

'I'm worried,' Naomi said. 'If the sex is wrong, the other genes might also be wrong. There must be some one hundred per cent accurate way we can check on the sex without waiting a month. Surely? What about a DNA test – wouldn't that be a possibility?'

'Other than this free foetal method, it's invasive to do that. I looked up a load of stuff on the web the other day about testing foetuses. There's a risk of miscarriage. It's a small risk, but – do you want to take any chances?'

Did she? Any chances? She tried desperately to think straight. If Rosengarten had made a mistake, it would be crazy to risk everything by panicking. But—

'If it comes to it, we'll fly back to the clinic. Confront Dettore.'

'You think Dettore would tell us the truth? You think if he's made a mistake he's going to admit it to us?'

John started to say something, then fell silent for some moments. Then he said, 'He – he doesn't have any reason—'

Swallowing back a knot of fear in her throat, she said, 'Reason to what?'

'To give us a girl when we've asked for a boy.'

'Phone him,' she said. 'You have his number, phone him now.'

They were less than half a mile from home, but John pulled off the road onto the forecourt of the small shopping mall. He looked up the number on his BlackBerry then, holding the phone to his ear, dialled.

Naomi watched his face. After some moments, he said, 'This is John Klaesson. I need to speak to Dr Dettore very

urgently. Please ask him to call me back on my cellphone.'
He gave the number, then he hung up.

'Voice mail?' she asked.

'Yes.' John looked at his watch. 'They're on East Coast time – which means they're three hours ahead. It's twenty after twelve. Twenty after three on the ship. Maybe there's some problem with the switchboard. I had this difficulty getting hold of him a few times in the past.'

'I didn't see any switchboard on the ship, John.'

He wedged the phone back into the cradle. 'There's a lot of things we didn't see.'

She said nothing.

16

When he was eighteen, John had to make a decision that would shape the course of his life. He had already decided he wanted to make a career in academic research, but had a hard time deciding which field. He was torn between his love of biology and his fascination with mathematics, physics and technology.

There was something mystical to him about all mathematical problems. Sometimes he felt he was reaching out through time into some new, as yet undiscovered dimension, to meet an intellectual challenge placed by a vastly superior intelligence. As if each of these big problems was part of some cosmic puzzle, and if you could solve them, you would understand the key to human existence.

In biology, also, were keys to the riddle of existence, but they were more limited. The world of genetics excited him, but ultimately genetics boiled down to mechanics. It seemed to him that genetics could help you understand everything about a human being, except for the one key question that had fascinated John all his life: why do we exist? Ultimately he found biologists too narrow in their thinking. Relatively few biologists believed either in the notion of God or any higher form of intelligence. He found far broader thinking among mathematicians and physicists, and that was ultimately the reason he opted to study computer sciences.

But when he began at Uppsala, Sweden's premier university, he hadn't realized that, despite the exploding technology revolution, life for most academic researchers was not changing, and that when he went out into the real world afterwards, he would be faced with a constant struggle for funding. If you weren't employed by a corporation or an institute, the research programme you were on would likely have funding for a limited period, often as short as just three years. This effectively meant that instead of concentrating on your research, you had to put a huge amount of energy into writing letters to companies, institutes, foundations, and filling in applications, trying to find your next tranche of funding.

This was where John was at again now. He'd stayed on at Uppsala doing his PhD, then as a postdoc, but ultimately found Sweden too limiting – as well as disliking the short daylight hours of winter there. At the age of twenty-six he had jumped at the opportunity to relocate to Sussex University in England, to a lecturing post that gave him the opportunity to work in a lab as part of a research team in cognitive sciences. It was headed by a man he considered to be a real visionary, Professor Carson Dicks, under whom he had worked when the scientist had spent a year as a visiting lecturer at Uppsala.

John enjoyed the science they were doing at Sussex and working under Carson Dicks so much, he didn't mind that the pay was poor, but he was depressed by the indifferent attitude in Britain towards research. Then, after three years, Dicks left the university to take a post at a government research establishment. Shortly after, at the age of twenty-nine, John was offered the chance of a tenure track faculty lecturing post at the University of Southern California, with his own lab in a department headed by Dr Bruce Katzenberg – another scientist whose work he admired hugely. He jumped at it.

John's work at USC involved the creation and study of virtual life forms – something that married his interests in both physics and biology, and was a dream project for him. After six years he was now up for tenure – something that would have been a certainty for him had Dr Katzenberg still been head of his department.

But a year ago, Dr Katzenberg was headhunted by a software company in Silicon Valley, which made him an offer he apologetically told John that not even God could have refused. Now, with less than a year of the project to run, the prospect of further funds did not look good, and nor did the likelihood of tenure for many of his colleagues on the project, who were starting to file applications elsewhere.

John had been brought up in Örebro, a small, beautiful university town in the centre of Sweden that was built around the banks of a river, and had a moated medieval castle in its centre. In summer he'd cycled through a park to school, and in winter when there was thick snow he'd skied there. He liked to walk, he liked open spaces, feeling free. In LA he sometimes felt hemmed in.

Even more than Naomi did, he missed the big changes in the seasons. He loved the long hours of daylight, and the summers were great, but he really hankered at times for the cold sharp tang of autumn and the sense of the approach of winter. And he missed the snow most of all. Sure, they could drive to the mountains and go skiing at weekends, or take a short, cheap flight to Telluride or Park City or any of a whole bunch of great ski resorts, but he missed that snow falling outside the windows, covering the garden and the cars. He missed the spring. He missed the sense of community.

Perhaps it was the same in any large city.

He turned off Jefferson into Gate 8, nodded at the attendant in his booth and pulled into a parking bay. Then, hitching his laptop bag over his shoulder, he walked back onto Jefferson, and crossed McClintock, a short distance from the Shrine. This area was fine in daytime, but at night students and staff either walked in a large group, or got escorted by a security guard back to the parking lots. It was that kind of a neighbourhood.

The dark and violent underbelly of the city had, mercifully, never touched either him or Naomi and he rarely gave it any thought. It was the constant reminders of Halley all around, everywhere in the city, that affected both of them. Santa Monica was the worst. For the best part of a year, St John's Hospital in Santa Monica had become a second home for them. He and Naomi had taken turns at sleeping on a cot in Halley's room. Watching him deteriorate. Hoping for some miracle that was never going to happen.

Sometimes, even just hearing the name *Santa Monica* brought pain. He had hoped that would change when Luke was born, that they could start living their lives forwards again, instead of always being in the shadow of the past. But now, with Dr Rosengarten's pronouncement, even their hopes for a new beginning were in a mess.

Christ, what the hell have I got us into?

Deep in thought, he entered the four-storey building and took the elevator up to the third floor, where the department of cognitive sciences was housed. Several students were milling around in the corridor as he emerged, familiar faces, but only a couple he could put a name to. It was lunch time. Ordinarily he'd be taking a break now, instead of arriving to start his day.

A pretty Chinese-American girl suddenly blocked his

path. 'Hey, Dr Klaesson – could I talk to you for a moment? I have a real problem with something you said in your lecture last Thursday about Neural Darwinism, and I need to—'

'Could we do this later, Mei-Ling?'

'Sure – shall I stop by your office?'

'About four – would that work for you?' He had no idea of his schedule this afternoon, but he just didn't want to talk to anyone right now. He needed some time alone.

To think.

To get hold of Dr Leo Dettore.

'Four's good,' she said.

'Terrific.' He walked on, down a shiny linoleum corridor lined on one side with grey metal filing cabinets and on the other with closed doors.

The last door on the left opened onto a room of ten computer workstations, four of which were occupied by some of his graduate and postdoctoral fellows. One was sitting back, semi-comatose, a can of Coke in his hand. Another was hunched over the screen in deep contemplation. His young postdoc, Sarah Neri, her head a mass of tangled red hair, had her face inches from her screen, studying some graph. John tiptoed past into the sanctuary of his office, and closed the door behind him.

It was a decent, if soulless office, a generous size, with bland modern furnishings and a window, set a little high, with a view out over a quadrangle onto two other campus buildings. There was paperwork strewn over every flat surface in the room, including the visitor chairs and much of the floor, a Mac monitor and keyboard, and a whiteboard on the wall that was covered in scrawled algorithms and a barely legible diagram from an illustration he had made for a student.

Without removing his jacket he sat at his desk, pulled his laptop out of the bag and downloaded the files he had been working on last night at home, then checked his agenda for the afternoon.

'Shit!' he said out loud.

There was a six o'clock appointment he had completely forgotten about. A journalist from *USA Today* wanted to do a piece about his department. Normally it would have been handled by Saul Haranchek, who had taken over as head of the unit after Bruce Katzenberg's departure, but Saul was out of town and had asked him to take the interview. John didn't need this, not today of all days when he wanted to get home early, back to Naomi.

He tried Dettore's number, but again got the answering machine. Then he rang Naomi at the production office.

She sounded low. 'Did you try Dettore?'

'Yes, I'm going to keep trying.'

'What about a second opinion?'

'Let me talk to him first. I'm afraid I'm going to be a little late back, I have to do an interview.'

'It's OK, I have to go to a screening I'd forgotten all about. Need it like a hole in the head. I won't be back till at least nine. What do you want to do about food tonight?'

'Want to go out? Have a Mexican somewhere?'

'I'm not sure I could handle Mexican at the moment. Shall we see how we feel later?'

'Sure,' John said. 'Love you.'

'Love you, too.'

He hung up with a heavy heart, then opened his email inbox.

He had Dettore's email address, and typed out a curt email, stating Dr Rosengarten's diagnosis and asking him to phone him as a matter of great urgency.

He sent the email, then walked over to the window. Despite the cold wind and the spats of rain, quite a few people were out there. Some sitting on benches eating their lunches, some in groups, talking. One or two smoking. Students. No longer kids, but not yet adults. Their whole lives in front of them. Did they know what was coming up behind them?

He looked at one particularly hip group standing in their baggy clothes, with their topiaried heads, laughing, fooling around, so goddamn carefree. None of their parents had messed with their genes. But when their turn came, what would they do?

Did they know they were the last generation of kids left to chance? Did they realize that however smart they might think they were, they were going to grow up to find themselves a genetic underclass? That they were going to be faced with the chance to make their own kids infinitely smarter, stronger, healthier than they themselves could ever be?

What choices would they make?

Then he turned away from the window, afraid. Rosengarten could have made a mistake, sure, but if he hadn't? If it was Dettore who had made the mistake, just how many other mistakes had he made?

Twelve weeks. You could abort right up until how long? Sixteen weeks? Or was it eighteen?

At half past four, he rang Dr Dettore's number again, and left a second message, a considerably more assertive one than before. He also rang Dr Rosengarten, and left word with his secretary that he wanted to speak to him urgently.

By six o'clock there had been no response from either Dettore or Rosengarten. He rang Naomi's office, but was told she was in a meeting. He looked at his watch. If Dettore was on board his offshore clinic, he would be on Atlantic time, three hours ahead of Pacific time. Nine o'clock in the evening. Angry now, he was about to pick up the phone to dial again when it rang. He snatched it off the cradle, but it wasn't Dettore.

It was the reporter from *USA Today*, a breezy-sounding young woman called Sally Kimberly. She was held up in traffic on the 101 and would be with him in fifteen minutes. Had the photographer arrived yet?

'I didn't realize there was a photographer coming,' he said.

'He'll be very quick – just a couple of shots in case we need them.'

It was another thirty-five minutes before she knocked on his door. The photographer had arrived and was busy rearranging his office.

Dettore had still not called back and nor had Dr Rosengarten.

17

It was cocktail hour, which meant the lights in the hotel bar were dimmed and an endless loop of Chopin played from the speakers, giving the impression that in some alcove behind one of the banks of potted palms lurked a pianist. The air conditioning was too cold, but the tables and chairs were well spaced out, making it a good place to talk – although John's real reason for bringing the reporter here was because it was one of the few places in walking distance from the campus that served alcohol.

He followed Sally Kimberly in through the revolving door. She was a polite, quiet-spoken young woman in her early thirties, and dressed in a conservative suit. Her body was a little plump, but her face was attractive, and she had a pleasant, caring manner about her, unlike some reporters he had encountered.

He glanced at her hands, looking for an engagement or wedding ring. There were a couple of plain bands, but not on the marriage finger. It was a strange instinct men had, he thought, some reproductive dynamic that was hardwired into the species. He could never help it himself – one of the first things he looked for was always the wedding-ring finger.

She picked a corner table at the far end of the room from the bar, and not directly beneath a speaker, so her recorder wouldn't be muffled by the music, she explained. She ordered a Chardonnay, and he ordered a large beer for himself. He needed some alcohol to steady his nerves, already shot to hell and back by the day's news and made worse by the prospect of this interview.

USA Today was a huge newspaper. A good article would enhance his chances of tenure, and it could catch the eye of a possible sponsor for their department. But he knew from past unhappy experiences that as a scientist you always had to be wary of the press and media.

Sally Kimberly set her small tape recorder on the table, but didn't switch it on. Instead she asked, 'Is your wife called Naomi?'

'Naomi? Yes.'

'Of course! I've made the connection now! She works in television PR? Naomi Klaesson?'

'Film and television, yes.'

'You're not going to believe this! We worked together about six years ago on the PR for a biology series for the Discovery Channel!'

'How about that!' John said, wracking his brains, trying to recall if Naomi had ever mentioned her. It was quite possible; he had a lousy memory for names.

'She's great, I really liked her. She was pregnant—' Her voice braked. 'I – I'm sorry. That was not very tactful. I heard about your son. I'm really sorry for you both. I'm sorry I brought it up.'

'It's OK.'

After a brief silence she said, 'So, how is Naomi?'

'Oh – she's doing great now, thanks. She's got through it.' He wanted to add, *And she's expecting again!* But he held back.

'Still in PR?'

'Uh-huh. Right now she's at a documentary company called Bright Spark.'

'Sure, I know them. Wow! I must give Naomi a call,

have lunch with her! She has the most wicked sense of humour!'

John smiled.

Their drinks arrived. For some time they chatted easily, graduating from the good and the bad about life in LA, to the merits of different eBook readers. Sally Kimberly sipped her white wine, John drained his beer in minutes, and ordered a second, warming to just being here with her, enjoying talking to her, feeling – if for just a short while – he was escaping from his pressures. There was something so sincere and vulnerable about her that made John wonder how on earth she survived in the rough and tumble world of newsprint.

She was single and found it hard to meet men in this city who weren't either totally vain or totally screwed-up, she told him. And her body language hinted, very subtly, but very definitely, that she found him attractive.

He found her increasingly attractive himself, and immediately saw warning flags. In eight years with Naomi he had never strayed; although he had found himself flirting with other women at the occasional party, he had never been tempted. He needed to play this young lady very carefully; flirt, yes, but in no way lead her on.

Suddenly his glass was empty again. 'Get you another white wine?' he offered, turning his head for the waitress.

The reporter looked at her almost-full glass. 'No, I'm good, thanks.'

The beer was giving him a pleasant buzz, making the problems with Naomi's pregnancy seem easier to understand, easier to cope with. Mistakes happened all the time in medicine. Rosengarten was in a rush, he hadn't been concentrating, and he was being arrogant saying he could determine the sex at such an early age. He wished he'd quizzed the obstetrician harder about why he was so sure, but he'd been so shocked, as had Naomi, that he had barely said anything.

'OK – I'll just have another—' He tapped the side of his head with a grin. 'Need some rocket fuel to get my brain going for you.' He detected what might have been a slight frown of disapproval. Or had he just imagined that?

'You have an accent,' she said. 'Kind of slight.'

'Swedish.'

'Of course.'

'Ever been there?'

'Actually, there's a possibility I may get sent to Stockholm to do a piece on the Nobel Prize awards—'

'You're getting one for journalism?'

She laughed. 'I wish.'

'It's the most beautiful city, all built around water. I'll give you some names of restaurants you should visit – do you like fish?'

'Uh-huh.'

'They have great fish. Best seafood in the world.'

'Better than here in LA?'

'Are you kidding me?'

'There's great fish here,' she said, a little defensively.

'You call me and tell me that again after you've eaten fish in Stockholm.'

She gave him an unambiguous *take me there* look.

Smiling at her, then hastily turning away, he finally caught the waitress's eye and ordered another large draught beer.

Sally Kimberly reached forward and switched the recorder on. 'I guess we should start. OK?'

'Sure, fire away,' he assented. 'I'll do my best not to incriminate myself!' He was aware the beers had gone to his head; he'd drunk them too fast. *Need to slow down, just take a few sips from the next one, and no more.*

She switched the machine off, wound the tape back and played a few moments. 'Just checking it's recording,' she said. John heard himself say, ... *my best not to incriminate myself!*

She set the machine down again. 'OK, my first question, Dr Klaesson, is what were the influences that made you decide to become a research scientist?'

'I thought you wanted to talk about my department and the work we're doing, rather than individuals?'

'I'd just like a little background.'

'Sure.'

Giving him an encouraging smile, she said, 'Are either of your parents scientists?'

'No, we don't have any other scientists in our family. My father was a salesman.'

'Did he have any interest in science?'

John shook his head. 'Not remotely. Fishing and gambling were his things – he was a walking encyclopedia of rods, lines, weights, lures, floats, bait, poker odds and race-horse form. He could tell you where the fish hung out at what time of day in every stretch of water within thirty miles of our home, and what horse was running in any race just about anywhere in the world.' He smiled. 'I guess he was into the science of fishing and betting.'

'Do you think there's some analogy between fishing and the methodology of scientific research?' she asked.

John was torn between trying to keep the reporter happy and trying to steer her on to what he really wanted to talk about. 'I think my mother was a much bigger influence,' he said. 'She used to be a mathematics teacher – and she's always taken a great interest in everything.

And she's a hugely practical woman. She could take an electric motor to pieces to show me how it worked one day, and another day sit me down and discuss the religious writings of Emanuel Swedenborg. I think she gave me my curiosity.'

'Sounds like you have more of her genes than your father's.'

The remark brought his thoughts abruptly back to Dettore. 'Perhaps,' he said, distractedly.

How the hell could Dettore have got it wrong? How? How?

'OK, Dr Klaesson, I wonder now if you could describe in – like – a couple of sentences, the broad beats of your research team's work?'

'Sure, absolutely.' He thought for some moments. 'How much do you know about the construction of the human brain?'

Her expression hardened, just a fraction, just enough for him to receive the message loud and clear. *Don't patronize me.*

'I did my PhD on "The Nature Of Consciousness",' she said.

That whacked him. 'You did? Where?'

'At Tulane.'

'I'm impressed.' He was surprised, too. He had not been expecting her to have anything beyond a working knowledge of science.

'I just didn't want you thinking you were talking to a no-brainer.'

'Not for one moment did I—'

She leaned back with a big smile, her face all warmth again. 'You did! I could see it!'

He raised his hands in surrender. 'Hey, give me a

break! I've had a hard day – I don't need you beating up on me at the end of it!'

His beer arrived. He took it from the waitress's hand before she'd had a chance to set it down and drank a deep gulp. 'Right. Your question. We're examining human organs, and in particular the human brain, trying to understand better their pathways of evolution to our present state, and how much further evolution will change them in the future.'

'And you are hoping one of the results will be to lead you to understand what human consciousness is?'

'Exactly.'

'Is *Neural Darwinism* a way to describe your simulation programs?'

'That's Edelman's phrase.' He drank some more beer. 'No, there's quite a difference.' A smear on the right lens of his glasses was irritating him. He took them off and wiped them with his handkerchief. 'You must have covered this field at Tulane. Neural Darwinism relates to when you build a robot that doesn't actually have a program – it has to learn from its experiences, the way human beings do. That's taking steps towards building thinking machines by copying some of the ways human brains work. We're not doing that – our field is different.'

He held his glasses up to the light and still wasn't satisfied. Wiping them some more, he said, 'Our methodology is to simulate millions of years of evolution in our computers, making virtual replicas of primitive brains and seeing if, by replicating natural selection, we can arrive at far more complex models that are closer to our own brains. At the same time we make virtual models of current human brains and let them keep evolving way into the future.'

'I'm puzzled by something there, Dr Klaesson.'

'Call me John.'

'John, OK, thanks. You say you make virtual replicas of *primitive* brains?'

'That's correct.'

'How primitive, John? How far are you going back? Palaeolithic? Jurassic? Cambrian?'

'Before then, even. Right back to Archaean.'

The third beer was kicking in now. He noticed to his surprise he had drunk nearly two thirds of it. He knew he had to slow down, but it was really making him feel good.

'And when you do finally understand how the human brain was formed, then you'll understand consciousness?'

'Not necessarily – you're making a big leap there.'

'Oh, right.' She was grinning and her voice was cynical. 'You're going to switch off your computer one day and say, *Hey, I just finally figured out how the human brain was formed. Now I'm going to go home and feed the cat.* Is that it?'

John smiled back.

'From the way you work, for you to have figured out how the brain was formed, you'd have a virtual model of it in your computer. Then the next step is going to be improving it, right? What will you do – add on more memory? Some kind of interface with humans?'

'Whoa! You're going too fast.'

'I'm not, Dr Kl— John, I'm just quoting from a paper you published three years ago.'

He nodded, remembering now. 'Ah yes, OK.' He smiled. 'You've done your homework – but that wasn't the theme of the paper – I was hypothesizing.' He was getting concerned suddenly that this interview was heading the wrong way. He needed to get a grip and steer it. 'Listen, this speculation about the future – I'm happy to talk about it, but could we keep that whole area off the record?'

'Hi, how you folks doing? Get you some more drinks?' The waitress had suddenly materialized and was standing beside him.

John saw that the reporter's glass was almost empty. 'Sure,' he said. 'Sally – another one?'

She hesitated a moment. 'How's your time? I'm not keeping you too long?'

He glanced at his watch. Half seven. Naomi wouldn't be home until after nine, she'd told him. 'I'm fine,' he said.

'OK, I'll have another Chardonnay.'

John considered his empty glass for a moment. As a student in Sweden he could easily manage upwards of half a dozen of these – and stronger beer too. 'Same again – I'll live dangerously!'

Sally reached forward and pressed the stop button on the tape machine. 'Off the record for a few minutes – tell me what you feel about the future – I'm really fascinated.'

He would never know why he said it – whether it was the alcohol that had lowered his guard, or whether it was the thought that if he opened up to her a little, he might get a better piece from her – or whether it was just the natural action of a man to show off to a woman who seemed genuinely interested. Or whether it was simply the release of stuff bottled up in him for too long. In any event, he felt comfortable; she was a friend of Naomi's. He could trust her.

'Designer babies are the future,' he said.

'Like – cloning?'

'No, not cloning. I mean selecting the genes that your child will have.'

'To what end?'

'To enable man to take control from Mother Nature – to be in a position so we can steer our future evolution to our needs. So that we can be looking at a human lifespan of hundreds of years, if not thousands, rather than a meagre three score years and ten.'

'I'm very uncomfortable with that whole notion of designer babies,' she said. 'I'm sure it's going to happen but I find it scary. How many years do you reckon before it starts happening – I mean, like, before it's possible. Ten?'

'It's possible now.'

'I don't believe that,' she said. 'Not from what I've heard. Not from anyone I've talked to.'

The alcohol was kicking in now and he felt good in the company of this increasingly attractive woman, and he really felt relaxed, perhaps too relaxed. All this secrecy had been hard; surely it wouldn't hurt talking to Naomi's friend? He glanced at the tape recorder. The tell-tale red light was not showing. 'We're off the record? Strictly off the record, right?'

'Totally.'

With a smile he said, 'You're not talking to the right people.'

'So who should I be talking to?'

He tapped his chest. 'Me.'

18

The building was moving. Definitely. For a moment, as the floor rose up beneath him, John thought he was back on the *Serendipity Rose*. Then the wall came in towards him, clouting him on the shoulder, sending scalding black coffee slopping out of the cup he was holding and onto his hand, his clothes and the floor.

He staggered sideways, everything in front of him blurry. He had to sober up, somehow. He'd been all right in the bar, he'd been fine there, no problem, it was the walk in the cold fresh air outside that had done it.

A chunk of time was missing. There was a blank from when he went into the bar to now, walking down the corridor towards his office. He couldn't remember saying goodbye to the reporter. When had she gone?

How much did I drink?

It hadn't been that much, surely? Just a few beers – then he'd moved on to whisky on the rocks. Just a couple of whiskies, just enough to relax him, that was all. Christ. Empty stomach, that was the problem, he realized. Skipped lunch after seeing Dr Rosengarten. It was now – he looked at his watch – *ohmygod* – almost a quarter after ten. He'd been with the reporter for over three hours. *Not like I was having an affair or anything. I was only talking to the woman. Trying to get her to write a good piece, one that would help me get funding – that's all I was doing.*

Except. Something dark inside his head was stalking him, something elusive was shadow-boxing him, taunting him. It was the sense that something was wrong, that he had made a terrible error. He hadn't made a pass at her, nothing as crass as that – although he had some memory of escorting her to the car park and some clumsy clashing of their lips when she'd suddenly darted her head forward to kiss his cheek, he had thought.

But that wasn't what was worrying him.

He unlocked his door, switched the light on and put the cup, which was now less than half full, on his desk, and sat down more heavily than he had intended, sending his chair trundling back on its castors.

He checked his voice mail, and there was a message from Dr Rosengarten, received at ten to seven, the curt nasal voice of the obstetrician informing him he was returning his call, and was about to leave his office for the day.

John felt cheered up by the fact that he had at least bothered to return the call – and had done so personally. He would try him again in the morning. He ran through the rest of his messages; there were a couple from earlier in the day that he hadn't yet listened to, both from Sweden. One from a friend from Uppsala University, who was coming over to Los Angeles this fall, and another from his mother, chiding him for not calling her to tell her how the visit to the obstetrician went today. It was now early morning in Sweden; too early to call either of them.

He hung up and checked his email. Over a dozen new ones since he had gone out to the bar, but nothing that looked important. Nothing from Dettore.

Bastard.

Suddenly he looked around, puzzled, aware that the room did not feel right. There seemed to be something missing, but he couldn't figure what. Or maybe it was just that the photographer had messed some things around.

His cellphone rang, startling him. It was Naomi. She sounded so scared, so vulnerable. 'Where are you?'

'Offish. In the offish. Jush leaving.' *I got you into this*, he thought. *Anything that happens is my fault.* 'I'm sorry – been tied up – I had to do shish interview – she knows you – still feel like going out? A Mescixian – ah – *Mexican*? Or some shush – *sushi*—?'

He was aware he was slurring his words but there was nothing he could do about it.

'John, are you all right?'

'Sure – I – I sh – shhhure—'

'Are you drunk? John – you sound drunk.'

He stared at the receiver, helplessly, as if waiting for some guidance to come out of the ether. 'No – I—'

'Have you spoken to Dr Dettore?'

Very slowly, taking great care over each word at a time, John said, 'No. He – heesh – I'll try in – in – morning.'

Oh Christ. John closed his eyes. She was crying. 'I'm coming darling – I'm – on way home now.'

'Don't drive, John. I'll come and collect you.'

'I could – cab – call cab.'

After a few moments, her voice sounding more composed, she said, 'I'll collect you. We don't have money to burn on cabs. We can pick up a takeaway. I'll be there in twenty minutes.' Then she hung up.

John sat very still. He had a bad feeling; that shadow in his mind was growing. There definitely was something missing in this room. What the hell was it?

But that wasn't the source of the bad feeling. Nor at this moment was it Dr Rosengarten's diagnosis, nor the fact that Dettore was unavailable. He was fretting about what he had said to the journalist. Trying to remember exactly what he had said. She was a nice lady, kind, sympathetic, fun to be with. He sensed he'd been a bit indiscreet, said a bit too much, more than he had intended.

But it was off the record, wasn't it?

19

Naomi's Diary

I can't sleep. John is snoring like a hog. I haven't seen him drunk like this in a long time. Why did he get so smashed? Sure, we're both upset by Dr Rosengarten, but getting drunk like this doesn't solve anything.

And he had lipstick on his face.

I spoke to my mother and to Harriet. Both of them rang, wanting to know how it went today. I told them that the obstetrician was happy, that everything was fine. Harriet lent us her entire savings – what could I say to her? That everything is fine except – oh, yes – one small detail – it's not a boy, it's a girl?

Surely the gender genes are the easiest of all the genes to manipulate? As I understand it, females have two X chromosomes, males an X and a Y. Separation of these is being done around the world in the most primitive of labs. If Dr Dettore can't get even this simplest element right, what assurances do we have about everything else we've discussed with him?

And, just supposing that everything else is fine, what problems would a girl have with the genes we've selected? We asked for our child to be six foot tall because we had a male in mind. We chose height and physical build for a male.

It's all wrong.

John is pretty certain Dr Rosengarten has made a mis-

take. It's possible – I didn't like the man and he wasn't interested in us. As John said, we're just little people to him, we don't matter.

God, I hope he has made a mistake.

And there's something else that's on my mind. Sally Kimberly. He says she told him we were friends. That's rubbish. It's true that we worked together, and normally I get along with most people. But she was a bitch. Hard as nails. We disliked each other intensely and made no bones about it.

In fact, there are very few people I've ever disliked quite so much as Sally Kimberly.

And now her lipstick is on John's face.

20

Naomi was awake; John could hear the faint crushing sound of her eyelashes as she blinked. The light from his alarm radio seemed intense, bathing the room with a spectral blue glow that was irking him. Outside in the distance a siren skirled, a familiar mournful solo, the discordant music of a Los Angeles night.

His head was pounding. He needed water, tablets, sleep. Desperately needed sleep. He swung his legs out of the bed, carried his empty glass to the bathroom, ran the cold tap, swallowed two Tylenol and padded back into the room.

'What's going to happen to us?' Naomi said suddenly as he got back into bed.

John felt for her hand, found it, squeezed it, but there was no pressure back. 'Perhaps we should think about termination – an abortion?'

'It never mattered to me, John, whether it was a boy or a girl. All I wanted was for our child to be healthy – I would have been perfectly happy not knowing the sex, like a lot of other people, just knowing that he or she is normal. I don't want an abortion, that would be ridiculous – you can't make a decision to abort your baby because you wanted a boy and you are getting a girl.'

There was an uncomfortable silence. The issue was far deeper than that and they both knew it.

'Ships have communication problems sometimes,' he

said. 'They rely on satellites and can't always get a link – I'll try again in the morning.'

There was another siren out there now, and the bass horn blasts of a fire truck.

'I don't want you to have an abortion,' he said. 'Not unless it's—'

She waited some moments and then she prompted, 'Unless it's what?'

'There are some tests that can be done now in labs here in the States – they can pick up all kinds of stuff about the foetus.'

She snapped the bedside light on and sat up, angrily. 'This isn't some disposable product, John. This isn't some lab experiment in a Petri dish or a bell jar – some – some fruit fly or something.' She pulled the duvet up and crossed her arms protectively over her belly. 'This is my child – our child – that's growing inside me. I'm going to love her, or him, no matter how he – it – turns out. I'm going to love this creature whether she grows to four feet tall or seven feet. I'm going to love her whether she's a genius or retarded.'

'Darling, that isn't—'

She interrupted him. 'You brought up this whole idea in the first place and you talked me into it. I'm not blaming you; I came to this with my eyes wide open; I'm as responsible for the decision as you are. What I'm saying is that I'm not walking away from this. Maybe whatever is going on – Dettore screwing up on the gender – maybe this is Mother Nature's way of keeping some kind of a lid on the sanity of the world. I think the day mothers start aborting their babies at the first sign that they're not turning out how they expect them to be, that's the start of a very slippery slope.'

John sat up too. 'If you'd known about Halley – about

his condition – before he was born – would you have gone ahead and brought him into the world knowing what future he faced?'

She said nothing. Then, turning to look at her, he saw a tear trickling down her cheek. He dabbed it with his handkerchief. Her face was all clenched up in misery.

'I'm sorry, I shouldn't have said that.'

There was no reaction.

Easing himself out of bed again, he pulled on his towelling dressing gown, padded out of the bedroom and across the narrow corridor, feeling even worse than a few minutes ago. Entering his den, he stepped carefully around the piles of papers, box of discs, cables, camera lenses and stacks of unread magazines, switched on the desk lamp and sat down. His laptop was still in the bag where he had dumped it when he came in. Removing it, he set it on the desk, opened it, and logged into his computer at the university. Then he checked his email.

Fifteen new ones, including a chiding one from his online chess opponent, Gus Santiano in Brisbane. The man had a nerve, he thought. Santiano regularly used to take up to a week to move. But if John took longer than a couple of days over his own turn, the Australian would start chasing him. *You'll have to wait,* he thought, blearily watching the rest of the email headers appear one after the other. Then suddenly he was wide awake.

Dr Leo Dettore – response.
This is an automated reply to your email from the office of Dr Leo Dettore. Dr Dettore is away at a conference in Italy, returning on 29 July.

The twenty-ninth of July was tomorrow, he realized. Or rather, today.

He hurried back into the bedroom. 'Dr Dettore's been away, darling. There's an email. He's back tomorrow!'

But instead of acknowledging this she remained motionless, tears still trickling down her face. After a long silence she finally spoke, very quietly.

'Is Sally Kimberly a good screw?'

21

John arrived in his office shortly after nine, cold and shivery, with a maelstrom of bad stuff going on inside his head. He sat at his desk with a cup of black coffee and a cup of cold water, prised two Tylenol capsules from their foil and swallowed them.

Rain rattled against the window. It was blowing a gale outside, his jacket was damp, his chinos were soaked and clinging to his legs, and his loafers were sodden after stepping off the sidewalk into a deep puddle.

At eleven o'clock he had to give a lecture to thirty students, in which he was to talk about the areas where the advances of medicine were having a bad impact on human evolution. Because of a whole range of scientific and medical developments during the past few thousand years, from primitive dentistry and optical lenses, through to organ transplants and new controls for chronic killer diseases like diabetes, it was no longer the fittest or best-adapted humans who survived.

Once, the gene lines of people with no teeth would have died out because they couldn't eat, and similarly those with bad vision would have more easily fallen prey to wild animals or enemies, and died out also, but this was no longer the case. These people survived with their defects and continued breeding, passing the defects to their offspring. Likewise people with the genes for organ failure or chronic diseases survived and bred. Every year more defective people were coming into the world rather than fewer. Science was already, stealthily and unwittingly, taking over from Darwinian principles of natural selection.

John had done experiments with his students on computer models of evolution with and without the impact of medical advances. Left unimpeded, humans would have evolved, naturally, into a far stronger species than they were now. He told his students that in the next experiment they designed they would add something new into the equation: genetic engineering. That was the only way to counteract the gradual erosion of our species by medicine. Without genetic engineering, over the next hundred thousand years – a mere three hundred generations' time – the computer models had shown that those people who lived in affluent societies would be dangerously weakened.

He had been looking forward to this talk, but now with the events of the past twenty-four hours, he had lost all enthusiasm. He just wanted, desperately, to try to sort everything out.

Naomi's accusation really hurt him. He buried his head in his hands. She was in a state and would calm down; he hadn't done anything other than talk to the reporter, he had a clear conscience about that. But just what the hell had he said to her?

The reporter had lied about their friendship. Why? To get him to talk?

Off the record. It had been *off the record.* Hadn't it?

He dialled Dr Rosengarten, then logged on to his email while the phone was ringing. The obstetrician's secretary answered. Dr Rosengarten was in theatre all morning. She took down John's number and told him she would have him call him back when he was free.

He glanced down the fresh list of emails in his inbox.

He'd put a few speculative feelers out to a number of universities and institutions over the past weeks, but there were no responses this morning. In a year's time if he didn't get tenure here, he would be out of a job. With almost all his savings gone on the baby Naomi was now carrying, he was feeling panicky. His book would still take another year to finish – and in any event he would not make anything like enough from it to live on. He faced the very real possibility that he might have to move out of his field altogether and take a research and development job in some place like Silicon Valley with a computer company. Not a prospect he relished.

Twenty past nine, Los Angeles time. The East Coast was three hours ahead. Twenty after midday. Dettore might be back by now. He dialled his number.

Four rings and then the voice mail again: 'You've reached the Dettore Clinic. Please leave your name, number – don't forget your country code – and any message, and someone will call you back shortly.'

He left another message, and replaced the receiver. His secretary came in with a pile of mail and he asked her if she'd go get him another cup of water. Then he fished Sally Kimberly's card from his wallet and dialled her direct line.

It didn't even ring. Instead he heard her recorded voice. 'Hi, you've reached Sally Kimberly. I'm out right now, but leave a message, or reach me on my cellphone.'

He left a message asking her to call him urgently, then dialled her cellphone, but her voice mail kicked in instantly on that, too. He left a second message.

Then, as he hung up, he realized what it was that had been bugging him last night – the feeling he'd had that there was something missing from the room: it was the photograph of Naomi that was normally on his desk. One of his favourite pictures of her, taken a couple of years back when they'd revisited Turkey. She was tanned, her fair hair bleached almost blonde by the salt and sun, standing on the prow of an elderly gulet, sunglasses pushed up on her head, arms outstretched, doing a parody of Kate Winslet in the film *Titanic*.

He stood up and looked around. The photographer must have moved it last night; he'd rearranged a load of stuff. But where the hell had he put it?

His secretary came in. He asked her about the photograph, but she assured him she had not touched it. Then he sat back down and sipped the water, switching his thoughts to Dr Rosengarten.

What he needed to understand was, if Rosengarten had been right and it was a girl, just how easy would it have been for Dettore to have got the sex of the child wrong? Was it harder than the other genes that he had altered – or easier? Was it just one slip, or was their baby a total mess?

He called up his addresses file, typed in a key word, and a name and a phone number came up. Dr Maria Annand. She was an infertility specialist at Cedars-Sinai. He'd been to see her with Naomi six months ago for tests, at the request of Dr Dettore, before being accepted by him. Dettore had wanted confirmation that it was still viable for Naomi to conceive, before putting them to the expense of coming to see him.

He dialled the number. By luck, he caught her just as she was leaving for an appointment.

'Look, Dr Annand, I have a quick question I want to ask you. If you have an embryo sexed, what are the percentage chances of getting it correct?'

'You mean like selecting a male or female?'

'Exactly.'

'That's done regularly on people carrying sex-specific disease genes. It would normally be done through pre-implantation genetics – when you are creating the embryo. When it gets to eight cells, you take a single cell from the blastocyst of the developing embryo, and the embryo doesn't notice. You have it sexed. It's very simple.'

'What margin of error is there?'

'I don't understand what you mean,' she said.

'Let's say a couple want a boy. They have pre-implantation genetics to select the sex – but later they discover they are not having a boy, but a girl. How likely is that to happen?'

She sounded adamant. 'Extremely unlikely. Any error on the sexing of a foetus is remote – it's so basic.'

'But it must happen? Surely?'

'You look at the chromosomes, look at the numbers. There's no way you're going to make a mistake.'

'There are always mistakes in science,' John said.

'OK, right, you can get a mix-up in a lab, sure. That happened recently. A fertility clinic mixed up the embryos of a black couple and a white couple – they put back the wrong embryo – the white couple had a black baby. That can happen.'

'The wrong embryo?' John echoed.

'Uh-huh.'

'You are saying that's the only way it could happen?'

'You'll have to forgive me,' Dr Annand said. 'I have to rush – I'm really late.'

'Sure, appreciate your time, thanks.'

'Call me later if you want to talk this through further,' she said.

'I may do that. So – just to get this right – the wrong embryo – that's the only way? The entire wrong embryo?'

'Yes. That would actually be more likely than getting the sex wrong.'

22

Somehow John got through his lecture. He fielded the barrage of questions from students that followed, answering them as briefly as possible, then hurried back to his office and closed the door. He sat down and checked his voice mail.

There was a message from Naomi. Her voice sounded tearful and panicky. 'Call me, John,' she said. 'Please call me as soon as you get this.'

He put the phone down. What the hell was he going to tell her?

He called Dr Rosengarten, insisting to the secretary he *had* to speak to him right now.

After several minutes on hold, listening to Vivaldi's 'Four Seasons', Dr Rosengarten came on the line, sounding his usual hurried, irritable self.

'The diagnosis you gave us about the sex of our baby,' John said. 'How certain are you that it is a girl?'

The obstetrician put him on hold again while he checked his notes, then came back on the line. 'No question about it, Dr Klaesson. Your wife is having a girl.'

'You couldn't have made a mistake?'

There was a long, chilly silence. John waited, but the obstetrician said nothing.

'In your diagnosis,' John added, a little flustered, 'is there any margin for error?'

'No, Dr Klaesson, there is no margin for error. Anything else I can do for you and Mrs Klaesson?'

'No – I – I guess. Thank you.'

John hung up, angered by Rosengarten's arrogance. Then he tried Dettore once more. Still the voice mail. He rang both of Sally Kimberly's numbers again but this time left no message. Then he rang Naomi.

'John.' Her voice sound strange, trembling. 'Oh God, John, have you heard?'

'Heard what?

'You haven't seen the news?'

'I've been giving a lecture. What news?'

He heard the rest of her words only intermittently, as if he were catching some bulletin on a badly tuned radio station.

'Dr Dettore. Helicopter. Into sea. Crashed. Dead.'

23

'We have this eyewitness report from a yacht off the coast of New York State earlier today.'

John stared at the newsreader with his sharp suit and solemn face. Naomi sat beside him on the sofa, gripping his hand tightly. The camera cut to a static picture of a Bell JetRanger helicopter, identical to the one that had flown them to Dettore's clinic.

A man's voice, a clipped New England accent, came through, crackly and intermittent on a ship-to-shore radio.

'Watched the . . .' Sound lost then restored. 'Flying low, just below the cloud ceiling . . .' Sound lost again. 'Just erupted into a ball of fire like a flying bomb . . .' Sound lost again. 'Then it came back and, oh God . . .' His voice was choked. 'Was horrible.' Sound lost again. 'Debris in the sky. Came down about three miles away from us. We headed right over . . .' Sound lost again. 'Nothing. Wasn't anything there. Nothing at all. Just the eeriest feeling. Horrible sight, I tell you. Just gone. Gone.'

The picture of the helicopter was replaced with a photograph of the *Serendipity Rose*, which now became the backdrop behind the newsreader.

'The billionaire scientist was returning to his offshore floating research laboratory and clinic, where he offered the prospect of designer babies for those able to afford his six-figure prices. Dr Dettore had this past weekend delivered a no-holds-barred paper to a Union of Concerned Scientists conference in Rome, in which he denounced the

Vatican's latest call for international regulations against experimentation on human embryos as a crime against humanity.'

The newsreader paused and the backdrop changed to a recent photograph of Dettore on a podium behind a bank of microphones.

'No stranger to controversy, Dr Dettore has had his work compared to Hitler's eugenics programme, and had featured on the front cover of *Time* magazine.'

John hit the mute button on the remote and stared grimly at the screen, feeling in a state of shock.

'What do we do now, John?'

'I called the clinic six times today, hoping I could speak to someone else – his colleague, Dr Leu. I got a *number not in service* message. I emailed twice. Both times the emails got bounced back, not able to be delivered.'

'We have to get a second opinion.'

'I spoke to Dr Rosengarten.'

'What did he say?'

'He was adamant he had not made a mistake.'

'He's hardly going to admit it, is he?'

'No, but—' He hesitated. Naomi, white as a sheet, looked terrible. How could he tell Naomi what Dr Annand had told him? That Dettore had most probably made a mistake, but not over the gender – over the entire embryo?

How could he tell her she might be pregnant with someone else's child?

'Why would a helicopter explode, John?'

'I don't know. Engines can go wrong – jet engines can blow up sometimes.'

'The man said it was like a bomb.'

John stood up, walked the few paces across the small room to the Deco fireplace and looked at a photograph of

Halley sitting in a toy police jeep, beaming happily. One of those rare moments of respite in his short little life. He felt angry, suddenly. Angry at Dettore for dying – irrational, he knew, but he didn't care. Angry at the loss of the chance of the funding for his own research that Dettore had discussed with him. Angry at Dr Rosengarten. Angry at God for what he did to Halley. Angry for all the shitty hands he seemed to be picking up in life.

He heard what Naomi was saying; the implication was loud and clear.

Bomb.

There were plenty of crazy people out there. Fanatics who hated progress, who believed only their way was right. And irresponsible scientists, too, who believed the whole world was their laboratory and that they could do what they wanted, blow up small Pacific atolls, design generation after generation of biological weaponry, tamper with the germ line of the human species, all in the name of progress.

And in between were people who just wanted to live their lives. Some of them innocents like Halley, born into a living hell.

Science could prevent the tragedy of little children like Halley. Progress could one day eliminate diseases like his. Dettore was right when he said that preventing scientists from being able to do their research on embryos was a crime against humanity.

'Don't ever forget why we've done this, Naomi,' he said, his voice raised in anger that was spawned from utter, helpless frustration.

Naomi stood up and walked over to him and put her arms around his waist. 'You'll love our baby, won't you? Whatever happens, you'll love her?'

He turned and kissed her lightly on the lips. 'Of course.'

'I love you,' she said. 'I love you and I need you.'

She looked so scared, so vulnerable. His heart felt wrenched. 'I need you, too.'

'Let's go out tonight – some place cheerful.'

'What do you feel like? Mexican? Chinese? Sushi?'

'Nothing spicy. How about that place Off-Vine?'

He smiled. 'That was the first place I ever took you to eat in LA.'

'I like it there. Let's see if they have a table.'

'I'll phone.'

'Do you remember something you said to me there? Sitting out in the courtyard? You said that love was more than just a bond between two people. It was like a wagon-train circle you formed around you that protected you against all the world threw at you. Do you remember?'

'Yes,' he said.

'That's what it is going to have to be like from now.'

24

Shortly before midnight, Naomi was violently sick. John knelt beside her in the bathroom, holding her forehead, the way his mother used to hold his when he was a child.

She had thrown up everything inside her, and now it was just bile coming out. And she was shedding tears.

'It's OK,' he said gently, struggling hard against the smell not to retch, too. 'It's OK, darling.'

He wiped her mouth with a wetted towel, dabbed her eyes, then helped her back to bed. 'Feel better?' he asked anxiously.

She nodded, eyes open wide, bloodshot, expressionless. 'How much longer's this bloody sickness going to go on for? I thought it was meant to be *morning* sickness?'

'Maybe it was something you ate?'

She shook her head. 'No.'

John turned off the light and lay still, feeling the damp heat coming off her body, his stomach still queasy from the smell of vomit.

'What do you really think it was?' she asked, suddenly.

'Think *what* was?'

'What made the helicopter crash. Do you think it was a bomb?'

There was a long silence. John listened to her breathing; it was steadily becoming less jerky, more rhythmic. Then, just as he thought she was deeply asleep, she spoke again.

'He had enemies.'

'A lot of scientists have enemies.'

'Do you have enemies, John?'

'I'm not well enough known. I'm sure if I was, there'd be a bunch of fanatics violently opposed to my views. Anyone who dares to stick their head above the parapet and be counted is going to have enemies. But there's a big step between disliking what someone does and blowing them to pieces.'

After some moments she said, 'What do you suppose is going to happen to his lab – ship?'

'I don't know.'

'There must be someone there dealing with admin. They're going to have to cancel new patients – there must be someone you can get hold of who can look at our records and find out what's happened, surely?'

'I'll try again in the morning. I'm going to try to speak to Dr Leu – he seemed pretty on the ball.'

He closed his eyes but his brain was racing. Dettore would have kept detailed records of exactly what he had done to every foetus. It would all be there in his files. Dr Leu would have the answers; of course he would.

'Maybe it's God's way.' She spoke so gently, like a child.

'*God's* way – what do you mean?'

'Perhaps He's angry about – you know – about what we did – about what people are trying to do. And this is His way of balancing things up.'

'By making you sick and by killing Dr Dettore?'

'No, I don't mean that. I mean—'

There was a long silence.

John climbed out of the bed. He needed more water, tablets, sleep. He desperately needed more sleep.

'Maybe God decided we should have a girl, not a boy,' Naomi said.

'What's this talk about God, suddenly? I thought you weren't too impressed with God?'

'Because – I'm wondering – maybe Dr Dettore didn't make a mistake. Maybe God intervened?'

John was aware that pregnancy messed around with a woman's hormones and they in turn could mess around with the brain. Maybe it was that. 'Darling.' He sat down on the bed. 'Dettore screwed up. I don't think this is God intervening. This is a scientist doing something wrong.'

'And we don't know how wrong?'

'We don't know for sure it's wrong at all. I still think Rosengarten is an arrogant man and he could have made a mistake that he won't admit to. We'll get a second opinion. I don't think we should worry too much at this stage.'

'Why don't we have its – *her* – entire genome read?'

'Apart from the cost, it's not just getting it read, it's the analysis that's complex. There are over twelve hundred genes responsible for the prostate; seven hundred for breasts; five hundred for ovaries. It's a massive task.'

'If Dr Dettore was able to do it, surely – I mean, how could he have done it so far ahead? And kept it quiet?'

'Happens in science all the time. You get someone way ahead – sometimes so way ahead people don't appreciate the discovery. He is – was – awesomely smart. He had unlimited money to throw at it.' And, he thought, but did not tell her, not wanting to worry her more, Dettore very definitely had some kind of a hidden agenda. He wasn't covering his costs of running the floating clinic – and that was without his own fees. Let alone the huge time commitment.

Altruism? For the good of mankind? Or—

He drifted into troubled sleep.

It seemed only moments later that the phone was ringing.

25

John woke with a start, feeling groggy and confused. What the hell time was it?

6.47, the clock told him.

Naomi stirred. 'Wasser—?'

Who the hell was ringing at this hour? Sweden, probably. Even after eight years here, his mother never could figure out the time difference. Several times when they had first come out to LA she had called at two and then at three in the morning. Three more rings and the answering machine kicked in.

He closed his eyes and was back asleep in moments.

At five past seven the phone rang again.

'Jesus, mother, we need to sleep!' he yelled.

'It might be important,' Naomi slurred.

'I don't care.'

The answering machine picked it up. Was it his mother? Some problem? It could wait, it would have to wait, whatever it was. He had a nine o'clock faculty meeting at the college and desperately needed a bit more sleep. He'd set the alarm for seven fifteen. He closed his eyes.

Moments later, it rang again. He lay there with his eyes shut against the bright daylight in the room. Felt the bed move. Naomi getting up. The ringing stopped.

'I'll see who it is,' she said.

'Leave it, darling, just leave it!'

She went out of the room. Moments later she came

back in. 'KTTV,' she said. 'Three messages from some woman called Bobby.'

'Bobby? I don't know anyone called Bobby. What do they want?'

'She didn't say – wants you to call. Says it's urgent.'

KTTV was a Fox affiliate, one of the Los Angeles television stations. He had done an interview with them a few months back for a show they were doing on evolution. 'What the hell time of day is this for them to call?' he said, wide awake now, despite his brain feeling leaden from tiredness and the pills.

The phone began ringing again.

'I can't believe this!' he said, and grabbed the cordless that was right by the bed.

A breezy male voice said, 'Hi, this is Dan Wagner from KCAL, is that Dr Klaesson?'

'Do you know what time it is?' John said.

'Well – ah – sure, it's early, but I was just hoping you might do a quick interview for our morning show—'

John hit the button, ending the call. Then he sat up. 'What the hell's going on?'

Naomi, draped in a towel, was looking at him in bewilderment. 'Some breaking news story – maybe they've got a big new discovery in your field. This could be a chance to get publicity – you're acting crazy, come on!'

John got out of bed and went through to the bathroom. He pulled on his dressing gown and stared into the mirror. Some deranged, sheet-white face, with dark rings beneath the eyes and hair sticking up like freshly harvested straw, stared back. He had about an hour to get himself together, to shower, shave, swill down some coffee, throw himself in the car and haul his ass over to the campus.

And now the damned phone was ringing again.

'LEAVE IT!!!' he bellowed at Naomi.

'John—'

'Leave it, I said!'

'John – what's the matter with—?'

'I didn't have any sleep, that's the matter with me, OK? I didn't have any sleep, I haven't made love for three months, and my wife is pregnant with God-knows-what child. Anything else you want to know?'

The phone stopped and immediately began ringing again. Ignoring John, Naomi answered it.

'This is Jodi Parker from KNBC news. Is that the Klaesson residence?'

'This is – can I help you?'

'May I speak with Professor John Klaesson?'

'Can I tell him what this is about?' she asked.

'Sure, we'd like to send a car over, bring him into the studio – we just need a quick interview.'

'I'll pass you over to my husband,' she said.

John gave a cut-throat sign with his finger.

Covering the receiver with her hand, Naomi hissed, 'Take the phone.'

He shook his head.

'John, for God's sake—'

John snatched the phone from her hand and hit the disconnect button.

'Why are you doing this?' Naomi demanded.

John looked at her, exasperated. 'Because I'm tired, OK? I'm very tired. I have a faculty meeting on campus at nine o'clock, which I have to be at, compos mentis. There will be at least two senior staff members at this meeting who will have a lot of sway over whether or not I get tenure. And as of this moment, if I don't get tenure, then in a year's time I'm going to be out on the streets, playing a banjo or washing car windshields at stoplights to pay for our baby's food. Any part of that you don't understand?'

She put her arms around him, her throat sore from vomiting when there was nothing more to vomit, worn out herself from barely sleeping all night, and worry.

After all they had been through, all the pain of the injections, all the discussions, the choices, the indignity, the heartache, the cost, the death of Dr Dettore, she was more scared than she could ever remember.

Everything was changing. This life she and John had together, this little home, this world they had created, all the good things they had together, this wonderful love between them, it was all different, suddenly.

John seemed like a stranger.

The baby inside her, this creature, growing in her womb, tiny arms and legs, so frail, so utterly dependent on her, was she going to turn out to be a stranger, also? *I saw you inside me, saw you through the scan, wiggling your cute little arms and legs. I don't mind if you are a girl, not a boy. I don't mind. I just want you to be healthy.*

She sensed, although she knew it must be her imagination, the tiniest sensation of movement inside her. Like an acknowledgement.

'John,' she whispered. 'Don't let this destroy us – this thing – this baby of ours – don't—'

The phone was ringing again.

John held her tightly. 'We have to be strong, darling. You and I. Wagon train, remember? Wagon-train circle? I love you, more than anything in the world. Please, ignore the phone, take the damned thing off the hook, just for ten minutes. I can't be late for this meeting. Please, there's no damned interview that's as important as this meeting.'

Naomi took the phone off the hook. John showered

and shaved, gave her a peck on the cheek, grabbed his car keys and his laptop bag, and hurried out of the front door.

The morning newspaper lay where it had been chucked, on the damp lawn. John picked it up, unrolled it and glanced at the front page. His eyes were drawn to a photograph of someone familiar. Incredibly familiar. An attractive woman, in tight close-up, with sunglasses pushed back on her head. She had a confident, rich-bitch-without-a-care-in-the-world expression on her face. Then he realized why she looked so familiar.

It was Naomi.

And his own photograph, twice her size, was above. His face, staring at the camera with a DNA double helix superimposed behind.

The newspaper was the one he received every morning. *USA Today.* The front page headline said:

> **LA PROFESSOR ADMITS,**
> **'WE'RE HAVING A DESIGNER BABY'.**

26

Four news vans were parked outside the university entrance as John approached, hurrying for his meeting. In front of them stood a gaggle of people, some holding cameras, some microphones. He heard his name called out. Then again, more loudly.

'Dr Klaesson?'

He heard a different voice say, 'Are you sure that's him?'

'That's Dr Klaesson!'

A short, dark-haired woman he vaguely recognized, with an attractive but hard face, thrust a microphone in front of him. Then he remembered why she was familiar: he saw her face often on a news show. 'Dr Klaesson, could you tell me why you and your wife made the decision to have a designer baby?'

Another microphone was thrust in his face. 'Dr Klaesson, when actually is your baby due?'

Then a third microphone. 'Dr Klaesson, can you confirm that you and your wife have preselected the sex of your child?'

John weaved through them and, more politely than he felt, said, 'I'm sorry, this is private, I have nothing to say.'

He felt a moment's relief when the elevator doors closed behind him in the lobby. Then he began to shake.

We still retain many of our primitive instincts, he thought, arriving in a harassed state ten minutes late for the meeting. Before man had learned to speak, he relied so much on his eyes, observing body language. The way people held their bodies, shifted in their seats, positioned their arms and hands, moved their eyes, told you everything.

He felt like he'd just entered a room that had been skewed ever so slightly out of kilter. The ten colleagues with whom he had worked closely for the past two and a half years, and thought he knew reasonably well, all seemed to be in a very strange space this morning. He felt like an intruder who had entered a private club.

Mumbling an apology for being late, John sat at the conference table, dug his BlackBerry out of his pocket and his laptop out of his bag and placed them in front of him. His colleagues waited for him in silence. John didn't want to be in this meeting at all right now; he wanted to be in his office and on the phone to the reporter.

Sally Kimberly.

Wow! I must give Naomi a call, have lunch with her!

He was almost beside himself with anger at the woman.

Off the record. It had been *off the bloody record.* She'd no right to print a word of what he'd told her.

'Are you OK, John?' Saul Haranchek asked in his nasal Philadelphia accent.

John nodded.

Nine pairs of eyes flashed doubt at him, but no one commented and they got on with the business of the meeting, which was to review their current curriculum. But after only a short while, as had become the norm these past few months, the meeting turned to the more pressing question on everyone's mind: what was going to happen to the department collectively, and to themselves individually, at the end of the next year? Saul Haranchek had tenure, but for the rest the future was still bleak. None of the government funding agencies, institutions, charities, companies or other universities they had approached had yet shown any interest.

John contributed nothing to the discussion. With the newspaper headline this morning, and the expression on his colleagues' faces, he wasn't sure he had any kind of a future in academic research.

He wasn't even sure he had any future in his marriage either.

At half past nine he pocketed his phone, picked up his computer, grabbed his bag and stood up. 'I'm sorry,' he said. 'Please excuse me, I—' he hurried out of the conference room without finishing his sentence.

He walked down the corridor towards his office, his eyes brimming with tears, hoping to hell not to bump into any of his students, unlocked the door and went in, closing it behind him.

There was a pile of mail on his desk, and thirty-one new messages on his voice mail.

Christ.

And fifty-seven new emails.

His phone rang. It was Naomi, sounding livid.

'I'm being bombarded with calls here. Your new lover's done a great job circulating my office number.'

'Jesus, Naomi, she is not my bloody lover!' he yelled, then immediately felt terrible. This wasn't her fault, she had done nothing to deserve this; it was his own stupid goddamn fault. No one else's. 'I'm sorry, darling,' he said. 'I—'

She had rung off.

Shit.

He dialled her direct line number but it was busy.

He looked despairingly at the phone, at his computer screen, at the bare walls of his office. His secretary had stuck this morning's post on his desk and near the top of the pile was a hand-written Jiffy bag with something hard inside. Curious, he ripped it open with the silver letter knife Naomi had given him for Christmas, and pulled out the contents, two stiff sheets of card held together by elastic bands, protecting something.

Inside was the photograph of Naomi that had been missing from his desk, the one of her taken in Turkey. The photograph that was on the front page of *USA Today*.

A folded slip of paper was also in the envelope. A short, hand-written note, with no address and no phone number. It said:

Hi John! It was great meeting you. Thanks for lending me this! All the best. Sally Kimberly.

You bitch! My Christ, you bitch!

His door opened. Saul Haranchek came in. 'Can I – er – bother you for a moment, John?' He hovered, rocking on his beat-up trainers, wringing his hands as if he bore news of the end of the world.

John looked at him and said nothing.

'You're a dark horse,' he said. 'I ah – we – I mean – like – none of us – you know – we didn't have any idea that you and—' He wrung his hands again. 'Look – your private life is your affair but I – someone showed me the newspaper – *USA Today*.' He shook his head nervously. 'If you don't want to talk about it, that's fine – just tell me?'

'I don't want to talk about it,' John said.

Nodding like some kind of automaton, Saul Haranchek turned back towards the door. 'OK, right—'

Interrupting, John said, 'Saul – look, I don't mean it that way, it's just – I guess – I've blown my chance of tenure, right?'

His phone was ringing again.

'You want to take that?' Haranchek said.

John answered it, in case it was Sally Kimberly. It wasn't. It was a woman called Barbara Stratton asking if he could do a quick down-the-line radio interview. He told her again more politely than he felt that he couldn't, and replaced the receiver. 'I've been an idiot, Saul,' he said.

'Is it true what I read? Did you and Naomi really go to Dettore?'

The phone was ringing again. John ignored it. 'It's true.'

Haranchek put his hands on the top of a chair-back. 'Oh boy.'

'Do you know something about him?'

'He was right here at this university back in the eighties for a couple of years. But no, I don't know anything about him – only what I read – and now he's dead, right?'

'Yes. Do you have a view on his work?'

'He was a smart guy – had an IQ that was off the scale. Having a high IQ doesn't necessarily make you a great human being, or even a good one. It just means you can do shit in your head that other people can't do.'

John said nothing.

'Look, it's none of my business. I'm rude to ask about it. But the real problem is, John, that this article doesn't do your credibility as a scientist much good – nor our department, by implication.'

'The truth is not at all how the paper put it, Saul. You know how things get distorted. Papers love to claim that science is more advanced than it really is.'

His colleague looked at him dubiously.

'You want me to resign? Is that what you're saying?'

Haranchek shook his head adamantly. 'Absolutely not. No question. It's unfortunate timing – let's leave it at that.'

'I'm sorry, Saul,' he said. 'Is there anything I can do to salvage my tenure chances?'

Haranchek glanced at his watch. 'I have to get back to the meeting.'

'Apologize for me, will you, Saul?'

'You got it.' He closed the door.

John stared down again at the note from Sally Kimberly. Although angry at her, he was even more angry at his own stupidity. He'd been nice to her, opened up to her in the hope she would do a good piece on his department. Why the hell hadn't he remembered the world didn't work that way?

He got himself a coffee then sat down. Almost immediately his phone rang again. It was Naomi and her voice was very small and quavering. 'John, have you seen the news – in the past half hour?'

'No,' he said. 'Why, what it is?'

'Dr Dettore. He was killed by religious fanatics – they're claiming responsibility, saying Dettore worked for Satan. They're called the Disciples of the Third Millennium. They're saying they put a bomb on the helicopter. And they've announced that anyone tampering with genetics will be a legitimate target. I'm really frightened, John.'

27

In the small editing suite, Naomi sat watching the rough cut of the first episode of the new series on disaster survivors she had been hired to promote and then left to drive home.

She needed to concentrate, somehow to blank out the news about Dr Dettore, blank out her anxiety over the child growing inside her and blank out her suspicions that John had slept with the bitch reporter Sally Kimberly.

And blank out the looks she got from everyone she worked with. She wondered which of them had read the piece or heard about it. Some of them must have, for sure, but no one said anything to her, and that made it worse. Lori was the only friend who contacted her. 'Darling, what amazing news!' she said, her voice different to usual. Still as bubbly as ever, but today almost too damned bubbly, as if it was an act, as if she was doing her best to mask distaste but not quite succeeding. 'You didn't tell us!'

It seemed that in the past two days her entire world had been turned upside down. She was having a girl, not a boy. Dettore was dead. Fanatics were making threats. Her face was on the front of America's biggest newspaper. And she could no longer trust her husband.

She wished desperately she was back in England. Back with her mother and her sister. John always talked about marriage being a wagon-train circle you formed against the outside world, but he was wrong. Your flesh and blood were that wagon-train circle. They were the people you could trust. No one else. Not even your husband.

She remembered a poem she had read a long time ago, which said home was the place where, when you have to go there, they have to let you in.

That's where she wanted to be now. Home.

English home.

Real home.

'Shit.' She braked sharply, bringing the elderly Toyota to a halt by a fire hydrant, and stared in horror at the sight greeting her. Cars, news vans and news trucks were parked along the tree-lined street either side of their house. A small crowd of people stood on the grass verge brandishing cameras and microphones.

She was surprised to see John's Volvo already in the narrow carport. It was twenty past six. He was never normally home before eight at the very earliest. The reporters surged across her path, closing in around her like pack animals as she turned into the drive and pulled up alongside John's car. As she opened the door, voices were yelling at her from all directions.

'Mrs Klaesson!'

'Hey, Naomi – look this way!'

'How do you feel about carrying the world's first designer baby, Mrs Klaesson?'

'Will Dr Dettore's death have any affect on—'

'What is your reaction to Dr Dettore's death, Mrs Klaesson?'

She pushed her way through, tight-lipped, and made it to the porch. As she pulled open the fly screen the front door opened. She stepped inside and John, wearing shorts and a singlet, slammed it shut behind her.

'Get rid of them!' she said angrily.

'I'm sorry.' He gave her a kiss but she turned her face away so sharply he barely touched her cheek.

During the morning, the rain had cleared up and it was a hot Thursday afternoon, with the forecasters predicting a scorching weekend. John had switched the air conditioning on and the interior of the house at least felt pleasantly cool. Stirring music was playing loudly, Mahler's Fifth – John liked to immerse himself in music when he was troubled.

'Just ignore those bastards,' he said. 'They'll get bored and go away. We mustn't let them get to us.'

'Easy to say, John.'

'I'll fix you a drink.'

'I'm not allowed to drink.'

'OK, what would you like? A smoothie?'

Something in his voice and his expression, some boyish naivety, reached out and touched her, reminding her of one of the many things she had always loved about him. He could infuriate her, but he could instantly disarm her, too.

They just stared at each other. A couple lost. A couple under siege. Anger wasn't going to get them anywhere. They couldn't row, they could not be divided right now. From somewhere they had to find the strength to deal with it.

'Great,' she said, more calmly. 'Do that. Something without alcohol that will get me smashed. I'm going to change.'

A few minutes later, wearing just a long T-shirt, she peered out through the blinds. Some reporters were chatting, some were on cellphones, a couple were smoking. A cluster of them were sharing out what looked like burgers from a large carrier bag. *You bastards*, she thought. *Can't you just leave us alone?*

Out in the hall, the music was playing even louder now. Above it, she heard the rattle of ice cubes coming from the kitchen, and walked through.

John was standing close to the sink, barefoot. He had a cocktail glass out, a bottle of vodka, a jar of olives, and a bottle of dry Martini, and was jigging the silver cocktail shaker hard. He hadn't heard her come in.

She saw a single cube of ice lying on the floor, knelt and picked it up. Then, quite spontaneously, she crept up behind him and rammed it down inside the back of his shorts, pressing it against his buttocks.

He shrieked, dropping the shaker in shock, and spun round, straight into her arms. 'Jeez!' he said. 'You scared the hell out—'

She had no idea what was inside her head, suddenly she just wanted him, now, this minute, absolutely desperately. Pulling his shorts down over his knees, she knelt and took him in her mouth. Gripping his buttocks, she held him firmly for some moments, then slid her hands up his lean, strong body, hearing him gasp with pleasure now, feeling his hands pushing through her hair, grappling her head, desperately turned-on herself, aching for him.

She tilted her mouth up, stood and kissed him hard on the lips, put her arms around his neck then slowly pulled him down, onto the floor, on top of her. They rolled, kissing furiously, each fuelled by the other's crazed turned-on desire, John naked now, tugging away at her clothes, then he was above her, entering her, forcing himself in, feeling him pushing, feeling his huge – wonderful – gorgeous – incredible – thing – sex – filling her, filling her body.

She pulled him even harder into her, gathering him tighter and tighter against her, pushing back against him as he slid deeper and deeper in, heady with the scents of his skin, his hair, his cologne. They were safe like this, totally safe, inside their wagon-train circle here, no longer two people but one, solid, incredible, beautiful rock. She murmured, almost delirious with pleasure, as he gripped her with his arms, thrashing her body against the hard tiles of the floor, pressing deeper and deeper inside still, until both of them began to judder together. She heard him crying out and clutched him still tighter, whimpering with pleasure, wanting this moment to last, to never end, wanting them to stay locked, to stay as one body, one rock, forever, right to the end of time and never move.

Afterwards they lay back on the floor, looked at each other, grinning and shaking their heads. It had been that good.

28

Later, the house was filled with the sweet smells of burning charcoal and hickory chips. John, out on the deck, was fiddling with the barbecue. Two thick tuna steaks he had brought home were lying in a marinade on the kitchen table. Naomi was mixing a salad, and feeling a rare moment of tranquillity. Peace inside herself. All her fears locked away – if only for a few fleeting moments – in another compartment.

Got my life back.

The phone was ringing for about the tenth time. John, prodding the coals with a toasting fork, didn't react. She debated whether to let it go to the answering machine, then suddenly wondering if it might be the Dettore Clinic, picked up the cordless receiver and pressed the switch.

'Hallo?'

She was greeted by the hiss of static.

'Hallo?' she said again, her hopes rising that it might be the ship-to-shore phone with a bad connection. 'Hallo? Hallo?'

Then a woman's voice, American, unfriendly with a hard Midwest twang, said, 'Is that the Klaesson home?'

'Who is that calling?' Naomi asked, on guard suddenly.

'Mrs Klaesson? Am I speaking with Mrs Klaesson?'

'Who is speaking, please?' Naomi said.

More insistent now. 'Mrs Klaesson?'

'Who is that, please?'

'You are evil, Mrs Klaesson. You are a very evil woman.'

The line went dead.

Naomi stared at the receiver in shock. Then, hands trembling, she switched it off and hung it back on the wall. She shivered. It suddenly felt as if the sky had clouded over, but through the window the strong evening sun was printing sharp, clear shadows like stencils across the yard.

She was about to call out to John, then held back. It was just a crank. A nasty crank.

You are evil, Mrs Klaesson. You are a very evil woman.

The woman's voice echoed in her head. Anger clenched her up inside.

'It's ready,' John said ten minutes later, presenting Naomi at the candlelit table on the deck with her favourite dish, and slicing it open to show it was cooked exactly the way she liked it, seared on the outside, pink in the centre.

'Tuna goes on cooking after you take it off the heat, that's what people don't realize; that's the secret!' he said proudly.

She smiled, not wanting to tell him that the smell was suddenly making her feel sick, and that he told her the same thing every time he cooked tuna.

He sat down opposite her, spooned (his secret recipe) mustard mayonnaise onto her plate, then helped her to salad. 'Cheers!' He raised his glass, sweeping it through the air is if it were a conductor's baton.

She raised hers back, touched his glass, her head swimming with nausea, then ran to the bathroom and threw up.

When she came back he was sitting waiting, his food untouched.

'You OK?'

She shook her head. 'I – I just – need—'

Peas, she thought, suddenly.

She got up again. 'Just need something to settle—'

She went into the kitchen, opened the freezer compartment and took out a bag of frozen peas and carried it back out to the table.

'You want peas? Want me to cook them for you?'

She tore open the pack, separated one pea from the frozen mass and popped it in her mouth, letting the ice melt, then crushed the pea between her teeth. It tasted good. She ate another, then another, and felt a little better. 'These are good,' she said. 'Eat yours, don't let it spoil.'

He reached out a hand and took hers. 'Remember, women get cravings during pregnancy; maybe that what's happening.'

'It is not a craving,' she said, more irritably than she had intended. 'I just want to eat a few frozen peas, that's all.'

The phone rang. John stood up.

'Leave it!' she snapped.

He looked startled. 'It might be—'

'Leave it! Just leave the bloody phone!'

John shrugged and sat back down. He ate some of his tuna, and Naomi broke off and chewed more peas, one at a time. 'How was your day?' he asked.

'Lori rang. She'd read the piece.'

'And?'

'Why the hell did you have to tell that woman, John? The whole city knows; the whole of America knows – probably the whole bloody world knows. I feel like a freak. How are we ever going to bring our child up normally out here?'

John looked at his food in awkward silence.

'Maybe we should move, go to England, or Sweden, just go to some other place.'

'It'll calm down.'

She stared at him. 'You really think that? You don't think Sally Kimberly – and every goddamn television station and radio station in the country – hasn't got a date marked down in their diary for six months' time, when the baby's due?'

He said nothing. In his mind the question was swirling, *Who the hell are the Disciples of the Third Millennium?*

There were all kinds of fanatic groups out there. People who believed their religious convictions gave them a right to murder. And he was thinking about the faces of his colleagues earlier this morning. The enormity had only really struck him today. He and Naomi were doing something the world wasn't ready for. It would have been fine if they'd kept it a secret.

But now the genie was out of the bottle.

A car door slammed. Nothing unusual about that, except—

Both of them heard it. Sensed something.

More press, probably.

He got up from the table and crossed the hall to the living room, which looked down onto the street, without switching on the lights. Through the window he could see several news cars and vans still out there. But there was a new vehicle among them, a plain grey van with no radio, television or newspaper insignia, parked right outside the house, beneath a street lamp. It was old and tired-looking, with a dent in the side, and dusty. The rear doors were open and three people stood behind it, a man and two women, unloading something that looked like wooden poles. The small gaggle of reporters still out on the sidewalk had made a space for them and were eyeing them warily.

John felt a prick of anxiety.

The man was tall and thin, with long grey hair pulled back into a ponytail, and shabby clothes. The women were shabby, also. One, also tall, had long, lank brown hair, the other, plump and short, had her hair cropped, almost a crew cut. They raised their poles in the air and now he could see they were placards.

They formed a group on the sidewalk, each of them holding a placard aloft, but he couldn't read the wording.

Somewhere in his study, he remembered, he had a pair of binoculars. It took him a few minutes of rummaging through the chaotic jumble to find them. Pulling them out of their carrying case, he went back into the living room and focused on the placards.

One read, SAY NO TO GENETICS.

Another read, TRUST IN GOD, NOT IN SCIENCE.

The third read, CHILDREN OF GOD, NOT OF SCIENCE.

Then he heard Naomi's voice, trembling, right behind him. 'Oh no, John, do something. Please, do something. Call the police.'

'Just ignore them,' he said, trying to sound brave, not wanting her to see that he was as disturbed by them as she was. 'Bunch of loonies. That's what they want: publicity. They want us to call the police, cause a confrontation. Ignore them; they'll go away.'

But in the morning the protesters were still there. And they had been joined by a second vehicle, an ancient, very battered green Ford LTD station wagon with darkened windows, and two more very tough-looking women holding placards:

ONLY GOD CAN GIVE LIFE.

ABORT SATAN'S SPAWN NOW.

29

John had an old school friend, Kalle Almtorp, from his home town of Örebro, who now worked as an attaché at the Swedish embassy in Washington. They rarely met up, but kept in touch by email. Kalle had good connections.

John had contacted him now to see what further information he could find out about the death of Dr Dettore, and the total silence from his ship. He also asked him for anything he could find out about the organization who called themselves the Disciples of the Third Millennium.

This morning, John had almost two hundred emails, as well as a whole barrage of voice mails both at his home and office numbers. The story of their designer baby had hit Sweden and, it seemed, just about every other country on the planet. There were phone messages from family and friends, as well as three from publicists begging to take him and Naomi on as clients, assuring them their own personal story could be syndicated globally for vast sums.

There was a reply from Kalle Almtorp. It was in Swedish – they always communicated in their home language.

Kalle had barely more information on the death of Dr Dettore than John had seen on the news. Like the ship, the helicopter had been registered in Panama and the crash had happened in international waters. However, because both the pilot and Dettore were US citizens, the FAA were taking an interest. A full air-sea search was underway and a salvage vessel had been sent to the crash area. So far there had been no reported communications from the *Serendipity Rose*, nor any sighting of wreckage.

As for the organization calling themselves the Disciples of the Third Millennium, Kalle had no information on them, either. It could just be a hoax, he suggested, some crank learning about the helicopter crash – maybe some religious nut – and claiming responsibility. However, he advised John and Naomi to be extra vigilant for a while, and he said he would be in touch again when he had any further news.

John typed a brief reply, thanking him, then another email caught his eye. It was from his old mentor in England.

John,
This is a long shot, because I imagine you have been totally seduced by the Californian sunshine. But I've seen on the internet the stir you've caused with designer babies and thought you might want to get away? We have a great opportunity here. UK government funding, Sussex countryside, pretty well-assured lifetime employment and ample funding. This is a real boffin establishment. Two-hundred-acre campus. Six hundred research staff. A particle accelerator to rival Cern under construction. Micro Writing department – there's a machine here that can write three hundred lines on a human hair . . . I've just been recruited to head up a new department, and we are actively looking for bright scientists in the virtual life field. I could offer you a lab of your own with great facilities and total freedom.

In any event, tell me how you are, you old
Viking sod, and what's new?
Carson Dicks.
Professor. Dept of Virtuality. UK Government
Morley Park Research Laboratories. Storrington.
West Sussex. United Kingdom

John leaned back in his chair and stared at it thoughtfully. If he mentioned this to Naomi, he knew exactly what
she would say; she'd bite his hand off for the chance to go
back to England. Back home.

But for him it was less appealing. Sussex was where he
had lived before, and he had liked it well enough. It was
close to London, it had the sea, it had Brighton, which was
a handsome and vibrant city, it had great countryside.

But it was England. Dismal weather. Dismal attitudes
towards scientists. It was hard to believe that a country
which had been responsible for so many of the world's
greatest inventions had such an indifferent and miserly
attitude towards research. Tenure at USC might be a
problem, thanks to Sally Kimberly, but he could remain in
the US, sell his soul and get a job in industry, with a
software or maybe a pharmaceutical company.

He liked Carson Dicks. But the thought of going back
to England depressed him. Although, he conceded, it
might be the answer to their present predicament.

He typed a guarded response back, telling the professor it was good to hear from him, and he would think
about it.

30

Naomi's Diary

Lori and Irwin have been brilliant to us. I still don't think either of them really approves of what we've done, but they're not showing it. They insisted we come and stay with them in their guest annex until everything dies down.

They have a great property on Lago Vista, just off Coldwater Canyon. It sits right on top of a canyon, up above the Beverly Hills Hotel with views west towards the ocean, and to the east across to downtown LA, and their guest house is heaven – bigger than our own house!

It's like being out in the country, tons of wildlife, and across the canyon we can see an enormous place – Irwin says it was built by Aaron Spelling (creator of Dynasty!*), but Lori's not so sure, she thinks that place is further east. Whatever. The house must be fifty thousand square feet and there are two tennis courts. Awesome! I've made a note to check it out for them, and I keep forgetting – I know just the person to ask.*

It's now four days since the news of Dr Dettore's death, and three days since John and I featured on the front of USA Today. It's really hard. Everywhere I go I feel people staring at me; even sitting in the car at stop lights I see people looking and I wonder if they saw the paper. I try to think, if I had read that article, would I remember the woman's face four days on? What makes things stick in people's minds? Every publicist would love the answer.

Maybe I'm being paranoid, but I'm sure I'm getting some strange looks in meetings.

John's had no response from the Serendipity Rose. Emails get bounced back, and the phone is constantly unobtainable. John's friend at the Swedish embassy in Washington, Kalle Almtorp, says the US Coastguard has found no wreckage from the helicopter and no sign of the ship. There are moments when I can't believe Dr Dettore is dead – he was such an inspiring, larger-than-life character – and other moments when I feel that I'm – that John and I both are the victims of some conspiracy.

John is very subdued. That worries me, because he's always been such a positive person, always known what to do. He seems lost at the moment.

When I was pregnant with Halley I never had any of the cravings you hear about, that you're meant to have. But now, this frozen pea thing I have is driving me insane! I wake in the middle of the night and go down to the freezer and take out a handful of cold peas. Irwin took us all out to the Ivy last night, and I managed to convince the waiter I was serious, I wanted a side order of unthawed frozen peas. He brought them, beautifully presented as if they were oysters or something, on a bed of crushed ice.

Going nuts? Moi?

31

This place truly was to die for, Naomi thought, reclining on a lounger on Irwin and Lori Shapiro's marbled pool terrace, the sky cloudless, the warmth of the sun feeling good on her body.

It was midday, Sunday. Irwin had taken John to his club for a round of golf, which Naomi was glad about – John needed to get out in the fresh air and away from their problems for a few hours. He was severely stressed, tossing and turning all night, and she could tell he was having problems concentrating in the daytime. He seemed to be in a daze, unsure what to do, and that scared her. In the past he had always been so mentally strong – in a world of his own at times, maybe, but in control.

She watched the Shapiros' two small girls, Chase and Britney, splashing around with an inflatable chair in the pool, and their son, Cooper, hunting for bugs in the shrubbery at the edge of the patio. He was six, born three weeks after Halley. If Halley had lived he might be here, wearing a hat that was too big and carrying a bamboo pole, hunting bugs with Cooper right now, she thought wistfully.

Lori called out to her. 'We have to leave in ten minutes!'

They were going to lunch at Barney's, with another girlfriend of Lori's. Reluctantly, she climbed off her lounger and headed inside. As she entered the cavernous open-plan living area, she glanced at the television, which was permanently on. A police officer was standing outside a colonial-style mansion, in front of a line of crime-scene tape, surrounded by emergency vehicles, talking grimly to a reporter.

'This is horrible,' Lori said, looking up from going through a list with her Hispanic maid. 'Have you been watching?'

'No, what's happened?'

'Get changed, I'll tell you in the car.'

*

Twenty minutes later, as they waited in Lori's black, convertible Mercedes at a stop light at the bottom of Coldwater Canyon, Naomi said, 'Killed – with their babies? Those people on the news?'

'Yes.' Then Lori said, 'Want to go by your house? See if the crazies are still there this morning?'

Naomi looked at her watch, feeling a dark slick of fear spreading through her. 'We have time?'

'Sure. Marilyn's always half an hour late.'

'OK,' she said hesitantly. Every morning Naomi had driven to the end of their street and seen to her dismay that the five weirdos with their placards were still camped there. She felt safe staying with Lori and Irwin. They had electric gates, surveillance cameras and ARMED RESPONSE signs all around the perimeter of their property. 'What exactly are they saying's happened?'

The lights changed. Lori made the turn and accelerated down Sunset. 'The guy, Marty Borowitz, was seriously rich,' she said. 'Irwin had actually met him one time. He owned a string of shopping malls, and a motel chain. He was found dead with his wife and their twin one-year-old babies in the burned-out wreck of their automobile – in the drive of their house. They're saying it was a car bomb. Just horrible.'

'Why?' Naomi asked. 'Does anyone know the reason?'

'They didn't say.'

They took Doheny South, down past the Four Seasons hotel, crossed Wilshire and Olympic, then Pico, Naomi saying little, just watching the traffic and the road ahead and the places they passed, but barely seeing them. She was lost in her thoughts.

There was so much violence in the world; so much hatred. Your son died in agony from a hideous disease. You tried to make a better life for your next child, but no matter how hard you tried, there were people who reckoned they had a right to kill you or drive you from your home because they didn't approve of what you had done.

The freaks with their grey van and their old LTD were still on the sidewalk, a few hundred yards in front of them right now, the weirdo man with his ponytail and the silent women self-appointed custodians of their faith.

All the news crews had gone now; there were just a couple of cars. One contained a photographer sitting in the driver's seat, snapping them through a long lens as they approached. From the second, a young woman emerged holding a small microphone.

'You want to go in?' Lori said, slowing right down as they approached the house.

'No.'

'We should just both walk in, show them we don't care. All the time they know they've driven you away from your home, they'll believe they've won.'

'Maybe they have won,' Naomi said. 'I just wanted to be a mother, Lori. I never set out to be a martyr.'

'If that's how you really feel, then you'd better book yourself an abortion,' Lori said. 'Because, boy, it's not just now that you're going to have to be brave, it's going to be for the next twenty years – and probably beyond that. You might find yourself having to battle hostility for the rest of your life. You do know that, don't you?'

'Pull up in the carport,' Naomi said.

Lori obeyed.

The two of them got out of the car.

'Hallo, Mrs Klaesson? I'm Anna Marshall from—'

Lori turned on her with a venom Naomi had never seen in her friend before.

'SCREW OFF, BITCH,' she yelled at her, startling the young woman so much she retreated several paces. Naomi emptied the mail box, and moments later they were inside the house, with the door locked shut behind them.

Naomi looked at Lori. 'That was pretty effective.'

'Speak to them in a language they understand.'

She laughed, uneasily.

'And the religious freaks didn't bite.'

'Probably vegetarians,' Naomi said. She sifted through the stack of mail, then went over to the living-room window and stared out. Hate was an emotion she had never felt before, not in any real, true sense. Dislike, yes, anger, yes, blind fury even. Hatred was something new. But it was what she felt for these people with their placards. A deep hatred she never knew she had within her.

At five in the afternoon, after a lunch and then following Lori around the shops on Rodeo, unable to muster enthusiasm for anything, they returned back to Lago Vista, to be greeted at the front door by John, white-faced, totally drained of colour. He put on a cheery greeting but Naomi could tell something was very seriously wrong.

A few minutes later, in the privacy of their annex guest rooms, he told Naomi.

'I've had a call from Kalle Almtorp. This couple who were murdered with their twin babies, the Borowitzes? You saw it on the news?'

'Yes?'

'He says it hasn't been released to the media, but the FBI are taking very seriously a claim that they've been murdered by the same people who murdered Dr Dettore – this bunch of fanatics, the Disciples of the Third Millennium.'

Naomi sat down on a sofa, her legs shaking. 'Oh God.'

John dug his hands into his pockets; he seemed about to say something, but then remained silent.

'How – I – I mean – is – is he – sure?'

'Yes.' He walked around the room, then placed his hands behind her, on the back of the sofa. 'I've had a job offer in England, from Carson.'

'Carson Dicks? A job? England?'

'If I took it, they'd be happy for me to start right away. I think – with all that's happening – maybe we should consider leaving America.'

'I don't even need to think about it,' she said.

32

Lying back in the soft leather seat, tired after the eleven-hour transatlantic flight, Naomi was lulled close to sleep by the soporific rocking motion of the large Mercedes that had collected them from London's Heathrow Airport. John had his laptop open, but was slumped back, eyes shut.

It was a long time since she had been back, and she had forgotten how green England looked compared to Los Angeles. She felt an enormous sense of relief at being on English soil again; everything looked so peaceful, even the traffic on the motorway seemed so much calmer than the turbulent freeways.

She was longing to see her mother and her sister. And she was longing, also, for the bitter, salty taste of a Marmite sandwich – a new craving she'd had during the past twenty-four hours.

The hostess on the Virgin plane must have thought she was nuts, she realized, when she'd asked her if she had any frozen peas and then Marmite.

The car had been arranged by Carson Dicks, and Naomi appreciated the gesture. They were going down to Sussex, to stay in a hotel in Brighton. Tomorrow, John had a meeting at the Morley Park Research Laboratory with Dicks and the team he was going to be working with. Then he was going to have to fly back to LA to tie up his loose ends at work there and organize the shipping of all their possessions over to England.

Meanwhile, she was going to have to start house hunting. Everything seemed to be happening at a speed that was hard to keep pace with. It was just two weeks since that newspaper article in *USA Today*. Two weeks since their whole lives had been turned upside down.

Her mother always said that things were meant to be. Naomi didn't believe that; she believed people controlled their own destinies. But she was an optimist. You just had to keep positive and eventually, somehow, things would work out OK.

Like now.

What do you think, Phoebe?

They hadn't had a second opinion yet – it was another two weeks before they would do that – but already in their minds they were reconciled to the fact that they were having a girl. They'd started going through lists of girls' names and last night, on the plane, they had settled on Phoebe.

Phoebe was one of the Titans in Greek mythology, who were of enormous size and strength. It seemed fitting.

She turned and looked through the rear window at the traffic behind them on the M23, watching for any vehicle that might be following them. There was a blue van immediately behind them in their lane, the middle lane. But then its indicator began blinking and it moved over and headed towards the ramp of the next exit. A small sports car was behind it. Then, a considerable way behind, a small green saloon and a red Range Rover, but both were slipping away into the distance.

Paranoia, she knew. It had been the same on the plane. She'd walked down the aisle, studying the faces of the passengers, watching for someone who might be following them.

What did a Disciple of the Third Millennium look like?

She lowered her window a few inches, and the roar of air intruded into the clubroom quiet of the interior. August. Summer in England. The air was close and damp. Small chinks of blue sky amid the darkening grey. She remembered that it often looked like this before it rained. But she didn't mind. Rain was hell in Los Angeles, but it was OK in England. Here it could rain as much as it wanted; just so long as she and John could move back here, she didn't care how much sun she had to sacrifice.

They were heading south. In the far distance she could see the green folds of the South Downs. This was where she and John had come not long after they had first met and fallen in love. She had brought him to England, first to Bath to meet her mother and to meet Harriet – and they had been charmed by him. Then he had brought her to Sussex to meet Carson Dicks and his other friends from the university. He had shown her off proudly, like a trophy, and she hadn't minded at all. They had both been almost deliriously happy.

And, she was thinking, she felt happy again now. Happier than she had felt—

The pain struck with no warning at all. It felt like a jack-in-the-box had sprung open inside her and a fist on the end was trying to punch its way out of her abdomen. Every muscle inside her seemed to contract, twist, then spring free. She convulsed, jerking so harshly into the seat belt it felt like it was cutting her skin, and screamed. Then she emitted a series of terrible low, juddering moans that got louder as the pain worsened, then worsened again, so acute now she was closing her eyes, biting her lips, aware of the Mercedes doing a violent swerve, aware of John's laptop falling to the floor. John, sprung awake, stared at her in confused terror, thinking for one moment they were having an accident. Then he saw Naomi's face. Heard her voice again.

'Darling? Darling?'

It was getting even worse, as if her entire insides were being ripped out with a white-hot knife.

'Pleasssssee . . . oh . . . pleeaaasssssssss . . . no . . . no . . .'

'STOP THE CAR!' John bellowed.

Violent braking. Horns.

'Help me-help-me-help-me-help-me . . .'

They were pulling over, onto the hard shoulder. A truck thundered past inches away. Her face was grey, twisted, tears streaming down it, and blood was coming from her mouth. She was shaking like a deranged caged animal, hair flailing, the terrible moans coming faster and faster.

Blood coming from her mouth. Oh Christ. She's dying. Oh Jesus, no, what the fuck have you done to her, Dettore?

'Darling – darling – Naomi – darling—'

The moans stopped.

The blood was coming from her lip, not her mouth.

A moment's silence. She turned to face him with unfocused eyes as if she was staring at some demon, her face clenched up into an emotion he could not read, it could have been pain or hate, or both. Then her voice dropped to a whisper.

'Help me. Please help me, John. I can't – I can't – take – I can't take another – aaaaaaaaaaaaaaaaaaaaaaaa—'

Then she jerked violently upwards, her eyes rolled, she began juddering and let out a single moan that went on and on, for thirty seconds, maybe a minute, maybe even longer, John didn't know, he was trying desperately to think straight, to work out what might be happening inside her. *Miscarrying? Oh God.*

He put a hand on her brow. It was clammy with perspiration. 'Darling,' he said. 'It's OK, you are going to be OK.'

She yammered incoherently at him, shaking her head violently, but he couldn't understand what she was saying, nor interpret the message in her wild eyes.

'Darling,' he said. 'Calm down, please, calm down, tell me, what is it, tell me?'

She tried to speak but her voice choked in her throat as she began juddering again, then she rammed the back of her wrist against her mouth, biting on it, eyes clenched shut.

John turned to the driver. 'We need an ambulance – or – are we near a hospital – how—?'

'Crawley. We're ten minutes away – less – there's a big hospital there.'

'Go!' John said. 'Just go as fast as you can, I'll – take care – any fines you get – please, just go!'

33

In the small white room, curtained off from the Accident and Emergency admittance ward, banks of monitors beeped as digital displays of numbers and jagged spikes charted Naomi's vital signs.

She was lying on a leather-padded table. John, standing beside her, stared anxiously at the EEG. The bright fluorescent lights gave her pallid face an even more ghostly complexion. Desperate with worry for her, he didn't care at this moment if she miscarried, he just wanted Naomi to be OK, that was all. And he was feeling utterly useless.

White shelves on the walls were lined with vials, bottles, syringes in plastic bags. There was a smell of disinfectant. A nurse in a blue scrub suit was adjusting the flow valve on a drip line. Another said, 'Eighty systolic, rising.' Naomi stared up at John, bewildered. She was a horrible colour, calm one moment, then the next she was all contorted again, shuddering, screaming in pain.

Please let her be all right. Please don't let anything happen to her. Please—

Another woman in blue nursing uniform entered the room. 'Dr Klaesson?'

'Get a doctor here! Jesus!' he shouted at her. 'My wife is losing our baby – get me the duty obstetrician!'

She wore a badge that said: A&E, ALISON SHIPLEY, HEAD OF NURSING, and held a clipboard in her hand.

'Dr Klaesson, could I please ask you a few questions?'

'GET ME A FUCKING OBSTETRICIAN, FOR GOD'S SAKE!'

Unfazed, she gave him a gentle smile. 'Dr Klaesson, Mr Sharpus-Jones is on his way down from theatre. He'll be here in just a few minutes.'

'John.'

Naomi's voice. So calm. Serene.

He stared down at her.

'Just some admittance formalities, please,' the nurse said.

'John, please calm down,' Naomi said, panting, almost breathless. 'I'm fine now, I'm OK, really I am.'

John stared at the lines connected to Naomi's chest and wrist, then kissed her on her clammy forehead. Nothing mattered in the whole world except stopping her pain. 'I love you.'

She nodded, whispering, 'Love you too,' and held out her hand. He took it and she squeezed him hard. 'I'm OK,' she said. 'Honest injun, I'm OK.'

The curtains suddenly swished sideways, and a tall man entered, dressed in surgical scrubs and white clogs, with his mask dangling below his chin. 'Hallo, Mrs Klaesson?' he said.

Naomi nodded.

He shot a glance at John then looked back at Naomi. 'I'm sorry to have kept you. How are you doing?'

'I'm fine,' she said.

John wanted to scream out, *You are not fine, you have been in unbearable agony, you are not fine at all, tell him the truth!* But instead he stood there and said nothing, while Sharpus-Jones examined her carefully, externally first, pressing all around her abdomen, then internally, all the time firing questions about her medical history, some of which Naomi answered directly, and some of which she answered after prompting by John.

Finally, pulling off his gloves, Sharpus-Jones said, 'Well, the good news is that your cervix is closed and you're not bleeding, which means that you are not miscarr—'

He was cut short as Naomi suddenly convulsed violently, sending the obstetrician stepping back in shock. She threw her arms in the air, arched her back, her eyes rolling, and let out a scream that tore through John's soul.

Moments later – barely seconds, it seemed to John – there was a whole team of people hoisting her onto a gurney, then they were wheeling her out of the room and along the corridor.

'Where are you taking her?' he asked in sudden, blind panic.

No one answered.

John followed them, but after only a few paces the nurse, Alison Shipley, took his arm and stopped him.

'Please wait here,' she said.

'No way!'

John shook his arm free and hurried after them. Then his path was blocked by the obstetrician.

'Please, Dr Klaesson, I know your anxiety, but I must ask you to wait here.'

It was a command, not a request; non-negotiable, said with a mixture of kindness and authority.

'Where are you taking her?' John said. 'What are you going to do?'

'I'm going to do an ultrasound scan and I'll take it from there. I may have to open her up to see what's going on inside. It would be better for everyone if you waited here.'

He went outside to call Naomi's mother and tell her what was happening; he needed someone he could share his distress with.

*

An hour later the obstetrician came back into the room, still gowned-up, mask dangling, looking deadly serious. John stared up at him in terror, and was about to stand, when the obstetrician sat down beside him.

'That was a close call.'

John stared at him, wide-eyed.

'Are you a doctor of medicine, Dr Klaesson?'

'No – I'm a scientist.'

'OK. We had to do an emergency laparotomy—' He raised a calming hand. 'A little incision in her tummy – called a Pfannenstiel incision. She's fine, everything is fine. The pain she was experiencing was caused by a cyst in the right ovary that had twisted, obstructing the ovary's blood supply, so that the ovary had become gangrenous. It was a dermoid cyst that she probably had all her life, and I'm surprised it wasn't found on the ultrasound scans. I don't know if either of you were aware of it, that your wife has a congenital abnormality of her reproductive organs?'

'Abnormality? What kind of abnormality?'

'She has a double uterus.'

'Double uterus? What – I mean – what does that—?' John's brain was racing. *Why the hell hadn't Dr Dettore told them this? He must have known. He must – perhaps he was hiding it from them. Why hadn't Rosengarten told them? That was easier to answer – he was in a hurry when he had carried out the examination, his mind elsewhere.*

'It's relatively common – about one in five hundred women has this, but in your wife's case it was not immediately apparent. But anyhow, your wife is now fine and the babies are fine.'

'Babies? What do you mean, *babies*?'

'She has one on one side and one on the other.'

Seeing John's expression, he hesitated a moment, then said, 'Your wife is having twins. A boy and a girl. You do know that, don't you?'

34

Naomi's Diary

Twins!

Mum and Harriet are over the moon. I'm still in a state of total shock. I've had enough surprises and I don't know how I feel emotionally about this. I'm trying to understand just what having twins involves. There's a website that gives a week-by-week account of what to expect during pregnancy and the first year after giving birth – it isn't going to be easy.

Last weekend Harriet brought down a newspaper article talking about an epidemic of twins. The article said it was caused by fertility specialists putting back clusters of eggs into the womb. I tried to explain to Harriet that it wasn't like that at the Dettore Clinic, there should have been only one egg. But I don't think she was really that interested in listening.

I sense she's a little jealous. She's thirty-two, hugely successful at her bond-dealing job, but single. I know from the many conversations we've had over the years that she's always maintained she's not particularly interested in having children – maybe she's hoping that by my having twins it'll take pressure off her from Mum to produce grandchildren!

Sometimes I lie awake at night thinking about Halley lying in his tiny coffin in his grave in that pretty cemetery off Sunset. He's all alone. Lori takes him flowers once a week for us. I wonder though if he's even more lonely now that we've moved so far away?

When I was carrying Halley I mostly enjoyed my pregnancy – right up until giving birth itself, at any rate, which was pretty hellish. I felt well, excited, confident. But now I don't feel any of those things. I just feel heavy, clumsy, sick all the time, weak. Very scared of what is really going on inside me. And when John tries to cheer me up, is he trying to hide some truth that he knows?

I've always trusted John. Did he and Dettore have some secret deal between them? One minute he seems to be as shocked as I am, but the next it's almost as if he's quite excited.

The only person I've really discussed this with is Rosie. We go back to ten years old together. Rosie Miller now Whitaker. She's always been much more savvy than me. John would be furious if he knew I'd told her – we have a pact not to tell anyone, but I need to talk to someone or I will go nuts. I have to say I was surprised at her reaction. Rosie is normally enthusiastic about everything. But I could see in her face she's worried about what we've done.

Why twins, Dr Dettore? Have you made a mistake? Have you done it deliberately?

Am I ever going to find out the truth?

35

'This is fabulous, the master bedroom. You won't see many like this, I can tell you,' Suzie Walker said.

Naomi, trailing behind her sister and her mother, followed the estate agent into a huge room gridded with oak beams. Midday sun poured in through the south-facing window, which looked across an expanse of farmland to the soft escarpment of the Downs.

'The views have to be experienced to be believed,' Suzie Walker continued. 'You could look at houses for the next thirty years and not find a view to rival this.'

'What about wind?' Harriet quizzed the agent. 'This is quite exposed, isn't it?' As a child, Naomi had looked up to her elder sister. Harriet had always been prettier than she was, and today, with her elegant bob of jet-black hair and English rose face, she looked even more attractive than ever. She had savoir faire, wisdom beyond her years, and she knew how to dress correctly for any occasion. Today she wore a shiny new Barbour, a tweedy Cornelia James scarf, jeans tucked into green wellies, as if she had lived in the country all her life, although in reality this was one of her rare ventures beyond her perceived urban sanctuary of London.

By contrast their mother, Anne, looked as bewildered by life as she had that terrible night, eighteen years ago, when she had come into Naomi's bedroom to tell her that her father wouldn't be coming home any more because he had gone to heaven. Her face still had pretty features, but it was lined beyond its years with strain, her hair was grey and old-fashioned, and, as much as Harriet knew how to dress to blend in with her surroundings, her mother was always a little too stiff, too formal. Today she wore an elegant black coat and town shoes; she would not have looked at all out of place arriving at a cocktail party.

'If you want a view, then you have to accept that you will have some wind, yes,' Suzie Walker said. 'But wind is good. It dries the land. And, of course, being in an elevated position like this means you have no worries from flooding.'

Naomi loved the house. She watched her mother and her sister expectantly, wanting them to like it, too. *Willing* them to like it. Still the baby of the family, she had a need inside her for their approval.

The agent was petite, with long fair hair, and neatly dressed. She reminded Naomi of a china doll. After viewing eight rental properties in the area in the past week, each of which was more horrible than the last, she had been in despair three days ago when she'd walked into Suzie Walker's tiny agency, close to the ruined castle precincts in the county town of Lewes in East Sussex, and plonked herself down in a chair.

The agent had leaned conspiratorially across her desk, raised a finger to her lips and said there was a property, a quite wonderful property, not yet officially on the market, but she would like to take Naomi to view it anyway, she had a feeling it would be ideal. A bargain price for a quick let – at the top end of Naomi's price range, perhaps – but anyone who saw this place was going to fall in love with it.

Dene Farm Barn was at the end of a half-mile metalled drive that threaded through wheat fields into the Downs from a quiet country lane, five miles east of Lewes. The property consisted of a wooden barn that had been converted into a four-bedroom house, and a separate flint granary that had been converted into a double garage. Perched on a ridge of a hill, there were views across miles of open farmland in all directions. The nearest community was a small village, two miles away.

The isolation was the one negative. But in trying to weigh this place up, there was a positive to that as well. The downside was that the nearest house, a farm cottage, was a good half mile away. Would she be nervous here on her own? How would it be at night? On the plus, they would be tucked away, no neighbours to ask awkward questions about the babies if and when the newspaper piece about them, or follow-ups to it, resurfaced. And it would be a total haven for children.

And on the double plus, it was simply, awesomely beautiful. Naomi could see herself and John living here, raising their family here, making a life here. There was an acre and a half of garden, mostly lawn and shrubs, with a young orchard of apple, pear, plum and cherry trees. She imagined barbecues with friends on the flagstone terrace. She imagined the wood-burning stove alight in the huge, open-plan living area. She imagined snow falling, watching a white landscape stretching away for miles in all directions.

It felt so incredibly peaceful here.

Safe.

John was enthusiastic also, after she had described everything in detail over the phone. He had one month to go in Los Angeles, to work out his notice at the university, and to organize the shipping of their belongings over to

England. He told her it was hard to imagine how much junk they'd accumulated in the past six years. She said to throw away anything he wasn't passionate about keeping.

'So, who actually owns this place?' Harriet asked, eyeing the vast Indian carved mahogany two-poster bed.

'I was explaining to your sister on – er – Wednesday. It is owned by the man who did the conversion, Roger Hammond. He's just gone to Saudi Arabia on a three-year contract. They are considering moving to Australia at the end of the contract. That of course would mean an opportunity to buy this place – be a wonderful investment – the garage block could be converted into a separate dwelling. This kind of property comes up once a decade, if that.'

'Well-designed bathroom,' Harriet said approvingly. 'Twin sinks. That's good.'

The agent led them across the corridor. 'And of course this next room would be perfect for your twins!'

After they had done all the rooms, Suzie Walker told them she would leave them to have a wander around by themselves, and went out to her car.

Sitting in front of the bright red Aga, at the ancient oak refectory table in the kitchen, Naomi looked at Harriet, then her mother. 'So?' she asked.

Her mother said, 'There seems to be lots of cupboard space. Very good cupboard space.'

'What will you do when it snows?' her sister demanded.

'Well – we may spend a few days trapped. I think I'd find that quite romantic!' Naomi replied with a smile.

'Not if you have to see a doctor urgently.'

'What about schools?' her mother said. 'That's what you need to think about.'

'She needs to think about the isolation,' her sister said. 'John's going to be at work all day. How are you going to cope with no one to talk to except sheep?'

'I like sheep,' Naomi said.

'You'd need a dog, darling,' her mother said.

'Dogs are a pain,' Harriet said. 'What do you do if you want to go away?'

'I like dogs,' Naomi said. 'Dogs don't judge people.'

36

There was something snagging in John's throat, tugging at it from the inside, a muscle twitching from nerves; there were muscles twitching in his guts, also. He couldn't stay still for more than a few moments. He wanted this all to be over, yet at the same time he was truly scared. Scared for Naomi, for the babies inside her. Scared about what lay ahead.

They had given him a chair beside the operating table, and he was sitting there now, stroking Naomi's forehead, staring at the green cloth screen that had been clipped across her chest, blocking their view of everything that was going on beyond in the operating theatre.

They were waiting for the epidural block that had been injected into Naomi's spine to become fully effective. John glanced at the round white clock face on the theatre wall. Five minutes had passed. He smiled at Naomi.

'How are you feeling, darling?'

She looked so vulnerable in the loose gown, with the drip line in her wrist and her plastic name tag. A tiny bubble of spittle appeared in the corner of her mouth and he dabbed it away with a tissue.

'OK,' she said very quietly. 'I'll be glad when—' She mustered a smile back at him, then swallowed, a nervous gulp. Her eyes were wide open. Sometimes they were green, sometimes brown; right now they seemed to be both at the same time. Her smile faded and doubt flickered, like a guttering candle, in its place.

'Me too,' he said. 'I'll be glad when—'

When what? he wondered. *When this waiting is over? When the babies are born and we can start to find out what Dettore has really done? When we can start to discover the wisdom of what we have done?*

'What are they doing?' she asked.

'Waiting.'

John stood up. The theatre seemed crowded; it had filled with figures in green gowns, most of them just chatting through their masks as if they were at a cocktail party. He was trying to remember who they all were. The consultant obstetrician, the registrar obstetrician, the consultant paediatrician, anaesthetist, assistant anaesthetist, nurses, midwife. Harsh white light burned down from the overhead lamp onto Naomi's exposed swollen belly. Banks of electrical equipment were giving off readings.

The anaesthetist, a cheery, thorough man called Andrew Davey, touched her belly with cotton wool. 'Can you feel this, Naomi?'

She shook her head.

Next he gave her a tiny prick with a small pointed instrument. 'Feel anything now?'

Again she shook her head.

He picked up a water spray and gave a hard squirt, first onto her belly, then either side of her navel. Naomi did not flinch.

'OK,' the anaesthetist said, turning to the obstetrician. 'I'm happy.'

The consultant obstetrician at the Royal Sussex County Hospital, Mr Des Holbein, was a solidly built, bespectacled man in his mid-forties. He had dark hair shorn to stubble, with a serious face that had the air of a benign bank manager. Like everyone else, he knew nothing about their background with Dettore. But he had done a great deal to bolster their morale, in particular Naomi's, over the past seven months.

It seemed to John that for the past seven months, doctors' offices, clinics and hospitals had become part of the rhythm of their lives.

Naomi had had a rough pregnancy. John had made it his business to try to understand more about the double uterus, and the conversation he and Naomi had had over and over, to the point of exhaustion and then beyond, was why Dr Dettore had never told them about this abnormality – and why had he implanted two eggs?

And why hadn't Dr Rosengarten in Los Angeles seen she was expecting twins on the scan? When they discussed this with Des Holbein, he told them that at that early stage, if he hadn't known about her second uterus, and if the boy had been out of position, possibly screened by the girl, and if he had been rushed, as it sounded Rosengarten was, it could quite easily have happened.

John kept in regular contact with his friend, Kalle Almtorp. The FBI were still no nearer to solving who had killed Dettore, and the *Serendipity Rose* had not been sighted. It was possible, he told John, that the Disciples of the Third Millennium, if they really existed, had sunk it at the same time as they had murdered Dettore – presumably killing everyone on board. They were no closer, either, to finding the killer of Marty and Elaine Borowitz, despite the original claims that it was done by the same Disciples of the Third Millennium. Just as silently as they had surfaced and struck, the Disciples of the Third Millennium seem to have faded back into the ether.

The FBI and Interpol were baffled. His best advice, Kalle told John, was for them to keep a low profile, avoid all publicity, be ex-directory and vigilant at all times. Kalle felt that moving from the US, as they had done, was sensible.

In England they had made the decision to tell no one about their visit to the Dettore Clinic, other than Naomi's mother and sister. Some of John's old colleagues, and some of Naomi's friends, had seen the press mentions when the article had been syndicated around the world, but John and Naomi had successfully played it down saying that, as usual, the press had got the wrong end of the stick and had tried to make a sensational story out of nothing.

By her eighteenth week, instead of the morning sickness having gone, as she had been told it would, it had worsened. Naomi had been vomiting all the time, unable to keep any food down, despite constant cravings for frozen peas and Marmite sandwiches. Suffering severe dehydration, with her electrolytes up the creek, short of sodium and potassium in her blood, she had been admitted to hospital four times over the next two months.

In her thirtieth week, Naomi had been diagnosed with pre-eclampsia toxaemia – pregnancy-induced hypertension – with rising blood pressure. There was protein in her urine, causing her very uncomfortable swelling of her hands and ankles, to the point where she could no longer get her shoes on.

When, at thirty-six and a half weeks, Mr Holbein advised them Naomi should have an elective lower segment caesarean section instead of going the full term, because he was worried about the function of the placenta being impaired and possibly causing death of the babies or bleeding behind the placenta, Naomi had taken little persuading; as had John.

The conversation in the operating theatre suddenly quietened and in unison the gowned medics seemed to close ranks around Naomi. John sat down and took her hand. His mouth had gone dry. He was trembling. 'Starting now,' he said to her.

He could hear the clatter of instruments. Saw figures leaning over the table, eyes above the masks all serious in concentration. He craned his neck around the screen and watched Mr Holbein drawing a scalpel across the base of the huge bump that took up the whole of Naomi's abdomen. Squeamishly, he looked away.

'What can you see?' Naomi asked.

Then suddenly the obstetrician popped his head around the screen.

'Would you like to see the babies delivered?' he asked, cheerily.

John looked at Naomi, bolstered by the confident tone of Holbein's voice. 'How do you feel about that, darling?'

'What do you think?' she said. 'Would you like to?'

'I – I would, yes,' he said.

'I would too.'

Moments later, the anaesthetist undid the clips and let the green sheet down.

'You can hold up her head to give her a better view,' Holbein said to John.

Gently, John obeyed. They could see a lumpy ocean of green sheets and the surgeons' gowned arms.

It seemed just moments later that Phoebe Anna Klaesson, tiny, coated in the slimy curds of yellow cream of the vernix and blood, eyes open, crying, trailing her umbilical cord from her belly and gripped firmly in a rubber-gloved hand, was pulled clear of the warmth and bustle of her mother's womb. She was lifted up into the comparative freezing cold and eerie silence of the operating theatre.

As John watched, totally mesmerized, she was turning, *right in front of his eyes*, from bluey pink to bright pink.

That crying. That sweet sound of life, their baby, their creation! He felt joy and fear at the same time. Memories of Halley's birth swirled in his head. All the pride and hope he had had. *Please be all right, Phoebe. You will be. Oh God, yes, you will be!*

The obstetrician held Phoebe up, while another gowned figure fixed the cord with two clamps, and a third figure cut it between them.

Holding the cord with the baby, Mr Holbein placed them into the green sterile sheet the midwife was holding out. Then, wrapping the sheet around Phoebe, he brought her close to Naomi.

'Your daughter looks lovely!'

Phoebe cried lustily.

'Listen to that!' Holbein said. 'That's a healthy cry.'

John's eyes were sodden with tears. 'Well done, darling,' he whispered to Naomi. But she was staring at her daughter with such exhausted rapture she didn't even hear him.

The obstetrician handed Phoebe to the midwife, who in turn took her over to the paediatrician, who was standing by the resuscitation trolleys, two small mobile tables each with a large flat overhead lamp. 'And now the next child,' he said.

As the surgeon moved back down to the abdomen, he said, 'The second baby is further back and higher up – this is not going to be quite so easy. It's a breech presentation with the head tucked up in a corner of the womb.'

Still supporting Naomi's head, John's anxiety returned. He watched the obstetrician concentrating. The man was moving his hands around inside Naomi, but John could see from his face something was wrong. Sweat was glistening on the man's brow.

The atmosphere in the room seemed to change. Every pair of eyes now looked tense. The surgeon was still moving his hands. He said something to the scrub nurse, too quietly for John to hear.

A bead of sweat fell from the obstetrician's head onto the lens of his glasses.

Suddenly the anaesthetist said to John, 'We're having a little difficulty here. I think, Mr Klaesson, you should leave us now.'

Holbein nodded. 'Yes, that's sensible.'

'What's going on?' John said, glancing anxiously at Naomi, who seemed to have lost what little colour she had in her face.

The obstetrician said, 'This is really difficult and the baby's heart rate from cord pulsation has gone right down. It would be better if you went out into a waiting room.'

'I'd prefer to stay,' John said.

The anaesthetist and obstetrician exchanged glances. John looked anxiously at Mr Holbein. Was the baby dying?

The anaesthetist pinned back the screen, blocking Naomi and John's view. John kissed her. 'Don't worry, darling, it'll be OK.'

She squeezed his hand. Then he stood up. Des Holbein came up to Naomi again. 'I'm sorry, Naomi, I've been trying to restrict the incision to what we call the bikini line, but I'm going to have to cut you vertically now.'

She gave a faint nod.

'The epidural block isn't high enough,' the anaesthetist said. Then his assistant suddenly called out, in alarm, 'Sixty!'

There was an air of panic in the room.

'I can't wait,' the surgeon said.

The anaesthetist raised his voice almost to a shout, 'I have to get her asleep! Give me a minute!'

John looked at both men in horror as the obstetrician imperiously said, 'Goddammit man, the baby is already hypoxic!'

The anaesthetist was struggling with a needle in a vial.

'I'm going to have to start if we want to save the baby!' Holbein shouted, with desperation in his voice.

'Wait, for God's sake, let me get her intubated and paralysed.'

The obstetrician, dripping with sweat, lifted the green sheets, and folded them back, exposing all of her tummy. 'How long will it take you?'

'A couple of minutes.'

'We don't have a couple of minutes.' He walked back up to Naomi. 'I'm afraid if you want to save the baby this is going to hurt a little. Are you OK with that?'

'Don't hurt Naomi,' John said. 'Please – it's – much more important—'

'I'm OK,' she said. 'Do what you have to do to save the baby, please, I'll be OK.'

'I don't want you to hurt her,' John said.

'I really do think it would be better if you went outside,' the surgeon said.

The anaesthetist spritzed the needle, then swabbed Naomi's arm and injected her.

John stared in horror as, seconds later, transfixed, he watched the surgeon insert the scalpel upside down into her abdomen, and with one steady upward sweep, trailed by a ribbon of bright red blood, he cut from just above where her pubic hairline had ended, right up to her umbilicus.

Naomi screamed in pain, her fingernails cutting into the palm of John's hand. She screamed again, then again. John stood, stunned, open-jawed, helpless, feeling blood draining away inside him, his head swimming. He took a deep breath.

The anaesthetist snapped a line onto the cannula in Naomi's wrist, and instantly she began calming down. Seconds later, she appeared to have stopped breathing altogether, with her eyes wide open, staring glassily.

Instantly the anaesthetist took the airline from his assistant and tried to intubate her. But he was having problems getting the clear plastic tube down her throat. 'Can't get it in,' he said. Perspiring heavily, he pulled it out, tried again, then pulled it out again, with all the elegance of a fisherman trying to get a hook out of the gullet of a pike.

John fainted.

37

It felt like he had a meat cleaver embedded in his head. John was aware he was lying down and that something cold was pressing against his right eye. He opened his left eye and all he could see for a moment was a blur. The light hurt and he closed it again.

A cheery female voice said, 'How are you feeling?'

He opened his eye again and focused. A face. A young woman he vaguely recognized. She had wavy blonde hair and was pretty. The junior midwife; her name was Lisa, he remembered, suddenly.

And then he remembered everything else.

In panic he tried to sit upright. 'My God, what's happened?'

'Just lie back down and rest, I want to try to keep the swelling down.'

He stared at her. She was holding what looked like a surgical glove packed with ice in her hand. 'My wife – what's happened? Is she all right?'

Cheerily, Lisa said, 'She is absolutely fine. And both your babies are out and fine – they're all doing really well.'

'They are? Where are – is—?'

For an instant he felt giddy with relief and excitement. The room swam; then, as if the blade of the cleaver was twisting in his skull, the pain in his head suddenly got so bad that John felt sick. He desperately wanted to stand, tried for an instant to lever himself up, but that made him feel worse. All he could do was close his eyes and lie back.

Moments later, he felt the ice-packed glove over his eye. It was like soothing balm.

'Your wife's in the recovery room at the moment. She's been fully anaesthetized and it will take a few hours before she's completely recovered. Your babies are asleep in the Special Baby Care Unit.'

'It was a boy? The second one?'

'A lovely little boy.'

He tried to sit up again but the pressure against his eye was too strong. 'And my wife's really all right?'

The junior midwife nodded vigorously.

John felt relief flooding through him. He heard a door open and a moment later heard the voice of the consultant obstetrician.

'Well, you're going to have a nice shiner there, Dr Klaesson!' he said cheerily.

He came into John's line of vision, clogs slapping on the floor, hat and mask removed, gown slack. 'Four stitches in your head and a black eye – still, you'll be able to tell everyone in years to come that at least you didn't let your wife suffer alone during childbirth!'

John managed a thin smile. 'I'm really – I—'

'No, listen, old chap, I'm sorry about the kerfuffle, but your wife is doing well, and the babies are absolutely fine. How are you feeling?'

'A little rough.'

'I'm sorry you had to go through that but there was no alternative – and your wife supported me. The second baby was definitely starting to suffer from lack of oxygen and I had to deliver him quickly otherwise we'd have lost him for sure.'

'Can I see them?'

'You've taken quite a crack on your head – you caught

the edge of the table and the anaesthetics machine as you went down. They're going to take you for an X-ray just to make sure everything's tickety-boo inside. By the time you've done that, Naomi will be all tidied up in her bed, ready for you to come down and see her and the babies.'

Aware that his voice was sounding a little strange, slurred, as if he had been drinking, John said, 'Special Care unit – did you say?'

The surgeon nodded.

Edgy now, John said, 'Wh-why?'

'Perfectly normal for any premature baby. Your little girl weighs two point six five kilograms and your boy weighs two point four three – both around five and a half pounds in old measurements. That's a good weight for twins at thirty-six weeks. They seem jolly healthy – in fact, remarkably robust – and they're breathing on their own. We've been lucky the toxaemia hasn't affected them.'

He gave John a knowing smile, and John, uneasy suddenly, wondered if Holbein knew, if he'd seen a piece in an English newspaper and remembered their names or faces.

Then the consultant turned and walked from his line of vision. 'I'm afraid I'm due back in theatre. I'll pop by later on this evening and see how Naomi's doing.'

John heard the door close.

'You're not the first person to have passed out,' Lisa said.

'It was the brutality – I – I couldn't believe—'

'At least your wife is all right, and the babies are fine. That's the main thing, isn't it?' the young nurse said.

John took a long while to answer. He was thinking about how, up to this point, none of this had seemed totally real. Of course Naomi had been suffering for months, but all the time the babies had been inside her, he could imagine they might wake up one morning and find her bump had gone, that it was all a misdiagnosis, just a phantom pregnancy, that was all.

Now, through his aching brain, the true reality of it all was finally dawning. The irreversibility. They had brought two human beings into the world whose genes might have been tampered with by Dettore in ways they had not wanted, and there was not a thing they could do about it, except pray that they were going to be fine.

He looked back at the cheery young nurse and, in answer to her question, nodded uncertainly.

38

His head throbbing, John stared through the glass, watching Luke and Phoebe asleep on their backs, swathed in white bedding and intubated. They were even smaller than he'd imagined, more wrinkled, more pink, with tiny little hands like starfish.

More beautiful.

Utterly, utterly, incredible!

He was choked, close to tears with emotion as he watched these tiny people, these miniature copies of Naomi and himself, encased in clear Perspex, dwarfed by the high-tech equipment all around them.

Even in their scrunched-up faces he could see the likenesses. There were distinctive characteristics of Naomi in Luke. And he could see himself in Phoebe. Logically, it ought to be the other way around, he thought, but it didn't matter; there was only one thing that was important, and it was plain to see it in their faces:

Absolute confirmation that their worst fears were unfounded. These *were* their children, his and Naomi's, without question.

He closed his eyes in relief. For months this had been his biggest fear. Naomi's, too, despite all he had said to try to reassure her.

Now they faced another worry – just what other mistakes might Dettore have made? Or what other deliberate alterations had he done to their genes that he had not told them about?

But at least they were healthy! Strong. *Remarkably robust*, the obstetrician had said.

His thoughts went back to Halley, to the awesome sense of responsibility he had felt when Halley had been born, and all the hopes he'd held for his son, long before he knew anything of the time bomb inside him. He felt even more responsibility for these two, now, bringing them into the world knowing the risks he and Naomi faced. Just hoping and praying Dettore hadn't messed up with the one gene that mattered.

Phoebe, eyes shut, raised her starfish hand a little, opened out her fingers, then closed them again. Moments later, Luke did the same. Almost as if they were waving at him, acknowledging him.

Hi Dad! Hi Dad!

He smiled. 'Welcome to the world, Luke and Phoebe, my little darlings. You're our future, your mum's and mine. We're going to love you more than any parents ever loved any child,' he whispered.

Once more, in their sleep, first Phoebe then Luke's little hands raised a few inches, opened out their fingers and closed them again.

John went back to Naomi's room, to sit with her until she was sufficiently awake to be wheeled up to see them herself.

39

Mountain air is different to any other kind of air that you can find on this planet. Mountain air doesn't have all that shit that you have to breathe in.

Down below it is just one big sewer, my friend, and I'm not just talking about the air.

Hasn't always been that way, of course. And one day it's going to be all back to how it was. You'll be able to walk the streets of cities and smell flowers.

Seriously, when was the last time you smelled flowers in a city?

Maybe in a park, but only if the park was big and the flowers had a strong enough scent. And to have a strong enough scent they'd probably been genetically modified.

We can't keep our hands off anything, can we? I tell you something, you walk in one of those supermarket places, they've got berries the size of apples, apples the size of melons, and those tomatoes, you know the ones I mean, those like big, mutant things – they have pig genes in them, to give them their colour, to keep them riper longer, but you don't see that on the label.

I tell you, my friend, you step down off this mountain and you walk in the sewers of the valleys and plains, you're stepping into a world you think you might know, but you don't, trust me, you do not know any of it. Like, get this – there's a big burger chain, a national chain and they're mixing polyester into the bread in their buns – to make them puff out. They're making you eat polyester and all the time you are thinking, hey, bread that looks this good must be doing me good!

That's how cynical scientists are, my friend.

You know what science is really about? Scientists pretend it is about knowledge, but the truth is that it is partially about power and about death, but mostly it is about vanity and greed. People don't invent things for the greater good. They invent them to satisfy their egos.

Everyone is being seduced by science. All the world leaders. They're hoping science will find a cure for AIDS, forgetting science caused it in the first place. Scientists cured bubonic plague and smallpox, but what did that do for the human race? Overpopulation.

The Lord has his own way of dealing with overpopulation. He had the balance of nature just fine, until scientists came along and messed it all up.

And think about this, my friend, next time you take a walk down there in the sewers and feel your lungs getting all choked up. Who is responsible? God or scientists?

Just remember the words of St Paul to Timothy. 'Guard what has been entrusted to your care. Turn away from Godless chatter and the opposing ideas of what is falsely called knowledge, which some have professed and in so doing have wandered from the faith.'

Here endeth the 17th Tract of the 4th Level of the Law of the Disciples of the Third Millennium.

In a room in a house that was as spartan as a monk's cell, high up on a mountain in the Rockies, thirty miles north of Denver, the young Disciple, working out his forty days of solitude, seated on a simple wooden stool in front of a computer, was learning each Tract by rote. He was repeating the words that had arrived in an email an hour ago, and that would shortly be erased, over and over in his head.

Everything had to be remembered. Nothing was ever to be retained in writing. *Rule Four.*

His name was Timon Cort. His hair was shaven to ginger stubble. He wore a fresh white T-shirt, grey chinos, sandals and oval glasses. Twice a day he ran the two-mile dirt track to the bottom of the private mountain and back up again without stopping. A further two hours a day he spent working out on the exercises he had been given to strengthen his body. The rest of the time he divided, as he had been instructed, between learning, reading the Bible, prayer and sleep.

He was blissfully happy.

For the first time in twenty-nine years, his life had meaning. He was needed. He had a purpose.

When he came down from the mountain at the end of his initiation, he would be entrusted with a Great Rite. If he carried this out successfully, he would then become a full Disciple. He would be married to Lara, a woman beyond his dreams, with her long dark hair and skin like warm silk, with whom he had spent one night before coming up this mountain, one night that in part sustained him throughout his solitude, and in part tormented him. Sometimes, instead of prayer, he counted the days to the next time he might see her. And always, afterwards, he prayed for forgiveness.

The Great Rite, then the eternal love of God expressed through Lara. You had to understand what it felt like to be wanted and loved, after a lifetime of people telling you that you were no good. A lifetime of being passed over by your father because your brother was so much smarter, so much better at baseball and football and life in general.

By your mother, because you hadn't taken any of the career paths she dreamed of for you. Because you got caught stealing some no-big-deal bits and pieces from a drugstore. Because you got six months suspended for dealing cannabis.

Passed over by your classmates, who thought you were weird, because you were too short, too physically weak, and that you never had anything to say that was worth listening to. By your teachers, who never thought you amounted to anything, and who turned you into a stammering wreck whenever you tried to show them that you were not as dumb as they thought.

That was all changed now. The Disciples loved him. Jesus loved him. Lara loved him.

All he had to do was learn the Forty Tracts. Then come down from the mountain and perform the Grand Rite of Passage – a killing in the name of the Lord of some of Satan's progeny. A name that would be given to him. It could be a single child, or an entire family. Or maybe even several families.

And he would have done something towards making the world a better place.

And God would give him Lara as a reward. And they would live for the rest of their lives in the right hand of God. And dwell in God's house ever after.

40

Naomi's Diary

John swears Phoebe looks like him and Luke looks like me. Well, I'm sorry, I don't see that at all. At five weeks old all I see is Fat Face and Thin Face. Mr Grumpy and Miss Calm. Mr Noisy and Miss Quiet.

Now I'm beginning to think of all the things we should have asked Dr Dettore to do. Like some gene that would make a baby sleep twenty-four hours a day until it becomes an adult. And never need food.

I'm exhausted. I feel like I've climbed a mountain every day since Luke and Phoebe came home, four weeks ago. I haven't even had time for a bath! Seriously! I grab a shower when John is around, and that's about it. I'm spending all my time washing faces, feeding them, changing nappies, loading and unloading the washing machine, ironing clothes. And just to add to the fun, Luke got colic when he arrived home and screamed hour after hour for a week.

I wept with joy when we first drove them home from the hospital. I remember that same feeling when the nurse handed Halley to us and we suddenly realized he was our baby! Ours alone. It's an incredible feeling.

Mum is staying and that is a help (at times, anyway), and Harriet stayed a couple of days and was a big help, too. Otherwise there seems to have been a stream of visitors. Nice to see them all, but it just creates even more work. It seems everyone is fascinated by the idea of twins, as if they're some kind of freaks.

John's mother is coming over from Sweden next week to see her grandchildren. She's a nice lady but with her deteriorating eyesight she's going to be more work for me, rather than any help. She can't be left alone in a strange house for one minute. But she's so excited about seeing her grandchildren, bless her!

Our finances, already at a low ebb, are being drained further. Two of everything. I wish I could contribute, but there's no way I could think about a job at this moment. I just stagger from feed to feed. And they are growing at an incredible rate. The paediatrician is surprised, but he says it's a good sign.

Definitely beginning to regret our decision to live in such an isolated place. I'd like to see something other than sheep and birds, and trees bending in the wind. I feel peaceful for a while after visitors have left, but then I start to long for John to arrive home.

It's OK for him, he spends all day out in the real world, talking to colleagues, having lunch with them, then comes home to his recreational toys, to his little babies and his little wifey.

One of them's crying now. Which means the other will be crying, too, in a minute. Feed and change. Feed and change. My nipples hurt like hell. I'm some kind of a milk cow. A servant to them. I don't remember Halley ever being this demanding.

I'm sounding hacked off. Well, I am hacked off. Having twins isn't twice as hard as having one baby, it's ten times as hard.

41

Her voice startled him, cutting through the New Age music of a harp across breaking waves that wafted through the room.

'What is it you are looking at, John? What are you trying to see?'

He pressed the shutter then turned to Naomi. 'Phoebe's now very definitely a miniature copy of you!'

'That's not answering my question,' she replied tartly.

He looked away awkwardly, staring around the room. It was pretty and cheery; the high, beamed ceiling and west-facing dormer window made it feel light and airy, even on a gloomy morning like this. They had decorated it themselves, with candy-striped curtains, and a jungle frieze running around the walls.

It was Saturday morning. John had cancelled his regular tennis game with Carson Dicks because he had seen how exhausted Naomi was, and wanted to give her as much help this weekend as he could. Unlike Naomi, her mother was not very domesticated. She could barely cook, and most appliances remained enigmas to her.

She still lived a genteel life, and occupied herself working in an art gallery in Bath specializing in local, but obscure, water-colourists.

There were times when Anne Walters was extremely focused, but there were as many days when she seemed to be in a world of her own.

Lowering his camera, he put an arm around Naomi

and hugged her. Through the soft wool of her jumper he could feel her ribs. She'd lost a lot of weight in recent months.

Outside, trees and shrubs keeled over in the strong March wind, and pellets of rain rattled against the roof. Heat from the radiator shimmered against the window. He hugged her even harder, protectively, watching Luke and Phoebe sleeping in their fluffy bedclothes in their cots just a few feet apart. He smiled, bleary-eyed, down at their innocent faces, at their almost impossibly tiny hands. Luke made a tiny cooing sound. Moments later it was echoed by Phoebe.

The room had a sweet, milky smell that he'd come to adore. The scents of baby powder, freshly laundered clothes, bedding, nappies and another wonderful smell that permeated everything, which seemed to come from their skin. The smells of his children.

The health visitor was really pleased at the weight they were putting on and with how they were doing generally. They were great babies, she told John and Naomi, beautiful, healthy, bonny.

So far.

So far.

And that one fear hung like a cloud stretching out to the horizon of his life. How long before they could be sure their kids were really fine and healthy? Before whatever Dettore had done or had failed to do showed up in them? What hidden time bombs were they carrying?

Sure, he knew, all parents had fears about their babies. Many of them the same kinds of fears he was having. But none of them had done what he and Naomi had.

Above him, a fairground carousel mobile hung from a beam, each of the animals swaying very slightly in the draught. Strung across each cot were threaded taffeta rattles, and in several of the books he had read it said that by one month old, each baby should have learned to get sounds from it. So far, they hadn't shown any signs of interest. Not that that meant anything, he knew, nothing to worry about at all. Not yet, at any rate.

'Are you looking for some sign?' Naomi asked, her voice sour. 'Are you waiting for a mark to appear on their foreheads like some kind of designer label, telling the world these are not just ordinary babies?'

He tried to kiss her but she pulled away. 'Darling, I like to be up here with them as much as I can. I love just looking at them, talking to them, like it says in the books, the same stuff we did with Halley. Putting on music for them, playing with them when they wake, and helping you feed them, changing their nappies. I absolutely love being with them, really I do!'

'I asked my mother if she ever talked to me when I was asleep in my cot,' Naomi said. 'She didn't; nor did she play me any music. But somehow I survived. Guess I was the one that got away.'

Phoebe stirred, then Luke. Luke held out his tiny hand. John touched it with a finger and moments later Luke's own tiny fingers curled around it, gripping it for several seconds. It was one of the most amazing sensations John had ever felt in his life.

'See that?' he whispered to Naomi.

She smiled, and nodded.

Luke continued to hold his finger for several seconds, before releasing it. Then John leaned down and stroked each of their faces, one with each hand. 'Daddy and Mummy are with you,' he said. 'How are you doing, little angels?'

Phoebe opened her eyes suddenly, and in the same instant, Luke opened his. It was uncanny, he thought, how they always seemed to open them at the same time. Both of them were watching him.

'Hallo, Luke. Hallo, Phoebe. Hallo, darling angels,' he said, shifting his position, encouraging them, as both sets of eyes tracked him. He saw the curl of a smile on both their lips and smiled back. Then he leaned forward and pinged the taffeta cord of Luke's rattle. Both pairs of eyes remained fixed on him, but they stopped smiling.

He pinged Phoebe's rattle, hoping to encourage her to reach up and touch it herself. But like her brother, she lay still, just observing him. Then after a few moments, as if they had grown bored, both babies closed their eyes in unison.

Naomi turned and walked back out of the room. John followed her, gently pulling the door to behind him, and leaving it slightly ajar.

As his footsteps retreated down the stairs, the eyes of both babies opened in unison. Just a brief flicker, then they closed again.

42

'So congratulations, John,' Carson Dicks said, raising his glass. 'Here's to your first few months.'

John rarely drank at lunchtime. He never usually even went out for lunch, preferring to eat a sandwich at his desk. But today Dicks had wanted to discuss the design of an experiment with him, and had driven him to a nearby pub.

A short, tubby man in his early fifties, with a crop of wild, fuzzy hair, an unkempt beard, and glasses as dense as the bottoms of wine bottles, Carson Dicks was any cartoonist's dream caricature of a mad professor.

John raised his glass. 'Cheers!' he said. 'Thank you.'

'*Skål!*'

John grinned. '*Skål!*' Then he drank a mouthful of the Chilean Sauvignon Blanc.

'So, how are you finding life at Morley Park?'

He detached some of his sole from the bone with surgical precision. 'I'm very happy. I have a great team, and the place has the academic feeling of a university but it doesn't seem to have the politics of one.'

'Exactly. That's what I like. There's some, of course, as there is in all walks of life. But here it doesn't interfere. We have this huge diversity of departments and research, but there's a great sense of unity, of everyone pulling together, working towards common goals.' He paused to fork an entire battered scampi into his mouth, then continued talking as he chewed. 'We have the pursuit of science for

Health, for Defence, and for the far more intangible – and of course debatable – *Greater Good*.' He gave John a knowing look.

'And how do you define the *Greater Good*?' John asked, suddenly feeling a little uncomfortable.

Dicks swilled his mouthful down with some more wine. One shred of batter dangled precariously in his beard and John found himself watching it, waiting for it to tumble.

'It's something we haven't talked about. A lot of people here did read that unfortunate interview you gave in the States. But of course, being British, no one wants to embarrass you by raising it.'

'Why didn't you mention it before?' John asked.

Dicks shrugged. 'I was waiting for you to do that. I respect you as a scientist. I'm sure you wouldn't have done anything without a great deal of thought and investigation.' He broke off a piece of his bread roll and buttered it. 'And of course, I know the press must have got it wrong. Designer babies aren't possible, not yet, are they?' With a broad grin he again stared hard at John, as if for confirmation.

'Absolutely; they got it wrong.' John gave a hollow, phoney, uncomfortable laugh.

'How are Luke and Phoebe?'

'They're terrific.'

'And Naomi?'

'She's exhausted. But she's happy to be back in England.'

They ate in silence for some moments, then Dicks said, 'If you ever did want to talk about anything, John, in total confidence, you can always come to me. You do know that, don't you?'

'I appreciate it,' he said. 'Thank you.'

Dicks picked up his glass again. 'Do you remember something Einstein said, back in the 1930s? Why does science bring us so little happiness?'

'And did he have an answer?'

'Yes. He said it was because we have not yet learned to make sensible use of it.' Again he gave John a penetrating stare.

John looked down at his food, then fingered his glass, tempted to drink more to alleviate his awkwardness. But he was already feeling a little light-headed from the first glass, and he was determined never to make the mistake of opening up to anyone again, not even to someone he could trust as much as Carson Dicks.

He reminded himself, as he had to frequently, why he and Naomi had made the decision they had. And he thought of the two beautiful children they had now brought into the world. Two children who would never have been born if it hadn't been for science.

'Einstein was wrong about a lot of things,' he said.

Carson Dicks smiled.

43

John felt decidedly unsteady as he walked back from the car park with his boss, hands in his pockets and his coat buttoned against the March wind. He entered the shabby lobby of the tired red-brick building, four storeys high, known simply as B11, that housed the Artificial Life Centre.

He'd broken his resolution to have just one glass with Carson, and they'd managed to get through two bottles between them, followed by a brandy each. Somehow, through the haze of alcohol, they'd managed to crack the design for the experiment John would spend the next three months on. He wasn't sure how Carson had been able to drive back, although the man had always been a heavy drinker, so maybe it affected him less.

'It's Caroline's birthday next weekend,' Dicks said. 'We're having a little dinner party on Saturday – are you and Naomi free?'

'Sounds good – I'll check with my social secretary!' John said. 'Thanks.'

The paintwork was peeling, there was a row of Health and Safety Executive notices stuck to the walls, a yellow radiation warning sign, a poster advertising a concert, another advertising a car-boot sale, and a list for names for a three-day coach visit to Cern in Switzerland.

Ignoring the slow and decrepit lift, both of them climbed the four flights of stairs. At the top, Carson Dicks put an avuncular arm around him.

'I mean what I said, John. If there's anything you ever want to talk about, I'm here for you.'

'I appreciate it. You're a brick.'

'I'm just glad to have you on my team. England's lost too many good scientists to the States in the past fifty years. We're lucky to have won one back.' He gave John a reassuring pat and headed off towards his office.

John walked along the corridor and entered lab B111–404, a long room filled with computer workstations, seven of which were occupied by members of his team, most of them in such fierce concentration they barely noticed his arrival.

Back in his own office, he took off his coat and some-how managed to miss the hook on the back of the door, watching in surprise as the coat slipped to the floor in a heap.

'Oops,' he said to himself, bending down and picking it up. He felt very woozy. Not good. He had a heavy afternoon workload to get through, the first item of which was to try to analyse a very complex set of algorithms.

First, he rang Naomi, as he did several times each day. 'Hi, darling!' he said. 'How are you?'

Her voiced sounded cold and he realized he should have waited until he was more sober.

'Luke's just been sick,' she said. 'And Phoebe's scream-ing. Can you hear her?'

'Uh-huh.'

'That's how I am.'

'OK,' he said, 'right.'

'What do you mean, *OK, right*?'

He was silent for a moment, thinking. 'I – I – just – wanted to say that – I'll try to get home early. Oh – Carson asked if we could go to dinner on Saturday – it's Caroline's birthday.'

There was a long silence. 'Sure.'

There was a reluctance in her voice. John knew that Naomi found Carson's heavily intellectual wife a little difficult. 'Honey, I think we should go – if you don't mind?'

'I don't mind.'

'Great. See you about six.'

'Six? I'll believe it when I see you.'

'I mean it, hon—'

He heard a sharp click. She had hung up.

Shit.

He replaced the receiver. The buzz from the alcohol was starting to fade, leaving him feeling leaden, in need of a sleep, and with a slight headache. He stood up and walked over to the window. It wasn't a huge room, but it had just about enough space for his desk, filing cabinets and books, and to accommodate a small group of visitors.

Staring down almost directly beneath, he could see the construction site, where the massive steel-and-glass edifice that would eventually house Britain's largest particle accelerator was starting to take shape.

He watched two men in hard hats attach a girder in a cradle to a crane hook. Workers. Drones. *Genetic underclass.* Dettore's expression came back to him repeatedly. Would people be bred to do manual tasks like that, in the future? Had Dettore's prediction been right that there would be a whole genetic underclass created, to serve the needs of everyone else? How did it happen at the moment? What made today's workers? A combination of lousy genes and poor education? Just random chance, circumstance, natural selection?

Would it be any worse to deliberately create such workers? Some people thought so. But was it really so terrible to contemplate doing that? What kind of a world would it be if you bred everyone to be a rocket scientist? Wouldn't that be truly irresponsible of science? To have the power to create a balanced world and funk out of using it, and instead take the easy option of making everyone smart? Maybe that would appeal to some idealists, but the reality would be a disaster.

But how palatable would the alternative be to anyone?

He sat down, wondering whether to get some coffee. But he'd already had two double espressos in the pub. *Just deal with some easy stuff for a while*, he thought, *let the alcohol wear off, catch up on emails.*

He glanced down the twenty new ones that had come in while he had been out. Mostly they were boring internal stuff.

Then he saw one from Kalle Almtorp, with an attachment.

> **John,**
> **This has just come through to me. I'm sorry, I thought perhaps everything had died down, but this does not seem to be the case.**

John opened the attachment. It was a news cutting from today's *Washington Post*.

> **DESIGNER BABIES FAMILY DEATH LINK TO DISCIPLES OF THE THIRD MILLENNIUM**

His eyes frozen to the screen, he read on.

> Philadelphia Police are taking seriously a claim by a religious group, Disciples of the Third Millennium, that they were responsible for the

deaths of Washington property tycoon Jack O'Rourke, his socialite wife, Jerry, and their twin babies. With chilling echoes of the Manson gang Sharon Tate slayings, their mutilated bodies were discovered in the O'Rourkes' secluded $10m mansion in the exclusive Leithwood estate in Virginia. Last year the same group claimed responsibility for the deaths of billionaire geneticist Dr Leo Dettore and Florida businessman Marty Borowitz and his wife Elaine and their twin babies. Despite an extensive worldwide police hunt, no trace of this group has ever been found to date.

There was an icon for a photograph, and John clicked on it. Moments later the image appeared. A photograph of two good-looking people, a man in his mid-thirties and a woman in her late twenties. He recognized them instantly.

They had been on Dettore's ship. There was no mistaking them. It was the couple by the *Serendipity Rose*'s swimming pool who had totally ignored them. The couple he and Naomi had jokingly called George and Angelina.

44

George and Angelina. John sat at his desk, mesmerized by the two images of the couple on his computer screen.

One, which Kalle had emailed him, was a wedding photograph. Jack O'Rourke in a white tuxedo looked even more of a doppelgänger for George Clooney than he had on the ship. His wife Jerry, hair in ringlets, wearing a classy white dress, seemed less like Angelina Jolie now, thinner, harder. They looked vain, as they had done on the ship, as if they knew exactly how beautiful and rich they were, powerful enough to buy everything they wanted, including perfect children.

The other was a close-up from the photograph he had taken surreptitiously on board the *Serendipity Rose*, of the couple lying on loungers by the pool. The match was evident; no question it was the same couple.

Twin babies, he read again.

They had *twins* too?

He swallowed, his mouth dry suddenly, and his hand was shaking. He clicked on another icon and there was a photograph showing a driveway leading up to a swanky house with tall pillars.

> 'They were a wonderful and kind couple, devoted to each other, and the most adoring parents in the world to their two-month-old twins,' said Betty O'Rourke, the murdered man's mother, at her Scottsville home. 'They had wanted to start a family for a long time, and felt truly blessed by the arrival of their beautiful twins.'

John's door opened and his secretary came in with some mail to be signed. He hastily clicked up a different window, one containing his weekly diary, then scrawled his signature on each letter, barely looking at them, anxious for her to leave so he could get back to the story.

As she closed the door behind her, he read to the end of the story. Then he read it again.

John O'Rourke was a sharp boy who had built up a billion-dollar real estate empire. His wife, Jerry, had genuine *Mayflower* ancestry; they were active in Washington political circles, had given Barack Obama a massive donation and were big fund-raisers for the Democrats. John O'Rourke harboured political ambitions of his own.

Their twins were called *Jackson* and *Chelsey*.

Like their parents, the babies had been mutilated.

Slogans and obscenities had been written on the walls in their blood.

With hands shaking so badly he could barely hit the buttons on his phone, he rang Naomi. When she answered he could hear screaming.

'It's Phoebe,' she said. 'She won't stop crying. I don't know what to do, John, why won't she stop? Why is she crying?'

'Maybe you should call the doctor.'

'I'll see. What is it you want?'

'Want?'

'Yes – you just called – now you're calling again.'

'I – I wanted to see if you're OK, darling?'

'NO, I AM NOT OK,' she shouted. 'I'M DEMENTED. IT'S FINE FOR YOU IN YOUR BLOODY OFFICE.'

'Maybe she's got an infection or something?' he answered lamely. Then he said, 'Listen, are you—'

He stopped in mid-sentence. This was stupid calling her like this, stupid to worry her.

'Oh Christ,' Naomi cried out. 'Luke's being sick again. John – sod it – I have to call you back.'

She hung up.

John stared back at the screen, suddenly feeling very, very alone in the world.

He dialled Kalle Almtorp in Washington.

It seemed, he told John, that the Disciples of the Third Millennium were as elusive as they had been a year ago when they'd claimed responsibility for Dettore's death. There were no names of any of the members and no clues where the organization hailed from.

'I think you need to be vigilant. The police don't know whether this organization is for real or whether it's the work of some copycat sickos. This whole genetics issue brings out some strong feelings in people, for sure. It's good that you aren't in America any more, but my advice to you is to make your home as secure as possible. Keep your head below the parapet and keep out of the press.'

'Can you do me one favour, Kalle. Can you get your secretary to find me a phone number for a Mrs Betty O'Rourke, in Scottsville, Virginia? I need to speak to her very badly. She may be unlisted – if so, could you try to pull some strings?'

Kalle rang back an hour later. It was an unlisted number, but he had managed to obtain it.

John thanked him, then dialled it.

After five rings he heard a mature-sounding woman's voice. 'Hallo?'

'Could I please speak to Mrs Betty O'Rourke?'

'That's me.' The voice, cracked with grief, sounded guarded.

'Mrs O'Rourke? Forgive the intrusion, my name is Dr Klaesson, I'm calling from England.'

'Dr Gleeson, did you say?'

'Yes. I – my wife and I – we met your son last year at a clinic.'

'Clinic? I'm sorry, what clinic are you talking about?'

John hesitated, unsure how much she knew. 'Dr Dettore. Dr Dettore's clinic.'

'Dr Dee Tory?' The name sounded like it was a total blank to her. 'Are you a newspaper man?'

John felt increasingly awkward. 'No, I'm not. I'm a scientist. My wife and I knew your son and – and his wife. I'm very sorry about your sad news.'

'I apologize, Dr Gleeson, I'm really not up to talking with anyone.'

'This is important, Mrs O'Rourke.'

'Then I think you should talk to the police, not me.'

'Please let me ask you just one question. Did your son intend to have twins?' Realizing he hadn't phrased it well, he tried to recover the situation. 'What I mean is—'

'How did you get this number, Dr Gleeson?'

'This may have some bearing on what has happened. I appreciate it must be difficult for you to talk at the moment, but please, believe me—'

'I'm going to hang up now. Goodbye, Dr Gleeson.'

The line went dead.

Shit.

He stared at the receiver for some moments. Then he redialled. The line was busy.

He tried again, repeatedly, for the next half hour. The line remained busy.

Finally he gave up. From a drawer in his desk he pulled out a thick, heavy *Yellow Pages*, and turned to the heading marked Security Services and Equipment.

45

Chopin tinkled on the Saab's radio as John drove along the country road. It was eight o'clock. The wipers thud-thudded, smearing the drizzle into an opaque film. Headlights burst out of the darkness towards him, then, in his mirror, became red tail lights shrinking into the distance. Darkness in front of him now, and behind him.

Darkness, also, in his heart.

He drove at a steady sixty miles an hour, the head-lamps picking out the familiar landmarks. Inside his head he pricked at thoughts, trying to grab them, grasp them.

They had moved from America to here. Was there any point in moving again – and if so, to where? Sweden? Would they be any safer there, any further from the reach of these crazies? A few years back the Swedish Prime Minster had been shot in a busy street. Where in this world could you be safe from fanatics?

He passed a brightly illuminated pub on the right, followed by the sign for a farm shop. Then a long stretch of dark road again, bordered by hedgerows. In a fortnight the clocks went forward. Summertime would begin. He would be able to drive home in daylight. Daylight gave more protection than darkness. Didn't it?

His mobile rang. Glancing at the dial he could see it was Naomi. Jamming the phone into the hands-free cra-dle, he answered. 'Hi, honey, I'm almost home. Be there in five minutes.'

'You're so late – I've been worrying about you.' Her voice sounded strange, very strained.

'I'm sorry, I did try to call back a couple of times but you were on the phone.'

'You said you'd be home at six.'

'I got stuck in a staff meet—'

Then the line disconnected.

He cursed. Reception was always bad in this area. He tried to call her back but there was no signal. Minutes later he saw the lights of a garage forecourt and pulled into it.

The selection of flowers was poor. The best was a small bunch of red roses, wrapped in cellophane. He bought them then drove on. Five minutes later, he turned off the main road onto the narrow lane that led to the village.

Caibourne was ten miles east of Brighton and four miles from Lewes, the ancient historic county town of Sussex. It was more a hamlet than a village. There was a pub, used mostly by locals rather than tourists, a church badly in need of a major roof restoration, a tiny Post Office that doubled as a general store, a thriving primary school, a one-court tennis club, and a community that was mostly farm and estate workers in tied cottages that were owned by the nearby stately home of Caibourne Place.

John drove past a row of labourers' cottages, the schoolhouse and the church. A mile and a half beyond the village, he turned onto the single-lane farm track that led up to their house. A rabbit ran across the road in front of him, and he braked sharply as the creature darted back across his path again, then loped for some yards up ahead of him before finally diving through a gap in the wire fencing and into a ploughed field. Beyond his headlights was total darkness.

Slayings.

Mutilated.

The second couple this had happened to.

There was a ton of stuff on the internet about Dettore, and what was particularly concerning was a series of anonymous blog posts by someone claiming to be a former employee from the clinic. God knows what information from the clinic had been leaked.

If this organization – sect – bunch of crazies – whoever – or whatever – they were – if they had taken over Dettore's clinic, if they had enough information to find George and Angelina, and the Borowitzes, then almost certainly they had enough information to find everyone else.

He negotiated a sharp right-hand bend and could see the lights of the house a few hundred yards ahead of him. He drove over a cattle grid, onto the gravel drive and pulled up next to Naomi's Subaru station wagon.

As he climbed out of the car, Naomi opened the front door, looking pale. He grabbed his laptop bag off the back seat and the flowers, shut the door, and strode over to her. Barely acknowledging the flowers, she put her arms around him and held him tightly.

'I'm sorry,' he said. 'I did try to call you back, but—'

Her face was wet and her eyes were red from crying.

'What's the matter, darling?' he said, although he could tell what it was from her expression.

They went in. Naomi closed the front door, locked it and clicked home the safety chain. 'Lori rang, from LA.'

John heard a roar of laughter from the television in the kitchen. He dumped his bag on the tiled floor and wriggled out of his coat. He hung his coat on a hook on the mahogany Victorian stand. There was a good smell of cooking meat in the house. 'How are they? How's Irwin?'

She looked at the flowers, but said nothing.

They went through to the kitchen. The playpen was on the floor, a mess of toys lying beside it. John saw a half-empty bottle of red wine on the table and a glass that had a small amount left in it. 'How's Luke? Did you call the doctor?'

'I have an appointment for him tomorrow. He said he doesn't think it's anything to worry about, but to take Luke to him if he's still not well in the morning.'

'Is he still throwing up?'

'He stopped.'

She put the flowers in the sink and ran the tap. 'Thank you,' she said. 'These are beautiful. You used to buy me flowers all the time when we first went out. Remember?'

Guilt tugged at him. 'I did?'

'Yes.'

He went over to the baby monitor and listened. Silence. 'Are they asleep?'

'I think so.'

'Just quickly take a look at them.' He sprinted up the stairs, treading as softly as he could, went down to their room and gently pushed the door open. Both were sound asleep, Luke with his thumb in his mouth; Phoebe, her fists balled, had a tiny spot of drool running down her chin.

He blew each of them a kiss, then went back downstairs and into the kitchen.

She poured herself some more wine, then turned to face him, her eyes wide, full of fear. 'Lori said there's a big story in the press – all over the news. There's been another killing. Another couple who went to Dr Dettore and have had twins, just like us, John.'

'Kalle rang,' he said. 'He told me. That's what I was calling you about.'

She walked over to the window. 'Does Kalle have a suggestion about what we should do?'

'He said to be vigilant.'

He did need a drink, he realized, so he took a fresh bottle of white wine out of the fridge. 'We need to get an alarm system that goes through to the police. Get lights that come on if anyone approaches the house. Window locks. Stuff like that. And he said we ought to maybe think about getting a guard dog. And—' He hesitated.

'Yes?' she prompted.

'He thought we ought to have a gun in the house.'

'This is England, John, not America.'

'I thought I'd apply for a shotgun licence – could be useful for keeping down all the rabbits.' He pulled the cork out.

'You're too absent-minded. I don't think it's a good idea to have a gun in the house, and certainly not with young children. Maybe a dog, when they're a little older – we could get a guard dog of some kind.'

When they're a little older. Her words repeated in his head. *When they're a little older.* There was something innocent in her remark that struck him as almost childlike. Two families had been butchered. A bunch of crazies were out there, somewhere in the night, maybe in America, maybe even in Sussex. They didn't have the luxury of time to wait until Luke and Phoebe were *older*.

'I've taken tomorrow morning off,' he said. 'I've got a couple of security firms coming up to give us their suggestions and prices.' He poured himself some wine.

Naomi nodded. 'Good, let's do that. I'm sorry, I got

myself in a state with the kids, and with the call. I want to stay here, John, I want us to make a life here in England. We can't just go on the run – spend our lives in hiding.'

He kissed her. 'I was thinking the same, driving over.'

'These people will get caught – no one can get away with what they've done for long, can they?'

Privately, John thought, *They've got away with it for over a year, so far. Totally away with it.* But he didn't say this to Naomi. Instead, putting his arms around her, holding her tightly, he said, 'Sure. Kalle said the FBI are throwing a lot of resources at this. They'll find them.'

She looked at up him, with total, utter trust in her eyes. 'He said that?'

'Yes,' he lied.

'Kalle's a good man.'

'He is.'

Holding her even tighter, he nuzzled her ear and whispered, 'Luke and Phoebe are asleep. Why don't we take advantage of that?'

For an answer she took his hand and led him up to bed.

46

A pitiful shriek pierced the silence of the night. Naomi shuddered at the sound as she lay awake, too damned awake, eyes wide open, brain racing, the room bathed in ethereal moonlight through the open curtains. With no neighbours, they never bothered to draw them.

'A fox taking a rabbit,' John said quietly. He slipped an arm around her, pulling her closer to him.

'It's the most horrible sound.'

'Just nature at work.'

She rolled over and stared at him. There was one more outburst of shrieks, a long squeal, then silence.

'You study nature in your work,' she said. 'You simulate it in computer programs. Do you have rabbits squealing in your computers?'

He smiled. 'No.'

She kissed him. 'You're a kind man. I'm sure you wouldn't want to hurt even a *virtual* rabbit. I don't want you buying a gun. I don't want us to live in an atmosphere of fear, like we're under siege or something. We mustn't lose sight of why we've done what we have, John. We haven't done anything wrong or immoral, we haven't done anything to be ashamed of – have we?'

'No,' he said quietly.

'I am scared. There hasn't been a day since – since the news about Dr Dettore – when I haven't been afraid. I have dreadful dreams, I wake confused and exhausted and sometimes, when the sun is streaming in, or I hear birds singing, or just you breathing, I get a few precious moments when the dreams have faded, a few moments of private blue sky, of peace. And then it all comes back and I think – think – that maybe there's a car down the end of the lane with a bunch of religious freaks in it, and they have guns and knives, and they don't even have hatred in their hearts, they have some kind of deep inner peace because they know they're doing the right thing, that they're acting out God's will. Does that scare you, John?'

'I think about it all the time.'

'You still believe man should take control of nature, don't you?'

'Yes; nothing's happened to make me change my mind.'

There was a brief silence, then she said, 'You do love Luke and Phoebe as much as . . .' Her voice tailed off.

'As?'

'Doesn't matter.'

He caressed her hair again. 'Yes, of course. I love them – incredibly – I didn't know I was capable of such love. I—'

'If you had to make a choice,' she said, 'between saving them or me, who would you save?'

'It will never come to that.'

Her voice became a fraction more insistent. 'Just supposing it did – just supposing you had to make a choice – who would you save? Luke and Phoebe or me?'

John thought carefully, unprepared for the question.

'Who?' she probed.

'You,' he said. 'I would save you.'

'Why?'

'Because if anything ever happened to them we could have more children. But I could never replace you.'

She kissed him. 'That's a very beautiful thing to say –
but do you mean it?'

'Yes.'

'OK,' she said. 'Let me ask you another question. If
you had the choice of saving yourself or them, who would
you save.'

His answer came out almost instantly. 'Them.'

She sounded relieved. 'So you do love them, don't
you.' It was a statement, not a question.

'Why do you have doubts?'

'I wonder, sometimes. I wonder if you feel that if you
could turn back the clock, that—'

'Never.' He shrugged. 'OK, I wouldn't have done that
bloody interview. But—'

'You'd still have gone to Dettore?'

'Yes. And you?'

'Yes.'

'Hon,' he said, 'throughout history, people who have
tried to challenge established thinking have been perse-
cuted. Not everyone has been right, but if nobody had
tried – well – the human race wouldn't have progressed
very far. We might not even have survived this long. We'd
certainly be living in some kind of dark age right now.'

'And we aren't?' Naomi said. 'These people – the
Disciples of the Third Millennium – the fact that they can
be out there, roaming around, believing they have the
right to kill people for their own beliefs, and that no one
can do a thing about it – that doesn't signal to me what
we think is civilization is anything more than a very thin
veneer.'

'That's what we are trying to change. That is what
going to Dettore was all about.'

'Is it? I thought going to him was about having a child who wasn't going to die at four years old from an inherited disease. Is it about something else? Something you haven't told me?'

'Absolutely not. I tell you everything.'

She was quiet for some moments, thinking, then she said, 'You would have told me, wouldn't you, if—'

'If what?'

'If you and Dettore had discussed anything else about – the babies.'

'What do you mean by *anything else*?'

'All the options he gave us. All those boxes we had to tick. I'd have no way of knowing if you and he had decided to – to go behind my back.'

'No way,' John said. 'No way I would ever have done that, darling. Not in a million years. Don't you trust me?'

'Yes, I do, of course I do. It's Dettore. I look at Luke and Phoebe all the time, and wonder – you know – I wonder what he's done, what's inside them, what surprises we have in store. It would be great, wouldn't it, if we could get their entire genomes read. Then at least we'd know.'

'And if you found out something you didn't like, what would you do about it?'

She was silent. She had no answer.

47

Down here in the dark of the sewer there is only one light that shines, my friends. It is His light. He shows the path to those who follow, and if you choose not to follow, that's your call.

You are doomed.

You, who do not follow, call evil good and good evil. You turn darkness into light and light into darkness. You make what is bitter sweet, and what is sweet you make bitter. Isaiah 5: 20.

I have your names written down on paper, my friends. And I have you written in the memory of my computer. And written in my head. Today you are everywhere, basking in your self-importance. But, my friends, you are doomed. And not just here on the earth plane. Fear not me who can kill your body but cannot kill your soul. Rather be afraid of God, who can destroy both body and soul in Hell.

How are you finding it down in Hell, Mr and Mrs O'Rourke and your hideous spawn, Jackson and Chelsey? Have you repented yet? Don't worry, you have plenty of time, all the time in the world. Everything that happens in this world happens at the time God chooses. And God chose you first, Mr and Mrs O'Rourke. Soon others will be joining you.

The Disciple sat on the hard wooden chair in the shade of his cell in the monastery, and stared out through the window at the walled kitchen garden below. Tiny green shoots appeared in the furrowed earth. He had planted tomatoes, broccoli, courgettes, lettuces, potatoes. Organic.

Real vegetables. Not like the shit in supermarkets. Not like the shit growing in the wheat fields beyond the monastery's garden. You could see the fields that had real wheat and those that were spawned by the Devil. The real wheat glowed a golden yellow colour under the sun because it had God's blessing. The GM stuff stayed a murky brown colour; it grew, ashamed, in perpetual shade.

A sharp, mantric rapping sound rose through the tranquillity of the warm morning air. The midday call to prayers. He rose obediently and placed his black veil over his head.

The abbot had made him the Assistant Guest Master. His duties impinged little on his thoughts and his plans. Here in the wilderness of Iowa they did not have too many pilgrims visiting. His duties here were light compared to his duties to God.

The completion of the Great Rite.

And then God's blessing.

I look down the names on my list and I see you all. I read your names and I see your faces in my head. I see your homes, I see your children. There is never one moment when God permits me to stop thinking about you all in turn, in rota.

I see your name on my list, Dr Klaesson. Dr John Klaesson and Mrs Naomi Klaesson of Los Angeles, California. I am thinking about you at this moment, wondering how you are feeling right now. You will have spawned by now. How are the creatures, Dr and Mrs Klaesson?

How are you feeling about what you have done?

Are you proud? Or have you woken and seen the light and been sickened?

You don't have to worry for long. Soon I will liberate you from your shackles of guilt.

And hand you over to God. Who won't be so merciful as me.

Timon Cort walked down the stone steps, along the cloistered courtyard; then he crossed the small, grass lawn, past the fountain and joined the sombre queue of brothers at the chapel door.

Entering through the screen into the sweet smell of incense, he was enveloped by the deep golden light glowing in the nave of the church. A sign.

God confirmed the sign in his prayers. God told him it was time to take the next step in the Great Rite.

48

Naomi's Diary

Made a friend today! Her name is Sandra Taylor. She came up (in a green Range Rover, what else?) to ask if we'd like to subscribe to the Caibourne, Firle and Glynde parish magazine. Subscription three pounds a year. Bargain! Sandra has three young children, one just eight months old – the same age as Luke and Phoebe. There's a toddlers' group in the village, where the mums meet every Wednesday. I'm going to check it out.

Today, Mum came to stay and I went shopping for a pram. I hadn't realized there were so many different designs of prams for twins. The salesman in the store pointed out the advantages of a side-by-side, explaining that would give each child an equal view, and a shorter wheelbase, enabling it to get round tighter corners. But that needed to be balanced against the problem of width in some supermarket aisles . . .

I worry so much. One of my worries is about cot death, and I constantly listen to the babyphone speakers around the house when they are sleeping. I wake in the night panicking that I can't hear them breathing.

Another major cause for worry is that Luke and Phoebe seem to go longer between feeds than the books – and Megan, the health visitor – say is normal. The paediatrician thinks this is strange, too, yet he insists they seem totally healthy. And he says they definitely are bigger than normal for their age. Noticeably bigger. But I remember Dr Dettore telling us that they would grow and mature faster than normal babies, so that's not such a big concern.

We've been told it is important to give them separate identities, not to call them twins, and to be sure on their first birthday, which is fast looming up, that they have separate birthday cakes and presents.

I'm thinking it's strange how perspectives change. I know I should be grateful to have two such lovely, healthy babies. But how true that expression is about other pastures looking greener. Los Angeles seems a million years ago. A million years since I had a life.

49

Naomi, standing by the kitchen window at seven thirty in the morning, watched John drive off. She saw his brake lights come on as he reached the cattle grid, heard the clatter as he drove over it. Wednesday.

Baby and toddler group day today. Bliss! And it was, relatively speaking.

The highlights of her weeks weren't much. The Wednesday toddler group she had started attending with Luke and Phoebe, held in a house in the village, at which she met other mothers – and caught up on the local village gossip. Occasional visits from friends or her mother. A cup of tea with the health visitor. Then there was the Friday morning arrival of Ron, the World's Most Miserable Gardener, who came as part of the rental deal, and spent most of the morning tinkering around in the garage until it was time to leave. He was north of seventy and couldn't dig because he had a bad back. For the same reason he couldn't mow. He had no conversation and he smelled like damp furniture. Naomi had suggested to the rental agency that he be replaced. The agency had written to the owners out in Saudi Arabia and were awaiting a reply.

Her thoughts were disrupted by Phoebe banging on the side of her plate with her spoon, and moments later Luke began screaming, drowning out the theme tune of breakfast television. He hurled his cereal bowl onto the floor and the contents spattered all over the place.

She bit her lip in fury, staring at the mess, yet another

thing – on top of the nappies, the sheets, the pyjamas, all the regular laundry and all the regular housework, now she had to scrape sodding breakfast cereal off the floor and the walls.

She felt like screaming back at him. Instead she found a teething ring and tried to get it into his mouth, but he windmilled it away with his hands, screaming even louder, and almost immediately Phoebe threw her spoon on the floor and began screaming, also.

Naomi grabbed the remote and hit the volume button, turning it up to maximum. 'I'm listening to this interview!' she shouted back at them, defiantly. 'I like this guy, OK? He's one of my favourite actors. We're going to have some *Mummy Time* here. OK?'

Blanking out their screams, she stood right in front of the television and watched the interview all the way through, her ears ringing from the cacophony of sounds behind her.

Then, sinking the volume back down, she turned and, to her amazement, both babies were staring at her in total silence, mouths open, eyes wide.

Naomi grinned at them. 'OK. So now we've figured out who's boss around here.' Then she gave each of them a kiss, made Luke a fresh bowl and spoon-fed him. He ate it all in silence without protesting. Good. Almost too good. 'Very good!' she said.

He stared blankly back at her.

'And you've eaten all yours by yourself! Good girl!' she said, wiping cereal from the edges of Phoebe's mouth.

As if in some kind of synchronization with her brother, Phoebe stared blankly back, too, for a moment. Then they both smiled.

They remained silent as she carried them up and

placed them on the bathroom floor while she grabbed her morning shower. Normally, before she had finished, two little heads would be peeking around the shower curtain, watching her. But today they lay motionless, where she had placed them.

Back down in the kitchen, as she threw the first load of laundry into the washing machine, they continued to remain silent. Usually they would have rolled around on the floor together, sometimes Luke, sometimes Phoebe crawling on top of the other, pinning the other down. But this morning, nothing.

She began to be a little unnerved.

At nine thirty she changed their nappies; afterwards, lying in bed, she gave them a feed then snoozed for a while. When she woke, they were still both staring at her, still silent.

She carried them up to their bedroom, settled them in their cots and went down to the kitchen. After tossing the laundry from the washing machine into the dryer, she made herself a mug of tea, checked the sound of their breathing on the speaker of the baby monitor for some moments, then settled down at the kitchen table to read the *Daily Mail*. It was ten o'clock. With luck she would have a whole blissful hour to herself.

Soon after the dryer finished its cycle, she heard them giggling and calling out to each other in their cots, as if they were playing some game. First she heard Luke make a gurgling sound, followed by a burst of giggles from Phoebe, then Phoebe made a similar gurgling sound that was followed by a burst of giggles from Luke.

She went upstairs. It was time to give them one more feed, then get them dressed for the baby and toddler group. As she entered their room, she was expecting to hear them still making a noise. But she was greeted by total silence. Both of them were staring at her, the way they had been staring at her down in the kitchen, but with even more intensity.

She stopped in her tracks, spooked out. It really felt, for an instant, as if it was she who was the infant, and they who were the parents.

50

John was disturbed by the expression on Naomi's face as she opened the front door for him. She looked pale and strained.

'Kids OK?'

'They're fine. Upstairs. Asleep.'

'How was the toddler group?'

'Embarrassing.'

He heard a gurgle come through the baby intercom. Then another gurgle, like a response.

'Embarrassing?'

'Yes, it was embarrassing, John, I was embarrassed by my children – our children – our wonderful *designer* babies.'

He raised a finger to his lips.

'What are you telling me?' she demanded. 'Walls have ears?'

'We agreed we'd never say it – and it is dangerous to say it in their presence, they might start repeating it when they're older.'

'For Christ's sake, how paranoid do you want to be?'

He looked at her, taken aback. 'How *paranoid*?' He was thinking about the death of Dettore, about the entire Borowitz family, about the O'Rourke family. *That's how paranoid*, he was thinking. *We can't afford to stop being paranoid. We really can't.*

Ever.

He listened again for a moment to the baby-monitor

speaker. 'I don't hear music – you're not playing them music?'

'That's right, I'm not playing them music. I'm too exhausted to play them music, why don't you go up and play them music? Why don't you go and bring the entire London Philharmonic Orchestra down here to play them music?'

'Honey – darling—'

'I don't think this playing them music, playing them all this ditzy New Age crap, is doing them much good. You seem to think you can bring Luke and Phoebe on like – like – some kind of hothouse courgettes – that if you sprinkle enough music and words all over them, they're going to come bursting out of their cots and running into our room and recite the whole of Plato's *Republic* from memory.'

John went through to the kitchen, in need of a drink. He knew it was tough on Naomi at the moment, but things would change. Work was going well, they were starting to pay off their debt to Naomi's mother and to her sister – although both of them insisted they didn't need paying back. Soon they might be able to afford an au pair – his mother had already suggested the daughter of a family friend, but it was too much of an expense at the moment. And Naomi was still adamant she did not want anyone else looking after them.

He took a tray of ice cubes from the freezer and popped half a dozen into the cocktail shaker that was lying, disassembled, beside the drying rack from last night. 'What was this embarrassing thing that happened at the toddler group?'

'Oh, that?' She feigned a matter-of-fact tone. 'It seems something our friend Leo Dettore overlooked was the gene for basic social graces.'

'They behaved badly?'

She shook her head. 'It wasn't that, it was – the way they interacted – or rather, didn't. They just totally ignored the other kids – all delightful babies. Our two didn't want to know them. And there was something really strange – when any other baby came up to them, Luke and Phoebe would just give them a cold stare, and the baby would burst into tears and start screaming.'

'They are nine months old, honey. That's far too young to expect them to be social. I thought the point of the toddlers' group was for mums to have a break, for you to meet other mums, get to know the community a little?'

'They made the other babies *cry*, John. They're so much bigger than the rest of them, that's part of the problem.'

'Babies are always crying—' He hesitated, lifting his cocktail glass from the rack. Then, taking the olives out of the fridge, he said, 'I thought last week they got on fine?'

'They got on fine in the sense that they didn't really do anything. I thought maybe they were shy, or something.'

'What about the other babies? Were they all playing together?'

'No – not exactly *playing*. But there was some interaction. There wasn't any with Luke and Phoebe. It's as if after a while the others became scared of them.'

'More likely they were fazed because it's two of them. Naomi, you can't expect any interaction at this age. Jeez – and you're hitting on *me* for expecting too much – I think you're expecting way too much. And there's the twins thing,' John said. 'All the information we have says that twins prefer each other's company because that's what they're used to.'

'Mix me one of those, too,' she said. 'A large one.'

He looked at her dubiously. 'You know what that book says about alcohol when you're breast feeding, that it gets in the milk—'

The vehemence of her reply startled him. Clutching the Absolut Vodka bottle by the neck in one hand and the dry vermouth in the other, brandishing them like clubs, she screamed with pent-up fury, 'I don't give a toss, John, OK? I don't give a flying fuck about all these books, all these websites on how to have a smarter baby. Get a life, you sad man, and while you're at it, give your wife a life, too.'

He stared at her blankly and the next moment found himself holding both the bottles as she thrust them into his hands.

'Once a day, that's all I breast-feed them now. I'll have a very large one, John, a double, or maybe even a triple, right to the top, shaken, and I want four olives in it. Are olives OK, will they do something weird to my milk? Will four olives in my martini turn our babies into retards?'

A ripple of laughter came through the baby monitor. John and Naomi both turned to look at it. It was uncanny timing, as if both Luke and Phoebe were laughing in unison at them.

The sounds from the babies continued as he mixed their drinks and lanced the olives with cocktail sticks. Happy sounds, calling out to each other, giggling. Listening to them, and the first sip of her drink, seemed to calm Naomi.

They carried their drinks upstairs and along the corridor, then stopped outside the door. The sounds were continuing, happy little cries, giggles. But the moment John opened the door, they stopped.

Phoebe lay on her side, thumb in her mouth, surrounded by a pile of her favourite toys – her polar bear, a snake, a zebra and a lion – apparently fast asleep. Luke, too, lay on his side, teething ring clenched in his mouth, eyes shut, breathing the deep, rhythmic breaths of sleep.

Naomi and John looked at each other, then she signalled with her eyes for them to go back out.

In the corridor, John closed the door, softly. 'How can they be that noisy one moment, then sound asleep the next?'

It was a while before Naomi answered him. There was nothing she could actually put a finger on, it was just a feeling she had, a small current running through her like an undertow, that Luke and Phoebe were already smarter than they were letting on. 'I don't know,' she said, finally.

In his cot, Luke called out to Phoebe. It was a high-pitched sound, a higher frequency than a dog whistle, inaudible to a human ear, well outside the range of the baby monitor.

On the same frequency, Phoebe answered him.

51

Dr Roland Talbot opened his Wimpole Street consulting room door to greet John and Naomi, who were holding Luke and Phoebe by their hands. 'Dr and Mrs Klaesson,' he said. 'Nice to meet you.'

Then he peered closely at Luke and Phoebe. 'Hi, Luke!' he said. 'Hi, Phoebe! How are you doing?'

Luke had blossomed into an angelic-looking child, with a cute snub nose, cobalt-blue eyes and blond hair that flopped down over his forehead; Naomi had dressed him in a yellow button-down shirt, blue chinos and trainers. Phoebe, equally angelic, her hair a fraction darker and much longer than her brother's, was wearing a red dress over a white blouse, white socks and sandals.

They gave him the same response they gave most people. Silent stares that were somewhere between curiosity and hostility.

Still smiling, unfazed, he ushered them all to a toy-littered L-shaped sofa in front of a coffee table, then sat down in an easy chair opposite them.

Tall and gangly, with amiable good looks and threadbare hair, the psychiatrist was dressed in a rugby shirt that looked a couple of sizes too big, and brown corduroy trousers that stopped short of his battered trainers, revealing, as he lounged back in his chair, several inches of hairless ankle and baggy yellow Snoopy socks that had lost their elastic. Despite being almost forty, he might have been wearing hand-me-downs from an elder brother, Naomi thought. He looked like a big, goofy kid.

'Great-looking children,' he said.

'Thank you,' John said, looking down at his son proudly, then at his daughter.

Then with a frown he said, 'Nineteen months old, right?'

'Nineteen and a half,' John said. He smiled at Naomi and she smiled nervously back. They *were* beautiful and blossoming more each day.

'I'd have guessed quite a bit older than that,' the psychiatrist said. Then, leaning right forward and crossing his arms, he asked, 'OK, so, tell me, how I can help?'

Naomi and John looked at each other. 'Want me to start?' Naomi said to her husband.

'Sure.'

'OK,' she said. She told the psychiatrist their concerns, that whilst on the intercom they constantly heard Luke and Phoebe chatting away to each other in baby talk, and sounding like they were playing happily. But whenever they went into the room, the babies fell silent, almost as if they were pretending to be asleep. That they did not seem to be interested in playing or communicating with other kids. And, perhaps even more importantly, that after nineteen and a half months they were not showing any signs of talking, not even saying *Mama* or *Dada*.

Talbot put them at their ease. 'It's a twins thing, quite often,' he said. 'Because twins become absorbed with each other, they very often take longer to relate to the world around them than a single baby. There are plenty of twins who don't start to speak until well past the age of two, so that's not something you need to worry about – at this stage. How is their eating?'

John and Naomi glanced at each other, uncomfortable on this topic, and unsure how much Dettore had had an influence on this. 'They don't really seem interested in food,' Naomi said. 'They were hungry as babies, but now they eat about half of what our paediatrician and the books say they should be eating.'

Dr Talbot watched Luke and Phoebe alternately for some moments. 'They don't look undernourished to me. Kids find their own level with nutrition. How's their health?'

'So far, touch wood,' Naomi said, 'it's been excellent.'

'No colds, nothing!' John said proudly.

'I don't want to tempt fate,' Naomi cautioned. 'But they seem very robust.'

'Not one cold in nineteen and a half months?'

She shook her head.

'Remarkable.'

Dr Talbot engaged eye contact for some moments with Luke then with Phoebe. Then, staring down at the coffee table, he rocked back and forward. 'I can see curiosity – which is common with all infants. They're looking at me, trying to figure me out, trying to figure this place out. That's a pretty healthy sign.'

'There is one thing that I – that we – have noticed, in both of them,' John said suddenly. 'They are really fascinated by animals.'

Naomi nodded vigorously. 'They are. We were out in the garden yesterday and a neighbour's cat jumped down from the fence, and they both trotted towards it, giggling. And there was a rabbit in the garden one day last week – bloody thing was eating my roses – and they thought the sight of it was wildly funny.'

'Maybe when they're a little older you should think

231

about getting them a pet – something they can share between them and look after – pets are terrific for helping develop a sense of responsibility.'

'You mean, like a goldfish?' Naomi asked.

Talbot screwed up his face. 'Goldfish are pretty, but they're boring. I always advise something tactile, some creature that kids can connect and interact with, like a hamster or a gerbil, or a puppy or a cat – even a rabbit.'

'We thought about getting a dog,' Naomi said.

The psychiatrist nodded. 'A dog would be good. OK, what I'd like to do is run a few little problem-solving tests with them, relating to sub goals, and see how they handle them, if that's OK with you? I want to do this individually, which means you take one of them out of the room. Shall we start with ladies first?'

John went out into the hall with Luke and sat down on a chair. Naomi watched as, first, Roland Talbot laid two cloths on the coffee table. He held up a plastic cow, squeezed it and a mooing sound came out. He saw Phoebe's eyes widen, and her arms reach out to try to grasp it. He pulled it back sharply away from her. Then he laid the cow on one cloth, well beyond Phoebe's reach.

'Let her try to get it,' he told Naomi.

Phoebe moved closer to the table. In seconds, Phoebe grabbed the cloth with the cow on, yanked it sharply towards her, then grabbed the cow, and squeezed a *moo* from it.

'Well done, darling!' Naomi praised her.

Next, Talbot repeated the experiment, but this time he put a plastic barrier across the cloth, hiding the cow, still well out of Phoebe's reach. The barrier could only be moved by grasping a handle attached to it.

Within seconds, Phoebe had jerked the barrier out of

the way, and had the cow back in her hands, squeezing it excitedly.

Over the next fifteen minutes, the psychiatrist set Phoebe a series of tasks that seemed to Naomi to be progressively harder. Then he repeated the process with Luke.

When Luke completed the last task, the psychiatrist brought Naomi and Phoebe back into the room and sat them back down on the sofa. For some moments he looked pensive. Phoebe took a sudden interest in Naomi's hair and began twisting it into a tangle. Luke reached out towards a set of cubes he had been putting together, angry that his father was holding him back.

The psychiatrist leaned against his chair, arms behind his head. 'Well, John and Naomi, you do have something to worry about, but it's not what you've come to see me about, I can tell you that.'

'What do you mean?' Naomi asked.

'You're worried about Luke and Phoebe being backward, right?'

Both John and Naomi hesitated, then nodded.

'I can tell you this: they're not the slightest bit backward. You know what I would worry about if they were my kids? They're so damned smart, I'd be worrying about how the hell, in a few years time, I'm going to be able to keep up with them.' He looked at them, giving them a chance for this to sink in.

John and Naomi exchanged a brief glance.

'These kids have very advanced skills for their age. I would say unique in my experience. They even *look* advanced. They are good visual learners and very auditory learners, so they have it both ways. A colleague of mine is running a research programme on exceptionally bright children – with your permission I'd like—'

'No,' Naomi interrupted, very firmly, shooting a warning glance at John. 'I don't want my children under any kind of scrutiny like that.'

John, mindful of Kalle Almtorp's warning to keep a low profile, said, 'I'm sorry, but very definitely not.'

There had been no further word about the Disciples of the Third Millennium for a year now, but that did not mean they could start relaxing their guard. Until these people were identified and behind bars, they could never relax – and perhaps not even then. There were always going to be fanatics out there who would resent what they had done.

Roland Talbot put up his hands. 'No sweat, absolutely, I understand.'

'Thank you,' John said.

'But I do think you need to be prepared,' the psychiatrist added. 'When you start Luke and Phoebe in full-time school, it's likely they're going to get bored pretty quickly. You may have to fix it for them to get special treatment, otherwise you'll hold them back and they'll start resenting you for it.'

John looked at Luke and Phoebe, wondering how much of this they were understanding and taking on board. They gave no sign of any reaction at all.

As they left, ushering the kids along the hallway in front of them, John put an arm around Naomi and squeezed her, filled with immense pride and hope. Maybe, just maybe, all they had gone through was going to be worthwhile. Their children were healthy, and now a top psychiatrist confirmed that they were smart, way above average for their age.

Smiling, he turned to kiss Naomi on the cheek. But she pulled away, white-faced, looking deeply disturbed.

52

'Mrs Klaesson?'

The woman stood on the doorstep, holding a dribbling baby in her arms, was haggard and irritable. 'Glissom?' she retorted, her Cleveland accent sounding like an echo.

She looked nothing like the photograph he had memorized, not remotely. 'Mrs Naomi Klaesson?'

He got a blank expression back.

Politely, he said, 'I'm looking for the Klaesson family. You're not by any chance Mrs Naomi Klaesson?'

'Naomi Glissom? No way, not me, you got the wrong address, mister. There ain't no Naomi Glissom here.'

Behind her a small boy rode a plastic tractor across the hallway. A television was on, loud. The woman was in her mid-thirties, tiny, with a plump face and shapeless black hair.

'Maybe I have the wrong house. I was looking for fifteen twenty-six South Stearns Drive.'

'You got it.'

The woman stared at the man. He was in his late twenties, medium height, lean, serious-looking, with ginger hair shaved to stubble, a blue business suit, black shoes and a black attaché case. Out on the street there was a small blue sedan that looked very clean. He was dressed like a salesman but he lacked a salesman's confidence. Perhaps he was a Mormon or a Jehovah's Witness?

He frowned. 'I'm from Federal North-West Insurance; Mrs Klaesson owns a Toyota car registered at this address;

she was in a collision with one of our clients and she hasn't responded to any communications from us.'

'I wouldn't know nothing about that.'

The baby's face scrunched up, then it took several sharp intakes of breath. It was about to start crying. The woman looked down and rocked it. 'Glissom?' she said again.

'K-L-A-E-S-S-O-N.' He spelled it.

'Klaesson? Dr Klaesson!' she said, suddenly. 'OK, I got it now. I think they rented this place a few years back. Used to get mail for them.'

Timon Cort nodded. 'Dr *John* Klaesson and *Naomi* Klaesson.'

'They're not here any more. They went away. Long while back.'

'You have any idea where they went?'

'You could try the agency, the rental agency. The Bryant Mulligan agency over on Roxbury.'

'The Bryant Mulligan agency?'

The baby was crying louder. 'Try them,' she said. 'They might know.'

'Bryant Mulligan?' He spelled it as she had pronounced it.

'Uh-huh.'

'I'm obliged,' he said. 'Thank you.'

She closed the door.

The Disciple went back to his car, climbed inside and dialled 411 on his cellphone. He asked the operator for the number of the Bryant Mulligan agency. Then rang them.

But the Bryant Mulligan agency had no forwarding address for the Klaessons.

53

It was a gloriously warm Saturday afternoon, three days after their visit to Dr Talbot, and almost certain to be one of the last summer days of the year, Naomi thought.

She was standing on a stepladder in the orchard, holding a plastic bucket half full of plums. Through the branches of the tree she watched Luke and Phoebe a short distance away on the lawn. Earlier they had been splashing about with John in the tiny inflatable pool he had set up for them. Now they had brought out their Barbie Prince and Princess, and just about every stuffed animal they had, arranged them in a semi-circle and were serving them afternoon tea from the toy set.

Phoebe was being *Mummy*, pouring the tea, while Luke passed around the plate of plasticine cakes. They appeared to be chatting happily to each other and to their toys, which she was pleased to see. Normally they only ever seemed to chat to each other when they were alone in their bedroom.

A wasp buzzed around her face and she flapped it away, then reached towards a whole clump of beautifully ripe Victorias. She'd been on edge since their session with Dr Talbot. John had been thrilled that the psychiatrist thought they were so smart. She had been less enthusiastic; it reinforced her suspicion that John and Dr Dettore had agreed on more things than she had been privy too. Maybe even to having the twins?

She was increasingly worried, too, about how everyone

commented that the children looked so much older than their age, despite that original warning from Dr Dettore that this might happen.

Whatever the truth, I love you, darlings. I will always love you – just as much as you let me.

With luck it would be warm enough tonight to have drinks outside. They had invited Carson and Caroline Dicks over for one of John's Swedish crayfish evenings. Keeping his traditions was important to John and she always found that rather quaint, if somewhat contradictory in a man who believed so much more passionately in the future than in the past.

Climbing back down from the ladder, she knelt to pick up some windfalls. She liked it in here, in the dappled sunlight and the shade; it was like being in a secret world. It reminded her of when she was a child, and how she loved to hide in secret places and spend hours on her own. Then, flapping away yet another wasp, she carried the almost full basket over to John and the children.

He was sitting at the wooden table on the terrace, a copy of *Nature* magazine in front of him, staring down at Luke and Phoebe with a strange expression on his face. He was holding something in his hand that she thought for a moment was his camera, but then, looking again, realized was a tape recorder. He was aiming it at Luke and Phoebe. All part of his obsession with logging and record-ing almost every moment of their childhood, she thought.

'See these, Luke, see these, Phoebe?' she said, breezily.

Neither child seemed aware of her. Luke was talking to Phoebe, his speech sounding more fluent and confident than usual. Phoebe responded, equally chattily. Then she turned to her pink, floppy-eared elephant.

'Obm dekcarh cidnaaev hot nawoy fedied oevauoy.'

Naomi frowned, wondering if she had heard correctly.

Luke responded, 'Eka foe eipnod hyderlseh deegso-mud.'

Then Phoebe said, 'Olaaeo evayeh gibra snahele.'

Naomi looked at John who raised a finger, signalling her not to disturb them.

They continued speaking in this strange language for several minutes, oblivious to Naomi, chatting busily away to each other and their toy guests. Then, suddenly not wanting to hear any more, Naomi went inside, to the kitchen, and set the basket down on the table, feeling very disturbed in a way she couldn't quite get her head around.

It wasn't baby-talk, it was as if they were communicating in a proper language, speaking it fluently. As if, somehow, this language had ramped Luke and Phoebe's conversational skills up a whole notch.

They were still playing, still chatting, she could see them through the window, although she couldn't hear them from here.

John's voice startled her. Right behind her, suddenly. 'Have you ever heard them speaking like that before?'

'Never.'

He pressed a button on the recorder.

'Obm dekcarh cidnaaev hot nawoy fedied oevauoy.'

'Eka foe eipnod hyderlseh deegsomud.'

'Olaaeo evayeh gibra snahele.'

He paused the tape. 'I don't recognize the language at all,' he said.

'It's not some variation of Swedish?'

'No.' He played it for a few more moments.

'Children make up languages,' Naomi said. 'It's in all the books I've read – something that twins do quite often. You know, like *secret* languages?'

'Idioglossia,' John said. His voice sounded detached and distant.

'*Idioglossia?*'

'Invented speech.'

She picked up a printed napkin, refolded it and set it back down on the table. 'Is it a game, John? Just a harmless game? Or—'

'Or?' he prompted.

She refolded a second napkin. 'Are they doing it so they can say things they don't want us to hear?'

He smiled. 'At twenty months, I don't think they are old enough to be quite that devious.'

'Don't you? Are you sure about that?'

Their eyes met in an uncomfortable silence.

54

'Helan går, sjung hopp faderallan lallan lej . . .
    'Helan går, sjung hopp faderallan lej!
    'Och den som inte helan tar,
    'Han heller inte halvan får . . .
    'Helan gåaaaarrrrrr . . . sjung hopp faderallan lej!'

Amid a burst of laughter at the ragged singing, four glasses of Skåne aquavit clinked across the festive table in John and Naomi's dining area.

'*Skål!*' John said.

'*Skål!*' said Naomi.

'*Skål!*' Carson Dicks said, putting down his song sheet.

Then with a little less enthusiasm, as if she was embarrassed by such rowdy behaviour, Carson's wife Caroline added her own, small '*Skål!*'

The centrepiece of the table was a huge dish heaped with crimson freshwater crayfish, covered with sprigs of fresh dill. A small plastic Swedish flag was placed to one side of it, and several candles burned around it. Two plates were stacked with the traditional white toasted bread, and another with Greve cheese. In front of each place setting were glasses of schnapps, beer, wine and water. The tablecloth was paper printed with pictures of crayfish, and the theme was carried through on the napkins at each of the four place settings and on the bibs they were wearing.

John, fuelled by alcohol, felt good. Naomi had made the table look wonderful. She looked beautiful, and he felt intensely proud of her. He was with his favourite friends.

The air was balmy. How could you fail to be happy on a night like this?

He stood up and raised his glass. 'I wish to make a toast to you, my darling. You are a wonderful woman, a fantastic wife, an incredible mother, and I love you and adore you.'

Carson and Caroline raised their glasses. Naomi mouthed an embarrassed, 'Thank you.'

'To Naomi!' Carson said.

'Naomi!' Caroline said, leaning across the table and clinking glasses with her.

He refilled Carson Dicks's schnapps glass, but Caroline covered hers with her hand.

'I'm driving,' she said.

John looked at her as if she was mental. 'No one drives to a crayfish party. You should leave your car and take a taxi home!'

Then he got up from the table and staggered over to the baby-monitor speaker. Just a faint hiss of static. All quiet. Good. He hoped their singing down here wouldn't disturb the children, but hey, the annual crayfish party would become part of Luke and Phoebe's lives too, in time. An essential cornerstone of their Swedish culture.

'So, how are you finding life at the Morley Park Institute, John?' Carson Dicks said, breaking into his thoughts.

John nodded. 'Good. I'm glad you persuaded me. I'm very happy.' He looked at Naomi.

'I owe you a big thank-you for bringing us back to England,' she said.

'We're happy, too,' Carson said, peering at both of them through his bottle-thick glasses. 'We're lucky to have John working for us – and we're fortunate to have you both here. It's worked out well. You're married to a great man.'

Caroline picked up her glass. 'Who was it who said that behind every successful man there stands a truly astonished woman?'

They all laughed.

John beamed at Carson. He liked him so much. His boss had dressed for the occasion tonight in a blue and yellow striped T-shirt, the Swedish national colours, unbelievably baggy trousers and open-toed sandals. He looked a complete prat, and yet . . . so adorable. Suddenly he raised his glass and stood up again. 'Carson and Caroline – you've been truly good friends to us. You've helped us both in so many ways. I want to say thank you. I think Naomi and I are very fortunate to have your friendship.' He drank half the glass and sat down.

Caroline, looking a little embarrassed, smiled. Carson raised his own glass. 'You know the definition of a true friend, John?'

John shook his head. 'No, tell me.'

'It's someone who knows everything about you – and still likes you.'

John roared with laughter. 'I guess that makes you a true friend indeed!'

'Don't you think there is a lot of serendipity in life, John?' Caroline said. 'That sometimes things are meant to be?'

'I think that's a cop-out,' Naomi said.

John, sensing an argument about to happen, picked up his song sheet. 'Right! Time for the next song. Caroline, your turn to sing!'

Reddening with embarrassment, she stood up, holding her sheet, and made a valiant attempt at singing the Swedish words.

'*Tänk om jag hade lilla nubben . . .*' she began.

When she had finished, she sat down to raucous applause from John and her husband, who again drained their schnapps glasses.

John refilled the glasses. He was about to sit down again, when a sound from the baby monitor caught his attention. For a moment he thought it was just the static again, but then, listening closer, he heard a sharp buzzing sound. Naomi looked up at him, catching his eye.

'Problem?' she asked.

He listened again. A very definite angry buzzing sound. 'I'll go.'

He raised a calming hand and headed, unsteadily, out into the hall. Then, swaying from side to side, he hurried to the twins' room. Opening the door, he almost immediately had to duck as a small, dark object, barely visible in the weak glow of the night light, hurtled at him, buzzing angrily, batted against a wall, then shot away.

He blinked, his vision a tad blurry. *Shit.*

He snapped the main light switch down and the room instantly flooded with light. Moments later the insect zoomed low over the cots, then buzzed him again before racing up towards the ceiling. It was a very large wasp, a queen, or maybe even a hornet.

Jesus.

Luke and Phoebe were both awake, silent, staring at him.

'It's OK,' he said, looking around for something to whack it with. A story book lay on the floor beside the play ring, and he grabbed it, looking around for the insect, which had now disappeared. He scanned the walls, the ceiling, then the bright yellow curtains. Nothing.

He raised a finger to his lips. Slurring his words, he said, 'Sssh – issschhhstt's OK. Daddy's s-shhere.'

He wobbled unsteadily, brandishing the book. Took a step towards the window. The insect launched itself at him. He took a wild swipe with the book and missed. It batted off the wall behind him, then swooped low again over the cots.

As it did so, Luke's hand shot up. He saw Luke's finger and thumb close like pincers. And a moment later the insect fell, silent and twitching, to the carpet.

John stared in disbelief. He went down on his knees. The headless body of a huge wasp lay there, jerking in death throes, its sting sticking out then retracting, sticking out, then retracting again.

He stood up and stamped on it, once, then again, until it lay motionless. Then, still not able fully to believe his eyes, he went over to Luke's cot. His son's eyes were wide open and he was holding his arm up, finger and thumb outstretched, as if he was presenting a trophy to his father.

There was a tiny black mark on his thumb. And a definite black blob on his forefinger. It was the head of the wasp, John could see, looking closer.

Shaking, he removed it with his thumbnail, unsure what to say. 'Luke – that's so—'

There was absolutely no expression on Luke's face. Nor on Phoebe's. Both of them stared at him, as if it was he who was the object of curiosity.

He kissed them both, and it seemed there was a glimmer of a smile back from them. Perhaps they were starting to show a little affection. And as he dimmed the light and went back out of the door, he found himself wondering whether he had imagined the whole thing.

Or, as he thought much later, hoping he had.

55

Out in the night, concealed behind dense shrubbery, the Disciple could hear laughter. The light that spilled from the downstairs windows of the house spread out across the lawn, but faded into the darkness long before it could reach him.

But the laughter reached him, and the laughter angered him.

These were people who had no business to be laughing.

He could see them clearly through the lenses of his small binoculars, a man and a woman whose faces matched those in the photograph he carried in his pocket, and another man and woman who were the guests, who had come in a grey Jeep Cherokee that was parked in front of the house.

I said of laughter, it is mad: And of mirth, what doeth it? Ecclesiastes 2: 2.

He was dressed in black trousers, a black parka and black, rubber-soled shoes, safely invisible to anyone inside the house. Beneath these outer clothes he wore a full body stocking that covered all of his head except for his face, and was designed to minimize the chances of leaving behind skin and hair for forensic scientists to find. But he was regretting the warm top layer now. He had thought the night would be chilly but instead it was humid.

In the sagging pockets of his parka he carried a pair of thin leather gloves, a set of lock-picks, a gas cylinder, a gas mask, a canister of quick-drying foam, a canister of liquid propane gas, a toolkit, a beautifully engineered air rifle that was collapsed like a tripod, a night-sight, a torch, a lighter. And of course the photograph of the sinners. Around his neck hung a pair of night-vision goggles. Clipped to his belt was a small oxyacetylene cutter.

From his vantage point the Disciple could make out four people sitting at a table inside; they seemed to be having a good time. There was a weak glow around the edges of the curtains in an upstairs window, and he wondered if that was where the twins slept.

A bead of perspiration trickled down the nape of his neck.

Closing his eyes, he said the Lord's Prayer. Afterwards he stood in silent vigil, waiting for the other couple to leave. Although, he thought, since they were cavorting with the sinners in their house, they were undoubtedly in league with Satan, and it would be a service to kill them too.

But those were not his orders.

Behold, ye have sinned against the Lord; and be sure your sin will find you out. Numbers 32: 23.

It was ten o'clock. He felt a little nervous, but the Lord was by his side, and that certainty gave him strength. And what gave him even more strength was the knowledge that, by his deeds tonight, he was going to demonstrate to the Lord his love and absolute commitment to Him.

And this is the condemnation, that light is come into the world, and men loved darkness rather than light, because their deeds were evil. John 3: 19.

At a few minutes past eleven a fox slunk through the garden, triggering the powerful outside floods, which swept up the lawn, drenching the shrubbery all around him in brilliant white light. He remained motionless; the male sinner's face appeared at a window, looking out for some moments, then went away. Nothing else happened. After three minutes, the lights went off.

A short while later the four people got up from the dinner table and moved to sofas on the far side of the room. Through the binoculars he could see the woman sinner was pouring what looked like coffee. He could hear music now. It sounded quite loud out here, and it must be even louder in the house, he reasoned. Cole Porter. Decadent music.

It was a good time now. He clicked the air-rifle components together, slotted the night-sight into place, pressed in place the air cylinder, and inserted ten .22 pellets into the magazine.

Then, using a stiff branch as a rest, he squinted through the night-sight and saw, in close-up, the wall of the house in a soft green glow. Moments later he had the cross-hairs on the first flood lamp. The light bulb, still hot, glowed a brilliant orange colour, so bright it almost dazzled him.

A month on his own in the ranch on top of the mountain in Colorado had given him plenty of time to practise his aim, but it was God who really made the pellet strike its target. He squeezed the trigger, heard the *thunk* of the gun discharging, then a fraction of a second later a light tinkle; barely any sound at all; and a shower of glass that looked like sparks through his night-sight.

Moments later, God helped him take out the second bulb with a single shot, just as easily. In the grand scheme of things, a couple of broken light bulbs and two flattened airgun pellets were unlikely ever to be discovered.

An hour later the music stopped. They were all standing up. He watched them saying goodbyes, exchanging kisses. They moved out of the room and out of sight.

A short while later he heard a vehicle starting up. The Jeep, he presumed. It drove away. The sinners came back into the room and began to clear the table.

Then at long last the sinners left the room and switched off the lights. A light came on in an upstairs window. He saw the woman sinner framed, briefly. She was staring out into the night when her husband came up behind her, slipped his arms around her, and began nuzzling her.

Leave her alone, creep. Go to bed. Turn out your lights. You are being selfish, you are keeping me waiting too long.

The husband moved away and, a few moments later, the woman. Then, finally, after what seemed an eternity, the light went out.

The Disciple made his way across the lawn. With the beam of a mini Maglite torch he held in his teeth, using a pick, he worked on the lock of the kitchen door, which yielded easily. But he did not open it. Instead, he went around the side of the house and scaled a drainpipe, which took him up to the alarm box just below the eaves. Drilling a small hole in the box, he emptied into it the contents of his canister of fast-drying foam, then dropped back to the ground.

Skirting around the house, it took him some minutes to find the steel cover of the telephone cable. Firing the oxyacetylene cutter with his lighter, it took only seconds to sever the cable. Inside the house, he could hear the warning beeps signalling a line fault.

Swiftly now, he opened the kitchen door and went in. Immediately the phone warning beeps were accompanied by the much louder sound of the internal burglar alarm siren. There was no sound from outside. He took the gas cylinder from his pocket, pulled the gas mask on, and raced up the stairs.

Just as he reached the bedroom door it opened, and the naked figure of the male sinner stood in front of him. He fired the gas cylinder into his face and the man dropped to the ground without making a sound. Stepping past him he saw the female sinner groping for the light switch. He fired another long burst of gas at her and she dropped back against the pillow. Both of them would remain unconscious for a good thirty minutes. More than enough.

He went back down to the kitchen, ignoring the beeping alarm, which he figured would barely be audible outside the house. It took him only moments to spot the electric jug kettle. *Perfect.* He unscrewed the switch mechanism, disabled the cut-out, and screwed the switch mechanism back into place. Then he emptied the water out of the kettle, switched it on, pulled a couple of dry tea towels off a rack, bundled them around the base of it, stepped back and waited.

After a couple of minutes he could smell hot plastic. Another minute and he could see wisps of smoke. Then the jug kettle was on fire.

Standing well back, by the closed door, he took out the cylinder of liquid propane from his pocket, and twisted the valve. A jet of gas shot across the room towards the kettle, and almost instantly, a sheet of flame shot upwards towards the ceiling.

Then he opened the door and stepped back into the night. Within moments, the rush of air had turned the room into a fireball.

Safely back behind the shrubbery at the end of the

garden, he removed the gas mask, and stood and watched as the flames spread. Soon his nostrils picked up the scents of burning wood and paint. His ears picked up the crackling of the flames. And then an even sweeter sound. Two infants crying.

He climbed a fence, and took the route to safety that God had shown him two nights ago, across the fields to the parking lot behind a small general store, where his little rental car sat in the shadows.

56

To: John Klaesson. bklaesson@morleypark.org
Subject: Disciples

John,
I think you should be aware that the Disciples may
have surfaced again.

An Iowa couple, Drs Laurence and Patty
Morrison and their twins, Nathan and Amy, aged
thirty months, were found dead in their burned-
out ranch house two days ago. They too had been
to the Dettore Clinic. The fire damage was pretty
bad, and it is too early for the police to know the
cause of the fire – but I just thought you ought to
know.

Three deaths of three couples with twins, all of
whom had been to the Dettore Clinic, is not
enough to prove anything, but I would advise you
to continue to be vigilant.

Of course I will keep you informed. To date
there has been no progress in identifying any of
these so-called Disciples of the Third Millennium,
nor anyone behind them. They remain a mystery
and an enigma.

I hope this email finds you and Naomi and your
family well and thriving. I will be moving from

Washington at the end of this year to a new posting in Malaysia, but I will endeavour to maintain vigilance for you.

Hälsningar!

Kalle

57

Reggie Chetwynde-Cunningham looked like the kind of boffin a casting agency might have suggested to a film director in search of an archetypal eccentric English professor. From behind his tiny desk in his cramped office in the Linguistics Centre, housed in Building B4 at Morley Park, he squinted at John through his monocle like some hawkish bird of prey

In his early sixties, the linguist had a weather-beaten face, intricately shot with broken veins, and mad hair. He was dressed in a shabby green tweed suit with leather elbow patches and sported a flamboyant paisley bow tie over a check Viyella shirt.

On the walls of his cluttered office were a couple of maps of ancient Britain, a picture of him shaking hands with Prince Philip, and a framed legend proclaiming: A LANGUAGE IS A DIALECT WITH AN ARMY AND A NAVY – DR JOHNSON.

'Yes,' he said. 'Gosh, right, hmmnnn.' His cherrywood desk was littered with biscuit crumbs, and more avalanched down now as he reached out, offering the pack of digestives to John, then took one himself and dunked it in his coffee. 'Quite fascinating!'

One of the things John particularly liked about Morley Park was that, unlike at the universities where he had worked before where the average age was around twenty, making him horribly aware of his advancing years, the average age here was closer to fifty. It was a good feeling to be among the younger members of staff, even if only by a narrow margin. He chewed a mouthful of biscuit.

Reggie Chetwynde-Cunningham had been knighted some years earlier for services to national security. In his previous post he had worked at the Government Communications Headquarters, developing computer programs that could pick out the voices of known terrorists from among millions of landline and cellphone calls monitored daily. Now he headed a department on the Morley Park campus developing systems for controlling machines through either thought or speech.

'Play the original again!'

A complex hi-fi system behind the linguist kicked into life, and moments later the crystal-clear voices of Luke and Phoebe filled the room.

First Phoebe. 'Obm dekcarh cidnaaev hot nawoy fedied oevauoy.'

Luke responded, 'Eka foe eipnod hyderlseh deegso-mud.'

Then Phoebe's voice again. 'Olaaeo evayeh gibra snahele.'

'Stop!' Chetwynde-Cunningham barked. Then, looking at John and beaming, he said, 'This is pretty impressive, you know.'

'What language is it? Have you identified it?'

The linguist shook his head. 'I had a play with it yesterday, actually, got a few of my younger colleagues to listen to it. One, a woman with small children herself. Everyone agreed there are patterns distinctive of language, but no one could put a name to it. Just to be sure, we ran it in on a computer program that can identify every known language in the world – all six thousand, two hundred and seven of them,' he added with a touch of pride in his voice. 'But there was no match, and of course there wasn't going to be!'

'Why not?' John sipped some coffee and politely waved away the biscuit pack that the linguist again pushed towards him.

'Well, you do hear of children born with the ability to speak other languages – people talk about it as evidence of past lives, that sort of stuff,' he said with a rather dismissive tone. 'But I've never heard a small child speak a foreign language convincingly. Sometimes, as with you and your wife, when the child comes from parents of mixed races, they will pick up smatterings of each of the parents' languages.'

'Is there some Swedish in this? My wife and I want—'

The linguist interrupted him with a vehement shake of his head. 'Not Swedish. There's no Swedish there.' He helped himself to another biscuit and suspended it over his coffee cup. 'Of course, you do get the phenomenon with twins, more usually with identical twins, where they create their own language as a means of excluding their parents – and the outside world in general. This seems to be what's happening in your case.'

'Their own language?'

Chetwynde-Cunningham nodded.

'Can you make any sense of what they're saying?' John asked.

'Oh yes, once you know the key, it's a doddle – same with any code.'

'*Code?*'

The linguist turned to his computer. 'Print original on screen!' he commanded.

Moments later the words appeared.

Obm dekcarh cidaaev hot nawoy fedied oevauoy.
Eka foe eipnod hyderlseh deegsomud.
Olaaeo evayeh gibra snahele.

John peered at them closely, trying to see if he could spot what the linguist evidently had already. But after a couple of minutes he was forced to concede defeat. 'I can't spot the key.'

'No, well, I'm not surprised. Take a look at the first line.'

John stared at it.

Obm dekcarh cidnaaev hot nawoy fedied oevauoy.

Then the linguist gave another command. 'Reverse and sort into English!'

Moments later a second line appeared:

You ave o deide f yo wan to hve a andich r cke, Dmbo.

It was starting to become clearer to John but he still wasn't quite there. The linguist gave a third command. 'Insert missing letter through line!'

Now a third line appeared:

You have to decide if you want to have a sandwich or a cake, Dumbo.

John frowned. 'Jesus!' he said, after some moments. 'It – it was during a tea party – they—'

Chetwynde-Cunningham commanded the translation of the next two lines. John read them as they came up on the screen.

Dumbo's greedy, he's already had one piece of cake.
Elephants are big, they have to eat a lot.

'You're saying this was spontaneous?' he asked. 'Not something they'd worked out in advance, somehow, John?'

'They're not yet two years old,' John said. 'I don't think they'd have been capable of working this out in advance – I mean—' He shrugged, unsure quite what he was thinking about this. He felt totally thrown.

'The calculations to do this in their heads, in some kind of simultaneous translation, would be quite phenomenal. If it was just one child, one could think perhaps it was suffering from some brain disorder, some form of autism or temporal-lobe epilepsy, perhaps causing some glitch in the neural pathways. But the laws of probability rule it out for both children to have this.'

There was a long silence. John continued to stare at the words, thinking to himself, wondering how on earth they could be doing this. The linguist interrupted him.

'If they are doing this spontaneously, John, then I think you've got some pretty remarkable children. They have a skill that I would think is quite unique. I've never heard of it before, ever.' He gave John a look that should have filled him with pride.

But instead, John found himself feeling very uneasy.

58

'I think we should take them back to see the psychiatrist, Dr Talbot, again, don't you, John?'

John sat at the kitchen table, cradling his martini. He was unsettled and baffled by what the linguist, Reggie Chetwynde-Cunningham, had told him, and he was fretting about the email he had received from Kalle Almtorp.

Three couples who had been to the Dettore Clinic had been murdered.

Christ.

Three couples who had been to the clinic had all had twins. The murders had happened in America; that was one small blessing – the distance.

So far.

'Did your linguist chap at work have any explanation for – for how they could be speaking like this? Talking perfect English backwards with every fourth letter missing?' Naomi asked.

John shook his head. 'He didn't.'

'We've been waiting for them to speak their first words to us, for them to say *Dada* or *Mama*, and they've said nothing and yet they're speaking *perfect* English to each other in code. Doesn't that spook you? It sure as hell spooks me.'

He stared ahead, pensively. 'It does. It's just so strange.'

'Do you think that Dettore did something? That maybe he messed up some important gene and their brains are wired up wrong?'

'I think that's too early to speculate. I guess if they keep speaking like this we should take them to a neurologist.'

'Don't you think we should take them to one now?'

John walked over to the wall where the baby-monitor speaker was mounted and listened. 'Are they awake?'

'Yes, I was waiting for you to get back so we could bathe them together.'

She sat down looking pale. John watched her. He felt terrible. She buried her face in her hands. 'After all we've been through. God, why is life so bloody unfair?'

'We have two beautiful children, hon.'

'Two beautiful freaks.'

John walked back over to her, rested his hands on her shoulders and kissed her neck. 'Don't ever think that. Luke and Phoebe are what we wanted. They're smart. They're much smarter than other kids their age. We just have to learn to adjust.'

'Why are they speaking in this code? People talk in code when they have secrets. Why are they doing this? Are they wired wrong – or are they much smarter than we realize?'

'I don't know,' he said helplessly.

Naomi looked up at him. 'We've made a mistake, haven't we?'

'No.'

'I just wish – that we – had – you know – a normal life. Normal kids.'

'Normal kids like Halley?'

There was a long silence. John looked again at the silent baby monitor, then picked up his glass again.

'That isn't what I meant,' she said. 'And you know that.'

John twiddled the olives on their stick, studying them pensively as if trying to read them like runes.

'They just stare at me sometimes,' she said. 'Like – like I'm just nothing. Like I'm just some kind of a machine that exists to feed them and serve them.'

They went upstairs, and as they approached the children's room, Naomi said, 'I think we should consider giving them separate rooms soon. That was something Dr Talbot mentioned – to help them develop their own identities.'

'He said when they were a little older.'

'I know, but I think it might be good to start separating them now.'

John raised a finger to his lips to silence her, then stopped outside the door. Beyond, he could hear Luke and Phoebe chatting animatedly, and again it sounded like they were speaking in their code.

He opened the door and immediately they fell silent.

'Hi, Luke, hi, Phoebe!' he said.

Both stared up from the floor, where they were playing with wooden bricks. Luke in a striped sweatshirt, baggy jeans and trainers, his blond hair flopped over his forehead. Phoebe in a lilac tracksuit and barefoot, her hair looking neat. Both blue-eyed, the picture of utter, adorable innocence. He shot a glance at Naomi who was staring, as astounded as he was, at the intricate and geometrically perfect Mandelbrot pattern, like some elaborate miniature crop circle they had made on the floor.

'Ebohph eklih,' he said, his eyes darting from Luke to Phoebe and back. But there was no reaction.

'Pretty pattern!' Naomi said.

John left the room for a moment, hurried to the bedroom, grabbed his camera and came back.

'Bath time!' Naomi said breezily.

John snapped the children with their creation. 'That's beautiful, Luke. Beautiful, Phoebe. Did you design that together?'

They both continued to stare at him in silence. And then, as if pre-determined, they both started laughing and smiling at their parents. A rare occurrence and one they only shared with their parents, nobody else.

'Very pretty!' Naomi said. 'Aren't you both clever!' She looked at John as if seeking some explanation, but he had none. 'Mummy's going to run your bath!'

She went out of the room. John stayed and took some more photographs. Both children remained motionless, just staring up at him. After a few moments he heard the sound of running water.

Shoving the camera into his trouser pocket, he kneeled down and scooped Phoebe up in his arms and kissed her. 'Clever girl!'

'Mittab,' she said, with a smile

'Mittab!' he cooed back, then carried her through to the bathroom and handed her to Naomi. Then he went back to fetch Luke, who was staring, as if deep in thought, at the pattern of bricks on the floor.

'Did you design this, Luke, or your sister?'

Luke pointed to himself, and smiled.

John picked him up in his arms and kissed him on his forehead. Then he stared into his son's wide blue eyes. 'That's really clever, you know that? Really clever!'

Luke's face puckered into a grin, and for a moment, John felt a sunburst of happiness explode inside him. Hugging him tightly, he said, 'You're such a clever little boy, aren't you? Mummy and Daddy are so proud of you! So proud!'

As John carried him into the bathroom he saw Naomi, sleeves rolled up, testing the water with her finger. Phoebe, half undressed, was sitting on the floor watching her. He undressed Luke, waited until Naomi was happy with the temperature, then gently put him in the water. Luke splashed playfully with his hands, beaming, trying to sink the yellow plastic duck and little boat that were in with him. Then Naomi pulled off Phoebe's tracksuit bottom and lifted her up and lowered her into the water.

The phone rang.

'Can you get that?' she said to John.

John went through to the bedroom and grabbed the cordless. It was Rosie.

'Hi!' he said. 'How are you?'

'I had lunch with Naomi the other day and she looks terrible,' she said, in the direct way she always spoke. 'You have to get her away, give her a break, she's going to crack up.'

'I think we both are,' he said.

'Just go on a holiday, take her somewhere nice, somewhere in the sun and cherish her. She's a great person, John, she deserves cherishing. A little TLC wouldn't go amiss, you know?'

'It's not that simple.'

'You're wrong, it's very simple. You bring the kids to us, we'll look after them, and you take Naomi away.'

Then he heard the scream.

Oh Jesus.

'Johhhnnnnnnnnnnnnnnnnnnnnnnn!'

'Call you back,' he said, dropping the phone and running.

He burst into the bathroom. Luke was screaming. Naomi, eyes bulging in hysterics, her face and clothes spattered with blood, was holding Phoebe in her arms. The bathwater was crimson. Blood was running down Phoebe's legs and down the side of the bath.

'Help me!' Naomi screamed at him. 'John, for God's sake, help me!'

59

'It's OK, darling,' Naomi said. 'It's OK! OK!'

In the paediatrician's office, Phoebe clung to her mother's jumper as if it were a life-raft in a stormy ocean, screaming her lungs out.

Dr Clive Otterman, a short, mild-looking man, wore a permanently bemused frown that always reminded Naomi of Buster Keaton. He stood by his examining couch, eyebrows raised in a saintly air as if he had all the time in the world.

Wrapping her arms protectively around Phoebe, then kissing her, Naomi said, 'He's a nice man, darling, you've met him before lots of times, he isn't going to hurt you.'

Phoebe continued screaming. Naomi looked at John, who stood beside her helplessly. They had left Luke at home with her mother, who had come up for the day.

Dr Otterman stood patiently in his grey suit, hands behind his back, and gave the smile of a man used to any kind of behaviour a child could throw at him.

'He isn't going to hurt you, Mummy promises you!'

Phoebe's response was to howl louder. Naomi stared helplessly at John. She felt like screaming at him. *You're her father, for God's sake. Do something!*

But all he did was shrug back, equally helpless.

She carried Phoebe across to the couch, and tried to lay her down on it, but she screamed even more loudly, tugging so hard on her roll-neck that she was pulling it out of shape.

'Darling!' Naomi said. 'This nice doctor just wants to take a look at you!'

The screaming got even worse. Naomi looked despairingly at the paediatrician, whose eyebrows shot up in a winsome smile. *Come on, you're a specialist, for heaven's sake, you ought to know how to handle an infant!*

As if by magic, Dr Otterman suddenly produced a pink Barbie doll, which he held up for Phoebe to see. The effect was instantaneous. Phoebe reached out her hands and he placed the little doll in them. Phoebe grinned suddenly, her lips puckered, and she said, 'Barbie!'

For an instant Naomi could believe neither her eyes nor her ears. She stared at John as if seeking confirmation and he stared, equally startled, back.

Phoebe had spoken! Her first word.

John beamed.

'Barbie?' Dr Otterman said. 'Do you like Barbie, Phoebe?'

'Barbie!' Phoebe said, then giggled.

Through all her anxiety, Naomi felt a sudden burst of happiness exploding inside her. *She was speaking! Her baby girl was speaking! Speaking normally! This was incredible!* She stared at John, wanting to throw her arms around him in joy.

'You like Barbie dolls?' Dr Otterman said. 'You like playing with Barbie?'

'Barbie!' Naomi said to her. 'Darling, *Barbie!*' She turned to the paediatrician, elated. 'She's speaking! Her first words!' She was so happy she could hug the man!

'Barbie!' John said to Phoebe.

'Barbie!' Phoebe said again and burst into a fit of giggles, as if this was the funniest thing in the world. 'Barbie! Barbie!'

Tears welled in Naomi's eyes. John put an arm around her and squeezed her.

'Incredible!' Naomi said.

'I told you, they're fine,' John said. 'They're fine!'

Naomi nodded, tears welling in her eyes. 'Yes.'

Phoebe, giggling, gave no resistance now as the paediatrician, assisted by Naomi, removed all her clothes, repeating the word *Barbie* over and over, as if she had made the most important discovery of her life.

Dr Otterman examined her thoroughly externally, then to Naomi's surprise, Phoebe allowed him, without protest, to take a blood sample, followed by a brief internal examination with a laparoscope. After that he gently probed with a tissue between Phoebe's legs and when he withdrew it, Naomi saw spots of blood on it.

'Barbie! he repeated back to her like a secret code between them.

'Barbie!' Phoebe said.

The paediatrician removed his gloves, washed his hands, helped Naomi to get her dressed again, and went back behind his desk.

He made several notes with a fountain pen, then set it down and frowned. After some moments he picked it up again, then leaned back in his chair.

'Dr and Mrs Klaesson,' he said, 'this internal bleeding last night – was it a very hot bath?'

'No warmer than usual.'

'I'm going to send the blood away for analysis – the results will take a couple of days.'

'What do you think is wrong with her?' Naomi asked. 'Is she very sick? I mean – internal bleeding – do you think it could have been caused by the bath water being too hot, or is it something—'

He looked uncomfortable suddenly. 'I think we should wait for the lab tests before jumping to any conclusions.'

'Wh-what sort of conclusions?' Naomi said, alarmed.

Dr Otterman stood up. 'I really don't want you worrying needlessly. I'll call you as soon as I have the results.'

'But what do you think it could be?' John asked. 'What's your opinion?'

'Internal bleeding can't be good news, can it?' Naomi said.

'There are a number of possibilities – let's wait,' Otterman said.

'The other thing is this language she and Luke are speaking,' John said. 'What are your thoughts on that?'

The paediatrician raised his hands in the air. 'I'm baffled by that.' He glanced down at his notes. 'You saw the psychiatrist, Roland Talbot, a couple of months ago, didn't you?'

'Yes.'

'He thinks they are quite exceptionally gifted. I don't think I'd concern yourselves too much over that, although I have to say, the pattern on the floor, it's a pretty impressive mathematical feat. We're still in a very early stage of understanding how the human brain works. There have been a number of documented instances of quite extraordinary communication between twins. Mathematics is sometimes a feature of autism—'

Naomi interrupted him. 'Autism? Do you think they're autistic?'

'It's one possibility they could be somewhere on the spectrum, although I personally don't think so. But that is something we need to be aware of as a possibility.' He said nothing for a moment, then went on. 'Somehow, they've hooked into a set of neural pathways that can perform this feat. What they are doing seems unbelievable to us, but is probably perfectly natural to them. Between some point of development in the womb, and the age of seven, our brains hardwire themselves. This could be just a phase – you may well find they lose this ability in another year or so. If there is no change, then there is a very good child behavioural psychologist in Brighton who I would suggest you take them to – but I suspect that won't be necessary.'

'I sure as hell hope you are right,' Naomi said. 'I find it just a little too weird.'

The paediatrician showed them both to the door. 'I'll call you just as soon as I know. Meantime, don't worry.'

Dr Otterman telephoned two days later. The tone of his voice scared Naomi. He suggested that she and John should come to see him as soon as was convenient, on their own if possible.

60

The consulting room seemed to have changed in the three days since they were last here. On Monday morning, with its yellow walls and huge window, the room had felt light and bright. Now it was dark and oppressive. Naomi and John sat in front of the paediatrician's desk. Dr Otterman was outside, dealing with some enquiry from his secretary. Panes of glass rattled in the wind. Naomi watched rain lash the street, an autumn equinox gale asserting itself on the town, the countryside, the sea.

A cold wind blew through her. She shivered. Nature had so much in its damned arsenal. Hurricanes, tornadoes, earthquakes, volcanoes, tidal waves, floods, meteorites, asteroids. Disease.

She reached out and took John's hand. He squeezed back, and half turned to her as if he was about to say something. Then Dr Otterman came back into the room and closed the door. 'Sorry about that,' he said.

They both watched him anxiously, as the paediatrician eased himself behind his desk. As he sat down he peered at something on his computer screen, then plucked a pen from the black mug in front of him and rolled it backwards and forwards between his fingers. 'Thanks for coming in,' he said. 'I felt it was better for you to hear this in person because – well – it's a very unusual condition – not life-threatening, but it does of course give rise to concern.'

Naomi and John waited for him to continue.

'It – well, how can I put it – it affects a very small

percentage of all children born in the world. We're going to need an electroencephalogram to make absolutely sure, but I don't really have much doubt at all.'

Into the tunnel, Naomi thought bleakly. *We're going back into that damned, bloody tunnel we were in with Halley. Tests. Hospitals. More tests. More specialists. More hospitals.*

He put the pen back in the mug, deliberated for some moments, then retrieved it again, his eyes darting between Naomi and John. 'This bleeding – I didn't want to give you my diagnosis until I was pretty sure. Now I have the results from the pathology tests and they are still not conclusive. Phoebe is presenting some symptoms of a variant form of a condition known as McCune-Albright syndrome.'

John and Naomi exchanged a puzzled glance. Then John said, 'I'm sorry, I've never heard of this – MacEwan-Albright syndrome?'

'Yes,' Dr Otterman said edgily. 'That's right, yes, Mc-Cune-Albright syndrome.' His face reddened. 'It's also known as *precocious puberty*.'

'*Puberty*, did you say?' asked Naomi.

He nodded. 'It's a congenital abnormality that causes varying forms of early sexual maturity in children, as well as other physiological changes.'

Naomi raised her voice in disbelief. 'Sexual maturity? What exactly are you saying? Phoebe's not even two years old – are you telling us she's sexually mature?'

The paediatrician stared back with a helpless expression. 'I'm afraid what I'm saying is exactly that. Extraordinary though it may seem, Phoebe is having her first period.'

61

In the car afterwards, Naomi and John sat for some moments in stunned silence. John put the key in the ignition but did not turn the engine on; instead he rested his hands in his lap. The car shimmied in the wind.

Precocious puberty.

Naomi shook her head, staring at the rain-crazed windscreen.

Bone age will be advanced and serum oestrogens will be in the pubertal or adult range. Oestrogen halts growth. Many children with this syndrome are likely to end up with stunted growth. Early development of breasts. Untreated, a five-year-old girl will have the sexual maturity of a teenager.

'The pills *will* work,' John said. 'Don't worry.'

'He said they *might* work. They *might* slow down this syndrome, but they won't cure it, John, that's what he said. *Sometimes* it helps, that's what he said. *Sometimes.*'

'At least it's not life-threatening.' Then, after some moments, he added, 'And – everyone is telling us how big they are for their age. Phoebe wouldn't be this big if she had stunted growth.'

'And Luke? Why is he so big?'

'I don't know. I don't know why either of them are.'

'Dr Otterman said the children have physiology closer to three – even four – years old, not two.'

'But he did say their rate of growth will probably slow down.'

'And if it doesn't?' she asked.

'I'm sure it will,' John said.

'What makes you so sure, John? The integrity of Dr Dettore? That fills you with confidence, does it?'

He said nothing.

'I want the children to have every possible medical test,' Naomi went on. 'I want to find out just what other surprises we are in for; what else that madman has done to them.'

John started the engine and began manoeuvring the Saab out of the parking space. He spoke quietly. 'Dr Otterman said this won't affect her, and she will be able to lead a normal life.'

'For most women, John, leading a *normal* life means having children. Do you have any idea how she is going to feel when she reaches her teens and all her friends are entering their prime? When she starts dating? What happens when she falls in love? How is she going to explain to someone in twenty years' time, *Oh, by the way, I had my first period when I was not quite two years old and went through the menopause when I was fourteen?*'

'He didn't say that, hon. He said this condition doesn't affect the menopause, that she wouldn't have an early menopause.'

'He didn't *know*, John. He said he would know more after the scan. He said no two cases were ever exactly the same.' She rummaged in her handbag, pulled out a pack of tissues and blew her nose. '*Stunted growth*. That's great. After telling Dettore we wanted our son to be tall, our daughter is going to be a dwarf.'

'You're worrying at the moment that she's too big for her age. She's not going to be a dwarf.'

'How do you know?'

'Look, there will be a lot of advances in medicine over the next twenty years – if we find out that—'

'Sure,' she said, interrupting him. 'And Phoebe is a victim of one of them. Great to know that our daughter is a guinea pig – and a freak.'

'I think *freak* is a strong word. She's not a freak.'

'So what is she? What euphemism would you like? *Maturity challenged? Vertically challenged?* Perhaps it's a little too *realistic* a word. But that's what she is, John, that's the reality we have to face. Courtesy of Dr Dettore, our life savings and loans from my family, we have produced a freak. How does that make you feel?'

'Would you rather she hadn't been born? That neither of them had been born?'

'I don't know. I don't know what I feel. Tell me what you feel – I never know what you are thinking.'

'All I ever wanted was—' He lapsed into silence.

'Was what, John? What was it you wanted? Tell me, I'm all ears. And you ought to put the wipers on, might help you see where we're going.'

He put the wipers on then pulled out into the street. 'I don't know,' he said, after a while. 'I don't know what the hell I wanted. I guess, just the best for our kids, for you and I, I just tried to do the best for us.'

'Is that what you'd like to think?'

'What do you mean by that?'

'Did you really want to do the best for us? Or did you want to satisfy your cravings as a scientist?'

He braked more harshly than he needed at the end of the street. 'You don't trust me, do you?'

'I don't know what I think any more, John.'

'That's very hurtful.'

She shrugged.

'Naomi, I've always told you the truth. When I first found out about Dr Dettore, I told you everything I knew, and I warned you there would be a risk in going to him. We both agreed to take a chance.'

'Maybe you didn't spell it out quite loudly enough,' she said bitterly.

'Perhaps you didn't listen quite hard enough,' he replied gently.

She turned and stared at him. Stared at the man she had once loved madly, wildly, crazily. The man she had been through so much with. The man who had given her the strength to get beyond the loss of their son, and the will to go on living.

Stared at him with a hatred so intense that if she'd had a knife in her hand, she honestly believed at this moment she could have stabbed him with it.

62

The day began in the monastery of Perivoli Tis Panagias the same way it had begun every morning for the past eleven centuries. At two thirty in the morning, beneath a sky still crowded with stars, the knock of wood on wood rang out. The summons to matins.

In the marbled glare of moonlight, the stark drumming rose to a frenzied crescendo that was more a shamanic beat than a gong. It rang out across the shadows of the courtyard, echoing off the worn flagstones and the cracked, peeling fortress walls surrounding the mostly derelict buildings.

In his cell the Abbot rose from his narrow bed, lit the oil lamp on his dressing table, crossed himself beneath the portrait of the Virgin Mary, and dressed quickly in his black robes.

When he had first entered this monastery as a young novice, sixty-four years ago, it had been Yanni Anoupolis's task to rise first, and go out and call the brothers to prayer, by hammering with the mallet on the ancient teak plank hung from rusty chains in the cloistered courtyard. Then he had been a young man of twenty-two, whose heart had ached to serve God.

Now it wasn't just his heart that ached, but so much else, also, especially his knees and his hips. The body that housed him was decaying just like the buildings that housed the few remaining monks here. His eyesight was steadily failing, month by month, and so was his energy;

he did not know how much more time God would spare him, but at least he had the comfort of knowing that after years of uncertainty, the future of the monastery, perched high on this rock atoll in the Aegean Sea, twenty kilometres south of the Greek mainland, was assured.

Father Yanni pulled his cowl up over his head, then, supporting himself on his stick, walked down the stone steps and into the courtyard, the reek of burning oil from the lamps in the church porch offering scant but welcome relief against the sharp, damp sea air. Behind him he heard the footsteps of three of the four other monks who remained from an original community of one hundred and ninety, when he had first come here.

Entering the rear of the church he crossed himself again, then stood for some moments in humble silence in front of the beautiful Madonna and Child icon. The blessed Virgin Mary! She protected them all on this island. And she had rewarded him for his lifetime of devotion by bringing the American here to save them.

He wondered if the American would be joining them for matins. Some mornings the American sat beside him, usually accompanied by young novices. Other days, the American had told him, he preferred to hold his own private prayer vigil in his room.

Father Yanni loved to see these novices in here, all such gentle, polite young men. So sincere, so devout, so dedicated, praying with such vigour and fervour. The energy of youth!

The American's name was Harald Gatward. He was a good man, the Abbot knew that much, but he knew little else about him. Only that the Virgin Mary had brought him here – which was all that he needed to know.

The monastery of Perivoli Tis Panagias had been built

in the ninth century as a remote offshoot of the Holy Mount Athos, providing an alternative haven for Greek Orthodox monks. They lived an ascetic life here. Worldly pleasures were strictly forbidden – these were temptations by Satan to distract and corrupt. This included chatter. Conversation was strictly on a need-to-know basis. Idle gossip led to malcontent and sin.

The Abbot was the only monk on the island who spoke any English, and his grasp of this language was limited and mostly archaic. He assumed the American must be a very rich man. When the Council of the Greek Orthodox Church had made the decision that they could no longer justify the cost of running Perivoli Tis Panagias for just five monks and had placed the tiny island on the market, hoping to attract a property developer to turn it into a resort, the American had outbid everyone. And this wonderful man had assured the Abbot that it was God's will that he and his four fellow brothers should live out their lives in peace here.

Of course there had been a few changes. The biggest of these was the new buildings, and women arriving on the island. But they were housed beyond the monastery walls, and none of them had ever encroached on the church, nor entered the refectory.

*

In his tiny cell, even more modest than the Abbot's and lit by a solitary candle, Harald Gatward knelt beside his bed, face buried in his hands, communing with the Lord in a prayer vigil he had held, with only one short break to check his emails, since eleven o'clock last night.

Gatward was a shambling bull-necked giant of a man, six-foot-six-inches tall, with a baby face that belied his fifty-eight years, and a mane of shaggy, greying hair that hung down from either side of his bald dome. A former colonel of the 51st Airborne, Gatward had been decorated for courage under fire in Vietnam.

And later that same year, on that same field where he had earned his honours, he had held the charred body of his fiancée in his arms as she died. An over-enthusiastic US military helicopter had inadvertently dumped several gallons of self-igniting chemical defoliant onto a field hospital and its staff, just as he was arriving to collect Patty at the end of her shift.

She had run towards him, her clothes, her hair, her hands, her legs, her face all burning, screaming for help. He'd rolled her over on the ground, torn his own clothes off and bound them around her to smother the flames. But no sooner had they gone out than like some joke candle on a birthday cake they reignited.

Later, long after the flames had died and she had begun to cool, her skin suddenly slipped away from her chest and her arms, as if he was easing her out of a coat.

'Dear God,' Harald Gatward said as he kneeled against the bed, 'when you created man you made him in your likeness.' After a brief pause he repeated the same line. 'Dear God, when you created man you made him in your likeness.' And then he repeated it again.

No human being should ever have to die the way Patty died, Harald Gatward believed. Chemicals had killed her. Man messing around with chemicals caused all kinds of problems in the world. All the bad shit. It was Satan who put the formulae into people's heads. Now stupid, hubristic man was no longer messing around just with chemicals, he was fooling around with human life itself. Doing all kinds of shit with genes.

God had informed Harald Gatward throughout his life. He had told Harald how to turn the inheritance from his father, who had made a sizeable fortune with auto spares manufacturing plants in Asia, into a multi-billion-dollar global empire. He had told Harald that it was right to go to Vietnam and fight for his country. He had shared many secrets with Harald over the years, many insights, many visions. He brought Harald to the monastery of Perivoli Tis Panagias to save the monks. That was important but that was only a small part of the reason he had come here.

The real reason, God had explained to him, was that from his island, Harald Gatward must begin the work that would save the world from scientists.

The sun will never set again and the moon wane no more; the Lord will be your everlasting light and your days of sorrow will end. Then will all your people be righteous and they will possess the land for ever. They are the shoot I have planted, the work of my hands, for the display of my splendour. The least of you will become a thousand, the smallest a mighty nation. I am the Lord; in its time I will do this swiftly.

You will be named the Disciples of the Third Millennium.

63

Naomi had lunch with Rosie, and was so engrossed with discussing what had happened she forgot the time. She was now ten minutes late. *Shit.*

To her relief as she drove into Caibourne, in torrential rain, she could see she wasn't the last. Two large off-roaders were pulling up ahead of her outside the homely, slightly dilapidated-looking detached house close to the village church that hosted the twice-weekly playgroup, and there was a line of cars stationary in front of those.

She parked untidily, one wheel on the pavement, battled the driver's door open against a strong gust of wind, then as an afterthought hastily popped a chewing gum in her mouth to mask the alcohol on her breath. She didn't like being late – punctuality was one of John's Swedish traits that had rubbed off on her.

She shouldn't have drunk anything, because she was driving, but, *hey*, she thought, *these last two and a half years, since well before Luke and Phoebe were born, I've had no life. Now they're getting a little older, I'm damned well going to have one again. And anyhow it was just two glasses, with food, over a two-hour period. Not exactly reckless.*

The path to the front door of the house was a chaos of lashing rain, hurrying mothers, tangled children and tangled umbrellas. Muttering brief hallos to a few familiar faces, Naomi hurried through them, head bowed against the elements, and made it into the sanctuary of the building.

The hall walls were covered in children's paintings, stuck up haphazardly, and a row of framed certificates. Squeezing past a bunch of mothers trying to get their children into coats, Naomi went through an open door into the main playroom. A tiny girl, wearing Walkman head-phones, was bouncing up and down on the very beat-up-looking sofa. Another girl sat at one of the tables, engrossed with an assortment of plastic creepy-crawlies and prehis-toric monsters. Two small boys, one in a green hard hat, the other in a baseball cap the wrong way round, were arranging vehicles in a multi-storey car park on the floor.

No sign of Luke or Phoebe.

As she squeezed her way back into the crowded hall, Naomi saw one of the mothers she had met before, who had been very friendly to her. She was busy wrestling her small boy, Nico, into a red coat.

'Hi, Lucy!' Naomi said. 'Horrible weather – September is usually such a—'

The woman, in a plastic rain hat and drenched Bar-bour, gave her a cursory nod, then dragged her child out towards the front door. Before Naomi had time to react, Pat Barley, who ran the playgroup, a tubby, jolly-looking woman several inches shorter than herself, with a pud-ding-basin hairstyle, was standing in front of her.

'Hallo, Mrs Klaesson,' she said. 'Do you mind if we have a quick chat?'

'No – of course,' Naomi said, a little surprised at her sombre and formal tone. 'Where are Luke and Phoebe?'

Instantly, she detected awkwardness in the woman's face. 'Just in the small playroom, through there,' she said, pointing through another doorway.

Naomi peered in. Luke and Phoebe were sitting side by side on a settee in total silence, staring blankly ahead.

'Hallo, Luke, darling, hallo, Phoebe, darling,' she said.

There was no hint of acknowledgement from either of them.

She exchanged a glance with Pat Barley, who signalled Naomi to follow her.

They went through into the kitchen, where there was a long table covered in paint-spattered paper, Styrofoam cups of paint, and dumpy little dough figures covered in paint and glitter. A helper was sponging vivid red and yellow streaks from the face of a small girl in a blue plastic apron.

'Look, Mrs Klaesson, this is rather awkward for me,' Pat Barley said. She was wringing her hands and staring evasively down at the floor. 'I don't want you to take this the wrong way, please. But I'm afraid there have been complaints.'

'Complaints?' All Naomi's positive cheer suddenly evaporated.

'I'm afraid so.' Pat Barley seemed to be trying to wring water from her hands. 'You see, my problem is that parents are so sensitive these days. This really isn't anything personal—' She hesitated. 'Oh dear, I don't know how to break this to you. I know you are newcomers to this part of the world and we really should be trying to do all we can to make you welcome. But the problem is that I've had – well – not just one or two complaints, you see – but about half a dozen, actually.'

'About Luke and Phoebe?'

'Yes.'

'What sort of complaints?'

There was a long silence. The helper, a tall, reedy-looking woman with an inane smile, was evidently listening, which was fuelling Naomi's discomfort.

'Well, I suppose it's the way Luke and Phoebe interact with the other children here. They are among the youngest in the group but they don't look or behave that way. For their age they seem quite a bit older, physically – and the way they behave is really quite out of character for children this young. For want of a better word, they are – *terrorizing* – the others.'

'Terrorizing? That's ridiculous!' Naomi said.

The playgroup coordinator nodded. 'Yes, I know it sounds ridiculous, but I've been watching them myself all the time today, and I have to say that their behaviour is rather antisocial. They went straight to the computer the moment they arrived here, and they wouldn't let any of the other children near it. Whenever another child tried, either Luke or Phoebe snarled at them so fiercely it made most of the other children cry. I'm afraid it was the same last time. They simply won't share, or seem to accept that other children have a right to play with everything, too.'

'I'll speak to them,' Naomi said. 'They've got to learn not to be selfish – I'm really sorry about this, I'll—'

Pat Barley shook her head. 'I'm sorry – the situation is that two mothers didn't bring their children in today because Luke and Phoebe were going to be here. Several of the other mothers have said they will have to stop bringing their children.' She looked very embarrassed, suddenly. 'I'm really very upset about this, I know it's a terrible thing to do, but I'm afraid I'm going to have to ask you to remove them from this playgroup. Perhaps you should try them in an older group – really, they'd fit in with five- or even six-year-olds. I'm awfully sorry, but they won't be welcome here again.'

64

Naomi watched their faces in the mirror repeatedly as she drove home. Buckled into their child seats, Luke and Phoebe sat in silence. Every time she looked, two pairs of eyes were looking back at her. She was finding it hard to concentrate on the road.

'Mummy's not very pleased with you,' she said, shaking inside with a whole mixture of emotions. 'They said you weren't nice to the other children. Is that true, Luke? Phoebe?'

Silence.

She eased past two cyclists in the lane. 'Luke?' she said, more sharply. 'Phoebe? I'm talking to you to. I asked you a question. I expect an answer, yes or no?'

The silence in the back of the car continued. She turned into the drive and drove up to the house, braking sharply, angrily, by the front door. She got out of the car. 'You want to play games? Right, you sodding well play them.'

She shut the car door, hit the central locking button and marched to the house. In the shelter of the porch she looked at the car. The rain was still lashing just as hard, and through the side window she could just make out the motionless figure of Phoebe.

Then she went into the house and slammed the door. *You can bloody wait out there. See how you like it when it doesn't go all your way for once. Going to have to knock some manners and decent behaviour into you two, before*

285

you start growing into a couple of extremely unpleasant little people.

She hung her wet Barbour on the coat stand, picked the parish magazine up off the doormat and walked slowly towards the kitchen, in too much of a mist from her thoughts to read it. She put water in the kettle, switched it on and spooned coffee into a mug, then sat down and cradled her head in her hands, wondering what to do.

Expelled from bloody playschool. Shit.

She rang John, and got his voice mail. 'Call me,' she said. 'We have a problem, I need to talk to you.'

The kettle boiled and clicked off. She remained where she was, thinking, trying to figure out what to do. Take them back to the behavioural psychologist, Dr Talbot, who thought they were so smart? They had to find someone to help them, this was a situation that—

The phone started ringing. Hoping it was John, she stood up and grabbed the receiver off the wall. 'Hallo?' she said curtly, aware of the anger in her voice and not caring.

A pleasant, rather earnest-sounding male American voice said, 'Is that the Klaesson household?'

'Yes.'

'I'd like to speak to Mrs Klaesson.'

'Yes, that's me.'

'Mrs *Naomi* Klaesson?'

She felt the tiniest prick of unease. After a moment's hesitation, she said, 'Who is that, please?'

'Am I speaking with Mrs Naomi Klaesson?'

'I'd like to know who you are, please.'

The phone went dead.

Naomi stared at the receiver for some moments, her anger fast curdling into a knot of dread in her stomach. She pressed down on the cradle, then released it, listened for the dial tone and punched out one-four-seven-one. Moments later she heard the automated voice:

'You were called today at fifteen-eleven hours. We do not have the caller's number.'

She remembered that John had a caller-ID device in his study and she went through to look at it. A red light was flashing on the top and she pressed a button to bring up the display. On the tiny LCD screen appeared the words:

15.11 INTERNATIONAL

A shiver rippled through her.

It felt as if some terrible ghostly tendril had reached out across the Atlantic and gripped her soul.

Am I speaking with Mrs Naomi Klaesson?

Who the hell are you? What did you want?

Disciples? Disciples of the Third Millennium?

Hurrying back to the hall, she grabbed the car keys, ran out of the front door, pressed the central locking button, ran over to the car and pulled the rear door open.

Luke and Phoebe weren't there.

For an instant, time stopped. She stared dumbly at the empty child seats. Then, terror-stricken, she looked round, eyes darting everywhere, at the barn with the double garage doors, at the house, at the shrubs swaying crazily. 'Luke!' she screamed. 'Phoebe!'

Rain pelted down on her.

'LUKE!' she screamed again, louder, even more pan-icky. 'PHOEBE! LUKE! PHOEBE!'

She ran over to the cattle grid and stared down the long expanse of empty driveway. A white plastic bag flapped, trapped in brambles in the hedgerow. No sign of either of them. She turned in despair back towards the house. 'LUKE! PHOEBE!'

She ran, stumbling, down the side of the house, then all the way around on the wet, boggy grass, screaming out their names.

Then she stood, frozen with fear, soaking wet, by the back door to the kitchen.

They had vanished.

'Please, God, no, don't do this to me. Where are they? Please, where are they?'

She ran back into the house. The phone was ringing. She dived into John's study and grabbed the receiver. 'Yeshallo?'

It was John.

'They've vanished!' she shouted at him. 'I had a call from someone and they've vanished. Oh Christ—'

'Hon? What do you mean? Vanished?'

'THEY'VE VANISHED, JOHN, THEY'VE FUCKING VAN-ISHED. I LEFT THEM IN THE CAR OUTSIDE THE HOUSE – OH GOD—'

'Naomi, hon, tell me, what do you mean? What do you mean, they've vanished?'

'THEY'VE DISAPPEARED, YOU STUPID MAN, THAT'S WHAT I MEAN. VANISHED. SOMEONE'S TAKEN THEM.'

'Someone's taken them? Are you sure?'

'I don't know. They've vanished.'

'When? Where – I mean – where have you looked?'

'EVERYWHERE!'

'Have you looked in the house?'

'THEY WERE OUTSIDE IN THE CAR, FOR GOD'S SAKE!'

'Check the house. Have you checked the house?'

'Noooo,' she sobbed.

'Naomi, darling, check the house. Have a look around the house. I'll stay on the line. Just check all the rooms.'

She ran into the drawing room. Then upstairs along the corridor, water running down her face. Their bedroom door was closed. She pushed it open, and stopped in her tracks.

Luke and Phoebe were sitting contentedly on the floor, absorbed in a tower they were building from Lego bricks.

She stared at them with a mixture of relief and total disbelief.

'I – I've – found them,' she said. 'They're OK. I've found them.'

'They OK?'

Backing out of the room she said, quietly, 'Fine. They're fine.'

'Where were they?'

Feeling confused, foolish, she said nothing. *Had she brought them in, taken them to her room and forgotten?*

No way.

'Where were they, hon?'

'In their room,' she snapped. 'In their bloody room.'

'Are they all right?'

'Luke and Phoebe? Oh yes, John, they're fine, they're absolutely fine. They've been thrown out of playschool, now they know how to get out of my car all by themselves, and they refuse to say a bloody word to me. If that's how you define *all right*, then yes, they are *all right*. Our designer babies are *all right*. They've obviously been born with *all right* genes.'

'I'm cancelling my meeting and coming home, hon. I'll be there in half an hour.'

'Go to your meeting. Don't cancel that. We have enough problems. Go to your meeting.'

'I can come straight home.'

'Go to your bloody meeting, John!' she shouted. 'Your children don't need you. They don't need me. They don't need anyone.'

65

John sat on a chair in the children's room, preparing to read to them as he did every night. Over the past few weeks he had read them *The Gruffalo*, Pooh Bear stories, 'Cinderella', 'Rumpelstiltskin', and various Mister Men stories.

They just lay silently in their cots, eyes open; he had no idea whether they were listening. And they never gave any reaction when he finished.

After he had kissed them goodnight, he walked heavy-heartedly downstairs and mixed himself a drink in the kitchen. Naomi was on the phone to her mother.

A strange thought suddenly crossed his mind. Were the children *punishing* them for what they had done? For tampering with their genes? He dismissed that, instantly. Then he took his drink through to his den and sat down in front of his laptop, and watched a dozen new emails appear.

One was from his chess opponent, Gus Santiano, in Brisbane.

Damn. It must have been a week at least since the man's last move. Guiltily, he opened it.

> **You bastard! Where the hell did you come up**
> **with a move like that from? Have you been**
> **taking some tablets this past week? Having**
> **coaching? Getting some personal help from**
> **Kasparov? I concede, mate. Your turn to open**
> **the next game.**

John frowned. Had the man been drinking? His last move had been a defensive pawn against an early king's bishop attack. What on earth was he talking about? Was Gus Santiano playing with another opponent somewhere else and got them confused?

He emailed him back, saying he didn't understand.

To his surprise, ten minutes later he got a reply, with an attachment.

You must have early Alzheimer's, John. These are the moves you've sent me this week.

John opened the attachment. To his astonishment, there were six emails from him to Santiano, dated daily during the past week, each giving a fresh move, as well as six replies.

Impossible! There was no way he could have done this without remembering, absolutely no way.

He called up the chessboard program, and keyed in the instruction for it to go sequentially through this latest game. The moves Gus Santiano had attributed to him were smart, he could see that clearly. Very smart.

But he hadn't made them.

He double checked the emails again. All of them had been sent from him, from this computer. But no one else used this computer; and it couldn't have been Naomi, she didn't play chess.

Baffled, he pulled an olive out of his drink and chewed on it, thinking. *Six moves.* Was it a hacker? Possible, except he didn't leave the computer online either here or at the office.

He did a search through his Sent Items box, and sure enough, found each of the emails. Next, he highlighted one and checked the source. It showed the email was sent from this computer at 2.45 a.m. last Saturday. The next one was sent at 3 a.m. on Sunday. The next at 2.48 a.m. on Monday. The following three at similar times on Tuesday, Wednesday and Thursday, today.

Am I going nuts? Sleepwalking and playing chess?

He swallowed down most of the martini in one gulp. But the usual buzz he got from the drink didn't happen. In the middle of the night someone was using his computer, playing chess for him. Either it was a hacker or—

He looked up at the ceiling. *Oh, sure, John, your two-and-a-half-year-old son and daughter are creeping downstairs in the middle of the night and playing chess, beating the pants off a semi-finalist in last year's Queensland open chess championship. Explain that?*

He couldn't. He didn't have any explanation. He was baffled.

66

'I didn't want to worry you – but on top of everything else, I had a strange phone call this afternoon,' Naomi said hesitantly. 'Probably nothing.'

John chewed his mouthful of cod; as with almost everything she touched in the kitchen, Naomi had cooked it to perfection. Trying to keep one ear tuned to the television news, he replied, 'What kind of strange? By the way, this is delicious.'

'Thanks, it's a new recipe I'm trying out. You don't think the mushroom sauce is too rich?'

'No, it's delicious. Who was it that called?'

'Someone from the States, asking if this was the Klaesson household – and if I was Naomi Klaesson. A man. Then he hung up,' she said.

John looked at her; she had his full attention now. 'When was this?'

'About three o'clock his afternoon.'

'He didn't give a name?'

'No.'

John's eyes went to the window; unease, like silt in a disturbed pond, rose inside him. 'Three? Do you have any idea where he was calling from?'

'I checked the caller ID. It just said *international*. Why?'

He was calculating in his head. *East coast time. Central time. Pacific time.*

Yesterday, in the office, he'd received a similar call. A

young man with an American accent had asked if he was speaking with Dr John Klaesson. When he'd replied that he was, the line had gone dead. He'd had a colleague with him in the office at the time and although it had bothered him a little, with the distractions of work he hadn't given it any more thought.

Now, suddenly, it was bothering him a lot.

His call had come at 2.45 in the afternoon. West coast time, that would have been 6.45 in the morning. East coast time, more probably 9.45. New York, perhaps? Anywhere. A reporter trying to following up on the Dettore story? Perhaps. Hopefully it was no more than that.

Except a reporter would have called back.

He toyed with the fish, cutting off another piece, pushing it around in the sauce, wondering whether to tell Naomi. He decided that after her distressing time at the playgroup this was not the moment to tell her about the phone call. Nor was it the moment to tell her about his most recent chess game against Gus Santiano. Instead he asked, 'How much has Phoebe grown in the past year?'

'Two and a half inches,' she said.

'Which is the same as Luke, right?'

'Yes.'

'And how many periods has she had?'

'One.'

'The pills seem to be working,' he said.

'So far.'

'Yes. So far. Which means they might go on working. OK? And if they go on working, she'll keep growing normally. Right?'

A reluctant nod.

'Let's be optimistic.'

After the meal John went back into his den. He'd never

bothered setting up a password for his laptop before, but now he went into the control panels to create one.

When he had finished, he returned to the chess program, made his opening move for the next game with Gus Santiano and sent it. Then he settled down to work.

At a few minutes past midnight he shut his computer down, then went into the kitchen and listened to the baby monitor. The only sounds were the rhythmic breathing of sleep. He crept upstairs and tiptoed along the corridor to Luke and Phoebe's room, opened the door and peered in.

He could see them both, in the weak glow of the Bob the Builder night light, fast asleep. He blew them each a kiss, closed the door and went to his bedroom. Naomi was asleep, with the bedside lamp on and a book open on the duvet. She stirred as he entered.

'Wassertime?' she asked sleepily.

'Just after midnight.'

'I was dreaming – you and I were being chased by Luke and Phoebe; they were in a car and we were on bicycles; they kept telling us they didn't want to hurt us because they loved us, but if we didn't pedal faster they would have to run us over.'

He leaned over and kissed her. 'Sounds like a classic anxiety dream.'

'It was spooky. I kept telling them, *You're our children, you're meant to love us, you're not supposed to run us over.*'

'And what did they say?'

'They just giggled.'

'Go back to sleep,' he said softly. Then he removed his clothes, put on his dressing gown, went through into the bathroom and brushed his teeth.

But when he came back into the bedroom, instead of getting into bed, he took his torch from the drawer in his bedside table, switched off Naomi's lamp and made his way, as silently as he possibly could, back downstairs and into his study.

There, just by the light of his torch, he unfolded the sleeping bag he'd taken out earlier from the linen cupboard, climbed into it and curled up on the tiny sofa.

At five in the morning, after a few hours of very fitful sleep, and suffering painful cramp, he abandoned his vigil and went up to bed.

67

The Disciple was happy. That fear in the infidel woman's voice had felt so good. *Be thou in the fear of the Lord all the day long. Proverbs 23: 17.*

Her fear was still flowing through him, energizing him like fuel. It gave him strength, power; it was so good he was tempted to call her again and release some more from her, let that flow into him as well. But that would be greed; and greed was a sin. God had been good to him, leading him to where the infidels lived. He must not reward Him with indulgence.

So now, his head swimming with the pleasures of Mrs Naomi Klaesson's fear, he sat at his desk, his laptop open, logged on to the internet, on to Google Earth. He saw the globe of the planet.

He moved the cursor, entered the name *Sussex*, hit a key and zoomed in until the screen was entirely filled by Sussex and parts of surrounding counties. Eagerly, he devoured the names of the towns near to the infidels' home.

Worthing. Brighton. Lewes. Eastbourne.

He had never been to England. There was a Brighton in America, a Brighton Beach, he recalled. But otherwise, these names meant nothing to him. This place, Sussex, these towns, their names came out of the screen so solidly, so real, he felt he could hold them inside his heart.

He then entered: *Caibourne.*

Caibourne! He held the name, said it aloud to himself, then repeated it. 'Caibourne!' At this moment, it was the sweetest sound in the world.

He zoomed in, until he could see the aerial views of a small cluster of houses. One of these houses belonged to John and Naomi Klaesson. He typed in their postcode, and instantly zoomed in closer still.

The Disciple punched the air in excitement. Then his face flushed with guilt. This was a bad thing, to let himself get carried away by his feelings like this. He had to restrain himself. For now, all emotions were forbidden. Joy would come later.

Those who sow in tears will reap with songs of joy. Psalm 126.

But a small amount of pleasure, that could not be a sin, surely? And here, in this studio apartment God had found for him, in the low-rise building inhabited mostly by elderly people who kept to themselves, in this quiet suburban backwater of the town of Rochester in New York State, this is what Timon Cort was feeling now.

God's pleasure.

It had been a long time since he had come down from the mountain in Colorado, into the sewer of the valleys below and the plains beyond. Two and a half years since he had first gone to that internet café in Boulder, Colorado, to download the instructions that awaited him. The names of the first couple and their spawn he was to kill, and where he was to go to collect his next instructions.

Now there was just one more act of the Great Rite to be carried out. And then he would become a true Disciple, and God would give him the beautiful, loving Lara, who had waited patiently for two and a half long years for him, and would continue to wait for however much longer was needed, as a reward. And then they would live for the rest of their lives in Paradise in the right hand of God.

Time had passed since then, but time had also stood still. He continued to wear his hair shaven to a light fuzz. He was dressed in the same simple uniform that all Disciples wore. A loose white T-shirt, grey chinos and plastic sandals. He passed his days in prayer, reading the Bible, eating frugal meals, biding his time, repeating each of the Forty Tracts he had learned by heart.

He possessed a business suit, a shirt, a tie and black loafers for when he needed to blend in with people, but other than his clothes and his Bible, his one possession was his sturdy laptop, through which he maintained contact with his Master. And through which he was kept informed of progress in the Great Mission of Salvation.

All the technology inside the computer gave him power. God's hand was in this machine. God understood that man needed weapons to fight Satan.

I will send destroyers against you, each man with his weapons and they will cut up your fine cedar beams and throw them into the fire. Jeremiah 22: 7.

England was where Naomi Klaesson came from. England was where the Infidels had begun their life together. Now the Infidels would end it there!

In the county of Sussex. In the village of Caibourne.

In the house he was staring down at.

Timon Cort knelt and closed his hands in front of his face in supplication. His eyes ran with tears of joy.

'Thank you, God, for showing me where they live.'

He brings princes to naught and reduces the rulers of

this world to nothing. No sooner are they planted, no sooner are they sown, no sooner do they take root in the ground, than he blows on them and they wither, and a whirlwind sweeps them away like chaff. Isaiah 40: 23, 24.

68

John, his empty camera case slung from his neck, stood in the middle. Luke, in a fleecy anorak, was on his left, Phoebe, in a duffel coat, on his right. Behind them two gibbons leapt around their cage, shrieking.

John held Luke and Phoebe's tiny, gloved hands tightly. They were both wrapped up warm against the biting November wind. Flecks of sleet blew around them, like ash. There was a sour reek of dung and animal feed and straw in the air, tinged with the odours of frying onions and burgers.

Naomi, holding the camera, wisps of hair flapping beneath her bobble hat, called out, 'OK! Smile! Luke, Phoebe, everyone say c-h-e-e-e-e-e-s-e!'

She watched them through the viewfinder. John grinned; Luke and Phoebe, hesitant for a moment, both mouthed something back at her and then, to her absolute joy, grinned as well. She pressed the shutter. After some moments she lowered the camera, and looked at it, puzzled. 'I'm not sure if it took,' she said. 'It didn't make the right sound.'

'Try another, hon.'

'OK. Everyone, once again, ready?'

Despite the cold, and the fact that the sight of animals incarcerated in zoos always made her a little uncomfortable, Naomi felt happy this afternoon. The children were actually smiling at the camera! This was promising to be the first picture ever with them smiling!

She framed them again, adjusted the zoom, called out to them to get them to look at the camera. 'Great!' she said, and handed it back to John.

He pressed the display button and then showed the image to Luke and Phoebe. 'See those two little folk?' he said. 'Who are they?'

Luke studied the image for a moment. Phoebe turned around, more interested in the monkeys.

'Can you see?' John said.

Luke looked up at him with wide, baleful eyes and gave him a look that seemed to say, *Yes, fine, I can see, it's a picture, what's the big deal?*

'You stand with them now, hon, I'll take one of the three of you.'

'Let's find a different background,' she said.

'OK.'

Luke and Phoebe prised their hands free of his and walked back to the gibbons' cage.

'Don't get too close, darlings,' Naomi said, worried, hurrying after them. She put a protective arm around each of them. Luke and Phoebe stood giggling at their antics, then said something to each other that Naomi couldn't catch. It sounded like their usual code.

After a couple of minutes she could tell their attention was wandering. 'What would you like to see next?'

'How about owls?' John said. 'You want to see an owl? We hear them at night sometimes. Would you like to see what an owl looks like?'

Almost in synch, each of them gave him a nod. He caught Naomi's eye and they grinned at each other.

John gripped Luke's tiny hand, so frail, so warm, in one hand, and Phoebe's in the other. Naomi held her other hand. The wind gusted bitterly, but John barely felt it, he felt such a warm glow of happiness inside him. At long, long last he was starting to feel a connection with his children. They were reacting to this place, enjoying a day out at the zoo; seeming to be emerging from whatever strange space they had been in.

They headed towards the owl house. As they passed the meerkats, Luke and Phoebe tugged excitedly, pulling him over towards the cage. They all stopped and stared at the creatures, which looked tiny and cuddly. Naomi peered closely at the sign on the cage and read from it aloud.

'While the rest of the family are digging, sunbathing or playing, one meerkat will always be on guard.' She turned to their children. 'See that one looking at us, Luke? Phoebe? She's the one that's on guard!'

Luke giggled. Phoebe pointed, giggling too, and said, 'Maccat!'

'*Meerkat!*' Naomi corrected her.

'Maccat!' she repeated.

'Maccat!' Luke shrieked.

They saw the owls, then spent a long time watching a sloth, upside down, asleep.

'Would you like to be able to hang upside down like that, Luke?'

Phoebe burst into giggles again, then said something to Luke, and he started giggling, too.

John and Naomi exchanged another look. *This is great! This is amazing! Simply amazing! Maybe our fears have been unfounded!*

They went back outside, saw the llamas, then the camels, then the bears, then went into the insect house and stopped in front of a glass cage containing a pair of tarantulas. Luke and Phoebe moved closer to the cage, then shrank back, each squeezing John's hand hard.

'Not crazy about them? Me neither.'

'Nor me,' said Naomi, with a shudder.

They moved on and stopped in front of a giant East African hornet.

John knelt down and whispered to Luke, 'Hey, tell me, what do you think about bugs? Creepy-crawlies? See these – they're even bigger than the one you killed last summer. Remember that?'

He connected for a fleeting moment with Luke's eyes. Then Luke looked away as if he was evading the question.

'You guys hungry? Want to eat something? An ice cream? Want to go pan for gold? Play in the bubble tub? Go on a ride?'

'S'ceam,' Phoebe said.

'S'ceam,' Luke echoed.

They bought them each a huge ice-cream cone with a chocolate flake sticking out of the top. Within minutes, John and Naomi were fully occupied wiping the sticky mess from their faces. John put an arm around Naomi and hugged her, hard, and she hugged him back. Suddenly, standing out here, with the wind blasting his face with sleet and grit, he felt almost delirious with happiness. Finally he had a life that was as close to perfection as any man had a right to. A wife he adored, two beautiful children. A career that was going brilliantly.

Just seeing Luke's chocolate-smeared mouth plunge once more into the cone, and watching Naomi wipe away a blob of ice cream from Phoebe's nose brought feelings of joy deeper than he had ever thought a human being was capable of.

Then the shadows returned. The Disciples of the Third Millennium. The mystery hacker who played his chess moves against Gus Santiano for him. His concerns over the strange phone calls from the States that both he and Naomi had had last week.

But for the moment, for these few precious hours where they were just a normal family having an outing, he shrugged them aside.

69

On Monday morning the Disciple dressed warmly. It was cold outside, minus fifteen overnight and the temperature only expected to rise to two degrees during the day. He put on thick jeans, lined boots, a thermal sweatshirt, a heavy pullover, his fleece-lined anorak, bobble hat, woollen gloves, hoisted the straps of his backpack over his shoulders, then left his apartment.

He trudged through frozen slush to the Greyhound station, ten blocks from his apartment, and bought a single ticket to New York. One of the rules for Disciples was never to carry a return ticket. If you fell into the hands of the Enemy, let them have as little information as possible.

At four in the afternoon, with the light fading fast, Timon Cort left the bus in Times Square, purchased a street map, then set off on foot down Broadway. He walked carefully, economically, taking as few breaths as possible, the absolute minimum, the way any man might when treading through a sewer. It took him less than ten minutes to reach the internet café he had found on the net the previous day.

His first step after logging on was to open a Hotmail account, giving a false name and details. He had decided to combine an Old Testament name with a New. *Joel Timothy* he typed.

He addressed an email to the first account in a chain that would route it several times around the world, burying its origins in a complex electronic paperchase through dozens of anonymous servers in turn, before it reached its target destination. Then he typed out the email.

**If I rise on the wings of the dawn, if I settle on
the far side of the sea, even there your hand will
guide me, your right hand will hold me fast.**

He sent it, paid for his time online, left the café and quickly immersed himself in the crowds. Every few minutes as he walked he looked over his shoulder. He had never felt nervous before, secure in the knowledge that God walked by his side, but maybe it was the hope that this was to be the last task that was playing havoc with his inner calm.

Just this to do, and then Lara.

Just this.

So long since had seen her, since they had held each other. Sometimes, even with God's help, he had trouble remembering her face and had to take the creased photograph from his purse and look at it, to re-memorize it. And each time he did so there was a twist of pain in his heart almost too much to stand.

But now he had to concentrate not on Lara, but on where he was.

The noises all around disturbed him. The swoosh of tyres from the endless river of yellow cabs, the blaring of horns, the bass thump of music from speakers on the outside wall of a record shop, the thump of music from speakers in a van with blacked-out windows, the thump of heartbeats all around him, the busy *click-click-click* of leather heels on the sidewalk, the rustle of clothing fabrics.

He put his hands over his ears and boarded a bus. The engine whined. Behind him he heard a constant, tinny, *skitter-skitter-skitter-skitter* leaking from the headphones of an MP3 player. He turned. Met the stony glare of a massive black man with a Satanic Ankh tattooed on his forehead who was talking to himself. He turned back, faced the front, closed his eyes, tuning out everything except the swaying motion of the bus, and repeated the Lord's Prayer over and over until he reached his destination.

In Central Park he felt better, walking along a track, away from the smells and sounds of the sewer and the man with the Ankh. They called this place a city! How did they dare? There was only one city – the City of God.

You have come to God, the judge of all men, to the spirits of righteous men made perfect, to Jesus the mediator of a new covenant, and to the sprinkled blood that speaks a better word than the blood of Abel. Hebrews 12: 23–24.

70

Dr Sheila Michaelides was a petite, bubbly, very self-assured woman in her early forties, with an olive-skinned face, large, angular glasses and a shock of straight black hair. She was dressed neatly, in a tight-fitting jumper over a cream blouse and brown slacks.

Her consulting room, with French windows overlooking a well-tended walled garden, was at the back of an imposing red-brick Victorian house that had been carved up into doctors' offices. It was a generously sized room, with a high, stuccoed ceiling, but furnished in contrast to its period in a cheery, modern style, with a pine desk on which sat a computer and framed photographs of two laughing children, and cushioned sofas arranged either side of a pine coffee table, at which John, Naomi and the child psychologist sat.

Naomi wondered if it was mandatory for any medic involved with kids to have saccharine pictures of children on display.

John was talking her through the history of Luke and Phoebe, omitting of course any mention of their background with Dettore. With Naomi interjecting to add details, he covered the incident with the wasp, the strange language the children had developed, Reggie Chetwynde-Cunningham's opinion on their linguistic ability, their excitement on Saturday at the zoo, and their even bigger excitement yesterday, Sunday, when they had gone to a pet shop and bought each of them a guinea pig.

He said nothing about his suspicions that the children might be playing chess on his computer late at night – because he hadn't yet mentioned this to Naomi.

When they had finished, Sheila Michaelides's neutral demeanour seemed to have changed a little. She looked at both of them in turn with a distinctly sceptical expression. 'This language you say they are speaking – do you really believe that?'

'Absolutely,' John said.

'What you are telling me it just isn't credible.'

'Surely,' Naomi said, 'if it is some kind of autism—?'

The psychologist shook her head. 'Even if you had one child on the autism spectrum, and perhaps capable of strange mathematical feats, it is inconceivable it could be the same for both.'

'Not even in identical twins?' Naomi asked.

'Phoebe and Luke are not identical twins,' she said.

'So how do you explain it?' John asked.

She tilted her head. 'Are you sure this isn't wishful thinking?'

'What do you mean by that?' Naomi said testily.

The psychologist glanced at one of her own fingernails. 'You strike me as very ambitious parents – from the way you have been talking about your children. You're an academic, Dr Klaesson, and you are clearly a very intelligent woman, Mrs Klaesson. I'm getting a feeling from you both that you have great expectations from your children. Would that be correct?'

'I don't have any expectations,' Naomi said quickly, getting in ahead of John.

'All we want is for them to be normal,' John added.

'And healthy,' Naomi emphasized.

The psychologist bit her nail for a moment, then said,

'You lost your boy, Halley, at the age of four. You adored him. Are you sure you aren't searching for something in your twins that puts them above him, as a form of compensation?'

'That's ridiculous!' Naomi exploded. 'Absolutely ridiculous!'

'Totally!' John confirmed. 'Look, we want to try to understand our children, that's why we've come here – but you seem to be attacking us!'

'No, I'm not. All I'm trying to say is that what you are telling me about them speaking backwards with every fourth letter missing is impossible! No model exists for this! You are claiming a linguistic skill for your children that no human being on this planet is capable of. Just think for a moment about the mathematics.'

'So give us your explanation?' John responded.

'I don't have one. I wish that I did, believe me, but I don't.' She looked hard at each of them.

Naomi felt herself being scrutinized, and she was confused. 'How can a linguistic scientist tell us one thing and you tell us another?'

The psychologist nodded in silent thought for some moments, then she said, 'Does the expression *epistemic boundedness* mean anything to either of you?'

'*Epistemic boundedness?*' Naomi repeated, shaking her head.

'Yes,' John said, 'I know about it.'

'Could you explain it to your wife?'

John shrugged, as if hesitant for a moment, then turned to Naomi. 'What it basically means is that human intelligence has a ceiling. That humans are hardwired with a certain level of intelligence. That there are biological limits. Just as there are limits on other aspects of human beings.'

He looked at the psychologist for confirmation. She nodded for him to go on.

'For instance, the four-minute mile. We know it can be broken by a few seconds, but no human is ever going to run a one-minute mile. Probably not even a three-minute mile.' He exchanged an awkward glance with Naomi.

One of Dr Dettore's might, her face said.

'It's the same with height,' John went on. 'Most humans are within a certain range. You get occasional exceptions, but seven and a half feet is about the upper limit – you're never going to find a human who is fifteen feet tall.' He looked back at the psychologist. 'What you're saying, if I'm understanding you correctly, is that this feat of language by Luke and Phoebe is the equivalent of – like – a one-minute mile, or a fifteen-foot-tall human?'

'That's exactly right.'

John caught Naomi's eye, then looked away sharply. He had not realized the full significance of what Luke and Phoebe were doing before, and now he did, he wasn't sure how he felt about it.

'So how come Chetwynde-Cunningham didn't tell you that?' Naomi asked.

John looked at her, then at the psychologist, then back at his wife. 'He did. That is exactly what he said. I thought perhaps he was exaggerating, but now I realize that probably he wasn't.'

'You are saying that our children are performing a mathematical feat that is beyond the capability of any living human being?'

'Beyond any human being who has *ever* lived, I would

imagine, Mrs Klaesson.' The psychologist looked dubiously at John and Naomi. 'I think the next step would be for me to see Luke and Phoebe. Ideally I would like to observe them at playschool.'

Naomi felt her cheeks burning. 'The reason – the main reason that we came here is – because—' She glanced at John for support, then back at Dr Michaelides. 'Because I was asked not to bring them back to playschool.'

The psychologist nodded. 'Yes, but I think I could have a word with the playschool leader and ask if she would let them come back with me observing – I've done this quite a few times and it is not usually a problem.'

'Anything you could do, we'd be very grateful for,' Naomi said.

After they had left, the psychologist wrote up her notes on her computer. She also checked the notes that the psychiatrist, Dr Roland Talbot, had faxed through.

Pushy, ambitious parents, she wrote.

Father compensates for long work hours by giving them his interpretation of 'quality time'.

Intelligent people. Dr Klaesson a typical academic. Greater intellect than wife but less worldly. Nonsense about the language – clear indication of their over-ambition for Luke and Phoebe. Attitude highly likely to have harming effect on twins in some way – as is indicated by their behaviour. Could make them school-phobic.

Withdrawn behaviour of twins an indicator of abuse? Parents clearly hiding something, evident in their body language.

71

Like many of its counterparts that were on the mainland peninsula of Mount Athos, the monastery of Perivoli Tis Panagias was a huge cluster of buildings in different architectural styles, contained within the outer monastic walls. In the middle ages, poor monks inhabited cells in the main building, while wealthier arrivals constructed their own houses, in their preferred building materials – mostly wood or stone – and colour schemes.

Staring down from his cell window into the cobbled courtyard that was dominated by the domed church, flanked on one side by a row of terraced houses that would not have looked out of place in San Francisco or in parts of Boston, and on the other by turreted and crenellated walls, Harald Gatward thought, as he did often during his hours of contemplation, that the place at night felt a little like a deserted studio lot.

Except it was never deserted. The spirit of God was always present, and the eyes of their beloved guardian angel, the Virgin Mary, ever vigilant.

Father Yanni permitted very few intrusions from the outside world to pass the monastery's tall wooden gates. Pilgrims of course were welcome, in the monastic tradition of hospitality, but the Abbot recalled it had been twenty years, probably longer – he would have to check the registration book – since any pilgrim had made the twenty-kilometre boat trip from the mainland. Occasionally a cruise ship sailed past, or a yacht, but they always kept their distance, although more out of respect for the four unmarked submerged reefs than for the privacy of the monks, he suspected.

One intrusion was the laptop, which sat next to the Bible on the simple wooden table in Harald Gatward's narrow cell. The Abbot had considered it a strange request, but who was he to refuse anything to the American who had been brought here by the Virgin Mary to save their monastery?

All other trappings of the modern world were housed in the village a short distance below the monastery walls. There the Disciples lived with their women. The Disciples were welcome to worship in the monastery's church and to eat meals in silence alongside the Abbot and the four other monks in the magnificent refectory with its frescoed wall, but not the women. Out of respect to the customs of the monks, Gatward had never permitted women to enter these walls.

At midnight, as was his ritual, Harald Gatward broke off from his prayer vigil. He was well pleased with the work of his Disciples. Five sets of Satan's Spawn were now exterminated. Three had made the world press, but the fourth, in a car crash in Italy, had passed unnoticed, as had the fifth, in a helicopter crash in Singapore. Even so, he had thought it prudent to call his Disciples home, let the heat die down.

Just one Disciple remained out in the field at this moment. He was good, this one, he had true passion. Soon it would be time to summon him home, and give him his reward: Lara, sweet girl, waiting down in the village, so patient, so devout.

There was an email sitting in his inbox from Timon Cort now.

PERFECT PEOPLE

If I rise on the wings of the dawn, if I settle on the far side of the sea, even there your hand will guide me, your right hand will hold me fast.

Harald Gatward closed his eyes and asked the Virgin Mary to dictate his reply.

72

Luke and Phoebe were kneeling on the kitchen floor, totally absorbed with their two guinea pigs.

Fudge had beige and white stripes, Chocolate was dark brown and white; they were cute, with their sleek coats, their black, hairless ears, their tiny paws, and the strange little squeaking sounds they made.

Naomi lovingly watched Luke and Phoebe play with them, each feeding them a carrot. It was the first real affection she had ever seen from the children, although she worried how long it would be before they got bored with them.

Five weeks to Christmas. She loved Christmas, loved putting up the tree and the decorations and preparing all the food that went with it, and buying and wrapping presents. And this year, Luke and Phoebe were old enough really to start appreciating what was going on.

She hoped it snowed, a white Christmas out here would be awesome. Her mother and Harriet were coming down on Christmas Eve and staying until Boxing Day, and John's mother was coming over to stay from Sweden for the whole of Christmas week. Carson and Caroline and their children were coming over for a boozy Swedish Christmas Eve dinner, and Rosie and Gordon and their children as well. It was going to be great – chaotic, but great!

As she sat, some of the anger that had been boiling inside her, since their meeting with the child psychologist

Dr Michaelides this morning, was now starting to simmer down.

She felt belittled by the woman. In the car afterwards John had told her she was being over-sensitive, but she disagreed. She had felt that she and John were on trial. OK, of course they'd said nothing to her about Dettore but—

Her thoughts were interrupted by John arriving back, hot and sweaty in his tracksuit after a long jog up on the Downs. He'd stayed at home this afternoon after they got back from Dr Michaelides, and she was glad to see him go on his run; he'd been working crazy hours recently and doing much less exercise than he used to.

'Hi, Luke! Hi, Phoebe! Hi, Fudge! Hi, Chocolate!' he said, sounding puffed. The children ignored him.

'Good run?' she asked.

'Six miles! Wonderful!' He wiped his brow and sniffed. His face was glowing red from exertion, and his hair was awry. Naomi liked him looking rough like this. 'Fifty-two minutes, but that includes over half a mile vertical ascent.'

'Not bad!' she said. 'You had three calls – one from Carson, and a couple of others from your office – I put them on your desk.'

'Thanks.' He glanced at his watch, then stared down at the children. 'How's Fudge, Phoebe?' There was a long silence. Then, without looking at him, Luke said, 'Fudge is my ging pig. Phoebe's is *Chokkit*.'

'OK, right, Daddy got muddled. So how's Fudge, Luke?'

Luke was teasing the guinea pig with a food pellet tied to a length of cotton, constantly pulling it just beyond the creature's reach. The frustrated guinea pig made a squeaking sound like glass being polished. Luke laughed and tugged the cotton again.

John knelt beside him, pushing aside a book that was lying on the floor. 'You should let him have a reward sometimes, otherwise he'll get bored and stop playing.'

The guinea pig advanced and Luke tugged the cotton again, totally ignoring his father. Then again. Phoebe wound a length of cotton around another pellet and began teasing *Chokkit* in the same way.

John felt excluded. The children had put up that damned wall between them and himself and Naomi once more.

'Time to put them to bed now, darlings,' Naomi said.

No reaction at all from either Luke or Phoebe.

'Get them ready for bed, Luke and Phoebe, then you have to go to bed, too!' Naomi said.

Phoebe reached into the hutch, took out the drinking bowl, went over to the sink, stood on a chair and ran the tap. She tested the water with her index finger, waiting until it was cold, then filled the bowl for the animals and placed it in their hutch.

Despite his anger of a few moments ago, John watched proudly. This was his daughter, caring for her pet, all by herself!

Luke picked up the box of food, and poured pellets into their plastic tray. Then he knelt down, scooped Fudge up and placed him on the straw-covered floor of their hutch. Phoebe tempted Chocolate with one more pellet of food then picked her up, kissed her on the mouth and placed her, as gently as if she were laying a priceless china ornament, on the straw inside the hutch.

Together John and Naomi bathed the children and John put them to bed.

'Will you say g'night to Fudge?' Luke said.

'Sure.'

'Will you say g'night to Chokkit?' Phoebe asked.

'Of course, sweetheart.'

John left the room and closed the door, beaming. They had asked him to do something! Wow! Progress!

He skipped down the stairs, went into the kitchen and knelt down in front of the hutch. Both of the creatures were curled up on the floor.

'Luke and Phoebe said to say goodnight!'

There was a great smell of cooking. Naomi was standing over the Aga, stirring a pan. She gave him a bemused look.

'I'm starving,' John said. 'What are we having?'

'Our special today is pan-fried guinea pig on a buckwheat pancake, served with a side order of child psychologist's sweetbreads,' Naomi replied. 'I had intended making a goulash of her brain, but there wasn't enough of it to make it worthwhile.'

John put an arm around her. 'Don't be too harsh on her – at least she's going to give them another chance at playschool.'

'She was a bitch,' Naomi said.

'Put yourself in her position.'

She stared at him. 'Yes?'

'We're keeping stuff back from her.'

'John, she was accusing you and I of being responsible for the way they are. She didn't tell us in so many words, but she was implying that all the problems with Luke and Phoebe stem from us being crap parents. That's not true and you know that.'

'They're getting better. They are also talking a bit more as well. Maybe we don't need a psychologist, maybe all we need is time. Look at them – you saw the way they played with their guinea pigs – how much they adored them. Right?'

'It's nice to see it. It would be quite nice if they showed *us* that much affection, too. I know they have got a little better as they've grown older. It's a shame they don't smile more – they have such lovely smiles.'

73

The Disciple spent the night in a youth hostel on the Bowery, where he kept to himself, his departure into the bitter cold morning as low-key as his arrival had been. In a few weeks' time he would be gone from anyone's memory there.

He breakfasted simply in a busy café, then took the subway to the West Village and emerged into a street teeming with people, heady with a hundred different smells, and the discordance of a thousand different noises. It had started snowing. Pure white flakes fell and were corrupted into dirty grey slush as they landed.

It took him only a couple of minutes to find the second internet café on his list, but all the computers were taken and he had to sit in a line. A young woman in scruffy clothes tried to engage him in conversation. Her name was Elaine, she told him, but her friends called her Ellie. She asked him where he lived and he told her New Jersey. Persisting, irritating him now, she asked him what he did. He told her he worked for the Lord.

She talked more to him, looking at him in a way that made him uncomfortable, edging closer to him, giving him signals. Tempting him. Sent by Satan, you could tell, you could always tell, sent to destroy his love for Lara.

The next computer became free and he moved away from her, saying a prayer of gratitude to the Lord, and sat down in front of it. Joel Timothy entered his username and password and logged on to his Hotmail account.

One new email sat there, waiting for him.

**The Lord will protect him and preserve his life,
He will bless him in the Foreign land and not
surrender him to the desires of his foes.**

The Disciple deleted the email, logged off and left the café. He was smiling. Walking swiftly back to the subway, not caring about how much he breathed in, nor about the sounds, his head was filled now with more important thoughts. Travel plans. He had never travelled outside of the United States before.

Now he was going to England.

74

Christmas decorations were still up. On one wall hung politically correct posters of the Three Wise Men, depicting them with different ethnic origins, painted by the children. Sheila Michaelides, keeping her distance, watched Naomi help Luke and Phoebe out of their coats and hang them on the peg, then leave.

Immediately, the psychologist noticed a change in the twins. It was as if they had been energized by their mother's departure. Luke, followed by Phoebe, went into the main playroom. Sheila moved up to the doorway so she could observe, and was instantly horrified by what she saw.

There were about a dozen children in this room, mostly in small groups, and a supervisor, a woman in her early thirties wearing jeans and some kind of woolly ethnic top. As Luke and Phoebe entered, all the activity and noise instantly stopped, as if a lever had been pulled. Not one of the children made eye contact with the twins, but instead, without actually moving from where they were, seemed to shrink away. It was like a frozen tableau.

The psychologist stared at the woman supervisor, whose eyes were tracking Luke and Phoebe with deep mistrust.

Luke walked straight over to the table where two boys had, seconds earlier, both been tugging on the little knight on horseback, and lifted it out of their hands without a word; neither boy looked at him. Luke peered at it contemptuously, then tossed it back onto the table. Phoebe knelt on the floor and peered at some dolls. Two little girls, Michaelides could see, remained frozen, immobile, shaking.

Luke then went over to the table where four children were playing Lego. His hands moved so fast that the psychologist could not keep pace with what they were doing. She just saw a blur of movement, of coloured bricks, the stare of the supervisor, the other children all motionless with fear in their faces. Then Luke stepped away.

The psychologist put a hand in front of her mouth involuntarily. She could not believe this. The Lego tower that, less than a minute ago, had been ragged and distinctly lopsided, now stood perfect, several inches taller, all the bricks rearranged into a separate colour for each of the four sides, so that it resembled a vertical Rubik's Cube, with a perfect pitched roof.

Moments later, she had to step aside as Luke and Phoebe marched back into the corridor. Like creatures emerging from hibernation, the other children, one by one, turned their heads towards the door, as if to make quite sure they were gone.

Sheila Michaelides felt the hairs on the back of her neck rising.

She watched Luke and Phoebe approach the boy who was playing on the computer. They went and stood either side of him, then each turned and said something.

Instantly, the boy jumped down from his seat and ran down the hallway, shaking and bawling his eyes out. Pat Barley emerged from the kitchen. She shot the psychologist a worried glance, putting her arms around the boy.

'What is it, Matthew? What's the matter?'

He buried himself into her arms, as if for protection, screaming like a frightened animal.

His terror was infecting the psychologist now; goose bumps were breaking out on her skin. She listened, trying to hear what the boy said, but he was just babbling. At the same time she watched Luke and Phoebe, now totally engrossed with the computer they had commandeered.

Just what had they said to the boy?

After some minutes, Pat Barley slipped out to join the psychologist in the hall and signalled with her eyes for them to move further away from the twins.

'What did little Matthew say?' the psychologist asked the teacher. 'What did Luke and Phoebe say to him that upset him quite so much?'

'I don't know – it's always the same – and they upset the other children as well, just as much. I don't think it's so much what they say as the way they say it. And, the thing is, they *look* so much older.'

'I've seen a lot of children with quite appalling behavioural problems,' Sheila Michaelides said, keeping her voice low. 'Violent children, out-of-control children, seriously withdrawn children – but I've never seen anything like – like what I've seen here, just in these past few minutes.'

'I've never seen anything remotely like it,' Pat Barley said. 'And I've had a few terrors in my time, believe me.'

'Are they ever physically violent? Have either of them ever actually attacked another child?'

'No, not that any of us have seen. It's a mental thing; they're manipulative. If I try to talk to them they either say absolutely nothing or they spout gibberish at me.'

'I very much appreciate your letting me come here and observe them,' the psychologist said.

'Perhaps now you can understand why I had to ban them?'

'Yes.'

For some moments they both watched Luke and Phoebe. From behind, they looked like any normal, happy children playing together. Then Pat Barley said, 'God knows what they're going to be like when they're older.'

75

Snow! Four inches, just white as far as the eye can see! Great start to the New Year! John went out and bought a toboggan. Took L & P up on the Downs. L loved it, P grumpy. How can she not like snow? How can any child not?

They're starting at a new, special needs playschool next week that Sheila Michaelides (SM – appropriate initials for a sadist!!) suggested.

At least – in my darker moments, when I worry about what we've done – or rather, what Dettore's done – I'm able to convince myself that there really isn't anything so great or special about the human species. All this crap about life being precious, sacrosanct. Maybe for those of us – a percentage of us, anyhow – who live in the First World, you could make out a case. But what was it Dettore said? Less than 20% of the world can read or write? Not sure how special I'd find life if I spent my days up to my ankles in water in a paddy field, and my nights in a tin hut with nine children. Don't think I'd even call that living – I'd call it 'existing'.

Soon they'll be three. What to get them? Debating whether to have a party and invite local kids over. Not sure how many mums would send their kids – could be embarrassing. Especially if Luke and Phoebe ignore them.

76

On the living-room floor, Luke sat holding a PlayStation joystick in his hand, absorbed in concentration. Phoebe, kneeling beside him, was watching the television screen, equally absorbed, and every few moments giving an urgent command to her brother.

A man in a long cape was climbing a never-ending Gothic stairwell; oak doors opened and closed revealing strange creatures, some scary, some beautiful, some plain weird. Sometimes, at Phoebe's urgent command, Luke pressed a button and the man ducked. Other times the man did a snap one-hundred-and-eighty-degree turn.

Maybe it was her imagination, Naomi wondered, but Dr Sheila Michaelides seemed very definitely to have thawed a little towards her and John. The psychologist was standing unobtrusively at the rear of the room, observing all that was going on, occasionally making a note on a small pad, saying nothing. She'd spent two days at the special needs playschool observing Luke and Phoebe, and now she'd been a fly on the wall all day here.

But at least, she felt, for the first time they were going to get an accurate assessment of their children and, hopefully, some clear advice on how to handle them.

The psychologist stood in the doorway of the bathroom, watching her and John bathe and dry the twins. Luke and Phoebe seemed to accept her presence the way they accepted most things: by ignoring her. To the children, she could have been invisible.

Downstairs, they sat around the kitchen table. Sheila Michaelides put her notepad in front of her, looking uncomfortable. She stirred her coffee then accepted a ginger biscuit from the plate Naomi offered. Then she said, 'Dr and Mrs Klaesson, I have to tell you I'm extremely concerned about Luke and Phoebe. I think there are some improvements you could make in your own parental roles, but from my observations this is not the root of the problem.'

'What kind of improvements?' Naomi demanded defensively.

'What do you mean by the *root* of the problem?' John followed on.

'Well,' she said, putting the biscuit down on her plate, and staring pensively for a moment at the steam rising from her cup of coffee, 'I need some time to think about everything I've seen and I would like to talk to some of my colleagues. One immediate observation I have is that you are clearly not getting the levels of love and affection from your children that I would normally expect. There is a tendency for twins to be self-sufficient for much longer than single babies, but Luke and Phoebe are almost three now.' She hesitated, looking at their faces, then added, 'They seem cold and very withdrawn, something that ordinarily would signal something wrong with the parenting—'

'Wrong?' Naomi cut in. 'What do you mean by that?'

'The possibility of abuse,' Sheila Michaelides responded.

Naomi opened her mouth, about to explode; John gripped her arm. 'Honey, calm down!'

'I'm not in any way suggesting this is the case – nothing I've seen suggests any maltreatment by you both. I think you are very loving, very caring parents.'

There was a tense silence as she flicked through her notes, looking for something.

'What exactly do you mean by *improvements that we can make in our role as parents*?' Naomi asked.

'Well, let's take an instance the first morning I came here, before playschool. You went out of the kitchen and left me alone with them. They showed no fear of me – a total stranger – at all. Children who are well bonded with their parents have a much greater fear of strangers than those who don't.'

'But we've been trying to bond with them ever since they were born!' Naomi said.

The psychologist nodded, her worried frown deepening. 'I think that's an area where I could give you some guidance. But there are broader problems that I don't think stem from this lack of bonding.'

Naomi watched her, concerned about the woman's body language. When they had first gone to see her, she seemed supremely confident to the point of arrogance; but now she looked nervous, toying with the biscuit, playing with her hands, frowning, her whole face tightening up every few minutes as if she was struggling with some inner demon.

'I've seen Luke and Phoebe separately and together. I've watched them solving puzzles, and I've tried as best as possible, given their lack of verbal communication, to test their memory and reasoning. What I'm finding is that they seem to have an intelligence and skill levels far in advance of their age. They seem at times to be testing everything around them. Most of the time they're very withdrawn, at other times, they try to assert themselves over everyone they come into contact with – over the other kids in playschool, over you, and as they don't have any challenge in asserting themselves over their guinea pigs, they taunt them instead, seeing how far they can push them; it's as if they are constantly testing the endurance levels of everything. I'm having a big problem with their mindsets – they respond to totally different cues to the norm, and they have a different pattern of communication. It is outside of any kind of range I've ever experienced.'

'You mean this strange language they have?' John asked.

'That's part of it. I was sceptical when you first told me about it, now I'm beginning to believe it.'

'How do you explain it?' John said.

'For them to be so wrapped up with each other that they rarely respond to either of you, and never to other children, and to have these unique skills, is symptomatic of autism. I had dismissed that previously, but that is one possibility I would now like to explore. I'm going to suggest that we should have brain scans done.'

'Autism?' Naomi said, horrified. 'You really think they might be autistic?'

'I'm afraid it is one possibility. Clearly there is something going on that we need to diagnose.'

Naomi looked at John. He squeezed her hand.

The psychologist went on, 'There are very primitive perceptual systems in the brain that recognize and respond to patterns of social behaviour. One of the tests I did shows that in Luke and Phoebe this ability is either absent, or programmed differently.'

'What does that mean exactly?' John asked.

'I'm not sure that your children are able to make certain distinctions about some aspects of what constitutes *normal* behaviour in society.'

John squeezed Naomi's hand even more tightly and looked at the psychologist. 'Where do we go from here?'

'I need time to think about it,' she said. 'One option might be for you both to take a break, and let Luke and Phoebe go into a residential psychiatric facility for observation.'

'Absolutely no way!' Naomi said, turning to John for confirmation. He looked hesitant for a moment, then nodded in agreement with her.

'I'm not proposing this as any slight on you as parents,' she said. 'If your children are, as I suspect, super-bright and under-stimulated, it might do them good to be in a facility for gifted children. There's a very good residential facility I could suggest—'

'I'm sorry,' Naomi said. 'That is not an option. It's out of the question. We're their parents; whatever problems they may have, we are going to be the ones to get them through it, whatever it takes.'

'Well, the alternative would be for you to change the activities at home for them. Perhaps design a new regime for them to follow.'

'Such as?' John asked.

'Giving them toys and games that would be appropriate for much older children. I think you should get them a computer – they are fascinated by computers – that's why they monopolize the one at playschool.'

'Sheila,' John said. 'Give me your honest answer – what would you do if you were in our position – if these were your children?'

'I need to think about it,' she said. 'I need to talk about this with some colleagues – in confidence, of course. I'd like to do some research. I wish I could give you some magic solution, but I can't; there isn't one. Life's not going to be easy for you.'

77

The front door was opening. The Disciple put his finger on the stopwatch *start* button: 7.32 in the evening. Dark. Someone came out of the house holding a big umbrella. Watching through his night glasses he could see it was the male Infidel. Moments later, as the sensors picked up the Infidel's movement, the outside lights came on.

Now!

The Disciple pressed the button. He was standing well out of range of the lights, in the dark, in the wet field, in the same lined boots in which he had trudged through the snowy sidewalks of Rochester and New York City. He was wrapped up in warm layers, and his black baseball cap, pulled down tight, gave his face some small measure of protection from the brutal wind and the rain as sharp as needles.

It was the same rain endlessly falling, endlessly sucked back up into the clouds, then dropped again. Sucked up from the sewer, dropped, sucked up again, you could never escape, didn't matter where in the world you were, snow made from water from the sewers fell on you, rain from the sewers fell on you, there was no place you were free from it, there never would be, not until you had purged the sewers, not until you had ridded the cities and the valleys and the plains of every last atom.

He checked that the sweep hand was moving on the stopwatch, then watched through his night glasses again; the image burned red in the glare of the lights. The Infidel escorted a middle-aged woman in a flapping coat across to a small Japanese car, held the door for her, slammed it when she had entered, then hurried back to his porch. Now the Disciple could see the woman Infidel as well, standing back inside the doorway. Both of them waved as the car drove off. No sign of a dog; one less problem to have to deal with.

Wondering who the woman was, he watched the lights of the car brush along the hedgerow as it made its way down the long farm track, heading away into the night, into another part of the sewer. Then he raised his glasses and stared through the mist of driving rain at the house. The Infidels had closed the door.

He lowered his glasses, put his finger on the stopwatch button and waited. It seemed like an eternity before the outside lights went off.

Instantly he pressed the button and looked down at the watch. They were set for three minutes.

The Disciple moved forward across the field. By morning the rain would have erased his tracks. A light came on in a downstairs window and he raised his glasses and switched off the infra-red. The male Infidel was sitting at a desk in front of a computer; he switched on a desk lamp; he raised something, a glass, a tall-stemmed glass, to his lips, and drank.

Be still before the Lord and wait patiently for him; do not fret when men succeed in their ways, when they carry out their wicked schemes. Refrain from anger and turn from wrath; do not fret – it leads only to evil. For evil men will be cut off, but those who hope in the Lord will inherit the land. Psalm 37.

The Disciple was staying in a small, draughty room in an old hotel on the seafront in the resort city of Brighton and Hove. His room overlooked a windblown promenade, a rusting, ruined pier, and a sea that had been churning dark and restlessly, like his heart, during the three days that he had been here.

It would be so easy, just to wait until the lights went off in the house, make his move, do his duty and then leave, cross the Channel tonight on a ferry in his rented car. By tomorrow night he could be sleeping in the arms of Lara, and the Lord.

But no. Like Job, his patience had to endure further testing yet. An email from his Master, from Harald Gatward, instructed him to wait a little longer, to prepare more thoroughly, to bide his time until the time was right. That at the moment, God had warned, there was danger.

I will instruct you and teach you in the way you should go; I will counsel you and watch over you. Psalm 32.

The Disciple lowered his glasses. He listened to the sounds of the night, of air hissing in the winter grasses, of a gate creaking and the distant clatter of a train, felt the rain against his face, the damp chilling his bones, but in his heart burned a deep glow of warmth. Dr and Mrs Klaesson and their Spawn were inside the walls of that little building.

When the command came he would be in the arms of Lara and the Lord, before anyone had even discovered their bodies.

78

From: Kalle Almtorp, Swedish Embassy, Kuala
Lumpur, Malaysia.
To: John Klaesson bklaesson@morleypark.org
Subject: Disciples

John,
I trust this email finds you well and coping with
that terrible British climate! Life here in Malaysia is
good although the heat took a while to adjust to. I
am curious to know how you are. How is Naomi?
Luke and Phoebe?

I am writing with possibly good news. My
contact at the FBI tells me (very confidentially!)
that they now have a lead in their search for these
Disciples of the Third Millennium. Still early days,
but (and please don't repeat this) there is some
evidence pointing to a religious cult based in exile
in a remote part of Europe. These people may be
funded by the son of one of America's richest
families, but I understand the evidence is only very
tentative at this stage.

As soon as I have more news I will be in touch
again. Meantime, it would be good to hear from
you. Scary how time passes. How many years since
we last saw each other?

Hälsningar!
Kalle

John balled his fist and raised it in the air. 'Yes!!!!!'

Then he tugged the last olive off the cocktail stick, chewed it, and drained the rest of his martini.

Rain spattered against the window in front of his desk. It was a truly foul night and the wind seemed to be freshening. This was great news! They were going to get those bastards. And then they would be safe, at last.

He'd needed something to cheer him after the grim pronouncements of Dr Michaelides, who had just left half an hour or so ago.

He tilted the cocktail glass back and let the last drips of the drink roll into his mouth. Then reality set in. Oh Jesus, what the hell did they do now?

Wait. Wait for the psychologist to come back to them, that was all they could do.

In an attempt to cheer Naomi, he went through to the kitchen and told her the good news from Kalle Almtorp. He embellished it a little, telling her that the FBI were days away from an arrest. From scooping up the entire damned cult.

In just a few days, they would be free from their worries!

But Naomi had not just drunk an extremely large martini; she was stone cold sober. She did not share any of his joy or his alcohol-fuelled optimism.

She told him life sucked.

79

Shelia Michaelides hurried to her Victorian terraced house in the centre of Brighton, her tiny umbrella useless against the gale, and she was drenched by the time she reached the sanctuary of her hallway. Changing into a dry pair of jeans and a sweater, she made herself a coffee, took a Marks & Spencer tuna pasta salad out of the fridge, then carried a tray up to her little study, sat down at her desk and booted up her computer.

Her mind was churning as she dug her fork in to the pasta, and her stomach felt knotted with anxiety. *Haven't eaten all day, must eat something!* She chewed slowly, each mouthful a struggle, forcing herself to swallow, her throat tight and dry. Rain scratched the window, and through the darkness she could just make out the silhouette of her neighbour's house across from her back yard.

She stood up suddenly, leaned forward and unwound the cord from the hook, letting the blinds drop.

She was shaking. Shaking from a fear she couldn't define. Always she had been in control. Now for the first time she felt out of her depth. There was some syndrome that Luke and Phoebe Klaesson had which she had never encountered, and it spooked her, increasingly.

She began typing.

Luke and Phoebe Klaesson observations. Day Three. These are not human beings as I know it. They are manipulative, brooding, in a way that suggests the

normal restraints of human existence are absent. Clear signs of sociopathic behaviour, but something beyond that . . .

She stopped and thought for some moments. She needed to talk to other psychologists about this, but who?

The cheese plant filling the small space between her desk and the wall looked in a sad state, badly in need of watering. She went downstairs, filled the can, came back and poured the contents into the arid soil, thinking, thinking.

Thinking.

She typed again.

Autism? How to explain this speech between themselves?

How?

Then, reluctantly, she forked another mouthful of pasta into her mouth and chewed, thinking. Thinking . . . there must be other case histories out there somewhere, in papers, in books, surely?

She was a member of a child psychologists' newsgroup on the internet, that circulated a weekly summary of case histories, new treatments, new drugs and general information. It was a good group, with psychologists in over thirty countries participating, and in the past she had always received informed responses to any questions she had asked.

She typed out an email, summarizing her observations of Luke and Phoebe, asking if anyone else had ever experienced anything similar with a patient.

To her surprise, the following day she received emails from ten psychologists. Five of them in the United States, one in the United Arab Emirates, one in Brazil, one in Italy, one in Germany and one in Switzerland.

Four of the psychologists informed her, separately, that the twins they had seen with similar characteristics had been conceived in the offshore clinic of the murdered American geneticist, Dr Leo Dettore.

She Googled the name *Dr Leo Dettore*.

Among the first batch of hits that came up, one was indexed:

> Newspaper. USA Today. July 2007. Dr J. Klaesson.
> LA PROFESSOR ADMITS, 'WE'RE HAVING A DESIGNER BABY'.

80

Mr Pineapple Head wore striped trousers, huge shoes, a red nose and a leather hat shaped like a pineapple. He was going down a storm, at any rate for the four children who had come to Luke and Phoebe's third birthday, who were in fits of laughter. John and Naomi, her mother and her sister, Harriet, and Rosie were also finding his antics extremely funny.

Luke and Phoebe were the only ones who didn't. They sat on the floor, staring at the man in stony silence, rejecting all his attempts to get them to join in doing tricks with him.

It had been a struggle for John and Naomi to get any other children to come to this party. Jane Adamson, Naomi's friend in the village, had dutifully delivered her son Charlie, who had come in with evident reluctance, clutching a present in one hand and holding on to his mother with the other, eyeing the twins nervously. Naomi had also enlisted a timid girl called Bethany, whose parents had only moved into the village this week and didn't yet know anyone. Rosie had brought her youngest, Imogen, and a colleague of John had brought her spirited four-year-old son, Ben.

Suddenly, halfway through the performance, Luke and Phoebe stood up abruptly and walked out of the room.

Exchanging a glance with John, who was standing to one side, busily taking photographs, Naomi followed the children out into the hall and closed the door behind her. 'Luke!' she called. 'Phoebe! Where are you going?'

Ignoring her, they trotted upstairs.

Louder, now. 'Luke! Phoebe! Come back down at once! It's very rude to leave your friends! You absolutely cannot do this!'

Angrily, she ran upstairs after them, calling their names again. She saw them entering the box room and followed them in.

The computer she and John had given them for their birthday sat on the floor, where John had temporarily set it up after they had unwrapped it this morning. Both children squatted beside it.

'Luke!' Naomi called.

Ignoring her, Luke touched the keyboard, and the monitor came alive with a blank Word document.

Phoebe said something to her brother, then tapped several keys in rapid succession with the competence of a touch-typist. For an instant Naomi was too amazed to be angry. Then she walked over to the wall and yanked the plug out.

Neither child looked at her.

'It's your party, Luke and Phoebe,' she said. 'You have friends here. Mummy and Daddy have got you Mr Pineapple Head as a special treat, it was very rude to walk out on him, and very rude to leave your friends. Now get up and come back down at once!'

No reaction at all.

Furious now, she grabbed Luke and Phoebe each by an arm and hauled them up onto their feet. Still there was no reaction. They just stood, sullenly.

'DOWNSTAIRS!' Naomi bellowed.

It produced not the slightest response.

She tried to pull them towards the door, and to her shock, found she could not. They were resisting with a strength that was more than a match for hers.

Releasing Phoebe's hand, she pulled Luke as hard as she could, jerking deliberately to try to unbalance him. But he stood his ground, his polished black lace-up shoes slipping just a fraction on the carpet pile before digging in.

Close to losing it, she yelled, 'If you don't come downstairs right away, you're going to bed, both of you. No computer, nothing. DO YOU UNDERSTAND ME?'

John, camera in his hand, was standing in the doorway. 'What's going on?' he said.

'Dr Michaelides is right,' she said. 'We should put them in a bloody institution, miserable little sods.'

She released Luke's hand. John knelt down and stared at him, then gently but firmly took hold of both of his hands. 'Listen, little fellow, you and your sister are having a birthday party and you've got friends here and a great clown. I want you to come down and behave the way a host and hostess should behave. OK?'

Naomi watched Luke. In his navy trousers, white shirt and tie, black lace-up shoes and serious face he looked more like a miniature adult than a child. And Phoebe, in a floral dress with a lace ruff, had an expression like ice. *You're not children*, she thought, with a shudder. *You're bloody-minded little adults.*

God, just what the hell are you?

John stood up. Luke and Phoebe gave each other an unreadable look. Then, after a moment's further hesitation, Luke walked after his father back out into the landing. Tight-lipped, Phoebe followed.

They re-entered the living room. Luke and Phoebe

walked solemnly to the front of the little group and sat back down on the floor, crossed their arms and fixed their eyes on Mr Pineapple Head, who had engaged the help of Ben in spinning plates on sticks.

'Everything all right?' Harriet whispered to Naomi.

No, she wanted to say. *Not all right at all.* Instead she just smiled and nodded. *Fine. Absolutelysodddingfine.*

*

That night, after her mother and Harriet had both gone up to bed, Naomi stood wearily in the kitchen, unloading the dishwasher and passing plates to John, who stacked them back in the cupboards. Fudge and Chocolate were wide awake, both pressing their faces against the bars of their hutch, making their funny little chamois-leather-polish-ing-glass squeaks.

Naomi poured herself a large slug of wine. 'This residential facility that Dr Michaelides mentioned – maybe we should think about it after all. I'm at the end of my tether, John, I don't know what to do any more. Maybe they'd respond better to discipline if it comes from someone they don't know. Perhaps after a couple of weeks they'd start to see reason.'

She picked up her glass and drank half the contents in one gulp. 'I never thought in a million years I'd say that. But that's how I feel. I don't know what else to do.'

'They were bored today,' John responded. 'That was the problem, I think. That's what Harriet thought, too.'

'She doesn't know anything about children,' Naomi said, a little acidly. 'She dotes on Luke and Phoebe.'

'Does she ever say anything to you about them? About how they don't respond to her?'

'She thinks it's a phase they're going through.' He

concentrated for a moment on finding a place to put a jug, then said, 'Let's hope Dr Michaelides is right, that more intellectual stimulation is needed. Maybe we made a mistake having a clown, perhaps we should have had an astrophysicist talking about the molecular structures of rocket fuels, or climate change.'

She gave him a wan smile. 'That's almost funny.'

81

At six in the morning John was wide awake after a restless night. Naomi had tossed and turned continually, and he'd twice been woken by the rustle and popping of a blister pack as she took paracetamols. Now she was sleeping soundly, as usual right over his side of the bed, leaving him almost hanging over the edge.

He extricated himself as gently as he could, trying not to wake her, padded across the floor and peered out of the window into the darkness. It was still the best part of an hour before daybreak. Pulling on his dressing gown, he dug his feet into his clogs and tiptoed downstairs in the darkness.

Someone else was up, he realized, hearing the sound of voices on television, and seeing light seeping under the living room door. Was it Naomi's sister, he wondered, although Harriet was normally a late riser. He opened the door and peered in.

Luke and Phoebe, in their dressing gowns, squatted on the floor, backs against a sofa, utterly absorbed in a television programme. But it wasn't any of the kids' shows Naomi would ordinarily have put on for them; it was an adult science lesson, something to do with the Open University. A teacher, standing in front of a three-dimensional model of a complex atomic structure, was talking about the formation of halogen. He was explaining how a quartz halogen headlamp on a car worked.

'Good morning, Luke, good morning, Phoebe,' he said.

Both shot him a cursory glance as if he was some minor irritation, then looked back at the screen.

'Like any breakfast?'

Luke raised a hand, signalling with it for him to be quiet, to stop distracting them. John stared at him, unable fully to take this in. His three-year-old children were sitting in front of the television, at six o'clock on a Sunday morning, utterly engrossed by a man talking about halogen gas.

He backed out of the room and went through to the kitchen to make some coffee, deep in thought. Just how bright were they? Had it been them accessing his computer and taking over his previous chess game with Gus Santiano – and beating him?

They were going to have to let the psychologist carry out tests on them, for sure. And he was going to need to discuss with Naomi about sending them to a special educational facility. There must be places that were not residential, where they could just take them each day, and still have a family life with them outside of that – doing fun family activities with them, such as learning about the molecular structure of halogen gas together.

He filled the kettle and switched it on. Then he spooned some coffee into a mug, and took a bottle of milk out of the fridge. Something felt strange; it seemed too quiet in here, a sound was missing. There was a distinctly unpleasant smell, he suddenly realized, as well.

Bad meat.

He wrinkled his nose, opened the fridge door and sniffed. Just fridge smells – nothing bad in there, nothing that had gone off. He closed the door, sniffed harder, puzzled. He checked the freezer door as well, putting his nose close to the trays, but there was nothing bad there either.

The kettle rumbled louder, then clicked off. He poured boiling water into the mug, added milk and stirred it.

Then, turning round with his mug in his hand, he saw it.

The mug slipped from his fingers, hit the floor and shattered, spraying china fragments and scalding coffee everywhere. But he barely noticed. His eyes were riveted to the floor, to the two sheets of newspaper that had been placed beside the guinea pigs' hutch.

On one sheet of newsprint, amid a stain of dried blood, Fudge was laid out on his back, paws in the air, his midriff slit open from his neck to his tail, his internal organs placed in an orderly row beside him. On the other sheet of paper, Chocolate lay similarly opened up and eviscerated.

For an instant, his thoughts wild and ragged, John wondered if a cat had somehow come into the house and done this. But walking over, and peering closer, he realized that theory was a non-starter. A small pile of coiled intestines lay beside each; their kidneys, livers, pancreas, hearts, lungs, were laid in matching rows. The tops of their skulls had been removed with surgical precision, and their tiny little brains placed beside their heads. Some of the organs had been cut in half very cleanly, and the intestines sliced open in sections.

He turned away in revulsion, feeling very distressed, his mind in turmoil. Such sweet little creatures, so friendly, it had been such a treat to watch Luke and Phoebe playing with them, kissing them, caring for them. Who the hell had done this?

Who on earth would have wanted to do this?

The inevitable was in his mind, but he was refusing to accept it. He just wanted to clear this up, get rid of it before Naomi saw it; she wouldn't be able to handle this. He didn't want Harriet seeing it either, nor Naomi's mother. No one.

Opening the cupboard under the kitchen sink, he pulled a black bin liner off a roll, opened it out, then carefully picked up each of the news sheets in turn, holding his breath against the smell from the intestines and stomach, folded the paper and placed it in the bag. Then he knotted the bag, took it outside, put it in one of the dustbins and replaced the lid securely.

Back inside, he was shaking. He cleaned up the mess of coffee and broken china as best he could, then went over to the living room and opened the door. The television was switched off and so were the lights. The twins weren't there.

He went upstairs to see if they were back in their bedroom, and when he reached the top, he noticed a glow of light from the box room. Walking swiftly down the landing, he pushed open the door. The children's new computer was on, and he saw a web page was up on the screen. He knelt to take a closer look.

It was a page from *Gray's Anatomy*, the dissection bible of all medical students. It illustrated a section of a kidney that had been cut open, with a list of points for observation during a post-mortem.

82

John went for a run, feeling very distressed, trying to think clearly and make some sense of what had just happened. Should he have grabbed hold of the children, taken them down to the dead guinea pigs and shaken sense into them? Would it have done any good?

And, just what the hell had driven the children to that website? And to do what they'd done?

It was a clear, cold morning. Frost glinted in the early sunlight and glazed puddles crunched beneath his running shoes as he made his way along a rutted cart-track up into the hills.

Halfway up he stopped for breath and looked back down across the vast sweep of the valley, at the farmhouses, roads, lanes, the clock tower of a stately home on the ridge of a far hill. It was half past seven on a Sunday morning, and most people hadn't risen yet; there was a stillness in the air, almost preternatural. Somewhere, a long way off, he heard the bleat of a sheep. Then just as far off, the bass lowing sound of a cow. High above him up in the sky he could see the vapour trail of a jet heading out towards the Channel.

He could see their own house, looking tiny, in a direct line between himself and the village church. Everything looked tiny from here. Like some kind of toy-world. Miniature fields, miniature sheep, cows, miniature houses, barns, cars, roads, lamp posts, traffic signals, steeples. So small, so insignificant.

Guinea pigs were small and insignificant, too. Their internal organs were tiny, little specks, some of them, you really had to look quite hard to tell what they were. And yet . . .

No life was insignificant. There were insects you might kill, like mosquitoes, because they were a threat – or a wasp in your babies' bedroom, or something dirty and uninvited, like a cockroach, and there were wild animals you had to kill because they were a threat to you or your farm, or those you had bred for food and you were going to eat them.

But to kill them out of curiosity?

Sure, in labs. Fruit flies, mice, frogs, all kinds of creatures were dissected in the name of education, in the name of medical research. In order to learn, creatures were killed all the time. That part he had no problem with – not that he had ever liked seeing anything dead, but there was an arguable reason there.

And in truth, casting his mind back to his own childhood, there had been a time as a young boy when he had shot at wildlife with a catapult. Then one day he'd hit a sparrow and killed it outright. He'd watched it drop from its perch onto the grass. He'd rushed over to it and saw beads of blood in its beak. Held its warm body, tried to make it stand up, moved its wings, trying to make it fly away and be better. Then, crying, he'd put it back up in the tree to keep it safe from the cat. Hoping it might get better and fly off.

But it was still there the next morning, cold and hard, like feathers glued to a small rock. Ashamed, he'd carried it into the woods, scooped out a shallow grave with his bare hands and placed a stone and leaves on top of it.

It was normal for children to kill animals, he knew

that. It was part of growing up. One of the rites of passage. Probably something to do with the exorcizing of dormant hunter-gatherer genes. But could he have ever killed a pet? Something he'd nurtured, cared for, cradled in his arms, played with, hugged and kissed goodnight, the way Luke and Phoebe had with Fudge and Chocolate?

Something that Dr Michaelides had said was repeating over and over in his mind.

I'm not sure that your children are able to make certain distinctions about some aspects of what constitutes normal behaviour in society.

Was this her way telling them, in a thinly veiled way, that their children were psychopaths?

83

Back at home, the house was quiet. No one else up yet. Good. The children needed to be punished for what they had done, but how? What would show them that what they had done was wrong? What the hell would get through to them?

Still in his tracksuit, sweaty and cooling down fast from his run, he made Naomi her usual Sunday morning cup of tea, toast and Marmite, and took it up to her, with the newspapers, on a tray.

She was sitting up in bed, watching Andrew Marr interviewing the Chancellor. He picked up the remote, turned the volume down, and, reluctant to spoil her morning, told her about the guinea pigs.

After a long silence, her face pale, she gripped his hand and said, 'Can we not tell Harriet – or my mother? Can we keep this to ourselves?'

He sat down on the bed beside her, glancing at the headlines of the *Sunday Times.* 'I agree, I don't want them to know.'

'We could tell them that – that – they left the door open and they ran away – couldn't we?'

'I just put the hutch outside,' he said. 'Your mother isn't going to notice anyway. If Harriet says anything, I'll tell her I put them outside and didn't shut the door properly.'

'We need to speak to Luke and Phoebe. We have to explain to them that what they've done isn't right. We have to get through to them, John, we have to make them understand. They have to be punished for this.'

'Tell me how we do that? Because I don't know. Dr Michaelides said—'

'I remember very clearly what she said. But we're their parents, we brought them into this world, it's our responsibility. They're only three years old, for Christ's sake! What are they going to do when they're four? Or five? Start cutting you and I open to see what *our* vital organs look like?'

She went to the bathroom and closed the door. John flicked through the paper, but couldn't concentrate on any article. Some minutes later she came out, wrapped in her dressing gown, her hair brushed and her breath smelling minty from toothpaste. Her face looked like thunder. She dug her feet into her slippers, went out into the landing along to the box room. Luke and Phoebe sat on the floor in front of the computer, in their pyjamas, close together, peering at a chess game. Without any warning, she grabbed Phoebe's arm and started dragging her out of the room. 'You and me are going to talk, Phoebe, if it takes us all day, you and me are going to talk. And your Daddy and Luke are going to talk. If it takes them all day. If it takes them all day and all night.'

'Luke!' John said.

Luke, totally ignoring him, pursed his lips and moved the mouse.

Whether it was Naomi's fury transmitting to him, or his own pent-up anger finally bursting, John grabbed hold of Luke, more violently than he had ever done before, dragged him out of the door and followed Naomi and Phoebe down the stairs.

He pulled his son, who was silent and like a dead

weight, across the hallway, through the kitchen and out of the back door, still following Naomi, dragging him across the lawn to the dustbins.

Naomi, still holding Phoebe with one hand, lifted the lid of a dustbin and hauled out a black bin liner. She held it up and stared at John. 'This it? This the one?'

He shrugged. 'Might be.'

Releasing Phoebe, who lay motionless and expressionless on the frosted lawn, she unknotted the top of the bag, then tipped the contents out. The carcasses of Fudge and Chocolate tumbled out and lay, among the detritus of their innards, on the grass.

Fighting back tears, Naomi, staring at each of them in turn, said, 'These were your pets. You loved them. You kissed them. You were meant to be looking after them. You seemed like you loved them. Why did you kill them? Why did you do this to them? Why? Don't you realize what you've done?'

Luke, speaking more lucidly and calmly than either of them had ever heard him, responded. 'They're a very low life form.'

Naomi looked at John. John, astonished at his son's sudden lucidity, but trying to keep his calm, responded, probing, 'Why does that give you the right to kill them, Luke?'

'You gave them to us, Daddy,' he said.

John wanted to cry and laugh. Luke was talking to them! Responding to them! This was an incredible breakthrough – and yet, it was awful. The circumstances were nothing to be happy about. He shot Naomi a look and she acknowledged it with eyes that reflected his own bewilderment. 'Luke, we gave them to you to look after, not to kill,' he said.

'Guinea pigs only live five years anyway,' Phoebe chipped in.

Both John and Naomi found themselves looking at their children in a totally new light. They were communicating! That in itself was remarkable. But it didn't lessen what they had done. It didn't lessen the bizarre nature of what was happening here.

'So, don't you think they had a right to live for five years?' John said. 'You're a human being; humans live for eighty years.'

'Chokkit had a smaller liver than Fudge,' Phoebe said.

'Anyhow, Fudge would have died of kidney failure at two; he had abnormal creatinine levels,' Luke said solemnly.

And authoritatively.

Quite unbelievably authoritatively.

Naomi shivered. 'Really?' she said. 'What are creatinine levels?'

'It's a metabolite that's filtered out by the kidneys. Fudge's creatinine levels were too high, meaning he was predisposed to kidney failure,' Phoebe responded, staring at her as if she were a retard.

'And what about Chocolate?' Naomi asked. 'What about her *creatinine* levels?'

'They were OK,' Phoebe answered simply.

'So why did you kill her?' Naomi asked.

'I didn't kill her,' Phoebe said indignantly.

'I see,' Naomi said. 'You cut her open and took out her insides. But you didn't kill her. Right?'

'No, she died. She was disobedient. We didn't say she could die, we didn't give her permission to die.'

84

John followed Naomi inside, went straight to the box room, unplugged the children's computer and picked it up. He remembered when he had been naughty as a child, his father used to confiscate his bicycle, his most treasured possession. That used to hurt a lot, depriving him of his mobility, effectively confining him. Maybe taking away the computer might have an impact on Luke and Phoebe. They needed, desperately, to find something that would.

He set the computer down on the floor of his den, then plugged it in and booted it up, curious to see what else the children had downloaded from the net.

The command came up: ENTER PASSWORD

You've set a password, you little sods! he thought, with reluctant admiration.

He was about to go and find them and demand the password, but then he had another thought. He knelt back down and, concentrating hard, tapped a series of letters on the keyboard.

ebohpkul

But the message came up:

PASSWORD NOT VALID – RETRY.

After thinking for some moments, John reversed the order of their names.

eklebohp

Seconds after he hit the return, he was in. Yes! He grinned triumphantly. They were using their secret language, joining their names together, omitting every fourth letter, and reversing them.

Then he stopped smiling. *Terrific. I'm all excited because I managed not to be outsmarted by my three-year-old children.*

He went to the internet settings, which should have been blank. But as he had half expected, they weren't. There was a MobileMe account in Luke's name and a Hotmail account in Phoebe's name. They had set themselves up with free email accounts!

A while ago, a very, very short while ago, he would have been incredulous; but not any more. He wasn't sure how he felt. Some moments he wished desperately this was all some dream, and that he'd wake up and find that he and Naomi had normal, happy kids who crawled into their bed on Sunday mornings, and didn't sit in front of the television set hooked on programmes about halogen gas, and didn't murder their pets.

Other moments he tried to think positively, and put his mind to the awesome possibilities that lay open to Luke and Phoebe. Whatever tinkering Dettore had done, their hunger for knowledge and their skills were incredible. Maybe they just needed a firmer hand, firmer guidance, better understanding? He and Naomi needed urgently to get their heads around exactly how bright the children were, and learn to see it as a positive rather than a negative.

He double-clicked on the web browser and while he waited for it to open, he tried to cast his mind back to his own childhood, to remember if there had been some point at which he had understood it was bad to kill things. Surely it had been his conscience that made him know?

The guilt over killing that sparrow that he still carried in some small way to this day. You didn't need to teach children that killing was bad. Any normal child would instinctively *know*.

Wouldn't they?

He opened the site history, to look at all the web pages Luke and Phoebe had been to. And now he became really incredulous. It had been just twenty-four hours since they had been given the computer, yet there were pages and pages full of records of websites they had visited. All of them educational, mostly science sites, some geared at kids, some at teenagers, some very advanced. Medicine, biology, physics, mathematics, chemistry, biochemistry and, interspersed, a raft of anthropological, history and biographical sites.

As he knelt, totally absorbed in his task, he was unaware of two solemn little faces watching him from the doorway.

Basic Biology. The Laws of Entropy. Formations of Nucleoid Proteins. Advanced Logic. Calculus. He felt a cold, creeping sensation down his spine as he scrolled on down the list. It wasn't possible! There was no way three-year-old children could be reading some of this stuff – in fact, any of this stuff.

He was interrupted by Naomi calling from downstairs that breakfast was ready.

He set a new password, to prevent them from sneaking in here and using the computer. Then he realized he was still in his damp, sweaty tracksuit. Quickly peeling it off, he went into the shower. A few minutes later, as he hurried downstairs, changed into a roll-neck jumper, jeans and his battered old leather yachting slip-ons – his comfort shoes – he was still very deep in thought.

The rest of his family were already seated at the oak refectory table, which was laden with cereal packs, bowls of fruit salad, muesli, yoghurts, a basket of brioches and another of toast, and a heaped platter of fried eggs, bacon, sausages and tomatoes. Luke was pouring out Rice Krispies, managing the large pack with great precision. Phoebe, like a little madam, was spooning chocolate yoghurt from a pot.

John kissed his mother-in-law good morning, then Harriet, who was engrossed in the weekend *Financial Times*. 'How did you sleep?' he said, taking his seat.

His mother-in-law was dressed rather formally, in a two-piece, as if she was about to go to church. John had noticed over the years that she always dressed smartly on Sunday, a throwback to her strict, religious upbringing. In her timid voice, she said, 'Well, thank you. Like a log. I always sleep so well here.'

Harriet, in a chunky fisherman's sweater, black hair unbrushed, looked up from the paper and tapped at the page with her finger. 'Do you ever read Arnie Wilson's column? He's the best ski writer – quite a funny piece about carver skis.'

'No, I haven't,' John said. He smiled absently and helped himself to some fruit salad, watching Luke spoon an obscene amount of sugar over his cereal.

'I think that's enough sugar, darling,' Naomi said.

Ignoring her, Luke dug the spoon into the bowl.

Irritated, Naomi snatched the bowl away from him. 'I said enough!'

Luke gave her an insolent stare. There was an awkward silence.

'Did you sleep well, Luke and Phoebe, darlings?' his mother-in-law asked.

Both of the twins ignored her.

'Answer Granny,' Naomi said, pouring milk onto Luke's cereal.

Phoebe licked her spoon clean, then, holding it up in front of her as if inspecting it, said, 'Sleeping is silly.'

Luke chewed a mouthful of cereal, then said, 'I don't sleep.'

'Really?' his grandmother said. 'You don't sleep?'

He spooned more Rice Krispies into his mouth and chewed slowly, and for a moment the crunching of the cereal was the only sound in the room.

John and Naomi exchanged a glance. John was signalling, *Hey, at least they're talking, this is a breakthrough, this is progress! Some kind of progress, anyhow* . . .

Harriet turned the page. 'Why don't you sleep, Luke?'

'Coz only dead things sleep,' he said.

This time John avoided catching Naomi's eye. He forked a slice of mango and ate it without tasting it, his eyes now on Harriet, watching her reaction.

'I slept last night,' Harriet said. 'But I don't think I'm dead!'

'I slept, too,' Luke's grandmother said. 'But that doesn't make me dead, darling, does it?'

Luke dug his spoon into his cereal, then said nonchalantly, 'You will be soon, Granny.'

85

Naomi's Diary

Am I wrong, making constant comparisons between L and P and Halley? My poor, darling, sweet, innocent Halley. OK, everyone knows that children say strange things, and Mum took it in good humour. But . . . thank God neither she nor Harriet noticed the guinea pigs had gone. What a really observant family I come from!

Halley, my little darling, I miss you so much. This may sound crazy, but when we first went to Dr Dettore's clinic, you know what I was hoping? That we'd get you back, but all made better. That our new baby would really be you, in a new, healthy incarnation. But there is nothing of you in Luke or Phoebe, at least, nothing that I can see. You were so gentle, so sweet, so loving. You said funny things, some-times, but I can't imagine, ever, you saying what Luke said to Mummy at breakfast today. I can't imagine you ever killing anything.

You may think this sounds strange, but there are times when I really sense you around me, holding my hand, telling me not to worry. If I didn't feel that, I really think I'd crack up. John is so much stronger than me. I wish I had the calm he has, that inner strength, that confidence about how things are going to turn out.

You were born on a Sunday and you died on a Sunday. Lots of people love Sundays, but I don't. I feel so down, sometimes, on Sundays. I'm down today. It was such a beautiful morning, and then it was ruined by what happened to Fudge and Chocolate. Now, this afternoon, it's raining and windy. Granny's watching an Agatha Christie movie on television and Auntie Harriet has gone home. P is on the kitchen floor in front of me, doing a three-dimensional jigsaw, and John is playing chess with L in the living room. Four o'clock and it's dark already. At six thirty they have evensong in the village church. Every Sunday. There are times, like now, when I feel a pull to go there. Are you pulling me?

Or am I just clutching at anything, in desperation?

86

John was smarting over his total annihilation at chess by his son.

Naomi said, 'This is what you wanted, John, isn't it? All this *hot-housing* you did in those months after they were born? Those hours you spent up in their room, endlessly playing them all that New Age music, all that talking to them and that tactile stuff. You wanted them to be smart, well, you've got what you wanted.'

It was Sunday evening and they were alone in the kitchen. Naomi's mother, suffering a migraine, had excused herself and gone to bed early. On Sunday evenings John always made supper, mostly something light and simple, which they would eat off trays on their laps in front of the television. Tonight he was making mushroom omelettes and a Greek salad.

'Not like this,' he said. 'I never intended this.'

'You laughed at my objections at the time. Now you're miffed because Luke beat you at chess.'

Noticing the box of guinea-pig food was on the floor, she picked it up and put it away in a cupboard.

'Naomi, he's *three years old*, for God's sake! A lot of kids aren't even potty trained at three! And he didn't just *beat* me. He wiped the floor with me. And the speed at which he made his moves – that was awesome.'

'A few years ago when those Rubik's Cube things were popular, adults had big problems doing them, but small children could do them in minutes. I remember someone saying it was because no one had told them it was impossible! Do children have an aptitude for puzzles that they lose when they grow older? Chess is a kind of puzzle, at one level, right?'

Standing over the pan, he concentrated for some moments on closing up the omelette. Normally he loved the smell of grilling mushrooms, but tonight his stomach was knotted with anxiety, and he had no appetite. 'Part of it is that kids at that age think about things less, they intellectualize about them less, they just get on and do it.'

'Maybe the same applies to chess? Nobody told Luke it was impossible to beat you, so he did, do you think? You told me you beat your grandfather when you were seven, and he was some kind of a chess master, wasn't he?'

'I beat him *once*,' John said. 'And that was after months of playing him. And—' He shrugged. 'Who knows? Maybe he deliberately let me win that one time.'

He cut the omelette in two with the spatula, scooped each of the halves onto plates, removed the pan from the heat, and pulled down the hob lid of the Aga. 'All set.'

They carried their trays into the living room; John went to the kitchen and returned with two glasses of Shiraz, then they sat in silence in front of the TV while they ate. *Antiques Roadshow* was on, the volume low.

'You do make the best omelettes ever,' Naomi said, suddenly sounding cheerier. Then she added, 'Maybe we should take the kids out more. Dr Michaelides might be right, that we're confining them in too much of a childhood world. They enjoyed the zoo.'

'Yep, they picked up a real love of animals from it, didn't they?' John retorted.

Naomi ate for some moments in silence.

'I'm sorry, hon,' John said. 'I shouldn't have said that.'

Naomi shrugged. They watched a meek, bearded man standing in front of a tray of Victorian surgical instruments.

'Maybe we should take them to a post-mortem,' John said. 'I'm sure they'd find that lot more fun than Mr Pineapple Head. Or take them to a dissection room at a medical college department of anatomy.'

'You're being silly.'

'I don't think so – that's the problem, they might really enjoy that. I think they want to see adult things.'

'So, you work at one of the techiest places in Britain. Why don't you take them on a tour of Morley Park? Show them the particle accelerator, show them the cold fusion lab.'

John put his tray on the floor.

'What's the matter?'

'I'm not hungry. I can't eat, I feel really – I don't know – I just wonder how we're going to cope; where we go from here.'

He stared at the television for some moments. A little old lady in a velvet hat was being told the value of a small marquetry box.

'This is a most exquisite piece of Tunbridge Ware,' the tweedy expert said. 'What do you know of its history?'

'Have you ever noticed,' Naomi said, 'on this programme they make a big deal about an object's history – and its *provenance*? Imagine if we were on this show – what would we be able to say about Luke and Phoebe's provenance?'

'I think it's more likely they'd be presenting us on the show as antiques,' he said. 'Relics of an extinct species. *Early twenty-first-century* Homo sapiens. *One beautiful female, English, in mint condition. And one rather tired*

Swede, atrophied brain, in need of some restoration. But with a big dick.'

Naomi giggled. Then she turned and kissed him on the cheek. 'We *will* cope, we'll find a way. We'll make good people of them, because *we* are good people. You're a good man. This whole nature-nurture thing – we will have to find ways to steer and influence them.'

John smiled, but he looked sad, bewildered. 'Luke frightened me this afternoon. I mean that seriously, he *frightened* me, it was like – I wasn't playing against a child – or anything human. It was just like playing against a machine. It actually got to a stage where I felt there wasn't any point in playing any more, because it was no fun.'

She sipped some wine. 'Maybe we should consider putting him in a chess tournament, see what happens if he's given a real challenge?'

'And have him hit all the headlines? A three-year-old chess prodigy is going to be national news, hon. It would flag him loud and clear up to the Disciples. We can't do that. What we are going to have to think very seriously about is special schooling.'

'Do they have schools for *machines*?' she said, only partly in jest.

John put an arm around her and squeezed her shoulder. 'What are they going to be like in ten years' time, do you think?'

'Ten years? What about in another three years? They're like miniature adults already. What do you think they're doing up there now in their room? Just hanging around until we go to bed, so they can start surfing the net all night? Designing new rocket-propulsion systems? Re-drafting the British Constitution?'

She ate the last of her omelette. 'Are you going to call

Dr Michaelides in the morning? And tell her about the guinea pigs? I'd like to know her thoughts.'

He nodded and stood up. 'Going to my den.'

'Do you have to work tonight? You look tired.'

'The book proofs – they have to be back in the States by the end of next week.'

*

Upstairs in his den, John opened up the web browser of his own computer. Then he began to look back at the history, starting with the day before the children had been given their own computer, then going back over the past months.

There were pages and pages of sites he had never visited himself. Again, as he had found on the children's computer, scores of visits to maths, physics and other science sites. There were visits to history sites, anthropological sites, geological, geographical. It was endless.

Nothing frivolous. His little three-year-olds hadn't used their internet surfing skills to do anything as dull as log on to kids' websites or chatrooms. It was just as if they were on one continuous quest, or hunger, for knowledge.

Three months back he came across the chess sites. Luke, or Luke and Phoebe together, had visited dozens of sites, ranging from learning the basic game to advanced strategies.

Then he knelt and switched on the children's computer on the floor. It began booting up, then the password request came up. He entered the new password he had typed in this morning, to stop the kids having access to it while it was confiscated. The message came up:

PASSWORD NOT VALID – RETRY.

He had deliberately put in a hard password, one that would be impossible to crack by chance. Maybe he'd made a mistake typing it just now? He tried again.

b*223*&65&*
PASSWORD NOT VALID – RETRY.

He'd written it down on a slip of paper, which he had put in his back trouser pocket, and dug it out, to check. It was correct. He typed it in again.

PASSWORD NOT VALID – RETRY.

Shaking his head in disbelief, he tried one more time, with the same result. And now he was pretty sure what had happened.

The children, or one of them, at any rate, must have been in here and somehow cracked his password. Then changed it to a new one.

87

The room was small, the window panes so rotted and waterlogged that the paint barely still stuck to the wood, and the putty was crumbling. The glass shook in the wind. The sky was grey, flecked with rain, and the sea beyond the promenade railing a heaving, ominous slurry.

There was a single bed, a television he had never watched, a table, a washbasin, a mirror, a couple of chairs, and his Bible. His crucifix hung on the wall in place of a print of Constable's *Haywain*, which he had taken down and placed on top of the wardrobe.

Every morning he rose in this small, cold room, in this foreign city, said his prayers, then opened his laptop and logged on to the internet in anticipation. But so far, he had been disappointed. Every day he watched the flow of data in disgust. Effluent pouring into his mailbox. Every morning he was presented with fresh opportunities to make his fortune, to make the acquaintance of ladies who wished to lure him to their pages. He noticed them, oh yes, and they made him angry, and they made him sad and they made him glad.

Glad that soon he would be going away from all this, abandoning it to its own putrefaction. Soon he would be in the arms of Lara, and they would make children, make them their own way, God's way, not the Devil's Spawn's way.

Children, obey your parents in the Lord for this is right. Honour your father and mother – which is the first com-

mandment – with a promise – that it may go well with you and that you may enjoy long life on the earth. Ephesians 6: 1–3.

He should not have this possession, for it was a sinful object, but he could not be without it. It was all he had of her. Lara had given it to him the morning they had parted. A small colour photograph of her standing in a simple summer dress, on the deck of the Californian ranch house where they had met. She was smiling, her long black hair tumbling over her bare shoulders, over her skin that was like silk. It was more than three years ago, but he could still remember the scents of her body, every smell, every touch, every word, promise, every caress of her breath against his face. *I will wait for you, Timon, my darling angel, I will wait for you until the end of time.*

Soon, Lara, God willing, soon!

Seated at the wooden table, beneath the miserly warmth of the single bar heater on the wall, he looked down the list of new emails, sifting through the filth, and suddenly, today, Monday morning, he felt a beat of excitement as he read the email that came with no signature and from an address he did not recognize.

He turned rivers into a desert, flowing springs into thirsty ground, and fruitful land into a salt waste, because of the wickedness of those who lived there. He turned the desert into pools of water and the parched ground into flowing springs; there he brought the hungry to live and they prepared the foundations of a city where they could settle. They sowed seeds and planted vineyards that yielded a beautiful harvest; he blessed them, and their numbers greatly

increased, and he did not let their herds
diminish. Psalm 107.

It was the message for which he had been waiting six lonely weeks. It was the call for him to do his duty and then, finally, to come home!

He logged off, his heart soaring. Thinking hard and quickly. There was a lot to be done, so much, but he was prepared, it would not take long.

He ate breakfast downstairs at a table on his own, saying a silent grace, avoiding eye contact and conversation with other guests. As he ate, he ran through his mental shopping list. Some of the items he had obtained already, by mail order, via the internet. He had been taught of the need to buy everything separately, in separate shops, in separate towns. Being a foreigner, he would be remembered more easily than a native English person. He would stick out. An American in Sussex, in January. A curiosity.

But he would be gone long before it mattered.

88

At midday on Tuesday morning, Dr Sheila Michaelides sat at her pine desk in her consulting room. She looked distinctly frosty.

Through the window behind the psychologist, Naomi watched rain falling on the lush green walled garden. She could see a thrush on the grass, digging with its beak, tugging out a reluctant worm.

'Why didn't either of you tell me the truth about your children?' the psychologist said.

'I'm sorry,' Naomi said. 'I'm not with you.'

'Aren't you? *Dr Dettore?* I think that name means something to you, doesn't it?' Her expression hardened to ice.

John and Naomi looked at each other, increasingly uncomfortable.

'Yes, we went to him,' John said.

'But not for the reasons you might think,' Naomi added.

'What reasons might I think, Mrs Klaesson?'

Naomi twisted her hands together in silence. 'That – that we – wanted—' Her voice tailed.

'Designer babies?' the psychologist said.

'No,' Naomi said. 'Not that at all.'

'Oh?'

Naomi pointed at the photographs of the two small, laughing boys on her desk. 'Are those your sons?'

'Yes, they are.'

'And they're healthy, normal little boys?'

'Not so little. Louis is twenty and Philip is twenty-two.'

'But they are healthy, normal?' Naomi said.

'Let's concentrate on your children, Mrs Klaesson, if you don't mind, that's what you've come to me about.'

'Actually, I do mind,' said Naomi angrily.

'Hon,' John said, cautioning.

'Don't *hon* me,' she snapped. Then, turning her focus back on the psychologist, she said, 'We went to Dr Dettore because he offered us hope, he was the only doctor in the world at the time capable of offering us hope, OK?'

'What kind of hope did he offer you?'

'A *normal* child. One that would be free of the bloody awful gene that John and I were both carrying. That's all we went to him for. So that he could give us a child free of this gene.'

'He talked you into having twins?'

'No,' John said. 'We wanted a son, that was all. We never asked for twins.'

There was a long silence, then the psychologist said, 'Are you aware of any of the other children who have been born to parents who went to see him?'

'Some,' John said.

'Three sets of twins, all born to parents who went to him, have been murdered in the past couple of years,' Naomi told her. 'There's a link to some freaky religious group – a bunch of fanatics.'

'That's why we don't talk about it,' John added. 'We've been advised to keep quiet.'

'A little hard when it's out on the internet,' Sheila Michaelides said.

'That's why we keep a low profile,' John said.

'What difference does it make to you?' Naomi

demanded. 'Are Luke and Phoebe second-class citizens because they were conceived in a different way? Is that what you are telling us?'

'Not at all. But if you remember, I asked you both if there was anything you could tell me that might have some bearing on your children's behaviour; you never mentioned that you had designed their genetic make-up – I think that might have been helpful for me to know from the start. Don't you?'

'No, I—' Naomi stopped in mid-sentence as John raised a calming hand.

'Hon, she's right. We should have told her.'

Naomi stared down at the carpet, wretchedly. She felt like she was back at school, being scolded by a teacher. 'Dr Michaelides,' she said. 'This is not how it might seem to you at the moment. We just wanted Dr Dettore to make sure those bad genes were taken out.'

'That was all?'

'More or less,' Naomi said.

'More or less?' the psychologist echoed.

There was an awkward silence. Finally John said, 'We agreed to make a few positive changes – just to help enhance our baby's abilities in some areas.'

Dr Michaelides looked at him sceptically. 'What areas, exactly?'

John suddenly felt very defensive, as if he, too, were being carpeted by a schoolteacher. 'Resistance to illness – we boosted their immune system.'

Naomi butted in. 'When we say *their* – that – that's not strictly true. We actually went to Dr Dettore wanting to have one child—'

'A boy,' John said. 'Another son.'

'And yet he persuaded you to have twins?'

377

'He said nothing about us having twins,' John repeated. 'It wasn't until Naomi was advanced in pregnancy that we discovered she was carrying twins. All the modifications we selected were of a very minor nature. We wanted to ensure our son would be reasonably tall. That he would have good eyesight, good hearing. We accepted an option that would enable him to get by on less sleep when he was older. Another that would give him more energy from less nutrition.'

'And we agreed also to allow some enhancement to his learning abilities,' Naomi said.

'Less sleep,' the psychologist said. 'Enhancements to the children's learning abilities. And now you are concerned because they seem to be up during the night, trying to learn more? What did you expect was going to happen?'

'Not this,' Naomi said. 'We just wanted to give them a good start in life. We never intended turning them into—'

The psychologist waited patiently as Naomi bit her tongue.

'Freaks,' John said. 'I think that's the word my wife doesn't want to say.'

'That's how you are beginning to view your children, Dr Klaesson? As freaks?'

'Not freaks in – I guess – in a *circus* sense of the word. I mean in the sense that they are different to other kids. Almost – like – wired differently.'

'I think they *are* wired differently,' the psychologist said.

There was a long silence, then the psychologist continued. 'If I'm going to be able to help you, you are going to have to be totally honest with me from this point on.' She fixed her eyes on each of them in turn. 'I want you to tell me – when you went to Dr Dettore – was he offering you some kind of a standard package?'

'In what sense?' Naomi replied.

'In the sense that he had some kind of a deal that he offered to his patients – clients?' She raised her hand and ticked her fingers in turn. 'A certain IQ, a guaranteed height, specific sporting skills – did you get the feeling there were certain things that he could do that all went together?'

'No,' John said. 'We had a huge amount of choice.'

'Too much choice,' Naomi added. 'It was over-whelming.'

They took it in turns to go through as much of the list of options as they could remember. When they had finished, the psychologist turned to her computer screen for some moments. Then she leaned back in her chair and looked thoughtfully at John and Naomi.

'I've been doing some research. Since I saw you at the end of last week, I've heard by phone or email from twenty-six child psychologists – all of whom are seeing children who were conceived at Dr Dettore's offshore clinic.'

'I thought this information is confidential,' Naomi said.

'It is,' the psychologist replied. 'And that's why the people I contacted spoke to the parents about sharing the information and allowing me to make contact with them.'

She glanced back at the screen, then, putting her hands on her desk, leaned forward. 'All the children are twins, and in each case this was a surprise to the parents. All have identical advanced intelligence, advanced looks for their age, and identical behavioural problems to Luke and Phoebe.'

89

John and Naomi said nothing for a full minute, both of them absorbing what Dr Michaelides had just told them.

'Are you suggesting they are clones?' John asked, feeling the sudden tightness of panic in his throat.

'No. I had several of the parents send me photographs because I did wonder that. None of the children look the same.' She smiled. 'I see a lot of parents and children, and I can assure you that there are many very clear points of physical resemblance between yourselves and Luke and Phoebe.'

'Thank God,' Naomi said.

'The same intelligence, the same advanced looks, the same behavioural problems with all the twins – how can that be?' John asked. 'We only selected a specific number of options – other parents will have made different choices – some a lot more radical than ours. How can the children all be so similar?'

'Maybe for the same reason that you all wanted one child and ended up having twins?' the psychologist suggested, with a quizzical expression.

Naomi stared back at her. 'Meaning what, exactly?'

'That perhaps Dr Dettore had an agenda of his own, is what Dr Michaelides is implying,' John said.

Naomi nodded. 'You know, deep down I have felt that ever since they were born.'

'Your Dr Dettore seems to have a pretty ruthless reputation among scientists,' Sheila Michaelides said. 'You just have to read some of his press interviews over the years to see a man with complete tunnel vision and no regard for medical ethics, nor any of his critics.'

'You think he used Naomi – and dozens of other mothers – as a kind of unwitting *host womb* for an experiment?'

'It is a distinct possibility, I'm afraid.'

John and Naomi looked at each other, both momentarily lost for words.

'But this shouldn't affect your relationship with your children,' Dr Michaelides went on. 'Even if their genetic make-up isn't how you ordered it, they are still your children, your flesh and blood.'

'Where do we go from here?' Naomi asked grimly. 'Into some tunnel of perpetual social experiments? Are Luke and Phoebe going to become lab rats to a global bunch of shrinks and scientists?'

'What about the whole *nature versus nurture* argument?' John said. 'Dr Dettore told us that whatever we did with the genes of our child – children – that would only ever be a small element of it. He said the major part of shaping a child would always be down to us as parents. If we love them enough and care for them enough, can't we in time influence them and shape them? Won't it be my wife and I who matter more to them, in the long run, than anything Dr Dettore has done?'

'Under normal circumstances I would agree with you to a considerable extent. I talked to you last week about *epistemic boundedness*, the way that humans are hard-wired, and the limits of normal human brainpower. But the manipulative behavioural patterns of your children suggest that normal restraints of human existence are just not there. Your children at the age of three are showing characteristics I would expect to find in adolescents five times their age.'

She twisted the cap on a bottle of mineral water and filled a glass on her desk. 'The most important thing for any parent is to *connect* with their child. To establish a bond. It seems to me that's what you don't have and it's what you're seeking. Is that a fair comment?'

'Yes,' Naomi said. 'Absolutely. I'm their servant, that's all. I wash them, feed them, clean up after them. That's all I'm able to do – and it's all they seem to want me to do. The other day Luke cut himself – but he didn't come to me for a cuddle, he went and showed it to Phoebe. He never thanked me when I put a plaster on it.'

'I think it might be helpful for you to speak to some of these other parents, very definitely, if they are willing.'

'Are there any others in England?' Naomi asked.

'Not that I have discovered so far. But there must be quite a lot more out there that I haven't heard about.'

'I'll speak to any parent, anywhere in the world,' Naomi said. 'Willingly.'

The psychologist drank some water. 'I'll see what I can arrange – but I must warn you, don't set your hopes too high on getting any magical answers. All the people I have spoken to tell me the parents are in the same situation as yourselves.'

'Have any of these children killed their pets, like Luke and Phoebe did?' John asked.

'I haven't had in-depth discussions with many of them,' she said. 'But a pair of twins in La Jolla, Southern California, strangled the family's pet spaniel after their father had complained about its incessant barking. They thought their father would be pleased that they had solved a problem for him. A pair of twins in Krefeld in Germany cut the throat of their family cat after their mother had screamed when it brought a mouse into the kitchen. I'm afraid it seems that the inability to distinguish between what is alive and dead may be a common trait. It's not that they are wicked in any sense – more that they have a wholly different value system. What you and I think is normal, they can't see.'

'But we must be able to educate them, surely?' Naomi said. 'There must be ways we can deal with them as parents. That's what you have to show us.'

'I think it would be very helpful to speak with other parents,' John said. 'We should take her offer up, hon. I think we should talk to as many as possible.'

'You obviously have happy, successful children, Dr Michaelides,' Naomi said. 'You probably can't appreciate how – so – so bloody *inadequate*. That's what I feel. So empty. It's like I'm just some discarded container they hitched a ride in. I want the babies I gave birth to back, Dr Michaelides, that's what I want. I want my children back, not as freaks, but as *children*. That's what I want from you.'

The psychologist smiled at her sympathetically. 'I understand; it's what any mother would want. But I don't know that I can give you that. Before you can move forward in your relationship with Luke and Phoebe, your goals are going to have to change. We're going to have to do some redefining.'

'How do you mean?'

'In the first instance, it might help for you to stop thinking of them so much as children, and more as *people*. You hired a children's entertainer for their birthday party, right?' She stared at them.

'You think that was a mistake?' John asked.

'I think you are going to have to change your mindsets totally. If you want to connect to them, it may be that you've got to start treating them as if they are teenagers, because that's how old they are intellectually.'

'What about their childhood?' Naomi said. 'And what teenager is going to be interested in them? This is just – I mean—' She shook her head in despair. 'OK, I know there have been child prodigies who have gone to university as young as twelve, but you read about them years later, and they're usually burnt out by thirty. What you are telling us is that we should tear up the rule books.'

'Mrs Klaesson,' the psychologist said, gently but insistently, 'there are no rule books to tear up. I'm afraid you and your husband threw them all out of the window the day you went to Dr Dettore.'

90

Staring through the car windscreen at the sodden country-side, Naomi thought, glumly, *January*. Those flat weeks after the Christmas decorations had come down, when all the joy seemed to have gone from winter, and you still had February ahead of you, and much of March before the weather started to relent.

Two o'clock; already the light was starting to fade. In a couple hours of it would be almost dark. As John swung into their drive, the Saab splashed through a deep puddle and water burst over the windscreen. The wipers clouted it away. Naomi stared at the stark, bare hedgerows. A hen pheasant scuttled forlornly along the grass verge, as if it was a toy with a battery that was running down.

The cattle grid clattered, then the tyres scrunched on the gravel. John halted the car in front of the house, between Naomi's grimy white Subaru and her mother's little Nissan Micra.

With the wipers stopped, the windscreen quickly became opaque with rain. Naomi turned towards John and was alarmed by how bleak he looked. 'Darling, I know I've been against having anyone in to look after them, and last week I totally rejected Dr Michaelides's suggestion that they go to some special school – but after seeing her again now, I feel differently. I think she might be right, that they need specialist care – nurturing – teaching – whatever they want to call it.'

'You don't think that's admitting defeat?' John said.

'Us letting ourselves get down about Luke and Phoebe would be admitting defeat. We have to stop feeling we've failed in any way. We have to find a way to turn their lives into a positive for them – and for us.'

He sat in silence. Then he touched her cheek with his hand. 'I love you,' he said. 'I really do love you. I'm sorry for all I've put you through.'

'I love you, too. It was your strength that got me through Halley.' She smiled tearfully. 'Now we have two healthy children. We – we've—' She sniffed. 'We have to count our blessings, don't you think?'

'Sure.' He nodded. 'You're right. That's what we have to do.'

Ducking their heads against the rain, they hurried in through the front door. Peeling off her coat, Naomi called out, 'Hi! We're back!'

John could hear voices, American accents. He wrestled himself out of his wet coat, hung it on the stand, then followed Naomi through into the living room.

Her mother was sitting on the sofa, in an Arran sweater way too big for her, working on a tapestry in front of the television. An old black-and-white movie was on, the sound turned up almost deafeningly loud, the way she always had it.

'How did it go?' her mother asked them.

'OK, thanks,' Naomi replied, turning the volume down a little. 'Where are they?'

'Playing on the computer upstairs.'

'Anybody call?' she asked.

'No phone calls,' she said. 'The phone's been very quiet.' She frowned at something in her tapestry for some moments, then said absently, 'We had a visitor, though, about an hour after you left.'

'Oh?' Naomi said.

'A very pleasant young man. He was American, I think.'

'American?' Naomi echoed, a tad uneasily. 'What did he want?'

'Oh, he'd come to the wrong address – he was trying to find *something* farm – I can't remember exactly – I'd never heard of it.'

'What did he look like, this guy?' John asked.

Her mother took some moments of careful thought, then said, 'He was nicely dressed, very polite. He wore a shirt and tie, and a dark suit. But there was one thing – he did something your father did often, you know? Your father used to put on his tie, but forget in his hurry to do up some of the buttons on his shirt beneath. This young man had forgotten two buttons on his shirt and I could see, beneath his shirt, he was wearing one of those religious crosses – what are they called – gosh, my memory's so bad these days, I keep forgetting words! What on earth are they called? Oh yes, of course, how silly of me – a crucifix.'

91

American. Crucifix.

John sat in his den, his whole damned body shaking.

This man, it didn't have to mean anything bad. It didn't have to mean that—

Except that a bunch of crazed American fanatics, calling themselves Disciples, had been murdering couples who had been to Dr Dettore and had twins, and now an American wearing a cross around his neck had turned up to a remote English house where there just happened to be a couple who had been to Dr Dettore and had twins.

He tried to think what further security measures they could take. They'd had toughened glass put in the windows. Window locks. Security lights. High-quality door locks. An alarm that rang through to a control centre. Panic buttons. Maybe he needed to get Naomi and the children away from here, for a while, at any rate. Go to Sweden, perhaps?

Or check into a hotel? But for how long?

They were looking into getting guard dogs. And there was one other security option they hadn't yet taken. The firm who had done all their installations had included details and a quote at the time, but it had been quite expensive and they hadn't seen the point. Now he regretted that decision. He went to the filing cabinet, pulled open the bottom drawer and lifted out the file marked *Security Systems.*

Then he rang the firm and asked how quickly they

could install the security cameras they had quoted on. He was told it would be about ten days. John told them if they could do it tomorrow, he would order it now. After keeping him on hold for a couple of minutes he was told they would be along at nine o'clock the next morning to install them.

When he had hung up, he then typed out an email to Kalle Almtorp at the Swedish embassy in Kuala Lumpur.

> **Kalle, hope you had a good Christmas and New Year – no snow, I guess??**
>
> **In December you emailed that your contact at the FBI says they now have a lead in their search for these Disciples of the Third Millennium. I'm asking because a potentially worrying situation has arisen here and I need to know just how concerned I should be about it. Any further information you could let me have, as a matter of great urgency, would be much appreciated.**
>
> **Love to Anna and the kids.**
> **Hälsningar!**
> **John**

He sent the email then went upstairs to the box room, where Luke and Phoebe were sitting on the floor in front of their computer. They must have heard him coming, he thought, because he saw the screen flicker as he entered the room, as if they had hurriedly switched from whatever they had been looking at to something innocuous.

'Hi!' he said.

Neither of them looked at him.

More loudly now, he said, 'Luke! Phoebe! Hallo!'

Both turned their heads very slowly, in unison, and

said, 'Hello.' Then they stared at him, for some moments, smiling, as if they were reacting as they were expected to.

Cold air eddied through his veins. They looked too neat and tidy, too immaculate. Phoebe wore a bottle-green tracksuit and white trainers; Luke wore a navy roll-neck jumper, neatly pressed jeans, spotless trainers. Neither had a hair out of place. For a moment he had the impression he was looking at robots, not at real people, not at his children. It made him want to back out of the room, but instead he persevered, trying to put into practice what Dr Michaelides had just told them they should do.

As nonchalantly and cheerily as he could, he knelt down and presented his cheek first to Luke, then to Phoebe. Both of them drew their faces sharply back, in turn.

'No kiss for Daddy?'

'Kissing leads to sex,' Luke said, dismissively turning back to the screen.

'What? What did you say, Luke?' John asked, astonished, all kinds of alarm bells suddenly ringing, wondering, hoping, desperately hoping that he had misheard his son. But moments later, Phoebe confirmed that he hadn't.

'We don't kiss,' Phoebe said haughtily. 'We don't want to be abused.' Then she, too, turned back to the screen.

'Hey,' John said, floundering for a reply. 'Hey, you listen to me—' He stared at the shiny casing of the computer, at the keyboard, at the mouse, at the multi-coloured mouse pad, his nostrils filled with the sour reek of plastic. He felt numb.

Beyond numb.

Luke moved the mouse and John saw the cursor sweep up the screen and stop on a square. He double-clicked and the square opened, like a miniature window, to reveal a flashing sequence of numbers.

John stood up, went to the wall, and pulled out the plug. Both children looked up at him without even a hint of surprise on their faces. 'Excuse me,' he said. 'What is this talk about abuse? Where's this from? The internet?'

Neither of them said anything.

'Is that what you think about your mummy and I? That we're going to abuse you? Because it's not a very funny joke.'

Both of them stood up and walked out of the room.

'Luke! Phoebe!' John said, barely controlling his anger. 'Come back, I'm talking to you!'

He burst out of the door after them and yelled at them. 'LUKE! PHOEBE! COME BACK HERE THIS INSTANT!'

Continuing to ignore him, they went downstairs.

He started after them, then stopped. How was he supposed to deal with this? It was like dealing with moody teenagers. Is that what they were?

He was really trembling badly now, his brain misty with anger. He just wanted to grab hold of them, shake them, shake the little bastards until the truth fell out of them. But Sheila Michaelides had told them that confrontation with the twins would just drive them further into their shells – exactly like teenagers, he thought.

Oh sure, easy to say, Dr Michaelides – but how the hell are we supposed to avoid getting angry when they say something like this?

Remembering for a moment his reason for coming upstairs, he went into his bedroom, took the two keys that were hidden underneath his handkerchiefs, then opened his wardrobe, pushed his suits and shirts over to one side, the hangers clacking, to reveal the steel gun cabinet he'd had fixed into the wall. Then he unlocked the door and lifted out the heavy shotgun that nestled inside.

It was a Russian-made twelve-bore, which he had bought, second-hand, after a three-month wait for the licence, at the same time as they had put in the other security measures here. He had never used the gun, and Naomi had disapproved strongly at the time. Nonetheless, he had always felt better at night for knowing it was there.

It seemed heavier than he had remembered; the stock was warm, the barrels as cold as ice. He broke it open, admiring for an instant the finely engineered movement, and squinted down the shiny insides of the barrels. As he closed it again, he heard the reassuring click. Then, raising the gun, peering across the pinhead sight and down the top of the barrels, he pulled the trigger.

Nothing happened.

Safety catch! he remembered. He slid it off, pointed the gun at the window, gripped tightly and squeezed first the right trigger, then the left one, hearing the sharp click each time.

Kneeling, he pushed the gun under the bed, far enough in so that it was out of sight. Next he took the box of ammunition from the cabinet, broke it open and put four cartridges in the drawer in his bedside table. Then he put the box back in the cabinet, locked it, and put the keys back in place beneath his handkerchiefs.

He sat on the bed for some moments, thinking what else he could do, what other precautions he could take, and all the time hoping to hell he was just overreacting, that this American had been innocent. In all likelihood they were worrying about nothing. Hell, his mother-in-law had never been to the States, she didn't like to fly, so she could have mistaken his accent.

He went downstairs to the kitchen where Naomi was making a late snack lunch for them all and Luke and Phoebe were sitting at the kitchen table

Leaning against the Aga for warmth, he said to his mother-in-law, 'Anne, this man who came to the door – he was definitely American?'

'Very definitely.' She was emphatic.

John thought for a moment. 'You said he was looking for an address – he was lost or something?'

'Yes,' she said. 'John, it *is* pretty confusing around here, first time you come. I got lost, too. You're not very well signposted.'

'I don't think he was lost,' Phoebe said sharply, without looking away from the television.

There was a brief silence. 'Did you see this man, Phoebe?' Naomi asked.

'You don't have to see someone to know they're not lost,' Phoebe said scornfully.

'So why do you think he wasn't lost, Phoebe?' John asked.

Still without moving her eyes from the television, Phoebe flapped away his question with her hand. 'We're watching the show, please stop interrupting.'

John and Naomi exchanged a glance. He saw his mother-in-law smiling at her impertinence.

Insolence.

He should have slapped Phoebe down for it, so should Naomi, but it was still a major achievement to get the children to speak at all, still a novelty to hear them.

'It was a farm he was looking for?' John said.

'I think that's what he said. And – oh yes – feed!'

'Feed?'

'Agricultural feed – he was selling agricultural feed!'

Then her brow furrowed. 'Although I have to say he really didn't look a terribly *rural* type.'

John went to his study and phoned, in turn, each of the five local farming families around them whom he had met. Three of them answered and confirmed they'd not had any visitor fitting that description. They each promised to call him if the American did turn up. At the other two numbers, he got the voice mail, and left messages.

John then tried to turn his attention to his book and make use of this sudden extra time away from work. But it was hopeless, he couldn't concentrate; he was too worried about this American with his crucifix.

Naomi called him back down for his lunch. After he had eaten he put on his Barbour, a rain hat and wellington boots, and went out for a walk across the fields, circumnavigating the house, keeping close enough to be able to beat any car coming up the drive back to it.

A thought was going round and round in his mind:

What if they had been in when the American had come?

Later in the afternoon, there was a reply from his email to Kalle. It was an automated response, telling him that Kalle was away from the office for the next ten days. A short while later the two remaining farmers returned his calls. Neither of them had had any visitors today.

92

At half past five in the afternoon, John's mother-in-law set off for her drive back home to Bath. It was already pitch dark outside, and the rain was still tipping down. John put on his Barbour and wellingtons and, carrying a golfing umbrella, escorted her out to her car. He kissed her good-bye, then stood in the porch with Naomi until the tail lights had disappeared down the drive.

Although he got on fine with her, he normally felt a sense of relief when she had departed. It was good to have the house back to themselves.

Normally.

But this afternoon he felt a deep sense of anxiety, and wished she could have stayed longer. With a torch, he made a circuit of the house, checking that the sensors for all the outside lights were working properly, comforted a little by the sudden flood of brilliant light as each one came on.

In the living room, Naomi flopped down on a sofa, grateful for the chance of a few minutes to look at the paper. She had a headache that was getting worse by the minute. Luke and Phoebe were lounging back on the other sofa, engrossed in watching an old pop video of the group The Corrs on MTV.

'*Thunder only happens when it's raining,*' they were singing.

Suddenly Phoebe grabbed the remote and turned the volume down.

'That's not true!' Phoebe said. 'Thunder does not only happen when it's raining. Why are they saying that? Mummy? Why are they saying that?'

Naomi lowered the paper, pleasantly surprised that Phoebe was addressing her. 'Saying what, darling?'

'That thunder only happens when it's raining. Everybody knows that a thunderstorm is a storm with visible lightning and audible thunder. The arrangement of storms within any spectrum is determined by the updraught strength, relative frequency of the updraught strength, depending on category, and relative threats of the updraught categories. I mean, are they talking about single-cell storms, multicell storm lines or supercells? They're the kinds that produce severe weather elements, right? But that's only talking about a fraction of the bigger picture. There are forty thousand thunderstorms a day in the world, which is like a quarter of a million flashes every minute. So what the fuck do they know?'

'Phoebe!' She was staggered by the knowledge that came from her daughter's mouth. And horrified by the swearing. 'Don't say that word, it's horrible.'

Phoebe shrugged like an antsy teenager.

'Would one of you do something for me, please?' Naomi asked. 'I have a really bad headache. Would you run upstairs and bring me some paracetamol – there's a box in my bathroom cabinet – the one with the mirror on it?'

Luke turned to her. 'What kind of a headache do you have, Mummy?'

'A bad one, that's what kind.'

'Is it from trauma or from mental stress?' Phoebe asked.

'Or from intracranial disorder?' Luke added.

'Or migraine?' said Phoebe. 'That's really quite important to know.'

Naomi looked at her children for some moments,
barely able to believe her ears. She gave them an answer
she hoped Sheila Michaelides would have approved of.
'It's a two-paracetamol kind of a headache, OK?'

There was a moment of silence, then Luke said, 'Then
I don't understand.'

'Nor do I,' said Phoebe. 'Not exactly.'

'You don't understand what?' Naomi responded.

Luke puckered his mouth, clearly deep in thought.
'Well, it's like this, I suppose. You want one of us to go
upstairs to get you two paracetamol because you have a
headache, if we are understanding you correctly?'

'You are understanding me correctly, Luke, yes.'

Again his whole mouth puckered in thought. Then he
turned again to his sister and whispered to her. Phoebe
shot a glance at Naomi, frowned, then whispered back.

Luke again addressed his mother. 'We're really quite
confused about this, Mummy.'

Naomi swallowed her exasperation. 'What are you
confused about, darling? Exactly? It's quite simple.' She
screwed up her eyes as the pain worsened, lowered her
head and pressed her fingers into her temples. 'Mummy
has a really bad headache. She would really be grateful if
one of you would run upstairs and get two paracetamols
for her. That's all.'

'Let me explain what we don't understand,' Luke said.
'You have a headache. Headaches don't affect your legs,
Mummy. So you are quite capable of going up to the
bathroom yourself.'

She saw a cheeky, teasing grin on his face for a fleeting
instant, so fleeting she almost thought she had imagined

it. Then he got up, shrugged, went upstairs and came down with two capsules.

*

Some while later, Naomi woke, with a start, on the sofa. A rock band she did not recognize was playing on the television, but the sound was muted. She could smell a tantalizing aroma of cooking meat. Was John cooking dinner?

She hauled herself off the sofa and walked through into the kitchen. And stopped in her tracks, in amazement.

Phoebe was perched on a stool, minding a large frying pan on the hob. Luke, on another stool, was dicing peeled potatoes, a cookbook open beside him.

As if sensing her coming into the room, Phoebe turned, with a butter-wouldn't-melt-in-her-mouth smile. 'Hi, Mummy!' she said cheerily.

'What – what's going on?' Naomi said, smiling back.

'Daddy's busy working. Because you're not feeling well, Luke and I decided to cook dinner for us tonight. We're making Swedish meatballs and Janssen's Temptation – potatoes with cream and anchovies, which you have every Christmas Eve, and we know you love!'

For some moments, Naomi was speechless.

93

Lara was cold. Cold and wide awake in her bed in the dormitory building at the foot of the cliff, directly beneath the monastery. A storm was blowing. The Aegean Sea, crashing on the rocks less than a hundred metres away, sounded like it was about to swallow the building, maybe even the entire atoll. Massive explosions of water sounding like thunder.

God loves me, and Jesus loves me, and the Virgin Mary loves me.

And my Disciple loves me.

And I belong.

Those were the things that mattered to Lara. As a child, she had always felt herself belonging on a higher plane than others around her. She felt an outsider, disconnected from her family, unable to fit in at school and to relate to the others there. She was a loner, yet she hated being a loner. All she had wanted was to *belong*. To be a part of something, to be wanted, needed.

She loved these people she was with now, and the vision they shared. She agreed with every view they held. She loved the fact that they understood you couldn't just lock yourself away from the world, but sometimes you had to go out into it, tread along its sewers, carry out the Lord's fight against Satan for Him.

She could hear, suddenly, above the din of the waves, the faint drumming of the wooden gong that summoned the monks to matins, echoing around the monastery walls high above her. It was half past two in the morning.

This was her third January here, and each of them had been equally harsh. Despite the window in her room being shut, she felt the blast of the icy squall outside on her face, and pulled the bedclothes tighter around her.

Then she pulled her hands together.

Praying.

Praying for the man in the photograph on her wooden dresser. Praying with a warm heart and with cold hands that were red and coarse from manual work. That sweet, sweet Disciple, with his gentle voice and his soft touch, and all the dreamy promises they had made to each other.

Timon.

The memories of that week of praying side by side with him in the chapel, and that one night she had been permitted to spend alone with him, still sustained her over three years on. They were preserved in her heart by the love the Virgin Mary had for her, for all three of them, for herself, for beautiful Timon, and for beautiful Saul, asleep in his crib just beyond the end of his bed, who would be two and a half soon.

He had not yet met his father.

She smiled. Imagining Timon's expression when he saw his child, his son, his boy, his baby, this beautiful baby whom God and the Virgin Mary had given them. The same Virgin Mary who had spared her from having to kill the Infidel Cardelli family in Como. God had sent her to a convent there, while she was pregnant with Saul, to wait for His command to strike against the family and their twin boy and girl spawned from Satan.

But then the Virgin Mary had sent an avalanche of snow down on to the Cardellis' car as they negotiated a pass in the Dolomites, sweeping them off the road and down into a deep ravine, burying the wreckage beneath a quilt of pure, white flakes.

Come let us reason together, says the Lord. Though your sins are like scarlet they shall be as white as snow. Isaiah 1.

Now, every day and night her prayers were the same. *Please God, Sweet Lord Jesus and Blessed Mother Mary, bring Timon home to my arms.*

So I may feel his seed entering inside me and grow more babies who will become strong here, away from the sewers of the world. Babies that Timon and I can nurture, who will grow up alongside all the other babies here to be fine, strong people, to become, one day, soldiers in your army, who will go out into the world and destroy evil.

Please bring him home to me soon.

94

The rain beat down relentlessly on the Disciple's car. This was the weather he had prayed for. On a night like this, no nosey villager would be out walking their dog, wondering what a strange vehicle was doing in the car park behind the schoolhouse.

Inside the little rental Ford it sounded like a never-ending sack of pebbles was being emptied onto the roof. The car smelled of plastic and velour and damp clothes. His body itched all over; he had broken out in a rash.

Nerves.

He felt terribly alone, suddenly, as if God was putting him through this final test, here on this vile night, in this foreign land, with rain spiking the tar-black puddles all around him. But he would do it. For God and for his Master and for the love of Lara, he would do it.

Under the miserly glow of the dome light he unfolded the plans for the Infidels' house, which he had photocopied on Tuesday morning at the County Planning Office in Lewes, and looked at them carefully one final time. Ground Floor. First Floor. North Elevation. East Elevation. South Elevation. West Elevation.

The layout was simple, there wasn't anything to it: the master bedroom was evident, and the Spawn would be in one of the three smaller rooms. Speed was crucial. In his briefing, three years back – but as clear as if it had been only hours ago – his Master had impressed on him the need for speed. To remember the ticking clock. To never forget every mission has a ticking clock.

Six minutes on this one tonight. That was all he could risk. He had found out the name of the alarm company from the box on the outside of the house on his visit to the property on Tuesday morning. Then it had been easy. He had phoned the company, given his name as the Infidel's and explained a problem he was having with the system. From the reply the engineer gave him, he now knew everything about the system.

From this he could work out that he would have six minutes to be finished and out, across the fields, heading back to his car.

And then.

The 3.30 a.m. reservation on the Eurotunnel Shuttle. He had practised the route on Sunday and Monday night. With the minimal traffic at that hour, and adhering strictly to every speed limit, the drive should take comfortably less than two hours from here.

By 5.30 a.m. Continental time, he would be on the autoroute heading to Paris. There he would leave the Ford in the long-term car park at Charles de Gaulle Airport, and take the transfer bus to Orly Airport. Plenty of leeway to make the 11.05 a.m. flight to Athens. Then two hours later the connecting flight to Thessaloniki. From there, a taxi to the port of Ouranoupoli where, after dark, the Master's launch would be waiting to ferry him the twenty kilometres across the Aegean Sea to the monastic island.

To Lara.

He looked at his watch. It was half past ten. In a little over twenty-four hours he would be in Lara's arms, at the start of his new life, in the Promised Land. And in the sight of God.

He folded the plans and put them back into his pocket, then for the final time he went through his checklist. Air rifle and telescopic night-sight. Maglite torch. Swiss Army knife. Gloves. Toolkit. Canister of liquid propane gas. Canister of compressed ketamine (which he had purchased in Brighton), which would paralyse for thirty minutes. Lighter. Beretta .38 handgun, with full magazine and silencer.

He felt nervous now. Far more nervous than on any of his previous American assignments. Slipping his hand into his anorak pocket he pulled out the stubby, heavy weapon and looked at it for some moments, stared at the dull black metal. Gripped it in his hand and slipped his finger over the trigger.

His instructions from his Master were only to use the gun in a worst-case scenario. If you fired a gun, one day, someone would be able to connect you to that gun. To fire a gun was to cross the Rubicon. You could never go back; you could never be a Soldier in the army of the Lord again.

He was tired of being a Soldier.

He wanted to come home.

He wanted to sleep tomorrow night in the arms of Lara.

This was why, aided by the illumination of the dome light of the rented Ford Focus sedan, he attached the silencer, taking several goes to catch the threading correctly. Then with a badly trembling index finger he pressed the safety catch down, into the *off* position, and jammed the now much bulkier gun back into his anorak pocket.

On the three occasions he had checked during the past month, the Infidels' bedroom light went out around half past eleven. It was now half past ten. At midnight he would make his way across the fields and up to the house.

He closed his eyes, placed his hands in front of his face, and recited the Lord's Prayer. It was the start of his ninety-minute prayer vigil for strength.

95

Light suddenly exploded across the rain-drenched windscreen. Brilliant white one moment, blue the next, and for an instant the Disciple, hands clasped in prayer in front of his face, froze in panic.

Police?

The car slid past in front of him, splashing through the deep puddles of the pot-holed lot. He heard the bass beat of music. *Ker-boom-ker-ker, ker-boom-ker-ker, ker-boom-ker-ker, ker-boom-ker-ker.* It wasn't police, it was one of those fancy sports cars with those halogen lights that glinted blue when you caught them at certain angles.

Who the hell are you? What are you doing here? This is my car park, this is my space.

The fancy car moved away, down towards the far end of the lot, then stopped beside the oak tree that straddled the railings, beyond which was an expanse of parkland and the municipal tennis court.

All its lights went off.

The Disciple raised his night-vision glasses and stared through the rear windscreen of the car. In the bright green glow he could see a man and a woman. Their faces were turned towards each other. Each of them gave a quick glance back into the darkness, at him, then they began to eat each other's faces.

Fornicators. Sewer people.

He could still hear that bass beat. But it was faint now.

This is my space. God found this for me. You should not be here, you really should not.

He slipped his right hand down to his anorak pocket, clasped his fingers around the cold, hard butt of his gun. Eliminating them would be easy; he had enough spare bullets. God would OK that – anything that stood between him and the Infidels and the Devil's Spawn was a legitimate target.

Perspiration guttered down his back. These people here, this wasn't meant to happen. He could abort, drive off, come back again tomorrow. Except, the weather was perfect tonight and Lara was waiting, and why should these sewer people delay him for another day? He had already emailed the Master. Plans were made. Too much to change.

He was shaking so badly he could not think straight.

Something made him twist the ignition key, put the car in gear, switch the lights on, accelerate out of the lot and turn left, through the village, past the busy pub with its lot full of cars, up the lane towards the entrance to the Infidels' house.

He could just turn right, drive in, straight up to the house.

That was crazy.

He stopped outside the entrance, turned the car around and drove back down towards the village. Thinking. Thinking. Trying desperately to clear the red mist of anger out of his head. Thinking.

OK. OK. OK.

He drove through the village, heading back towards the main road, cut the apex of the right-hander at the end of the village and had to swerve violently to avoid oncoming headlights, so violently he hit the verge and the car slewed.

He slammed on the brakes. Closed his eyes for a second.

Please tell me what to do, God. Guidance. Give me guidance.

God guided him onto the main road. He drove up it for five miles until he reached a roundabout. He did two full loops of the roundabout. This was all going wrong, this wasn't the plan. This was God testing him.

Haven't you tested me enough?

A car cut out in front of him; he jammed on the brakes and his wheels locked, the little Ford yawing crazily, missing the back of the car by inches.

He took the first exit off the roundabout, not even sure where he was now, and swung into a lay-by. He pulled on the handbrake, then lowered his head, hyperventilating in panic.

The clock on the dash was blurred. His whole vision was blurred. Twelve minutes past eleven.

He switched on the dome light, took out the photograph of Lara and stared at her. *Sweet, sweet Lara.* Her face, smiling back at him, calmed him. Gave him strength. Helped him to collect his thoughts.

Headlights loomed in his mirror. He stiffened. Then moments later a car roared past.

Forty-five minutes. That was all. Just forty-five minutes to get through.

He drove on for a couple of miles until he reached the outskirts of a village he had never been to before. A signpost said ALFRISTON.

Braking sharply, he turned the car round, then drove slowly back, retracing his steps, and pulled into the unlit entrance to a farm, switched the engine and the lights off and sat, very still, trying to calm himself down and to think clearly.

The fancy car with the lovers, which had come into the lot behind the schoolhouse, was a test. God had tested Job and was now testing him. Or warning him. If it was still there when he drove back, it would be a sign to abort tonight; but if it was gone, it would be God giving him the all-clear.

At eleven forty-five he drove back into the village of Caibourne and turned into the schoolhouse parking lot.

The lovers had gone.

And the rain was easing off. Still falling, but lighter now, although the wind was getting stronger. Good. He pulled his thin leather gloves on, climbed out of the car, locked the doors, and took the air rifle from the boot. He made his way across the lot, past the school, checked very carefully that the coast was clear, then ran across the road and onto the muddy bridleway that would take him straight across a field of corn stubble, and up to the field of pasture grass that adjoined the Infidels' garden.

He held the torch, but only switched it on for an instant every few paces. The track was uneven, chewed up by horses' hooves. Several times he slipped, almost losing his footing, and twice he cursed as his anorak snagged on the brambles.

Although he was still extremely fit, the steep climb, nerves and the cold air were taking their toll. He was breathing heavily, perspiring inside his warm clothing and under his heavy load. But there was a deep glow in his heart.

And now, finally, he could see the Infidels' house! A looming shadow two hundred yards in front of him. There was just one light on, the master bedroom. And then, joy! Even as he was watching, it was extinguished.

Darkness!

Now the adrenaline was pumping and he could scarcely contain his excitement.

Something darted above him, a bat, or maybe an owl. He listened for a moment to the howl of the wind through the grass and the trees and the bushes, listened to a hinge shrieking as an unlatched farm gate swung open, shut, open, shut, and the steady banging of an unsecured door. So many noises to mask his own!

Looking up at the bitumen-black sky, he thought to himself, yes, this night has been ordained! Leaning against the gridded metal stock fencing, he raised his night-vision binoculars. Fixed them on the master bedroom window. Adjusted the focus until it was pin-sharp. Remembered his briefing, the words of the Master.

Watch the condensation. When the outside temperature is colder than inside there will be condensation on the windows. When the heating goes off the condensation will slowly cease. When the condensation has gone it is safe to assume the occupants are asleep.

The master bedroom windows of the Infidels were misted with condensation. But even as he watched, he could see it beginning to fade.

*

It was dark in their bedroom. Their parents no longer left the Bob the Builder night light on. That wasn't important. One sense always compensated for another. In darkness, smell kicked in stronger. So did touch. So did hearing.

They smelled him now. They heard him.

Soon they would touch him.

410

In their little side-by-side beds, in the darkness of the room in the house where they lived for now, but for not much longer, in a voice too high-pitched to be detected by the human ear, Luke called out to his sister. Just one word, spoken with the fourth letter, 'd', missing, backwards.

'Yaer?'

A split second later, in a voice equally inaudible to the normal human ear, Phoebe responded.

'Yaer.'

96

They observed him from a comfortable distance, the figure in the dark baseball cap, anorak and boots. At the moment he was staring at the house through his binoculars, his rifle leaning against the fence. They were too far away to tell whether it was just an airgun or a hunting rifle.

The gap between them was two hundred yards, a distance they had maintained since they had watched him emerge from the parking lot behind the schoolhouse, cross over the road and head off up the footpath. He had never once turned round.

Like him, they also had night-vision aids, but they were better equipped. Both of them wore goggles, and carried binoculars as well. With these goggles it was like walking in green daylight. They watched, for a brief moment, an owl swoop into a field and then rise with a wriggling mouse dangling from its beak.

Shielded by a hedgerow, just in case he should turn round, they continued to observe him as he lowered his binoculars then, a couple of minutes later, raised them to his eyes again. They wondered what he was waiting for and communicated this via an exchange of puzzled glances. Neither of them spoke; he was down-wind of them. Despite the covering noises of the raging gale, the faintest whisper was too dangerous to risk.

*

The condensation had almost gone! The Disciple felt calmer now; his heart was no longer crashing around out of control inside his chest, but was beating at a steady, strong level, circulating the adrenaline that was keeping him alert and sharp, pumping around those endorphins that were making him feel good now. He checked his watch.

12.22

Time!

For a glorious few moments, clambering over the fence into the field that bordered the Infidels' property, he felt invincible. Then, crouching low to minimize the chance of being seen from the house, and treading carefully, wary of damaging an ankle in a rabbit hole, he made his way as swiftly as he dared across the boggy, rain-sodden field.

Now his heart was really pounding again as he reached the boundary fencing, which was as close as he dared go for the moment. The house, just fifty feet away, loomed high and shadowy above him. All the lights were off and the windows closed. Good. He stared at the Infidels' cars on the gravel drive. Just the Saab and the Subaru. No overnight visitors. Good. Then he fixed his gaze up at the wall where he had seen the sensor when he had paid his visit.

He knelt, took the air rifle and, cushioning it on his hand, rested it on a wooden fence post. He pulled off the night-sight covers, crammed them into his anorak, then squinted through it. It took him only a moment to pick up the sensor for the intruder lights, a tiny, convex strip of glass or Perspex set in white plastic, about ten feet above the ground, and directly beneath one of the battery of floodlights it would trigger.

But his damned hands were shaking; they had never

shaken before like this. Taking a deep breath, trying to calm down, he lined the cross hairs up, but the instant he did, they had moved off the target. He shifted his position a fraction, making an even better wedge against the post, and aimed again. Better. Steadier, but nowhere near as steady as when he had been practising, nor anything like as steady as at the previous house in Iowa, where he had done exactly this same thing.

Curling his finger over the trigger, he took up the slack, allowed the cross hairs to move off the target, then slowly, concentrating desperately to try to stop the gun jigging from his damned nerves, jigging from the ferociously gusting wind, he brought the cross hairs dead centre over the target and increased his pressure on the trigger.

There was a sharp *phuttt!* as the gas cylinder expelled the first of the ten pellets in the magazine and almost simultaneously a hideously loud *thwakkk!* as the pellet embedded itself in the stained wooden cladding of the barn wall, several inches to the left of the sensor.

The Disciple held his breath, stared up at anxiously at the master bedroom window, shaking even more now. To his relief, there was no sign of any movement. How could he have missed so badly? Yesterday, he'd driven to a lonely spot in the countryside and set the sight up for this distance. He had ripped out the bullseyes in the targets with ninety-seven out of one hundred slugs.

He took a second shot now, and again hit the cladding, this time directly below his target. And now the perspiration was starting to run down his body again, and his head felt too hot inside his hat and his fingers sticky inside his gloves. He watched the master bedroom window for a light to come on, or a twitch of the curtains. But again, to his relief, nothing. So many noises from the wind right now, one tiny .22 pellet was probably insignificant; except it didn't sound that way from down here.

He fired his third shot.

Even wider. 'No!' the cry came out before he could stop it.

Now his eyes were beginning to blur with tears, from the savage, icy wind, and even more from frustration. Seven pellets left. Seven. Just needed one.

He opened his eyes, blinked away the tears, wiped them with the back of his leather glove, took careful aim, felt confident now, had the target absolutely square on as he pulled the trigger. The pellet went well to the left and must have struck metal because it made a hard ping, so damned loud. He ducked right down and waited, staring up at the master bedroom window, and at the other windows, really afraid he must have woken someone this time.

Only fifty feet! How can I miss from fifty feet? How? It isn't possible?

Please, God, don't desert me now.

He let a couple of minutes pass, until he was satisfied all was quiet inside the house. Then he took aim again. Squeezed the trigger. And almost shouted out for joy as the glass exploded and the shards tumbled down onto the gravel with a few barely audible tinkles. The white plastic sensor, split in two, dangled limply from its wires. He raised his binoculars and focused on the sensor, just to double check that it wasn't merely the outer casing that had gone. But the damage looked thorough. It was destroyed.

His mouth felt dry with anxiety. He laid down the rifle, then patted the handgun in his pocket. From his left pocket he pulled the leather pouch containing the tungsten lock-pick tools. His insides were jangling, the red mist of panic he'd experienced earlier was returning and he was having to make an effort to stay calm, to remember his plan.

He should make it look like an accident, like a fire, that was his brief. But that carried too many risks, the thought of being caught, of being incarcerated. No. Not an option. These scum sewer Infidels weren't worthy of such a risk. He would gun them down like the vermin they were, them and their Spawn. Then he would burn the place. His Master might not be happy with him, but he would never be able to send him out into the field again. There were times in life where you had to make your own decisions.

He climbed over the fence and onto the narrow grass verge on the other side. Stared anxiously up at the house. Put one cautious foot forward on to the gravel as if he were testing water. Then another.

Scccrrunnccccccchhhhh.

He froze. Took another step, then another, praying for silent footfalls and each time scrunching just as loudly as the last. *They won't hear it, not in this storm. Stop worrying.*

He reached the porch. He already knew what kind of lock it was, from his previous visit, a sturdy, mortise deadlock, and he had the right pick selected for the task, a full diamond. He had practised a thousand times on an identical lock he had bought earlier in the week.

From his breast pocket he pulled out his tiny torch, twisted it on, and held it in his left hand, pointing the beam on the lock. With his right hand, he inserted the tip of the tungsten diamond pick into the keyway. Navigating the wards, he pushed it firmly through the plug, feeling for the first pin. Then it came to a halt. He tried again.

And then he realized, to his dismay, what the problem was.

Someone had left the key in on the other side of the door.

Even as he was registering this, he heard a metallic sound right in front of him. The ratchety clank of brass pins lifting clear of a sheer line. The dull, leaden, unmistakable sound of a key turning in a lock.

Dropping the pick, his hand lunged for his Beretta. It was jammed in his pocket! As he tugged at the weapon in wild panic the door opened. It was so dark inside the house he could barely see the two small figures, in boots and in their winter coats.

The Devil's Spawn.

Standing in front of him.

Their eyes glinting with such curiosity he felt for a moment they were staring right through him. He stepped back several paces. Much too late, he realized they were in fact looking at the people behind him.

He never heard the gun fire. He sensed just one brief rush of scorching, arid wind, accompanied by an eerie *whoosh* that made his ears pop. He never felt the bullet, either, which entered through the base of his skull, partially severing his spinal cord. It traversed through his left cerebral hemisphere into his right cerebral hemisphere, on through his frontal lobe, exited above his right eye, and ricocheted off the brick facing of the porch, gouging a small hole in the cement pointing.

For an instant, he saw Lara, standing in brilliant, milky light at the end of a long tunnel; then the faces of the Devil's Spawn stood in front of her, blocking his view with their smirking faces, smirking *Victory!* at him, savage, graceless smiles stretched across their faces, while their eyes burned with hatred. They were moving towards him, or perhaps he was moving toward them. He called out, in desperation, 'Lara!'

Her name echoed in the hollow darkness, and dissolved into the Spawns' giggles, ringing, wracking, deafening, childish giggles. The only light now came from the four eyes, four pools of luminescent, colourless dry ice. They were receding. Soft gravel was cradling him.

There were faces above him now, two different faces, silhouettes in the darkness, something familiar about them. Slowly his ravaged neural pathways lightened their features for him, turning them a vivid night-vision green. And then through his addled thoughts and fading consciousness, as his blood drained out onto the gravel, memory began flooding in. Into his confusion entered a fleeting moment of understanding. He knew now why they seemed familiar.

In the fancy sports car in the parking lot behind the schoolhouse. Those profiles through his night-vision glasses as they had turned to kiss. The man and the woman.

It was them.

97

Halley was in his little battery-powered police jeep. Base-ball cap on back to front, huge grin on his face, driving around and around the lawn in the back yard of their house. Roaring around the inflatable rubber paddling pool, swerving to avoid stray toys, flashing his lights, hooting his klaxon. It was his third birthday; he was fine today, he was having a great day.

Naomi grinned, too, as she watched him. She gripped John's hand with joy beneath a warm Californian sun. It was a day that was as perfect as it was possible for any day to be – when you knew your son had less than a year to live.

The dream was slipping away. She kept her eyes shut, tried to sink back into it. But a cold draught of air was blowing on her face. And she needed to pee. She opened her eyes. The room was pitch dark and her clock said 6.01.

The gale was still raging outside. There were all kinds of creaking noises from the beams above her, rattling noises from the windows; draughts.

John was still deep asleep. She lay for some moments trying to resist that need to pee, pulling the duvet up over her face to shut out the cold air, closing her eyes, trying to return to that Californian summer afternoon. But she was wide awake and all her troubles were pouring back into her mind.

What day was it today? Friday. They were taking Luke and Phoebe to see Dr Michaelides, to talk about special schools. Then in the afternoon they were going to see a couple of dog breeders, one which had a litter of Rhodesian Ridgeback puppies, and another breeder who had a litter of Alsatians sired by a police dog.

Trying not to wake John, she slipped out of bed and padded into the bathroom, wrestled herself into her dressing gown and pushed her feet into her slippers. She peed, then washed her hands and face, brushed her teeth.

Horrible bloody bags under my eyes.

She peered closer into the mirror. More wrinkles. Every day there seemed to be fresh ones. Some were beginning to look like crevasses. *Let's face it, kiddo, you are ageing. Another decade and you'll be a wrinkly. A couple more after that and you'll be a crumbly. Next thing you know, Luke and Phoebe'll be pushing you along the seafront in a wheelchair with a tartan rug over your knees while you sit there, with mad white hair, drooling.*

Except.

Would Luke and Phoebe ever take care of John and herself? Would they ever care enough? Would they want to be bothered? Wasn't that what kids were supposed to do? Wasn't that the way life was supposed to work? How did that bumper sticker she'd seen go? GET EVEN! LIVE LONG ENOUGH TO BECOME A PROBLEM FOR YOUR KIDS!

She closed the bedroom door behind her and switched the landing light on. Luke and Phoebe's bedroom door was shut and the box-room door was shut. They were usually up at this hour.

But this morning, silence.

The stair treads creaked like hell, and she went down slowly, mindful of not wanting to wake John. Then, as she reached the hall, she felt a stab of unease. The safety chain on the front door, which they always kept in the locked position when they were indoors, was hanging loose.

Had they forgotten to attach it last night? She supposed they must have done, and made a mental note to tell John. Right now they needed to be more vigilant about safety than ever.

Then something else struck her. She turned and looked at the Victorian coat stand. It seemed emptier than normal. Where were the children's coats? Her eyes shot down to the ground, to the hollow in the middle of the stand where they all kept their boots. Luke's blue wellingtons and Phoebe's red ones were missing.

Her unease deepened. Had they gone for a walk? At this hour, in the pitch darkness, in the filthy weather?

She opened the heavy oak door, pushing hard against the strong, biting wind and flinching against stinging droplets of rain, and peered out into the darkness.

And froze.

Something was lying on the ground right in front of the porch, a sack or an animal, or something.

A slick of fear shot down her spine. She stepped back warily, looked at the panel of light switches, and pressed the red one.

Instantly all the exterior floodlights, except one, came on and she saw it was not a sack or an animal. It was a man, sprawled on his back. A handgun lay in the gravel near him. Barely registering more than that, she slammed the door shut, pulled on the safety chain, and threw herself up the stairs, choking with shock.

'John!' She burst into the bedroom and switched on the light. 'John, for God's sake, there's someone downstairs, outside, a man, a man. Unconscious, dead, I don't know. Gun. There's a gun!'

She ran out, along to the children's bedroom, threw open the door; but even before she had hit the light switch she could see the room was empty. The box room was empty, too.

John came out onto the landing in his dressing gown, holding his shotgun. 'Where? Where outside?'

Staring at him in wild, bug-eyed panic, she blurted, 'F-f-f-front – f-f-front door. I don't know where Luke and Phoebe are.'

'Call the police – no – hit panic button, quicker – by the bed, press the panic button. They'll come right away.'

'Be careful, John.'

'Where is he?'

'Front door.' Trembling. 'I don't know where Luke and Phoebe are. I don't know where they are, they may be outside.'

'Panic button,' he said. Then he switched the safety catch off, and headed cautiously downstairs.

Naomi ran to the side of the bed, pressed the red panic button and immediately the alarm began sounding inside and outside the house. Then she grabbed the phone and listened for a second. There was a dial tone. Thank God. She tried to stab out 999, but her fingers were shaking so badly that the first time, she misdialled. She dialled again and this time it rang. And rang.

'Oh Jesus, come on, answer, please, please!'

Then she heard the operator's voice. She blurted out, 'Police.' Then, moments later, she heard herself shouting into the phone, 'MAN! GUN! OH GOD, PLEASE COME QUICKLY!'

She calmed enough to give their address carefully, then ran down the stairs, passed John who was in the hallway peering out of a window, and into the living room, calling, 'LUKE! PHOEBE!'

No sign of them.

Back in the hall, Naomi stood behind John and stared fearfully out of the window at the motionless, rain-sodden figure in his anorak, bobble hat and wellingtons. His face was turned away from them so they could not make out his features. And she wondered, just for a fleeting instant, whether she had been overreacting. A tramp? He looked like a tramp?

A tramp with a handgun?

'I can't find Luke and Phoebe,' she said.

John was opening the front door.

'Oh God, please be careful. Wait. The police will be here—'

'Hallo!' John called to the man. 'Hallo! Excuse me! Hallo!'

'Wait, John.'

But John was already stepping outside, holding the shotgun out in front of him, finger on the trigger, staring at the brightly lit drive and lawn, and the pre-dawn darkness beyond, swinging the gun from left to right, bringing it back onto the man each time. He took a few more steps, the wind lifting the bottom of his dressing gown like a skirt. Naomi followed.

They were standing right over the figure, right over the man in his black cap and black anorak and black trousers and black boots. He was young, no more than thirty, she guessed. John crouched, snatched up the handgun and gave it to Naomi to hold.

It was heavy and wet and cold and made her shudder. She stared out warily into the darkness beyond the lights, then back at the man.

'Hallo?' John said.

Naomi knelt, and it was then that she saw the hole in his forehead above his right eye, the torn flesh, the bruising around it, and the plug of congealed blood inside that the rain hadn't managed to wash away.

She whimpered. Scrambled on all fours round the other side of his head. Saw the patch of singed hairs at the base of the skull, the torn flesh, more congealed blood here.

'Shot,' she said. 'Shot.' Trying frantically to remember a First Aid course she did when she was in her teens at school, she grabbed his hand, pushing back the cuff of the leather glove, and pressed her finger against his wrist. Despite being soaking wet, the flesh was warm.

She tried for some moments, but couldn't tell whether it was a pulse or just her own nerves pulsing. Then his eyes opened.

Her heart almost tore free of her chest in shock.

His eyes rolled, not appearing to register anything.

'Where are my children?' Naomi said. 'Can you hear me? Where are my children? For God's sake, where are my children?'

His eyes continued to roll.

'Where are my children?' she screamed, barely able to believe he could still be alive with these holes in his head.

Then his mouth opened. Closed. Opened, then closed again, like a beached, dying fish.

'My children! Where are MY CHILDREN?'

In a voice quieter than the wind, he whispered, 'Lara.'

'Who are you?' John said. 'Who are you, please?'

'Lara,' he said again and again faintly, but just loud enough for them to hear that he had an American accent.

'Where are my children?' Naomi said, yet again, her voice wracked with desperation.

'Call an ambulance,' John said. 'Need an ambulance—'

His voice was cut short by the distant whoop of a siren.

'Lara,' the man whispered again. His eyes locked and widened, for a brief moment, as if he was now seeing her, then they roamed again, lost.

98

A disembodied blue light strobed in the darkness, in the distance, not seeming to get any closer. A siren wailed but didn't seem to be getting any louder. Maybe it was going somewhere else, not coming to them at all, Naomi wondered, stumbling across the lawn, calling out with increasing desperation every few moments, 'LUKE! PHOEBE!', staring into the bushes, the shadows, looking back at John who was still kneeling by the man, then at the blue strobing light again, then at the dark, empty fields.

At the void that had swallowed up her children.

Now the siren was getting louder, and suddenly she was fearful that the children were in the drive, and the police in their haste, in this darkness, might not see them. Balancing her way across the bars of the cattle grid with difficulty in her sodden slippers, pointing her flashlight into the darkness, oblivious to the cold and the pelting rain, she stumbled along the metalled surface of the drive, calling out again, 'LUKE! PHOEBE! LUKE! PHOEBE!'

Headlights pricking the darkness ahead of her now. Twin blue lights streaking along above the hedgerow at the bottom of the drive. Electrifyingly fast. She stepped onto the verge, felt her dressing gown snag on a bramble, but ignored it, frantically waving her torch.

As the car came round the bend, she stood frozen like a rabbit in the dazzling glare. The car stopped right beside her, slivers of blue light skidding off the paintwork, skidding off the face of the uniformed policewoman in the passenger seat, who was lowering her window and peering out at her. A voice crackled on the radio inside the car and the male driver said something Naomi didn't catch. Heat and damp, rubbery smells poured out of the window.

Pointing frantically towards the house, Naomi said, near breathless, 'Man – there – need ambulance – you didn't see any children – down the drive – two children?'

Looking at her with a concerned expression, the policewoman said, 'Is someone armed? Is there someone with a gun?'

'Shot,' Naomi said. 'There's a man shot – there – he's up there – and my children, I can't find my children.'

'Are you all right? Do you want to get in?' the woman police officer asked.

'I'm looking for my children,' she said.

'I'll come back down to you in a few minutes.'

The car pulled away barely before she had finished speaking, accelerating harshly, clattering over the cattle grid. She watched the brake lights as it halted on the gravel, saw both driver and passenger doors open and the two officers stepping out purposefully.

Naomi turned away, carried on running down the drive, following the torch beam, her slippers slapping on the hard tarmac, her feet coming out of them every few steps. She went ankle-deep through a puddle, lost both her slippers, retrieved them and hooked them on her feet again, calling out, her throat rasping, 'PHOEBE? LUKE? LUKE? PHOEBE?'

Halfway down the drive there was an open gate leading into a field of stubble, where she sometimes took Luke and Phoebe for a walk. Several pheasants, bred on a shoot at nearby Caibourne Place, had made a refuge here. Luke and Phoebe took a delight in startling the pheasants out of their covers, giggling at the strange, clanky sounds of their beating wings and their metallic croaks. She went in there now, shining the beam of the torch around, calling out to them.

Silence. Just the wind and a creaking hinge. And another siren.

Moments later a second police patrol car ripped past her and up the drive. Then, seconds later, as if it were being dragged in its slipstream, a third car with four people inside, this one unmarked and no siren, just the urgent roar of its engine and the swish of its tyres.

She stumbled on, calling out their name every few moments, crying in shock and despair and exhaustion. 'Luke! Phoebe! Darlings! Where are you? Answer me! Where are you?'

Dawn was breaking now. Watery grey and yellow tints streaked the darkness. Like celluloid developing, the darkness turned into increasingly clear, shadowy shapes, and these in turn were lightening into the familiar sights of the buildings, trees, houses that were their surrounding landscape. A new day was breaking. Her children were gone and a new day was breaking. Her children were gone and a man was dying outside their front door.

She ran back onto the drive and, at the end of it, headed towards the village. She stumbled along a corridor of hedges and trees, the beam of the torch becoming less necessary with every step, fear clenching her throat like a fist, hoping desperately that suddenly she was going to see Luke and Phoebe in their winter coats and their red and blue wellington boots, walking hand-in-hand back towards her.

Another siren now. Moments later an ambulance with

all its lights blazing came around the corner. She waved the torch, frantically, and the ambulance stopped. 'Dene Farm Barn?' the driver asked.

She pointed, gulping air. 'Just back there, a hundred yards, turn right, the first entrance, up the drive. I can't find my children.'

Seconds later she stood, breathing in a lungful of diesel fumes, watching streaks of cold blue light dart like angry fish across the shimmering road, watching the ambulance turn right, slowly, ever so slowly, like one frame at a time, into their drive. Their home. Their sanctuary.

She stood still, blinking tears and rain from her stinging eyes, gulping down more acrid air, shaking, shivering so badly her knees were banging together. 'Luke?' she said, her voice feeble now, forlorn, lost. 'Phoebe?'

She stared at the lame yellow glow of the torch; the beam didn't even register on the road any more. She switched it off, swallowed, hugged her arms around herself to try to stop shaking. The rain hardened; she could have been standing in a shower, but she was oblivious to it as she turned, one way then the other, taking one last hopeless look, as if she might suddenly spot their little faces peeping out from behind a bush, or a tree or a hedge.

Where are you?

She was trying, desperately, to focus her mind. Who was the man? Who had shot the man? Why? How had anyone got into the house? How had anyone got Luke and Phoebe into their coats and boots and taken them away? Who were these people? Paedophiles?

The Disciples?

Could Luke or Phoebe have shot him? Then run away? Was that why they had run away?

Run away? Taken away – abducted?

In some space, way beyond her bewilderment at the moment, in some dark place deep inside her heart, she harboured a certainty, an absolute dead certainty, that they were gone for ever.

99

A grey van pulled up beside Naomi as she trudged back up the drive to the house, and a man asked her in a kindly voice if she was all right. For a moment, her hopes soared.

'Have you got them?' she said. 'Have you found them? Have you got my children? Are they OK?'

'Your children?'

She stared at him, utterly bewildered. 'My children? Have you got them? Luke and Phoebe?'

He opened the door and moved over, making space for her. 'Jump in, love.'

She backed away. 'Who are you?'

'Crime scene officers.'

She shook her head. 'I have to find my children.'

'We'll help you find them. Hop in, you're going to freeze to death like that.'

A two-way radio crackled. The driver leaned forward and pressed a button. 'Charlie Victor Seven Four, we have just arrived on scene.'

The man in the passenger seat held out his hand. Naomi took it and climbed in, then pulled the door shut. A fan was roaring; hot air began toasting her feet, blasting on her face.

She shook her head, the giddying heat making her feel faint and disoriented. 'Please help me find my son and daughter.'

'How old are they?'

'Three.'

'Don't worry, love, we'll find them.'

The van moved forwards. She watched the hedgerows passing as if in a dream. 'They weren't in the house when we woke up,' she said numbly.

'We'll find them, don't you worry.'

The kindness in his voice made her burst into tears.

The van clattered over the cattle grid and onto the gravel. Sobbing uncontrollably, she saw the ambulance, its doors shut, side window screened off from view, the first police car she had seen earlier, and two more. There seemed to be police everywhere. Three were standing in the garden wearing flak jackets and holding rifles. No sign of the shot man; she presumed he was in the ambulance.

There was a tape barrier sealing off a wide area in front of the house where the shot man had lain, with two uniformed policemen in caps standing in front of it. As the van pulled up, yet another car appeared, a dark Volvo saloon, bristling with aerials, this one with four uniformed policemen inside it.

'Where do you think they might be, your kids?' the crime scene man asked.

'I—' She shook her head, opened the door and clambered quickly out. This wasn't real, it couldn't be. In a daze, she mumbled a thank-you and walked towards the taped-off front door. One of the uniformed policemen raised a hand and said in a kindly voice, 'I'm sorry, madam, would you mind using the kitchen entrance.'

She went round to the side of the house. The kitchen door was shut and locked. She rapped with her knuckles. A uniformed policewoman opened it. It might have been the same woman she had spoken to earlier, in the car, her face streaked with blue light, she wasn't sure. Then John, still in his dressing gown, was walking towards her, hair matted to his head, face sheet-white. He put his arms around her.

'Where have you been, darling?'

'Have you found them?' Naomi sobbed. 'Have you found them?'

'They're around somewhere,' John said. 'They must be.'

She sobbed back at him. 'THEY'VE GONE! SOME-ONE'S TAKEN THEM, OH GOD, SOMEONE'S TAKEN THEM!'

John and the woman police officer traded glances.

'Our children have gone, John – don't you get it? Do you want me to spell it out to you? Do you want me to spell it out to you backwards with every fourth letter missing?'

Two uniformed officers came into the kitchen. One looked about nineteen years old, tall and very thin, and rather green. Slightly odd, still wearing his cap inside, Naomi thought inconsequentially. The other was older, stocky, with designer stubble and a shaved head. He held his cap in his hand and had a kind smile. 'We've searched every room, all the cupboards and roof spaces. We'll go and check on the outbuildings. Garage and greenhouse, right? And the dustbin shed? Any other outbuildings that we haven't seen, sir?'

John, soaking wet and shivering with cold, said, 'No.' Then to Naomi he said, 'Got to get you into some dry clothes. Go have a shower, I'll deal with everything.'

'We need to go back out,' she said. 'They might be down at that pond on the Gribbles' farm – they might have fallen in.'

'Get some proper clothes on and we'll go out and look. We'll find them, they'll be somewhere around.'

The stocky officer turned to the younger one. 'I'll check the outbuildings. You start a log of everyone who enters the house.'

Just as Naomi left the kitchen to go up and shower, there was a rap on the door. John opened it to see a tall man of about forty, with dark, wavy hair, dressed in an unbuttoned, rain-spotted mackintosh over a grey suit, white shirt, sharp tie and shiny black lace-up shoes. His nose, squashed and kinked, looked like it had been broken more than once, giving him the thuggish look of a retired prize-fighter.

'Dr Klaesson?'

'Yes.'

'Detective Inspector Pelham. I'm the duty Senior Investigating Officer.' His tone was courteous but brisk. Extending his hand, he gave John's a brief, firm tug, as if more would have been eating into valuable time, his sharp, grey eyes assessing John as he spoke. Then, a tad more gently, added, 'I'm sure you and Mrs Klaesson must be feeling a little shell-shocked.'

'I think that's an understatement.'

'We're going to do everything we can to help you. But I'm afraid we're going to have to seal this house up inside and out, as a crime scene, and I'd like you and your wife to pack a bag with your essentials and enough clothes to last for a few days, and move out.'

John stared at him in shock. 'What?'

'No one's been in the house,' Naomi said.

'I'm sorry, it's standard procedure for a major crime scene.'

Two men suddenly came in from the garden without knocking. They were wearing white suits with hoods up, white overshoes and rubber gloves, and each carried a holdall.

'Morning, Dave,' one said nonchalantly.

'Morning, Chief!' said the other breezily, as if they were just a pair of interior decorators turning up to paint a hallway.

The young uniformed police officer took their names and noted them down in his log.

'Where – where do we move out to?' John asked the DI.

'Do you have any relatives you could stay with nearby? Otherwise a hotel or a boarding house.'

'Relatives, yes, but not close. Look, we don't want to leave here, not without our children.'

Detective Inspector Pelham nodded in understanding, but not sympathy. 'I'm afraid you are both going to be required to come to the station and make statements. Someone will drive you. We're already looking for your children, and the helicopter will be overhead in a few minutes. I suggest you get dressed, and you and I and Mrs Klaesson have a cup of tea here in the kitchen and run through a number of things I need to ask you.'

'I want to go out and look for them.'

'I have officers out there looking in the immediate vicinity already. Your children are three years old?'

'Yes, but—' John checked himself.

The detective inspector raised his eyebrows, quizzically. As if in response John added, 'They are quite grown-up for their age.'

'All children are these days, Dr Klaesson.' The policeman's inscrutable expression eased fleetingly into a thin, wintry smile. 'Have they ever done this before?'

'Wandered off? No,' Naomi sobbed.

'We can't make any assumptions at the moment,' DI Pelham said. 'But I think at three years old, we should work on the likelihood that they are not far away – although in view of what's happened we've put out an alert to all airports, seaports and the Channel Tunnel as a precaution. It would be helpful if you could let me have a recent photograph of them. But don't worry, we'll find them.' He looked at each of them in turn. 'You've never seen this man – outside your front door – before? You have no idea who he might be?'

The Detective Inspector noticed the strange glance John and Naomi Klaesson gave each other.

100

Even after a hot shower and dressed in warm clothes, back in the kitchen Naomi could not stop shaking. It took all her concentration to fill the electric kettle and push the plug in. Moments later, as it began to hiss and rumble, she heard a much louder roar, like thunder, outside.

She stared out of the window and saw a helicopter clatter by overhead, barely higher than the trees. John came down in jeans, a roll-neck sweater and his fleece jacket, clutching two holdalls into which they had hurriedly packed washing kit and changes of clothing. Moments later, Detective Inspector Pelham came in from the garden.

'I do not want to leave, Detective Inspector,' she said. 'I want to stay here, this is my home. I want to stay until my children come back.'

'I'm sorry, Mrs Klaesson, we'll be as quick as we can.'

'How quick?'

'A couple of days, I would hope.' Then he said, 'I see you have a security camera, hidden up beneath the guttering. Does it record?'

'Jesus!' John said, slapping his forehead. 'Of course! It was only installed on Wednesday!' He looked at Naomi and her eyes brightened a fraction.

'Yes!' she said. 'Why the hell didn't we think of it?'

John led the way along the hall to his den, and opened the cupboard where the recorder was concealed. 'I – I haven't tried – let me check.'

Shakily, he thumbed through the instruction manual.

'Don't wipe the tape, darling,' Naomi said. 'For God's sake, don't wipe it.'

He pressed the stop button on the machine. Then the rewind. 'It's activated by movement,' he said. 'And it has night vision.'

The digital display counted back to 00.29, then jumped back further to 19.10.

He pressed play.

All three of them stared at the black-and-white image on the small monitor beside the machine. It showed a glare of headlights. Then, moments later in fish-eye wide angle, John's Saab pulling up next to Naomi's Subaru. John got out and walked up to the porch and out of sight.

Then.

A flash, indicating a time jump.

John held his breath.

Sweet Jesus.

Total stunned silence in the room.

A figure clambering over the fence from the field. Wearing a dark cap, an anorak, wellington boots, gloves. He put one cautious foot forward on the gravel, as if he were testing water. Then another.

'It's him,' Naomi said, in a strangled, tremolo voice.

The figure froze. Took another step, then another, coming towards the porch.

And then.

Coming over the fence behind him were two more figures, advancing stealthily. Both wearing dark bobble hats, jackets zipped, collars turned up, their faces almost totally obscured by goggles.

The figure in front stopped in his tracks. Then moved

on towards the porch. He stopped again, pulled something out of his pocket, something long and slender, some kind of a tool.

He disappeared from view into the porch. Then, moments later, he came back into view and now he was holding a gun – *the gun!* – in his hand.

And in the same moment, one of the two figures behind him ran forward, also holding a handgun, raised it at the base of his head and there was a burst of light from the muzzle.

The head of the figure in the cap snapped sharply upwards, then he collapsed back onto the gravel, arms outstretched, gun falling from his fingers and coming to rest a few feet away.

As they had found him, Naomi realized.

And then.

No.

This could not be happening. This really had to be a dream. Luke and Phoebe in their raincoats, in their wellington boots, trotted into view and threw their arms around each of the two figures in goggles in turn.

There were several moments of warm embracing. Then the four of them hurried across the gravel drive. The adult figures, still wearing their goggles, helped Luke and Phoebe over the fence into the field beyond.

Then a flash, indicating a time jump. John came into view, in his dressing gown, holding his shotgun, walking towards the motionless figure of the man in the bobble hat.

'No!' Naomi said. 'NO! PLAY IT BACK, JOHN, PLAY IT BACK! OH GOD, PLAY IT BACK!'

John rewound it a short distance. But the repeat was

the same. Luke and Phoebe clambering eagerly over the fence. Then himself coming out of the house with his shotgun.

He pressed the stop button.

For some moments none of them spoke. Then John turned to the Detective Inspector and said, without malice, without anything, just drained, bewildered, not even desperate, just utterly helpless, 'Do you still want to work on the likelihood that they are not far away?'

101

Naomi sat on her own in front of two police officers. Although no one had said as much, it was clear that whilst she and John were being treated with kindness and courtesy, they were not themselves beyond suspicion. Which was why they were being required to make separate statements.

A tiny red light blinked on a video camera that was bolted high up on one wall and pointing at her. The room was small, anodyne and windowless. Bare cream walls that looked recently painted. A carpet that smelled new and comfortable bright red chairs with just a coffee table in front of them.

Two detectives faced her. One, in his early forties, was a bruiser of a man, in a fawn suit, with a precise, rather wooden air. The other, a woman about ten years younger, with short ginger hair, had a podgy face with small, suspicious eyes. She was dressed in a blue blazer sporting a club emblem on the breast pocket, over a thin roll-neck, and slacks.

Naomi could scarcely believe the speed at which the media had arrived at their home. The police had cordoned off the driveway down at the entrance, but within not much more than an hour of their first arriving there had been photographers snapping the scene with long lenses from the surrounding fields, and down in the lane there must have been a dozen different news vehicles, including a cameraman, high up above everyone else on a Sky TV hydraulic crane.

The male detective switched on the tape recorder in front of him. 'This is Detective Sergeant Tom Humbolt and Detective Constable Jo Newman interviewing Mrs Naomi Klaesson, Friday, January sixteenth at—' He paused to check his watch. 'Ten twelve a.m.'

His tone was bend-over-backwards polite. 'I'd like you to start, Mrs Klaesson, if you wouldn't mind, with your taking us through the events that led to you calling the police this morning.'

With her shattered nerves made even edgier by the formal tone of the interview, she gave them, in a faltering voice, as detailed an account as she could.

'Why exactly did you get up so early today, Naomi?' the woman detective asked. 'You said you don't normally get up until seven on weekdays.'

Naomi gulped down a mouthful of hot, sweet tea and asked, 'Do you have children?'

'Yes.'

'So you'll know what I mean about a mother's instincts?'

She nodded. Naomi glanced at Humbolt, who signalled with his eyes that he understood, also.

'I just sensed something was wrong, I can't put it any clearer than that – and I needed a pee.' There was a brief silence. Naomi toyed with her cup. 'Someone will call, won't they? If they find them while I'm in here?'

'The moment there is any news, we'll be told,' Detective Newman replied.

'Thank you.'

Then tears welled up inside Naomi, and she began crying, deep, choking, sobs. Murmuring an apology, trying to compose herself, she pulled a handkerchief out of her handbag and pressed it to her eyes.

'Interview suspended at ten twenty-one a.m.,' she heard the DS say.

*

Half an hour later, feeling a little bit calmer, Naomi sat back down in the interview room, and the tapes were restarted. In her mind, a constant loop of the videotape of Luke and Phoebe was running, over and over. She saw them trotting across the driveway towards those strangers in their baseball caps and goggles, hugging them, embracing them, kissing them. Greeting them in a loving way they had never – ever – done with herself or John.

Greeting them like they were their parents.

And suddenly the deep, numbing cold that was in every cell of her body froze her rigid.

What if?

What if?

What if those people were their parents?

No. Unthinkable. Besides, Luke and Phoebe had so many of her and John's features, everyone said that, and it was plain, absolutely plain to see sometimes when she looked at Luke how much of his father was in him.

And now she had another, even worse, thought. This was the first thing that had gone through her mind when she'd seen the body on the gravel and her children's missing coats and boots. She stared down at the table, listening to the hiss of the air conditioning. This was the thought she had pushed away, tried desperately to push back into a chamber of her mind as she had stumbled down the drive, as she had staggered through the sodden fields.

The thought that she did not, absolutely did not—

'Mrs Klaesson?'

The voice of Detective Sergeant Humbolt cut through her thoughts. Calm, but insistent.

She lifted her eyes up to his face.

'Would you like a little more time before we start?'

'Would you like to see a doctor to give you something to help calm you?' Jo Newman asked.

Naomi closed her eyes and shook her head. 'Please, tell me something. These paedophiles – they target chatrooms, don't they? You get these sick perverts chatting to young children, they become friends, then they lure them to meetings. This happens, doesn't it?'

The two detectives glanced at each other, then Humbolt said, 'For older children it is a real danger, but I don't think at three years old that's likely. They'd be too young.'

'I don't imagine at three, your children are old enough to be going on internet chatrooms, are they?' Jo Newman said.

'Their mental age is much older,' Naomi said. 'They are far more advanced than you could imagine.'

The woman detective gave her a look, as if both being mothers they shared a secret between them. It was a look that said, *All mothers think their children are special!*

'Your children had full access to the internet?' Humbolt asked.

'We gave them a computer last Sunday, for their birthday. I've been very surprised at some of the stuff they've been looking at – most of it scientific.'

Humbolt raised his eyebrows. 'At three?'

'I mean it when I say they're advanced. They are very advanced. They're like – child prodigies.'

Jo Newman said, 'Mrs Klaesson, all the computers in your home will be taken away for analysis. If they have been on any chatrooms, everything will be traceable.'

'Look – I – I know these questions are important. But we're sitting here and my children have been abducted – I just want to get back and find them. I don't want to be here, answering questions, this isn't right, we're just wasting time; can't we do this later?'

'You have information that may be very important for us to find the children,' the woman detective said, with a sympathetic smile.

Naomi had read recently that out of ninety-eight children who had been murdered in England in the past year, only three had been killed by people who weren't either immediate family or friends. 'Is that the real reason I'm here?' she said. 'Or is it because I'm a suspect? Is that it?'

She could see the sudden discomfort in their faces.

'What's the matter with you people? You have the videotape, you can see that strangers have taken my children – why am I here? Tell me?'

'You're not a suspect, Mrs Klaesson,' Detective Sergeant Humbolt said.

'We have a dead man on our doorstep, our children are abducted by strangers and instead of looking for them you're treating me like a bloody suspect. You have John in another room, he's been interrogated, too, and you are going to see if our stories tally. Let me tell you something: they are going to tally, OK?'

Neither detective said anything for some moments. Then Jo Newman said, 'Mrs Klaesson, let me set your mind at rest. Everything possible that can be done to find your children is being done. Every available police officer is being called in to search the area around your home. The police helicopter is scouring the area.'

Naomi accepted what she said, but with considerable reluctance. What choice did she have?

More questions followed, a whole barrage of them, one after another. How was her relationship with her husband? With her children? With her neighbours? Friends? Their children's friends?

She tried to answer each of them truthfully. But the two detectives didn't seem to be capable of taking on board just how smart and advanced Luke and Phoebe were.

'You say your mother saw this man on Tuesday? The one who was found outside your house?'

She shook her head. 'No, I didn't say that. I said that she was concerned about a stranger—'

Then she thought of something. 'A crucifix! She said he was wearing a crucifix! I – I didn't think to look this morning. Can someone check?'

Humbolt made a note on his pad. 'I'll find out.'

Looking a little awkward, DC Newman asked, 'Do Luke and Phoebe have any birthmarks or scars?'

'I – I – I don't think so, no. No.'

'And can you remember what they last had to eat?'

'To eat?' she echoed. 'Why does—'

Then she remembered. A series on television she and John had been watching a while back, about a Home Office pathologist. In one of the episodes, a child had gone missing. The police asked the parents about birthmarks and about what the child had eaten.

That way, if they found the bodies, it would make it easier to identify them. Either from marks on their bodies – or from cutting open their bellies and seeing what was in their stomachs.

The door opened suddenly, and Detective Inspector Pelham came in, still in his raincoat. 'Sorry to interrupt you,' he said, fixing his eyes on Naomi. 'But I thought you should know we have some developments.'

102

Before their interviews, John and Naomi had been introduced to a family liaison officer, DC Renate Harrison. In
her early forties, with brown hair cut into a short, stylish
bob, she was dressed in a businesslike way, in a grey
Prince of Wales check suit over a lace-collared cream
blouse, but she had a gentle demeanour.

She now led John and Naomi along a corridor to the
Detective Inspector's office, and sat them down at a small
round conference table.

DI Pelham followed them in a few moments later. He
closed the door and hung his mackintosh on a peg. In the
three hours since Naomi had seen him, he was looking
more ragged. His shirt was creased, the knot on his tie had
slipped, and there was a patina of perspiration on his face.

'Right,' he said, sitting down. His eyes moved from
Naomi to John and back, repeatedly. 'To cut to the quick,
we've found a car in the Caibourne village car park that
we think belongs to the man on your doorstep. It's been
there overnight and was rented from the Avis office in
Brighton three days ago, by a man fitting his description,
using an American driving licence and credit card we
found in his wallet. The name on them is *Bruce Preston*.
Does that mean anything to you?'

Naomi and John shook their heads. 'Never heard of
him,' John said.

Glancing at his watch, Pelham said, 'It's still night time
in America – we won't be able to find out if that's his real

name until after the start of business hours. There was a laptop in the boot of the car and the contents of that and a mobile phone found on his person are being analysed. Hopefully we'll get something from them.'

Then, standing up and going over to his desk, he returned with a brown envelope, from which he removed a photograph.

'This is an enlargement of a snapshot we found in Bruce Preston's wallet. Have either of you ever seen her before?'

John and Naomi stared at a pretty girl, with Latin looks and long black hair, in a simple summer dress, standing on what looked like the deck of a house.

'No,' John said.

'Never,' Naomi said. 'Definitely not.'

'Does the name *Lara* mean anything?'

They both shook their heads.

'Only that *Lara* is what he seemed to be murmuring when we found him,' Naomi said.

'Nothing else?'

'No.'

'That was all he said in the ambulance too, before he lost consciousness.' He stared at both of them for some moments, then said, 'This cult you mentioned – the Disciples of the Third Millennium? We won't be able to follow that up until the US opens for business.'

'Is this man going to survive?' Naomi asked.

'He has the two top neurosurgeons in the county working on him but he's not in good shape.' He shrugged again. 'I don't know.'

There was a brief pause. Pelham studied each of their faces in turn for a few seconds before speaking again. 'OK, there's more news for you – I'm telling you this in confidence. If anyone from the press gets to you, I'd appreciate it if you don't mention this. Clear?'

'Yes,' John said.

'The press are going to be crawling everywhere. You say nothing to them, not one word, nada, unless DC Harrison here sanctions it. Got that?'

John glanced at Naomi for confirmation. 'Yes.'

'Are you willing to go on television to appeal for the return of your children?'

'We'll do anything,' Naomi said.

'Good. We're lining up a live appeal with the BBC and Sky and some other programmes. Now, last night a villager in Caibourne out walking her dog saw a Mitsubishi sports car drive twice through the village, very slowly, as if the driver was lost or looking for something. She noticed it but unfortunately didn't make a note of the registration. However, and here's what's interesting, at three o'clock this morning, a customs officer at the Channel Tunnel remembers a red Mitsubishi sports car going through, with a man and a woman in the front seats and two small children, a boy and a girl, in the back.'

'Jesus,' John said. He took Naomi's hand and squeezed it hard.

Detective Inspector Pelham removed his jacket and slung it on the back of his chair. His shirt, damp with patches of perspiration, clung to his muscular torso. 'Security cameras record every vehicle at the tunnel entry point and we're having the tapes checked. It may be nothing, but it's about a two-hour drive from your home to the Tunnel at that time of night, which fits. We've contacted Interpol and requested all European police check out every railway station and airport, including private ones, for any children matching Luke and Phoebe's descriptions.'

'You think they could be abroad?' Naomi said. 'They could be abroad already? Where are they going – being taken – I mean—'

Her voice dried up. Shaking her head from side to side, tears welling up in her eyes, she said, 'No, oh no, no, no, no.'

John squeezed her hand even harder but there was absolutely no response. He wanted desperately to comfort her, as if in easing her mind in some way he might be able to ease his own. But he could find nothing to say. Just a maelstrom of thoughts. 'Does this mean that you won't be searching for them locally now?' Naomi asked.

'We have someone on the way to the Tunnel now with a photograph of Luke and Phoebe. If the customs officer is able to positively identify them, we will scale down our search for them locally and concentrate on trying to find clues, but until then we continue with the full search.'

'When can we go back home?'

'Technically, as soon as the crime scene lads have finished inside your house and in the immediate vicinity. I would think tomorrow, or the day after at worst. DC Harrison will help you find somewhere – and she or a colleague'll be with you around the clock for the next few days, to shield you from the press and protect you.'

John nodded bleakly.

'I don't want to go to a hotel,' Naomi said. 'I want to go and look for my children.'

Pelham gave her an understanding look. 'I'm sure you do, but I have drafted every spare officer I have to get out there, doing that now. The most helpful thing you can do for me at the moment is to carry on with your interviews with us. We need family trees from both of you, complete lists of all your friends, business associates, neighbours.'

John squeezed Naomi's hand and she signalled, with a squeeze, back.

'Of course,' he said. 'Anything.'

Pelham stood up. 'Would you like us to arrange some counselling for you?'

'Counselling?' John said.

'No,' Naomi said vehemently. 'I don't want counselling. I don't need some bloody – some – some bloody inadequate social worker telling me how to cope with this. Getting my children back is what I need to cope with this. Please get them back for us. I'll do anything, anything in the whole world.'

Pelham nodded.

Channel Tunnel.

Red Mitsubishi sports car.

Children in the back seat, a boy and a girl.

Three o'clock in the morning.

She didn't need any further proof. She knew, in her heart, it was them.

103

With fishing boats coming and going continually during this early part of the night, no one paid any attention to one more set of navigation lights sliding past the ancient Moorish watchtower, at the end of the stone quay, that marked the entrance to the port of Ouranoupoli.

Pilgrims and monks came and went continually, also. This little town on the northern Greek coast was the embarkation point for the twenty monasteries of the peninsula called the Holy Mount Athos, a short ferry ride across a strip of Aegean Sea.

It was also the closest harbour to another monastery on a small island twenty kilometres south of here.

The launch backed up to the bustling quay, just long enough for its one passenger to jump ashore, before heading back out to sea.

Lara Gherardi, her long black hair bunched up inside a baseball cap, and dressed in a baggy anorak, jeans and trainers, her travelling essentials in a small rucksack on her back, walked swiftly past a row of moored fishing smacks, then up the steep, metalled road, past several busy restaurants and cafés, into the main street of the town.

The sea was calmer over towards the mainland than the skipper had expected and they had arrived here a quarter of an hour early. She went into a crowded bar and ordered a water, then drank it out on the pavement, staring distastefully at a shop display of Holy Mount Athos souvenirs. The taxi pulled up.

Lara dumped her rucksack on the back seat, then climbed in beside it. Moments later the taxi was heading out of town, towards Thessaloniki airport, two and a half hours' drive away. It was seven o'clock.

She caught an eleven o'clock flight to Athens, then slept, fitfully, on a bench in the airport departure lounge.

At eight o'clock in the morning, seven o'clock UK time, she boarded a flight to London Heathrow.

104

Naomi's Diary

I'm just lying wide awake here on the fourth floor of the Thistle Hotel. Listening to the rumble of traffic down in the street below, and the sound of the sea just beyond the promenade wall. I can't sleep a wink. Just waiting, waiting, waiting for the phone to ring. Got up twice already to check my mobile is switched on and that the hotel phone isn't off the hook.

I keep hearing a phone that keeps ringing in another room. I've phoned down to the front desk, just to make sure the night staff know which room we're in.

Several times today I've wanted to die. I felt like this when Halley was losing his fight. I just wanted to slip my moorings and drift off into death with him.

I just keep thinking about where L and P might be, what's happened to them. I know I've been finding them difficult, but that's all gone from my head now. I love them to death. I know in some ways they may be strong, but they are still infants, tiny, little people. What we've done, John and I, very stupidly, is to make them too smart for their own good (or Dettore did, or whatever). They've been made smart enough to communicate with the adult world, but not to understand its dangers. That's how this has come about.

That image, that video footage of the children trotting into the arms of these strangers, that is what really gets to me. After three years of doing all we could for Luke and Phoebe, they've run off willingly with strangers. That's the worst thing of all.

That they may have been groomed by paedophiles over the internet, is one of the police lines of enquiry, although they haven't found any evidence of that on their computer, so far. They think it's possible that the dead man was part of a rival paedophile group and they had a falling out.

Great.

My children are in the hands of some paedophile monsters who shot a man in the back of the head. And no one has any clue where they are.

105

At some point during the sleepless night they had made love. Maybe *screwed* would have been a better description, John thought, because that's what it was. A coupling borne out of some primal need. They hadn't even kissed, Naomi had just drawn him into her, and they had worked away until they had both come, then returned to their respective sides of the hotel room bed.

At seven o'clock he pulled on his tracksuit and trainers, slipped out of the room and down to the lobby of the hotel. Then, as he walked through the revolving doors and out into the dry, grey morning, a battery of flashlights strobed at him, and he immediately went back inside, in panic.

There was an entire army of reporters and news vehicles out there.

He ran across the foyer, following signs marked first to the ballroom, then to the conference centre, and moments later found himself in a large, empty, conference hall.

He made his way to the back of it and out of the rear exit, walked up a wheelchair ramp and came to double doors with a metal bar. He pushed them and to his relief found himself in a deserted side street.

He ran through the bitterly cold air, up a long hill, heading away from the reporters and the sea towards the town centre, and after a few minutes emerged into a wide, deserted shopping street. A police car went by, then a taxi, then a bus with just a couple of passengers. He ran along, past shop windows filled with mannequins, hi-fi, furniture, lights, computers, past a bank that had been converted into a bar, then halted at stop lights and looked at his watch.

Luke and Phoebe were in the hands of strangers. What was happening to them? Were they still alive? He closed his eyes, wishing he could do something more than just answer damned questions, wishing he had woken and looked out of the window and seen those bastards taking his children and torn them to pieces with his bare hands.

As he ran across the road, he saw a teenage boy on a bicycle pedalling away from a newsagent, and stopped as he reached the shop, then went inside.

It was a small, narrow space, lined on one side with magazines, several of them soft porn, and on the other with both British and international newspapers. The proprietor, a surly-looking man, watched him from behind the counter.

Every British paper had the story on its front page. Several international ones did, too. There was even a photograph of himself and Naomi beneath the splash of one newspaper printed in a language he didn't recognize.

DESIGNER BABIES ABDUCTED!
TWINS KIDNAPPED!
DOUBLE KIDNAP TRAGEDY FOR DESIGNER
BABY COUPLE.

He picked out one paper at random and opened it. His and Naomi's photographs stared out at him. Taken in front of their house. The image was a little soft – it must have been taken with a long lens by one of the photographers in the fields yesterday morning.

He started reading the article.

> Swedish scientist Dr John Klaesson and his wife, Naomi, are distraught after the kidnapping of their twins, Luke and Phoebe, early yesterday morning.
>
> In an emotional appeal on television last night—

'Hey.'

John looked up, startled, to realize the proprietor was addressing him.

'Either buy it, mate, or clear off.'

John held up the page showing his photograph for the man to see. 'They're my children,' he said lamely.

'What's that?' The man wasn't even looking at him, he was rummaging below the counter for something.

'These twins, in the headlines, these are my children.'

He looked up at him and shrugged. 'Suit yourself. Either buy it or clear off.'

John put the paper back on the rack and patted his pockets. He had no money on him, not a bean.

'I'm sorry,' he said, distraught. 'I'll come back.'

The man wasn't interested; he wasn't even looking at him any more.

John slunk out of the shop and ran, half-heartedly, back towards the hotel and in through the door he had exited and left open.

Naomi was in the shower when he came into the room. 'Renate Harrison rang to see how we were. She's going to be waiting outside the rear entrance just before nine,' she said.

'Has she any news?'

'She said there have been some developments overnight, we'll get details at the police station.'

'But they haven't found them?'

'No.'

Naomi switched off the shower and stepped out. John passed her a towel. She looked so vulnerable, he thought, with her hair plastered to her head, and water running off her body. He wrapped the towel around her and stood silently, for some moments, hugging her.

At least if they haven't found Luke and Phoebe, there's a chance they are still alive, he thought.

And in Naomi's eyes, he saw exactly the same thought reflected back at him.

106

As they sat at the round table in his small office, accompanied by Renate Harrison, it seemed to John much longer than twenty-four hours since Detective Inspector Pelham had entered their lives.

'Right,' he said, looking sharp and fresh. 'Did you manage some sleep?'

'Not really,' John said.

'None,' Naomi said.

'You'll be able to go back home tonight.'

'Thank you,' John said.

Addressing Renate Harrison, Pelham said, 'You'd better get them fixed up with something to help them sleep.'

'What news do you have?' Naomi asked.

'Some progress,' he said. 'Not as much as any of us would like, but some. OK, this is the latest position. Our mystery man Bruce Preston is still in a coma following sixteen hours of neurosurgery yesterday. He's under round-the-clock police guard in the Sussex County Hospital, and *if* he regains consciousness, we'll interrogate him as soon as we are permitted. But he has severe brain damage and his prognosis is not good.'

'Have you found out about his identity?' John asked.

'It's false. I've had the FBI check him out and the trail goes cold in Rochester, New York State.'

'No link between him and the cult we told you about?' Naomi said.

'The Disciples people?'

'Yes.'

'None so far. We've sent photographs of him and the woman in the picture in his wallet to the FBI, and we haven't heard anything back yet.' He paused to take a sip of coffee. 'An analyst from our High Tech Crime Unit, who's been working around the clock on your two computers, has a number of questions he wants to ask you – he's coming in at ten.'

'Did you find anything on Bruce Preston's laptop?' John asked.

'Not yet; it seems he was very careful – or very good at hiding his tracks.'

'How much longer do you need to keep my own laptop?' John asked. 'I need it back pretty badly.'

'The analyst is bringing it back for you – both your computers.'

'Thanks.'

'We got the registration of the red Mitsubishi from the security cameras at the Channel Tunnel late yesterday,' he announced. 'The plates are false.'

John and Naomi said nothing.

'At seven o'clock this morning I got a phone call from France. This car has been found at a small airport in Le Touquet. We've managed to ascertain between us that a man and a woman, in their mid-to-late twenties, boarded a Panamanian-registered private jet with a small boy and girl who fit Luke and Phoebe's description, at half six in the morning yesterday. The pilot had flown in from Lyons and filed a flight plan to Nice. But the plane never showed up there.'

'Where did it go?' John asked.

'It left French airspace, and disappeared into thin air.'

'Does anyone have information about who owns this jet?' Naomi asked.

'We're working on it.'

'What's the range of one of those aircraft?' John asked. 'How far could it travel?'

'I'm told it depends entirely on the size of its fuel tanks. It had taken on sufficient fuel, given that its tanks weren't empty when it arrived, for fourteen hours of flight. Apparently this particular aircraft has a cruising speed of three hundred and fifty knots. Which basically means enough to get to America and halfway back.'

Going back to his desk, Pelham produced a map of the world, which he laid out in front of them. It had a curved line drawn on it in red ink. 'This line covers all the destinations the plane could have made safely on its cruising range.'

John and Naomi stared at it bleakly. The line stretched from Bombay in one direction, to Rio in another. And that was without taking into account any refuelling stops.

Their children could literally be anywhere on the planet.

107

The high tech crime analyst had a pallid complexion, bloodshot eyes and a large gold earring. He was dressed in grubby jeans and several layers of T-shirts and reeked of cigarette smoke. Addressing the floor rather than John and Naomi's faces, he said, 'Hi, I'm Cliff Palmer,' then gave each of them in turn a wet-fish handshake.

Naomi noticed he had a slight nervous tic.

He sat down, placed John's computer in front of him, then pushed his hair back from his forehead with both hands. It immediately slid forward again.

Renate went out of the room to fetch him a drink.

'You've been looking through my computer and the kids' computer?' John said.

'Yes, uh-huh.' He nodded pensively, and pushed his hair back again. 'I've made copies of both hard disks, I thought that was the best thing to do. I'll go down to the car and fetch your children's computer in a minute. You'll have to forgive me, I've not been to bed yet – I worked through the night.' He looked at each of them in turn, as if expecting sympathy. Naomi gave him one tepid quiver of her lips.

'Have you found anything of interest?' John asked.

He put his hand in front of his mouth and yawned loudly. 'Yes, well, it might be of interest – stuff on both the computers, but I can't do anything without the keys.' He raised his eyebrows at John.

'Keys?'

'The encryption keys.'

'Do you mean for the passwords?' John asked.

Cliff shook his head. 'Not just those – although there are plenty of those in both systems that I haven't been able to get beyond, or bypass, yet. But it's the language they're using in emails and on chatrooms.'

Renate Harrison brought him a mug of tea and set it down, and coffees for John and Naomi.

John said, 'I warned Detective Inspector Pelham about that yesterday when the computers were taken to you – that they've developed a speech code of talking backwards, with every fourth letter missing.'

The analyst stirred sugar into his tea, then sipped it. 'Yes, I was told – but it's way more sophisticated than that. From the progress I've made so far, all I can tell you is that they've been in touch with quite a number of people all over the world for at least a year – that's as far back as I've gone at the moment. But all the addresses are encrypted and the language is impenetrable.'

He sipped some tea. 'I've tried all the usual encryption suspects but there's no match to any of them. There are ciphers out there that are just not breakable by anyone, you know that, don't you?'

'These are three-year-old children, Cliff,' Renate Harrison reminded him.

'Yes, I know,' he said, a tad irritably. 'But it's the same on both machines.'

'Are you saying they've devised these?'

'Someone who has been accessing these computers has either been devising them or borrowing them. I can't tell you who, all I can do is try to find out what they say, and I think I've hit a brick wall.'

Naomi looked at John. 'What about your guy, Reggie?'

'Reggie Chetwynde-Cunningham? I was about to say that. He'd be the person for this.' Addressing the analyst, he explained, 'I work at Morley Park. This man has an entire research facility there – he's the top encryption expert in the country.'

Cliff gave a nod. 'I wouldn't normally like to admit defeat to a pair of three-year-olds. But under the circumstances—' He gave a nervous laugh.

No one laughed with him.

108

Lara reversed the rental Fiat into the car park bay so that when she returned she would be able to drive out forwards, saving precious seconds, should she need them.

Figuring out the pay and display machine, she bought a ticket for the maximum time, four hours, and stuck it where the instructions told her, on the inside of the windscreen. That would give her until six o'clock this evening.

She tucked the straps of her rucksack inside the bag, then, carrying it like a holdall, she crossed the busy street and entered the front of the Royal Sussex County Hospital. From the little shop in the foyer she bought a small bunch of carnations wrapped in cellophane. Despite the terrible nervousness she felt, she tried to look nonchalant, to blend in, to be just another visitor coming to see a patient and bringing a few belongings for them.

She hovered for some moments near the information desk, looking for a plan of the place. There were plenty of people around to ask, but she didn't want to draw any attention to herself, so she just carried on walking, trying to appear confident, as if she knew where she was going, whilst silently and invisibly asking God for guidance.

She went up an incline and came to a junction of corridors. There were signs here. X-RAY. CARDIOLOGY. OUTPATIENTS. HISTOPATHOLOGY. RENAL UNIT. MATERNITY. PHARMACY.

NEUROSURGERY.

She climbed three flights of stairs, then walked along

another corridor. She strolled past medics, orderlies, nurses, visitors. She passed an elderly man in a dressing gown and slippers, inching his way on a Zimmer frame with grim determination, and a gurney on which another old man lay, mouth open, toothless, bewildered, as if someone had abandoned him out here.

Up another flight of stairs. Another corridor. Past a staff rest room. Peering through the window, she could see five female nurses in there. Lara understood the rhythms and beats and logistics of hospitals. She understood the chaos of shifts, the constant ebb and flow of strange faces, the impossibility in a large hospital of everyone being familiar with everyone else, or even recognizing everyone else.

When she was eighteen, her parents had her admitted to the psychiatric ward of a general hospital in Chicago. She had spent much of that time wandering the corridors, chatting to staff, generally hanging out with anyone who would talk to her, trying to find a little corner of the massive place where she could belong. She made friends with the kitchen staff and for a while belonged there; then she made friends with the laundry staff, and for a while belonged in the laundry. Then with the team at one of the nursing stations.

It was her sweet, gentle Master, Harald Gatward, who had broken the terrible news to her yesterday about her own beloved Disciple. The Master explained that this was a test from God of her love for Timon Cort and of her love for all the Disciples. There would never be a bigger test for her than this. After this she would truly *belong* for ever.

She walked on, saw the sign NEUROSURGERY right ahead of her now, and stopped.

Reality check.

She took a breath, said a small, silent prayer for strength and courage.

Timon was close. He was still alive, she knew that; she'd phoned the ward sister an hour ago, pretending to be a newspaper reporter, and she had confirmed that he was alive still, but she would say no more.

Inching forward now, one step at a time, pretending to be making an adjustment to the flowers every time someone came by, she reached an intersection. An arrow marked NEUROSURGERY pointed to her right. And she could see at the end of the corridor a nursing station and what looked like a reception area.

She walked down, and in the bustle of activity as she approached the station no one paid her the slightest attention. Then she froze.

To her left was a short corridor down to the double doors of a ward. But before those doors was another door, on the right. A uniformed policeman sat on a chair outside it, staring at a newspaper, looking bored out of his tree.

Her heart skipped.

Timon was in there!

Then she turned abruptly away before the policeman noticed her, and walked around to the far side of the island station. Thinking hard for some moments, she made a decision, began retracing her steps back to the stairs, and went down to the next floor, then on down, floor after floor, until she finally reached the basement.

The lighting was dingy and she heard the rumble of a furnace. There was a smell of boiled cabbage and fuel oil. Massive pipes ran along above her. Ahead she could see steam billowing through an open door.

'Has anyone given you tea?' she said aloud, to herself,

in what she was hoping sounded like an English accent. She said it again. And again. 'Hez ennyone given yew tee?'

And one more time, as she dumped the flowers on the floor and set off in search of the laundry storage area.

'Hez ennyone given yew tee?'

Most of the doors off the corridors down here were marked, and it took her less than five minutes to find the one marked STAFF UNIFORM STORES.

Putting down the holdall, she went through the door into a cavernous room that seemed out of another century. On one side were shelves stacked with every kind of hospital uniform, and accessories. On the other, a long work bench, at which about a dozen Oriental male and female staff were busily pressing and folding clothes. No one had even noticed that she'd come in.

She went over to the work bench and addressed an elderly Chinese woman. 'Hi, I'm an auxiliary nurse – doing an emergency locum in Maternity. They told me to come down here to get a uniform.'

The woman raised her hands. 'You go uniform have Personnel make request.'

In response to Lara's blank stare, the woman drew a rectangle with her hands. 'Form! You go request form Personnel. Upstairs. Seggon floor.'

'I'll take the uniform, bring the form down later!' Lara said. 'Emergency!'

The woman shrugged, muttered angrily and turned back to her labours.

Lara swiftly took a nursing uniform and blouse, but could see no shoes anywhere. Her trainers would have to do. Plenty of the nurses here were wearing what looked like plimsolls. Hiding everything inside her bulky anorak, she picked up her bag, hurried back up to the ground floor, then made her way to the first toilet she could find, locked herself in a cubicle and changed.

She carried her bag out of the hospital and over to the parking lot, locked it in the boot of her car, then returned to the hospital. She walked briskly, like any nurse who might be late for her shift, in through a side door this time, and made her way back up to the Neurosurgery ward.

So easy, she thought. *Nothing to it, just look confident!*

As she passed the nursing station, she pulled out of her pocket a hypodermic syringe and a vial, and now held both of these openly. The policeman was still reading his newspaper, and barely even glanced at her as she approached.

'Hez ennyone given yew tee?' she asked breezily.

His face brightened. 'Not for a while, I'd appreciate a cuppa.'

Giving him a special smile, she said, 'Two minutes!' then went into the room, closing the door behind her.

Then stood still.

Stared at him.

At the man she had thought about and prayed for every day and every night for the past three years. Timon. Sweet, sweet Timon, with his gentle voice and his soft touch. Stared at his swollen, distorted face; at the clear plastic breathing tubes in his nostrils. At the array of drip lines running up from his wrist, and at the battery of wires running from electrode pads on his head into a large machine with about ten different digital displays on it.

She stepped over to the bed, looking at the strip of white gauze on his forehead, and at his closed eyes. She touched his free hand, squeezed it. 'Timon,' she whispered. 'Listen, I have to be quick, I don't have much time. It's me, Lara. Can you hear me?'

To her joy, she felt her hand being squeezed, as if in response.

Then his eyes opened.

'Timon!' she said. 'Timon, my sweet love!'

His eyes rolled, as if he were trying to focus, but no longer had the motor functions to do so.

'Listen,' she said. 'There is something you need to know. You have a son, a beautiful boy called Saul. *Our* son.' A tear trickled down her cheek. 'He's nearly two and a half years old now. He's going to be so proud of you.'

The Disciple's eyes widened. His mouth opened. 'Lara!' he murmured. 'Lara!'

She shot a nervous glance at the door, then, freeing her hand, pushed the needle in through the seal of the vial, and drew the contents out until the barrel was full. She didn't bother to squirt out a bit, to ensure there was no air going into the vein. Instead she just leaned forward and kissed him on the forehead. 'I have to do this,' she whispered. 'I'm so sorry. It's just to make sure you don't say anything by mistake to anyone here. You understand, don't you?'

His eyes rolled, and for one fleeting instant, she was certain he had actually looked at her face. And signalled his understanding.

Then, rapidly locating a vein in his wrist, she pushed the needle in, then pressed the plunger all the way home.

'Goodbye,' she whispered, removing it. 'Goodbye my sweet, gentle Disciple.'

The door opened.

Lara turned, to be confronted by a nurse in her forties, with a stern face and black curly hair, wearing a badge that said, SISTER EILEEN MORGAN.

'Who are you? What's going on? What are you—'

471

Lara stabbed her in the neck with the syringe, then burst out of the room, collided with a man in a white coat, a doctor, pushed him out of the way, ignoring shouts behind her, and sprinted down the corridor, past the nursing station, along to the stairs, and threw herself down them.

She did not look round, just kept going, kept running, taking the stairs two, three at a time.

Down on the ground floor she crashed through a family with small children, dodged a woman wheeling a trolley laden with library books, pushed open doors marked EMERGENCY EXIT ONLY and instantly heard an alarm klaxon go off.

Then she was running across the road, digging in her pocket for her car keys. As she reached the car she looked back and saw that the policeman who had been on guard was already coming in through the car-park entrance.

She unlocked the car, got in, jammed the key into the ignition at the third attempt with her shaking hand, twisted it. The engine burst into life. The policeman was right in front of the car, holding his hands up, yelling at her to stop.

She floored the accelerator.

He hurtled onto the bonnet, his face striking the windscreen and buckling a wiper blade.

She swerved the car to the right, then left, racing across the parking lot, trying to shake him off. Then she made a sharp right to the exit onto the busy street, and she saw him slide off to the left and roll away out of sight.

A bus was bearing down from the right. If she went right now, she could make it, just, just. She floored the pedal, pulled out right across the road and made a sharp left, the little car slewing wildly, then picking up speed.

Straight towards a truck.

A truck on the wrong side of the road. *Asshole. You asshole!*

Saw the shock on the driver's face.

And then she realized. It wasn't the truck that was on the wrong side, it was her, forgetting she was in England, forgetting they drove on the left.

An instant later the front bumper of the truck exploded through the windscreen.

109

At five o'clock in the afternoon, travelling back in the dark from the Morley Park Research Laboratories, John and Naomi sat in silence, immersed in their thoughts, while Renate Harrison drove.

The detective's cellphone rang and she answered it. From her deferential tone it sounded like she was talking to a superior officer.

Reggie Chetwynde-Cunningham had been very decent to give up his weekend, Naomi thought. He had this afternoon seconded his entire team of encryptologists to the task of breaking the language codes in the two computers, and assured them he would lead the team through the night, if necessary.

The family liaison officer finished her call and put the phone back in its cradle. 'That was DI Pelham. There have been some developments.' Her tone sounded grim. 'He wants me to take you straight to see him when we get back.'

Naomi felt a whorl of fear spiral through her. 'What – what developments?'

'He didn't give me any details.'

Naomi, in the rear seat, looked at Renate Harrison's face in the mirror. Every few seconds it was illuminated by the headlights of an oncoming vehicle. The woman was lying, she could see it in her expression.

Was this it? Was this going to be the bad news they

were expecting? That their children had been found dead? Murdered by the paedophiles or Disciples, or whoever the hell had taken them?

John was sitting in the front passenger seat. Naomi laid a hand on his shoulder. 'Do you think this guy, Reggie, will be able to crack these codes?'

John turned his head, put his hand gently over her fingers. 'He's doing all he can, hon.'

'I know, but will he crack them?'

John was silent, wondering what to say to her. He knew that some modern codes were virtually impossible. 'If anyone can break them, it's him.'

Naomi responded, 'Is that another way of saying that if he can't, no one can?'

For an answer, John took her hand in his, and interlocked his fingers with hers.

She thought back to the expression he had used so often in the past. *Love is more than just a bond between two people. It's like a wagon-train circle you form around you that protects you against all the world throws at you.*

Their fingers closed that circle. She and John. They were that wagon train. Except. You were meant to have your entire family inside that circle. Wasn't that the point?

*

The tall, wooden detective sergeant, Tom Humbolt, who had been one of her two interviewers yesterday, was in DI Pelham's office with him when they arrived shortly after six. Humbolt was dressed as sharply as he had been yesterday, in a camel suit and a jazzy tie, with a warm smile on his face. Pelham was looking concerned.

They sat down at the round table.

'Right, to bring you up to speed, Mr and Mrs Klaesson,'

the DI said tersely, 'there have been a number of developments. At two thirty this afternoon, a woman masquerading as a nurse entered the room of the man we know as Bruce Preston, at the Sussex County Hospital, and administered a lethal injection. I'm afraid the medical team were unable to resuscitate him.'

John stared at him in silence, absorbing this, and the significance. Naomi was wide-eyed in shock.

Humbolt continued, 'She stabbed a nurse – not fatally – and drove her car at a police officer who had been guarding him, injuring him seriously, and she was subsequently killed in a head-on collision with a lorry. She was apparently on the wrong side of the road.'

'Committing suicide?' said Naomi, her voice barely above a whisper.

'Who – who – what – this woman – what . . . ?' John said, his voice tailing off.

'She matches the photograph of the woman that we found in Preston's wallet – the one I showed you.'

'This must be Lara, the woman he kept mentioning after he was shot,' John said.

'We don't know anything about her or what their relationship was,' Humbolt said.

'She was travelling on an American passport,' Pelham said, 'under the name Charlotte Feynman. The FBI have just informed us that the passport number corresponds with a woman of twenty-seven of that name, who died of meningitis in a hospital in Columbus, Ohio, eighteen months ago.'

He paused to let this sink in, then went on. 'What I'm now going to tell you is in complete confidence and you are not to repeat it to the press, or to anyone, is that clear?'

John and Naomi nodded.

'We've found three items of interest in her handbag, in the boot of her car. A boarding-card stub from a flight from Athens to London earlier today; a receipt – which looks like a bar receipt – from a location as yet unidentified, in euros, dated yesterday; and, what might be the best of all, a receipt for a left-luggage locker at Athens airport time-dated six fifteen a.m. today. I've had a copy faxed through to the Athens police headquarters and a request for them to open it and let us know the contents. There's always red tape involved with the Greek police, and if I don't get immediate cooperation, I have an officer on standby to catch a flight out there tonight with the original.'

'Killed him?' Naomi said. 'Went in the room and killed him?'

'We won't know until the post-mortem is done, but that's how it appears.'

'Wasn't he under guard?'

'Yes.' He gave an apologetic shrug. 'To report on other progress, our team have concluded their field search for clues at your home.'

'What have they found?' John asked.

'Very little to go on, so far. Footprints. A discarded cigarette butt in the schoolhouse car park that's been sent for DNA testing. Now, regarding the private jet, a Gulfstream, our colleagues in France have checked out all national and international airports within the jet's range and there've been no sightings. They are trying to obtain ownership details of the plane, but it seems there's a whole chain of companies involved, starting with half a dozen different ones in Panama. Someone's gone to great lengths to keep its owner invisible.'

'I know I keep asking this, but do you think it's a paedophile ring?' Naomi asked, looking at Pelham then Humbolt in turn. Neither of their faces gave away anything.

'We are keeping a totally open mind at the moment, Mrs Klaesson,' Pelham said. 'But if it is of any comfort, with the involvement of this aircraft and all the planning that seems to be behind this, it's too sophisticated for any of the paedophile rings we've ever encountered.'

'What about the Disciples of the Third Millennium?' John said.

Pelham shot a glance at the detective sergeant then stared back at John and Naomi. 'I understand from the FBI that they may be close to a breakthrough.'

'What kind of a breakthrough?' Naomi asked, her hopes rising.

'They won't tell us.'

'Great,' she muttered bitterly.

'One thing I'm not clear on,' John said, 'is how you are sure that it was Luke and Phoebe who went through the Channel Tunnel and were on that plane. You seem to be very certain it was them.'

Tom Humbolt responded, 'I went to Folkestone today and interviewed the immigration officer who claims he saw them. He said he had a bit of banter with them – they were all travelling on American passports and told him they were on a touring holiday of Europe. He said he'd commented that with the kids on the back seat of this small sports car, they couldn't have much luggage with them. The man he'd presumed was the father had joked back that because the car went so fast, they got everywhere that much quicker, so they needed less luggage.'

'He wasn't at all suspicious?' said John.

'He said that he felt afterwards that something hadn't been quite right. But couldn't put a finger on it,' Humbolt responded.

'And he had a really good look at them?' Naomi quizzed.

'He's one hundred per cent certain it was your son and daughter.'

'Did he say anything about how they were? Did they seem distressed? Anxious? Upset?'

'He didn't, no.'

'Prat,' she said. 'What a prat. He's suspicious and he does nothing? What the hell's he there for?'

Everyone was silent for a moment.

Then Pelham said, 'Under the current circumstances, I think it would be inadvisable to return to your home – at least until we know more about the identity of this woman who killed Bruce Preston. With your permission, I'd like to move you to safe accommodation under police guard. We have some facilities at Sussex Police Headquarters, in Lewes. It's not luxurious, I'm afraid, just a basic room with shower and TV. But I'd feel more comfortable if you were there, until I can be sure you're not in any danger yourselves. Are you OK with that?'

'Anything,' she said. 'I don't care.'

Pelham stood up, walked over to his desk and leaned against it, putting his hands behind his back. 'Dr and Mrs Klaesson, I want to ask you both something, and I need you to answer me openly, however difficult it may be for you. You have been telling me the truth, haven't you?'

'What on earth do you mean?' Naomi had to contain her anger.

'You haven't had a call from the kidnappers that you haven't told us about? No ransom demand? No communication of any kind?'

'Absolutely not!' declared John.

'Why would you think we would hold anything like this back from you?' Naomi asked.

'Because in my experience – and no offence intended – people under the kind of strain you are under do sometimes. Because, quite naturally and understandably, you will do anything to get your children back. Often, if people are told by kidnappers not to mention something to the police, they comply. You need to understand where I'm coming from, and likewise, the reverse.'

After some moments of collecting her thoughts, Naomi responded, 'Detective Inspector Pelham, so far as I am concerned you are coming from your life, and when you are finished today, you'll go back home to your life. Until the moment I have my children back, safe and well and in my arms, I don't have a life. Nor does my husband. Can I make that any clearer to you?'

110

The room in the Sussex Police Headquarters annexe building smelled newly decorated and had the damp chill of all rooms that are only occasionally occupied.

Naomi sat on one of the twin beds, hugging herself for warmth, while John fiddled with the electric radiator. The walls were painted a pastel yellow, there were chintz floral curtains, two landscape prints – a view of Lewes Castle, and of the river Ouse – a small sofa, a writing table and a television, which John had switched on. A door opened onto a tiny en-suite bathroom.

In the hall outside the room, two armed police officers guarded them. Their presence should have made her feel safer, Naomi thought, but it didn't. It just made her feel worse, even further divorced from reality.

Her phone beeped, telling her she had messages, and she played through them. Rosie. Her mother. Her sister. She rang home and checked the messages on the phone there. There were twenty. Some were from friends and neighbours in Caibourne, several from the press, and a couple of work ones for John, which she jotted down on the back of a receipt she dug out of her handbag.

'That's better, getting some heat now,' John said.

She read out the work messages to him.

'They're not urgent, I'll deal with them tomorrow.'

Tomorrow. She thought. *Tomorrow* was a million years away. Luke and Phoebe could be alive tonight and dead tomorrow. *Tomorrow* wasn't a luxury they had. *Now, this minute*, that's how it had to be. 'Will you call Reggie Chetwynde-Cunningham, see if he's made any progress?'

'He promised to call the moment he has any news.'

'He might not have been able to get through.'

'Hon, he has both our cellphone numbers, OK?'

One of their guards, a cheery Firearms officer in his late thirties, brought them their supper, a tray of lasagne and salad and rhubarb crumble and custard. He had three small kids himself, he told them, and knew what they must be going through.

Naomi, out of politeness, resisted telling him that no, he didn't know what they were going through, he had no idea, no one could have any idea. Just hold in your mind the worst thing in the world you could imagine and then multiply it by ten billion. And not even that would take you close.

A while later they had a phone call from a doctor, at DI Pelham's request, he said, asking if they would like sedatives or sleeping pills. Naomi politely declined, telling him she wanted to be fully alert if there were any developments during the night.

They watched each news bulletin in the forlorn hope that they might learn of some progress the police had not yet told them about. They were the lead item and the main story. The killing of the man in hospital. The death of the mystery woman with the false American passport. Speculations about paedophile rings, Disciples of the Third Millennium cult, the world adoption trade in small children. Excerpts from the broadcast John and Naomi had made yesterday. Pictures of Luke and Phoebe. A statement from DI Pelham saying little.

In between, Naomi made calls to her mother and

sister, John dealt with some emails, and they watched *Who Wants to Be a Millionaire.*

John managed to concentrate on the show for just one question, but within moments had lapsed back to his inner world. To the terrible guilt he felt for what he had done. *If* he hadn't spoken to that journalist, Sally Kimberly, then there would never have been all the publicity. Perhaps no one would have taken any notice of them. Whoever had taken Luke and Phoebe, and for whatever reason, he felt certain he was in some way to blame.

He didn't know what to say to Naomi, what to do about it, how to deal with it.

For the first time ever in his life he felt that if he were to die, it would be a blessed relief. And what he deserved. All that kept him going was the knowledge that somehow he had to be strong for Naomi, to keep every ounce of pressure on the police.

After the ten o'clock news Naomi said, 'Do you think they will ever find them, John?'

'Absolutely.'

'Alive?'

'Yes.'

She stood up, walked over to the window and stared out. There was no view, just a windowless brick wall the other side of an enclosed courtyard. 'They're too smart, too intelligent. People who think they've seized a couple of pretty children to abuse are going to find themselves with more than they bargained for. When Luke and Phoebe suss that these people they trotted off with so damned happily are actually monsters, then they're going to start resisting – and when that happens, what the hell are these creeps going to do? What would you do?'

John walked over to her and put his arms around her. 'Maybe they're smart enough to escape. Perhaps this is the time that the advantages we've given them in life will pay off.'

She looked at him. 'Really? Well, if you can explain all these wonderful advantages they have – how come they were foolish enough to go off with these people in the first place?'

111

'Did you manage to sleep?' Pelham asked John and Naomi.

'A little, thank you.' Naomi stared across the round table in the detective inspector's office through raw eyes and with a throbbing head. Her scalp felt tight and uncomfortable, as if it had shrunk around her skull.

Pelham was accompanied by Tom Humbolt and a third man, a lean, good-looking American in a dark suit, whom the DI introduced as Special Agent Dan Norbert of the FBI, who was based at the American Embassy in London.

'Thanks for coming down on a Sunday,' John said.

The agent spoke in rapid-fire bursts with a Southern twang, his lips barely moving. 'Not a problem, we're full out on this case. Real sorry 'bout your kids. Gonna get them back for you, that's what we're here to do. We're gonna get 'em back fast as we can.'

He spoke with a certainty that gave Naomi a spark of hope. 'What's happened?' she asked. 'Have there been some developments? Do you know where they are?'

'We believe we do,' he said.

Pelham said, 'I decided not to risk waiting for the Greek authorities to get around to opening up the left-luggage locker and sent an officer to Athens airport myself last night. He found a bag in the locker containing amounts of cash in a number of currencies, the business card of a taxi company in Thessaloniki, and the deceased woman's real passport sewn into the bottom. Her name is Lara Gherardi. That mean anything to either of you?'

'No,' John said.

'*Lara Gherardi?* No.' Naomi shook her head.

Pelham continued, 'The FBI say she was reported missing three and a half years ago by her family in Chicago, who believe she was linked to a religious cult. She had a history of mental illness and instability, and had twice in her teens run off and joined cults. On those occasions, her family used to get communications from her, but they've heard nothing in three and a half years – they say it's as if she disappeared off the face of the earth.'

Naomi looked at the American agent. 'Where do you think our children are? Have you found out anything about the plane?'

'We haven't gotten any useful information on the Gulfstream yet. But we're closing the loop in another direction. The man who was found with a gunshot wound on your doorstep on Friday morning – who was murdered yesterday – we believe is Timon Cort, a member of the Disciples of the Third Millennium cult.'

'It really exists?' John asked.

'The Disciples?' The agent tilted his head. 'Uh, you want to believe it exists. We're pretty certain we've located their base, and we've been monitoring all their electronic signals for several months by satellite, picking up all their digital communication packets. We've been tracking this Timon Cort character through emails – all coded in weird religious tracts of the Bible – for the past eighteen months. We linked him to Iowa, where there was a mass death of a family who had been to Dr Dettore, then to Rochester, New York State, where another family who had been to

Dettore were killed. Then we lost him. Turns out he comes to England and pitches up on your doorstep.'

'Who shot him outside our house?' Naomi asked, tightly, shivering.

'Can't answer that,' Dan Norbert said. 'You get seriously screwed-up people in these cults. Two factions disagreeing about what to do, that kind of stuff.'

'And you *know* where they are?' she said.

'Thanks to Miss Gherardi's left luggage ticket.' He chewed his gum for a moment. 'Our office in Athens has been on to the cab firm who told us where they picked this woman up from yesterday. Her photo was in Timon Cort's wallet. She got sent to kill him, presumably to keep him from talking, but that doesn't interest us. It's the connection between them, that's the thing, that's the absolute proof for us.'

'I thought the Disciples killed people – that they were dedicated to eradicating children conceived in Dr Dettore's clinic?' John said. 'Why would they abduct them?'

'Seems like they've had a change of policy. In the past week in the United States, three sets of *Dettore* twins have been reported missing by the parents. They've just vanished, leaving even less for us to go on than yours have.'

'*Three* sets of twins?' John said. 'They've kidnapped six kids in the past week?'

'We don't have evidence the others have been kidnapped, but it seems likely. They've all just slipped under the radar, vanished into thin air.'

'And you think they're in the same place as Luke and Phoebe?' asked Naomi.

'We're gonna find out pretty soon.'

'How soon?' she persisted.

'Well, ma'am, appropriations are really being pumped, and we're just getting our proactive procedural safeguards locked in – we want to ensure we don't give these bastards one inch of wiggle room, right?'

'Right,' she echoed blankly, barely understanding a word of what he had just said.

Then he went on. 'I'm sorry to have to make you go back over ground you've been covering with these good people for the past forty-eight hours, but I'm going to need to start at the beginning with you.'

'It's not a problem,' John said. 'We're very grateful for your involvement.'

It was three in the afternoon before Special Agent Norbert was done with his questions, and Pelham escorted him out of the door, back to his car.

112

John and Naomi sat in silence for some moments as they waited for Pelham to return. Naomi, completely drained, looked at Tom Humbolt, who had an expression on his face that seemed to be saying, *Why do guys like Special Agent Norbert treat everyone who isn't FBI like they just fell off the back of a truck?*

'Three other sets of twins?' Naomi said to him. 'Why – why would they be taking them?'

'Could it be to try to protect them?' John asked.

'Maybe to try to brainwash them?' Humbolt ventured.

'It seems positive, at least,' Renate Harrison said. 'If their agenda was to harm Luke and Phoebe, and these others, I don't imagine they would have gone to these lengths of taking them away.'

Her mobile phone rang. She answered it, then a moment later said, 'One moment, sir, I'd like everyone to hear what you have to say. Can we call you back on a speaker phone in a couple of minutes? Thank you.' Ending the call, she said to John and Naomi, 'It's Professor Chetwynde-Cunningham with some information. I suggest we wait for Detective Inspector Pelham to return.'

A few minutes later, with a starfish-shaped conferencing phone on the middle of the table, Renate Harrison dialled the linguist's number at Morley Park. 'We have Dr and Mrs Klaesson, Detective Inspector Pelham and Detective Sergeant Humbolt listening, Professor.'

'Jolly good. Good afternoon, everyone.' He sounded very tired.

They returned the greeting, then waited.

'I'm afraid I don't have any good news for you. It's a bit disappointing at the moment. We've all been working around the clock on this, and I'm afraid we haven't made much progress. You are probably aware from our conversations, John, that encryption techniques have moved forward enormously in recent years, with a great deal of research money being thrown at creating uncrackable codes for secure trading on the internet. Yes?'

'Sure,' John said.

'What we have here is way advanced from the code your twins were using a while ago, of reversing speech and deleting every fourth letter. I'm afraid what we are up against here is something none of us has encountered before and it's not decipherable within current capabilities. I'm not saying it won't be possible one day, but it could take us a month, or many months, maybe longer. Without the keys, we're stymied in the short term.'

Pelham leaned forward. 'This is Detective Inspector Pelham speaking, Professor.'

'Yes, hallo.'

'Are you willing to keep trying?'

'Of course, but I don't want to hold out any promises – you need to be aware of that.'

'We appreciate your candour, Professor.'

'With your permission, I'd like to send copies of these hard disks to one of my former colleagues at GCHQ – the Government Communications Headquarters at Cheltenham. He's willing to give his people a shot at it.'

Pelham looked at John and Naomi for confirmation,

then said, 'You have our absolute consent to explore any avenue you consider appropriate.'

'OK. I don't think there's much more I can add at present.'

'We're very grateful to you,' Pelham said.

'Thanks, Reggie,' John said.

'Perhaps I can offer you and your wife one small crumb in this awful predicament. If your children are smart enough to be able to communicate in this code, then they must have quite extraordinary intelligence.'

'Meaning what, exactly?' John asked.

'Well, just that. Perhaps their survival skills are equally honed.'

'They are still only three years old, Professor,' Naomi said.

'That may be, but they've got more wits about them than most adults.'

After a long silence, John said, 'We hear what you are saying, Reggie, thank you. We appreciate everything you and your team are doing.'

'I'll keep you posted.'

They all thanked him, then Pelham terminated the call.

'Maybe we should take a break,' the detective inspector said. 'I think we could all use a little air.'

113

It was a perfect night. They could have waited weeks for conditions like this, months even. No moon, heavy cloud cover, a light swell. They cut the motor and drifted, and within seconds, operating on synchronized watches, all the other outboards on the fleet of twenty inflatables had been cut, too.

Sudden hush. Just the slop of the ink-black ocean, the splash of oars, the creak of rowlocks, the sound of nervous breathing, the rustle of tough clothing fabrics.

Twelve miles to the south, the lights of the ships were now no longer visible. Out there in the darkness on the edge of the horizon, two aircraft carriers, one belonging to the Greek navy, one to the United States, were hove-to, on full alert. Helicopters sat on both their decks, crewed-up, waiting.

With all electronic equipment switched off, and all conversation forbidden, the crew in the flotilla of shore craft rowed the final three miles in silence.

*

At half past one in the morning, Harald Gatward knelt beside his bed, face buried in his hands, communing with the Lord in a prayer vigil more intense than any he had held in months.

He felt like he had hit a wall with his worship, the kind of wall marathon runners face after the first few miles, the wall of pain and despair you have to get beyond, because when you do, when you muster your resources and force yourself through, soon the juices start flowing, and everything becomes easier.

Satan had put up this wall and he needed God to help him find a way through it.

Father Yanni, the Abbot, had come to his cell and spoken to him last night, told him in that wise, lugubrious voice that the other monks had noticed he wasn't praying so well recently. Particularly the past couple of days. Father Yanni wondered if, perhaps, the American was sickening for something? Or having doubts?

'The man who has doubts is condemned if he eats, because his eating is not from faith; and everything that does not come from faith is sin,' Harald Gatward had replied.

The Abbott told him the monks would pray for his faith, then had said a short prayer with him, and left.

Gatward opened his eyes and stared into the darkness of his room. Soon it would be the drum call to matins and they would all see his troubled face. Might be better this morning to remain in his cell; he had to think through his problems, the ones he could not, dare not, share with the Abbot or any monk here.

Timon Cort.

Lara Gherardi.

What a mess.

Had Timon Cort said anything before he had died? Had Lara Gherardi? Was there anything in their possession that could yield clues to the enemy?

It had been a mistake sending Lara, and he was bitterly regretting it now. She had been a good person; he had acted out of panic, hadn't thought it through properly, and had not given her time to plan. It would have been better to have sent someone not emotionally attached; her love for her fellow Disciple must have affected her judgement.

In five years, through meticulous planning and discipline, rigorously following the guidance of God, none of his Disciples had made one slip. Now, in the space of less than forty-eight hours, two were dead.

He closed his hands over his face, and began to recite from Psalm 73.

'Oh Lord, when my heart was grieved and my spirit embittered, I was senseless and ignorant; I was a brute beast before You.'

Outside, he heard drumming. The sharp rapping of wood on wood, beginning softly, then rapidly rising in a frenzied crescendo, echoing across the flagstones below, and across the monastery walls.

The beat was getting louder.

As if a wooden gong was hammering inside his skull.

I'm coming, all right, yes, yes, to matins, I will come.

Louder still.

His door burst open. Shocked by the intrusion, he looked up straight into blinding white light. The next moment he heard a sharp hiss, smelled a sour reek like a perfume that had gone bad, then in the same instant, he was enveloped in a moist, acrid cloud.

It felt like acid had been thrown into his eyes. Crying out in pain, he squeezed them shut, pressing his hands back over his face, and now his throat and lungs seared as if he was breathing in flames.

He tried to remember his military training. To stay calm. No panic. Just think the situation through before acting. But he was suffocating; his gullet was on fire, his nostrils, his lungs. He tried to open his stinging eyes. Could see nothing, just a blur of blinding light. He was trying to think, to work out what was happening.

He stumbled against his table, fell to the floor with it, heard a sharp crack that might have been his laptop striking the floor also. Instinctively he curled up into a ball and rolled, *always present the enemy with a moving target.*

He crashed against something hard. A leg of the bed. Then against the wall. Lay still. Coughing, choking, his eyes burning, fighting for air.

Voices outside. Unfamiliar voices. The drumming had stopped. Instead there were strange footsteps, all kinds of new sounds. One very angry voice shouting down below. It sounded like Father Yanni.

He tried to sit up, forcing his eyes open, and saw through a wall of tears a figure, just a dark blur of a figure, towering over him.

His coughing eased; the acrid smell was fading a little; he took a deep gulp, but it was like sucking fire into his lungs and he coughed violently again. 'Who – who are you—?' he wheezed painfully, squinting, panic-stricken, desperately trying to blink his eyes clear, but to no avail.

The voice was American, with a faint Kansas twang, and sounded a little muffled. It said, 'Where are the children, motherfucker?'

Gatward tried to speak but had another coughing fit. The light that was shining in his face was making the pain in his eyes worse, and he put his hand over them.

'PUT YOUR HANDS ON TOP OF YOUR HEAD, MOTHERFUCKER. ONE ON TOP OF THE OTHER.'

Harald Gatward hesitated, then obeyed. *Who the hell was this man?* Except, the pain in his eyes and throat and lungs was so bad, he almost didn't care who the man was, he just wanted the pain to stop. He didn't care if he died at this moment.

'WHERE ARE THE CHILDREN?'

'What children?' he wheezed, before lapsing into more coughing.

'You want to make this easy, or you want to make this hard, you piece of shit? Because it would give me a lot of pleasure to make this real hard. Where are the children?'

Gatward, confused, shook his head. 'What children?' Moments later, someone was seizing his hands, jerking them behind his back; he tried to resist, but the moment he drew in breath, he began coughing. 'Wharachireren?' he managed to get out.

Something metallic closed around one wrist then the other. Handcuffs.

'Whoorrruyou?'

'Special Agent Norbert, FBI. I'm here in the presence of the Greek Police and the US Military.'

The air in the room was clearing now. The taller man lowered his gas mask, produced his ID from an inside pocket and held it out to Gatward, who, still suffering from the CS gas, was unable to see what it was, let alone read it.

Special Agent Norbert, dressed in a flak jacket, fatigues and a balaclava, with an HK MP5 sub-machine gun crooked under one arm, said, 'Colonel Harald Edgar Gatward, I'm arresting you on charges of conspiracy to murder and kidnap. You have the right to remain silent. You are coming back to the United States with us today; even as we speak your extradition papers are being stamped by the Greek authorities. They don't want a piece of shit like you polluting their country.'

His lungs a fraction better now, Gatward said, sullenly, 'I saved their monastery.'

'You saved their monastery? That's funny. Who'd you save it for?'

Gatward said nothing.

'For the children? That who you saved it for?'

'What children?'

Something in the way Gatward said that gave Special Agent Norbert a distinct prick of unease.

114

'I'm sorry, Dr and Mrs Klaesson,' Detective Inspector Pelham said. 'I was hoping to be able to give you good news. This is a big disappointment for you, I know. It is for us, too.'

It was Monday morning, and he was seated at the round table in his office, beside DS Humbolt and Renate Harrison. He looked drained. They all did.

John and Naomi stared at him in stunned silence. Then John said, 'Are you telling us it isn't the Disciples' people who have taken them?'

'The base of the Disciples of the Third Millennium was raided in the early hours of this morning by the Greek police, backed up by the Greek navy, a US SEALS squad and a British SAS squad. Agent Norbert told me on the phone an hour ago that they are certain beyond any reasonable doubt that they have the ringleader of the cult and the majority, if not all, of its members in custody in Greece, awaiting rubber-stamping of extradition papers.'

'But they don't have Luke and Phoebe?' Naomi said.

'I'm afraid not, no.'

She lowered her head into her hands and wept. 'They're dead, aren't they? They must have killed them.'

There was a long, awkward silence.

'Not necessarily,' Tom Humbolt said. 'You see—'

'NOT NECESSARILY???' Naomi raised her voice at him. 'Is that the best you can offer us? Not *necessarily*?'

Humbolt raised his huge hands in the air. 'We don't have any reason to believe they've come to any harm.'

'Don't you?' Naomi said. 'They were abducted in the middle of the night and two people are dead, and you don't have any reason to believe they might have come to any harm? What planet are you on, Detective Sergeant?'

'Hon!' John put a protective arm around her. 'Hear him out.'

'I'm all ears,' Naomi said. 'Tell me what you know about them. What do you know about the Disciples?'

'Very little more than is in the papers, at this stage.'

'Or than the Americans would tell you?'

Ignoring the barb, Pelham said, 'We know it is a religious cult dedicated to halting the progress of science. Its leader is now in custody, along with forty other members of the cult.'

'They were all on this island?' John quizzed.

Pelham replied, 'It could well be that their abductors hadn't got your children there before the raid and might be holding them somewhere en route.'

'And what do you think they're going to do with them now that their organization has been busted? Take them on a fun day out to Euro Disney?' Naomi said.

'All of the people arrested are being interrogated at this moment. I can assure you that if any of these Disciples has information about their whereabouts, they'll get it out of them.'

'I hope they torture the bastards to death,' she said.

115

Two hours later, in Sheila Michaelides's office, John held Naomi's hand, squeezing. Renate Harrison, their ever-present shadow, dressed in a smart two-piece and crisp white blouse, sat beside them.

Naomi stared past the psychologist, out through the window into the walled garden, as the policewoman brought Sheila Michaelides up to speed with the latest developments Naomi envied the psychologist the seeming tranquillity of her existence.

'I'm so sorry for you, John and Naomi,' she said, when Renate Harrison had finished. 'I saw two police officers on Saturday afternoon and gave them as much information as I could.'

Her head was sticking out of a fluffy, fresh-looking white cashmere sweater, but she looked tired. She had more make-up caked on than Naomi had seen before, and there were bags under her eyes. Even her hair lacked its usual bounce.

'You were going to try to make contact with some of the other parents around the world,' John said. 'Have you had any success?'

'Yes, I have—' She glanced at her computer screen. 'I'm getting emails coming in all the time – there's been a surge of them since yesterday morning. There's something going on that I can't explain, but perhaps you can?' She stared at Renate Harrison.

'Explain what, exactly?' the family liaison officer asked.

'Over the past five days, seven sets of twins conceived in the Dettore Clinic have disappeared into thin air.'

'Seven?' John exclaimed.

'I'm waiting for confirmation back about one set in Dubai; the total may be up to eight now. And I suspect there are a lot more.'

Naomi swivelled on her chair to face the policewoman. 'DI Pelham said three sets – he said *three*, yesterday. How could it be seven – eight?'

'When you say *disappeared*,' John asked, 'surely there must be people who have seen something?'

'Apparently not.'

'All about the same age?' he asked.

'Their ages range from three to five.'

'And—' John said. 'Are – Naomi – and I – the only people to have any evidence of their children's disappearance?'

'Incredibly, it would seem so. I've had telephone conversations with five of the parents – I've been up half the night with different time zones around the world – and in every single instance they tell me their twins have literally vanished. Not even one sighting so far by any security camera, anywhere.'

'Why us?' Naomi demanded. 'I mean, why do we have evidence and no one else?'

'There doesn't seem to have been any violence involved in the other instances,' Sheila Michaelides said.

'So who were these people who shot this Disciple on our doorstep then took Luke and Phoebe away? The Good Samaritan and his Best Friend?' Naomi said in an outburst of frustration. 'Did they just happen to be out for a stroll across the fields, carrying a handgun and wearing night-vision goggles?'

There was an uncomfortable silence. No one seemed to know how to respond. Finally the psychologist said, 'Naomi, I'm hoping during the course of the day to speak to more of the parents of the children who have gone missing. I can't believe it's coincidence, so there has to be some linking factor. Something will come to light.'

'Could we speak to these parents ourselves?' John asked.

'I can conference you in, with their permission,' she said, seeking and receiving a nod of approval from Renate Harrison. 'I think it would be a very good idea.' Then, again looking at the police officer, she said, 'Meantime, what is the next step you anticipate from your American colleagues?'

'I think at the moment,' Renate Harrison said, 'they're as baffled as we are.'

*

The policewoman drove through Caibourne, and on up the lane. Neither John nor Naomi had said more than a few words since leaving the psychologist's consulting room. They were both inside their shells, thinking, trying to pull together something that made sense out of all they had heard, and getting nowhere.

DI Pelham was allowing them to go home today, with the suggestion that Renate Harrison, relieved by another colleague during the night, stay with them for the next few days, and patrols would be stepped up around their house. They would be guarded as much as resources would allow.

They made a right turn into the driveway, and Naomi felt an immediate lump in her throat. They were coming up to their house.

Their *empty* house.

It was a fine day, sunlight glinting on the damp grass. She barely noticed. Barely even noticed the unmarked maroon police car parked in the drive, close to her Subaru and John's Saab, and a lone policeman in a uniform that looked too bulky for him sitting inside it.

Post and newspapers slithered across the tiled floor of the hall as John pushed open the front door. Naomi looked at her watch. As if on autopilot, she said, 'Almost one, lunchtime. I – I'd better – make something, I suppose.'

'Would you like me to do it?' Renate Harrison offered. 'If you just show me where everything is and tell me what you'd like?'

John set down their holdall and his laptop bag, and scooped up the mail and papers, sifting through those that were for him and Naomi, and those that were for the owners of the house, putting them aside in a separate pile. Then he went through to his den, set his computer on his desk and went back out again, to carry in the children's computer from the boot of the car.

Back in his den, and logged on, he saw that he had sixty-two new emails. Wearily, he slumped back in his chair and scrolled down through them.

Then he froze.

He leaned forward, hands poised over the keyboard, staring at the screen, barely able to believe what he was seeing.

It was an email from Luke and Phoebe.

116

From: Luke & Phoebe Klaesson
Subject: Safety

Dear Parents,

Please do not fret about our whereabouts.

We are here because we consider you incapable of providing us with adequate protection against the Disciples of the Third Millennium and other fanatical groups. And because you are unable to provide us with the levels of stimulus and education we require – although we know you have been trying and we are grateful to you for that.

Don't waste energy trying to trace the source of this email – as any geek will tell you, it will take you years. We are safe and well and happy for the first time in our lives and that is all you need to know.

You will not be able to reply to this email. If you wish to meet with us, we will grant you one visit because we believe as our birth parents you are owed that courtesy. We know it may be hard to believe, but we do love you – but in our own way, which you won't understand.

Two seats have been reserved for you on Alitalia flight 275 to Rome today, departing London Heathrow at 1810 hours. In Rome you

will take a taxi to the Hotel Anglo Americano
and wait in the room reserved for you for further
instructions. Come alone, bring no camera. If
you are accompanied or followed, there will be
no further instructions for you in Rome.

As proof that we are fine, a short video clip is
attached.

Your children,

Luke & Phoebe

117

On a computer monitor, in a room at Sussex Police Headquarters, Luke and Phoebe stood side by side, each with
an arm around the other. They appeared to be in a small
studio, with a plain grey background, which gave nothing
away about their location. Luke wore a sweat shirt, jeans
and trainers, Phoebe a purple tracksuit and trainers.
Clearly visible beside them was a television screen, with
the CNN morning headlines of today.

The children looked, Naomi had to admit to herself,
happy and relaxed.

'Hallo, Parents,' Luke said. 'See! We're fine!'

'Hallo, Parents!' Phoebe said. 'Actually, we're great!'

At the end of the clip the image froze. Naomi stared at
it through tears. *My children,* she was thinking. *Luke,
Phoebe, my babies.* Then she closed her eyes, unable to
look any more.

*Please, God, let me wake up and find out that this has
all been some horrible dream.*

Pelham, Humbolt, Renate Harrison and the computer
geek, Cliff, were in the room with John and Naomi, seated
around a table.

'What are your chances of tracing the email, Cliff?' the
detective inspector asked.

Cliff, in clothes as grimy and crumpled as before,
looked no less tired at two thirty on a Monday afternoon
than he had at ten o'clock on Saturday morning. Pushing
his hair back with his hands, he said, 'The thing is, if you

want to make an email anonymous and you know what you're doing, you can make it anonymous. It's not a problem.'

'Can you explain how to us?' Tom Humbolt asked.

The computer analyst gave a nervous laugh, then, blinking furiously at the table, said, 'There are several different ways. They mostly involve routing an anonymous email from server to server around the world, with software designed to delete its own footprints as it goes. If I'm right in the way I think this has been sent – and it's the way I would have done it – you'd have to physically send me round the world, tracking it back, trying to find the footprints in every server it's been through.'

'How long would that take?' Naomi asked.

'Assuming we could even find every server, gosh, I don't know.' He gave another nervous giggle. 'Months.' Then, staring at the table again and blinking furiously, he said, 'That's not the answer you want to hear, is it?'

Dave Pelham leaned forward, placed his elbows on the table, then pressed his fingers together to form a bridge. Resting his chin on it, he said to Humbolt, 'The lab have a copy of this?'

'Yes, sir.' The detective sergeant directed much of his reply at John and Naomi. 'They're enhancing the sound to see if they can pick up any background noise that might give us clues about where they are.'

John glanced at his watch, then caught Naomi's eye. They were going to have to leave soon for the airport.

Pelham said to both of them, 'I really think someone should accompany you, in the background.'

Naomi shook her head adamantly. 'You read their instructions, Detective Inspector. We can't take the gamble.'

John said, 'They haven't given us much time, have they?'

'That's deliberate,' Pelham said. 'We barely have time to get anything in place. OK, if we don't send anyone with you, then we need to get the cooperation of the Italian police.'

'NO!' Naomi was emphatic. 'You have to let us handle this the way they are telling us.'

'Mrs Klaesson, let me make this clear. We never accede to demands of kidnappers.'

'What demands? They're not asking for anything. They're saying *if we wish to meet them*. What kind of *demand* is that?'

'These people, whoever they are who have abducted your children, are clearly highly professional and well organized. If you do what they are requesting without adequate police back-up, you and Dr Klaesson would be taking an unacceptable risk with your safety.'

'My children come above everything,' she replied. 'I don't care what risks I have to take to get them back. With respect, doing anything less than they ask in that email is what I would call an unacceptable risk.'

118

The plane was sinking steadily on its landing approach. Naomi, gripping an empty bottle of mineral water, her tray still down, sat squeezing her eyes shut against a headache that two paracetamol had done nothing to relieve.

John had a science magazine open in front of him but hadn't turned the page in an hour. How could either of them concentrate on anything?

A stewardess, hurrying, took the empty bottle and slammed her tray shut. Minutes later, the plane touched down. The engines bellowed in reverse thrust. She felt the seat belt dig into her, then they were taxiing.

Rome. A short while ago they had been home; then they had been in a room at police headquarters; then in a speeding police car with a motorcycle escort. Now they were in Rome.

'OK, hon?' John said.

She eked out a tearful smile. In a hotel room in this city they would get instructions. They would be reunited with Luke and Phoebe. In her hopes, they would all go back home together, and this nightmare would fade away into the past.

The entrance was a busy modern lobby in an old building. They sidestepped a horde of Japanese tourists being marshalled towards a coach, and reached the front desk. John filled in the forms, handed over their passports and a credit card, and declined the offer of help with their luggage, which consisted of her handbag, a small holdall and John's laptop bag.

The clerk's lapel badge said, VITTORIO. 'Travel light, good thing, eh, very good!' Vittorio flashed a smile that was wasted on them, and handed them their door card and minibar key.

'Do you have any messages or mail for us?' Naomi asked, looking around, scanning faces in the lobby, wondering if the person Luke and Phoebe's email had said was going to make contact with them was already here.

'One moment, huh? I check.' He turned round and peered at the rows of pigeon holes, then pecked at the computer keyboard. 'Doctor Meeses Klayassion, no mail and – eh – no, no message. Anything come, no worry, straight to you room. Have a good stay in Roma!'

The room was narrow and gloomy, and even with all the lights on felt dark. Naomi sat down on the bed and looked at her watch. It was ten thirty local time, nine thirty in England. 'Do you really think they will contact us, John?'

'Yes.'

'Why haven't they yet? Why isn't there any message?'

'Hon, they – *whoever* – they'll know we've only just arrived. Give it time.'

'DI Pelham has contacted the Italian police, hasn't he? I bet he has.'

'He agreed he wouldn't, provided we sent him an email by midnight telling him we were OK.'

'I don't believe him. I think he's contacted them, and that's why we're not going to hear from Luke and Phoebe, or whoever's taken them. Pelham has blown it.'

'Give them time.' He walked over to the window. It was a huge, heavy old sash, double-glazed, with a view down on to a busy street. He unclipped the catch and slid the outer unit upwards. Immediately, he felt a cold draught from the chill night air, and heard the rasp of mopeds and motorcycles, the roar of car engines, the cacophony of horns, the endless crazed symphony of a Rome evening.

He let the window drop shut again, set his laptop up on the small writing table and took out his adaptor kit. After a couple of aborted attempts he was logged on.

There were twenty-seven new emails. Running his eyes down them, he felt a sudden beat of excitement, and instantly double-clicked the ninth. 'Hon,' he said. 'Come here.'

> **From: Luke & Phoebe Klaesson**
> **Subject: Travel**
>
> **Dear Parents,**
> **You have reservations on Alitalia flight 1050 to**
> **Dubai, United Arab Emirates, departing 13.45**
> **tomorrow. Collect your tickets from the Alitalia**
> **desk in International Departures. You will be**
> **met by your driver in the arrivals lounge at**
> **Dubai.**
> **The same warnings apply.**
> **Your children,**
> **Luke & Phoebe**

'What's in Dubai?' Naomi asked.

'I have absolutely no more idea than you do, hon. Anyhow, it's maybe not the final destination.'

'It sounds it, if we're being collected by car.'

John wrote the details down on a slip of hotel note-paper, then logged off, opened the earlier email from Luke and Phoebe and again played the video clip of them.

Staring at the screen, Naomi put an arm around his shoulder. 'I know they haven't been all we dreamed of, that they're not perfect, but I don't know how I could cope if anything happens to them. You do think they're still alive, don't you?'

'Yes, absolutely,' he said, trying to sound confident, trying to mask his doubts from her.

They must be alive, still, he thought. *In this clip, with this morning's CNN news they are alive. Whoever has taken them, and whatever their agenda, they must still be alive at this moment, and all we can do is keep obeying the instructions. And hope.*

Then, to try to keep Detective Inspector Pelham off their backs and to prevent him from involving the Italian police, he sent an email to him.

Communication received from Luke and Phoebe. They have advised us we are being kept under observation for twenty-four hours and we are to stay put here in the hotel, to await further instructions.

Twenty minutes later, when he logged on again, there was a reply from Pelham.

Will hold back from contacting Italian police provided I receive a further email by 1500 hours GMT tomorrow assuring me you are both safe.

John logged off again, then phoned down to the front desk and booked a taxi to the airport for seven in the morning.

119

A million placards, some from hotels, some from car rental companies, some in English, some in Arabic, were thrust at John and Naomi by a clamouring horde of people as they walked out through customs, into the air-conditioned cool of the cavernous arrivals hall. They looked around, increasingly anxiously: AVIS, HILTON, HERTZ, NOUJAIM, THOMAS COOK, DR HAUPTMAN. Then they saw it.

KLAESSON.

A short Middle-Eastern man in a grey suit with damp patches under the arms, a cheap white shirt and plain black tie, greeted them eagerly in bad English.

'I Elias,' he said. 'Come driving you.' Then, despite John's attempts to resist, he took both the holdall and the laptop bag, and led the way through the melee and out into the cloyingly warm evening air.

It was seven o'clock and already almost completely dark. Just a few bloody, red streaks stained the sky as they followed him across an open parking lot to a white Mercedes in a meter bay. 'Where are you taking us?' John asked.

The driver turned, grinning inanely, and said, 'I sorry, no good English, sorry, so sorry!'

He put their luggage in the boot, then scurried round to open the rear doors for each of them in turn. Five minutes later they were out of the airport complex, moving in heavy traffic along a wide boulevard of modern hotel buildings that reminded John of the streets around LAX airport in Los Angeles.

Leaning forward, he tried to question the driver again. 'Where are we going?'

Alarmingly, the man raised both hands in the air, then swivelled around on his beaded seat cover to face him. 'No-zactly!' he said, then to John's relief turned back to face the road.

They were heading away from the city. John decided not to ask the man any more questions. Soon they were on a pitch-dark highway, driving fast in thin traffic. And for the first time since they had started this journey, he began feeling seriously worried.

There was one concern he had simply not permitted himself to think about up until now – which was, what if not all the Disciples had been rounded up in Special Agent Norbert's raid? What if Luke and Phoebe were being dangled as bait to lure him and Naomi?

Had he really been so clever after all, in throwing a false scent at Detective Inspector Pelham?

As if reading his thoughts, Naomi leaned over and whispered, 'I don't feel good about this. Where do you think we're going?'

'I don't know.' He pulled his phone out of his pocket and checked the display. Five blots, a full-strength signal. At least he had some means of communication if need be. He put it back. Despite the air conditioning, he felt uncomfortable in his winter-weight jeans, roll-neck sweater and leather jacket. He wriggled out of the jacket and folded it on his lap. 'Aren't you warm—?' he started saying to Naomi, then noticed the car was slowing down, its indicator light winking on the dash.

They turned off the highway onto a long, dead-straight

road that seemed to be heading out into desert. Even more anxious now, he turned and peered out of the window. Nothing but total darkness behind them – and ahead of them.

After five minutes of travelling along this road at high speed, again they slowed, and now John could see a complex of industrial buildings ahead of them, inside a barbed-wire compound, the perimeter brightly illuminated. A factory or storage depot of some kind.

They stopped beside a security booth, in front of closed metal gates. The driver put down his window and spoke to an armed guard. Moments later the gates slid open and they moved forward, following a road that threaded around to the rear of the buildings. John, holding Naomi's hand, was feeling tense as hell now. Was this where Luke and Phoebe were?

But now they were moving away from the buildings, seemingly out into the desert again. And suddenly, catching a sudden whiff of kerosene, he realized where they were going.

A few hundred yards ahead of them, just a silhouette at first, but rapidly becoming clearer in their headlights as they drew closer, was a jet plane, not much smaller than a commercial airliner.

'Seems like the Magical Mystery Tour continues,' he said drily, feeling a strange sense of relief at seeing this plane, as if its presence confirmed that at least they weren't being brought out here to be executed.

Was this the jet Luke and Phoebe had boarded in Le Touquet? He could see cabin lights shining through a row of portholes, and more light spilling out through the open door at the top of the gangway. And now the smell of kerosene was much stronger.

The Mercedes stopped. The rear door opened and a brilliant flashlight beam straight in his face momentarily dazzled him. Outside he could hear a rapid exchange of voices. An argument about something, then calm again.

Elias, their driver, said, 'Coming please!'

They climbed out. It wasn't so warm now and John gratefully pulled on his leather jacket. The driver opened the boot and handed him the holdall and his laptop bag. Then an Arab gesticulating excitedly with both arms led them to the gangway.

He climbed up to the top step, then just inside the plane saw a young man and a woman standing motionless, on either side of the doorway, like sentries. They were tall, dramatically dressed in pure white jumpsuits and white trainers, and quite stunningly good-looking. Both were in their early twenties, John guessed. The man had exquisitely cut blond hair, and the kind of tanned, chiselled looks you only ever saw on male models in the fashion pages of magazines; the woman, a blonde, too, had the willowy features and perfect poise of a top model. Neither smiled; their expressions were of slight disdain.

John, waiting for Naomi, felt immediately intimidated by them. 'Hallo,' he said, throwing each of them a glance, trying to break the ice.

'Welcome aboard, Dr and Mrs Klaesson,' the young man said, in a cold, clipped New England accent that carried no hint of a welcome in it at all.

'You may select any seats,' the woman said in a similar accent and even cooler tone.

'Where are we going?' John asked.

'Please do not ask either of us any questions,' the man said. 'We have no mandate to answer you.'

'Can you just tell us one thing,' Naomi asked. 'You are taking us to Luke and Phoebe, aren't you?'

'I recommend the rear two seats,' the woman said. 'Those are the furthest from the engines. You get the least resonance.'

Naomi stared at her. The woman's face remained totally deadpan. Silent anger rose inside Naomi, but she stifled it. They just had to keep calm, do nothing to jeopardize their situation. Just hope, that was all they could do. Hope.

To their left, the door to the cockpit was closed. They turned right, walked through an area laid out like a small boardroom, with an oval conference table and eight chairs fixed to the floor around it. Then on, past a galley, and into the rear section of the cabin, where there were twenty seats, plushly upholstered in leather and with extravagant leg room, laid out in a row of ten either side of the wide aisle. Naomi realized it wasn't just for the noise levels that the woman had recommended the rear seats; the cabin was narrower there, making them the only seats that were actually next to each other.

Moments later, the young man pulled the cabin door closed.

Then John heard the whine of the engine turbines starting to rotate. A seat-belt sign flashed above him. He looked out of the window to his left. Saw the reflection of his pale, anxious face in the glass. Tiny balls of white light strobed in the darkness beyond. The aircraft's own navigation lights, he realized. Moments later, as if put on by a single flick of a switch, he saw runway lights stretching out into the distance.

Then he heard a metallic whirring sound. In seconds his reflection, the strobing light and the runway lights had disappeared. His own surprise was mirrored by a frightened cry from Naomi.

Electronic metal shutters had come down. Across every window.

120

After take-off, the stewardess served them a meal in a pre-packed tray, of the kind they might have had on any airline. A Caesar salad with prawns, scalding-hot poached salmon beneath a foil lid; chocolate fudge cake; a triangle of soft cheese and biscuits. The steward brought them each a glass of Chardonnay, and mineral water.

John ate most of his food, but Naomi just picked at hers. Afterwards they tried to sleep for a while.

Naomi was thinking about the steward and stewardess. Their silent, hostile attitude reminded her so strongly of the way Luke and Phoebe behaved towards her and John. These two could almost be their older siblings.

After five hours, they were given another meal, this time sandwiches and fruit. And then, an hour later, John and Naomi both noticed that the plane was losing height, as if it was starting on a landing path.

The seat-belt light started flashing.

The steward and stewardess remained out of sight, somewhere beyond the galley, as they had all the time when they weren't bringing John and Naomi water or serving the meals.

They were very definitely losing height.

Then, just as suddenly as they had whirred down, all those hours back, the shutters over the windows were rising back up. Daylight flooded in. Brilliant, dazzling, early-morning daylight.

John and Naomi stared out of their windows.

They were flying low, no more than three or four thousand feet, above hilly terrain, covered in lush, tropical vegetation. Through John's window there was only a view of land, and the sun rising into a cloudless sky. But through Naomi's they could see a wide, white sand beach, cobalt-blue sea. A sharp *clunk* echoed through the plane, followed by a series of thuds. The undercarriage going down.

Like a current of electricity, excitement suddenly coursed through Naomi, perking her up despite her tiredness. *Going to see my children. Going to see Luke and Phoebe. They're here, they're here in this beautiful place! They are OK, they are not harmed. Going to see them, they're going to come in this plane with us, back home.*

'Do you have any idea where we might be?' she asked John.

He wished he had some knowledge of botany, then he might have been able to figure from the vegetation roughly where they were. He shook his head. 'I have no real idea how fast we've been travelling, nor in what direction we've been going, or anything. I just know we're nine hours' flying time from Dubai. If this is the same plane Luke and Phoebe were taken on, I remember DI Pelham telling us it has a cruising speed of three hundred and fifty knots. So we've covered about three thousand, five hundred land miles. We could be bloody anywhere.'

He stared out of the window again. It looked like early morning, which meant they must have travelled west. If they were flying slower than he had calculated, it could be the west coast of Africa. Faster, and they could be off the east coast of South America.

'We took off from Dubai at about seven thirty p.m. UK time. So our body clocks are now on about four thirty a.m.,' he said. He needed a bath, a shave, a change of clothes. He felt grungy and exhausted. Naomi looked beat, too. It hurt him to see her suffering like this, hurt him almost as much as the pain of his missing children was hurting him. And he felt angry at himself, bitterly frustrated, that he wasn't able to do anything to help her. All he could do was sit here like a lame duck, accepting graceless hospitality from these cold young people.

The hills suddenly dropped sheer away beneath them, as if they had surfed over a ledge, giving onto a flat valley that was a good two miles wide and several long. It was like a secret valley, he thought, as it if had been hewn out the centre of the hills. Probably formed by a volcanic explosion thousands of years ago.

As the plane dropped lower still, it was as if a lever on a lens had suddenly been rotated, turning a foggy blur into pin-sharp focus. One moment there had been a flat valley floor, just a mass of shimmering vegetation, the next it had suddenly become a complex of shapes rising from the ground. Buildings, mostly single-storey, interconnected, he could see now, by pathways, like a university campus stretching away into the distance in every direction, each of them camouflaged, to be invisible from the air, by vegetation on their roofs.

The plane was even lower now. Just a few hundred feet above the buildings. He was looking hard, trying to see people or vehicles, but there was no sign of any life.

It felt almost as if they were coming down to land in a ghost town.

'What is this place?' Naomi said.

'Luke and Phoebe's winter vacation resort. Bought from millions they've secretly made trading stocks on the internet?'

She did not smile.

121

The plane touched down on a runway that was painted a sandy green. It taxied for a few hundred yards and then, without slowing, entered a cavernous hangar, the roof of which, John noticed, was also covered in vegetation, and came to a halt. The place was brightly illuminated and appeared completely deserted.

'Please come this way.'

The stewardess stood, solemn-faced, in front of them.

Unbuckling his belt, John asked her, 'What country are we in?'

'Our mandate is not to answer questions. You must exit now.'

Carrying their luggage, John and Naomi followed her, past the steward who stood by the exit door, down the gangway onto the blue-painted concrete floor. The air was hot and humid, and reeked of spent kerosene, and there was a high, dull whine of the turbine blades spinning down.

John glanced around, intensely curious. He saw a smaller executive jet and a helicopter parked in the hangar, a gantry on rails, a forklift truck, dozens of large containers, and pallets stacked up to the ceiling, a good hundred feet high.

There was no sign of the pilot or any other crew, nor of anyone working in here. Surreptitiously, John slid his cellphone out of his pocket, switched it on and looked at the display. There was no signal.

The stewardess pressed something on a device she was holding and stainless-steel elevator doors, a short distance ahead, slid open.

The steward said, 'Please step in, Dr Klaesson and Mrs Klaesson.'

The four of them travelled down for several seconds in silence. Then the doors opened onto the gleaming platform of an immaculate underground railway station. A solitary, bullet-shaped carriage, its door open, sat on a monorail.

As they boarded it, feeling as if they were in some surreal dream, Naomi and John exchanged glances but said nothing. They were beyond surprise at this moment, just running on adrenaline. They had come too far to question or challenge anything any more. They were running on hope.

They took two seats and their escorts sat in the two opposite them. The doors hissed shut, and moments later the carriage began to accelerate silently and without vibration, into a dark tunnel.

After two minutes they emerged into a station that was identical to the one they had just come from. The doors opened and they followed their escorts out and into another elevator. It seemed a long ride up. John's stomach dropped. Then, moments later, the floor pressed up against his feet, and before he was fully aware of it, they had stopped.

The doors opened onto a wide, handsome corridor that had a corporate feel, as if it might be the head offices of a bank or of some major global company.

Naomi shot John a quick glance. *What is this place?*

And he shrugged back, *I have no more idea than you.* Then he took another look at his cellphone display. Still no signal.

Now they were being led along the corridor. Past closed, windowless doors. At the far end, the stewardess opened a door and led them into an ante-room. Another exquisitely beautiful woman, also in her early twenties, at most, with short brown hair and a deadpan expression, sat at a desk. She, too, was wearing a white jumpsuit.

'Dr and Mrs Klaesson,' announced the stewardess.

In contrast to their escorts, she gave them a pleasant smile, stood up, walked across to grand, double doors and opened them. Then, in a clipped Boston accent she said, 'Will you please go through,' and stepped aside for them to pass.

John let Naomi go first and followed her into a large office, with a white carpet and striking modern furniture, the centrepiece of which was an oval, slate-grey desk. And from behind which a figure was rising.

A tall, lean, tanned man, dressed also in dazzling white, with dark, luxuriant hair swept immaculately back and tinged with elegant grey streaks at the temples. Stepping around the side of his desk, he strode across the room, arm outstretched, to greet them. He did not look a day older since they had last seen him four years ago. If anything, he looked younger.

'Hi, John! Hi, Naomi!' he said in his warm, assertive Southern Californian accent.

Naomi took a step back as if she had seen a ghost. Then both of them stared at the doctor in stunned silence.

122

'What the hell's going on?' John said. 'Do you want to explain to us?'

Beaming at them and ignoring the question, Leo Dettore shook each of their hands, saying, 'So great to see you guys again!' He beckoned them to a seating area around a coffee table. But John and Naomi stood still. Behind the geneticist, a wall-to-floor window the width of the room looked out across the campus of buildings, and over to the mountains beyond.

'You died,' Naomi blurted. 'You died – it was on television, in the papers, you—'

'Please, sit down; you must be shattered. Let me get you something to drink. Water? Coffee?'

'I don't want a drink,' Naomi said, emboldened now. 'I want to see my children.'

'Let me have a chance to explain and then—'

'I WANT TO SEE MY CHILDREN!' Naomi shouted, close to hysterics.

'Where the hell are we?' John said. 'Just tell us where the hell we are?'

'That's not important,' Dr Dettore said.

'WHAT?' Naomi exploded.

'Not important? We've been travelling for twenty-four hours, and it's not important?' John marched up to him and raised his fist threateningly. 'We want our children. We want Luke and Phoebe. If you've harmed them in any way, I'll kill you, I swear it, you bastard, I'll tear you apart!'

Dettore raised his hands in mock surrender. 'John, I'll take you to see them right now. They are safe here. OK?'

'Yes, *right now.*'

Unperturbed, Dettore said, 'Do you think I went to all this trouble to bring you here if I wasn't going to let you see them?'

'We have no idea what's in your sick mind,' John said. 'If you're capable of faking your death then what the hell else are you capable of?'

'WHERE ARE OUR CHILDREN?' Naomi yelled.

Dettore waited a moment before replying. Then, calmly, he said, 'Your children came here in order to be safe. Having them here was the only way I could guarantee their safety. You both know that crazy religious sect was on a mission to kill all the children who had been through my programme. There wasn't an option. But you need to understand that I brought you here because, as Luke and Phoebe's parents, you have an absolute right to see your children, and to take them home with you – if they want to go with you.'

'*If* they want to go with us? What do you mean by that?' demanded John. 'You've kidnapped them – and God knows what your agenda is. *If* they want to go home with us? What kind of arrogance is that? We're their damned parents!'

Dettore walked back to his desk and picked up a thick document. 'Did you never read properly the contract you signed on board the *Serendipity Rose* – either of you?'

John felt a sudden sick, empty sensation deep inside him.

Dettore handed it to him. 'It has both your signatures on it, and you have initialled every page.'

There was a moment of silence. Then Dr Dettore went

on, 'Just so that you both understand, Luke and Phoebe were taken into safe custody at their own request. You may of course see them, and spend as much time with them as you like. But I think in your own interests you should first take a look at clause twenty-six, paragraph nine, subsection four of this agreement. You will find it on page thirty-seven.'

John laid the document on the table, and turned to page thirty-seven. He and Naomi both read down, found paragraph nine, which was in tiny print, then subsection four, which was microscopic. It read:

Birth parents agree at a time in the future to be determined by the child or children to cede all rights to parental responsibility, should the children so expressly wish, to Dr Dettore, and Dr Dettore shall have the absolute right to adopt said children. In any dispute the wish of the children shall be final and absolute.

At the top and at the bottom of the page were John and Naomi's initials, boldly written in blue ink.

She was silent for a moment, then said, 'This can't be legal. It cannot be binding. They're three years old! How can a three-year-old have the right to decide its parents? This is rubbish! There isn't a court in the world where this would stand up.'

'Let me make something very clear to you guys,' Dettore said, sitting down opposite them. 'I didn't go to the trouble of bringing you here in order to show you a clause in a contract you signed four years ago. I want you to understand that your children have not been coerced or abducted or kidnapped, but are here by legal right, that's all.'

'Legal right—'

PETER JAMES

He raised a hand to silence Naomi in mid-sentence. 'Hear me out,' he said. 'I want to make something important very clear to you. If you want to take your children home, I'm not going to stop you. They're your kids. I don't care what agreement we have between us – I'm not a monster, regardless of what the press may have called me over the years. If you insist on taking them home with you, not only are you free to do so, but you'll have my private aircraft at your disposal. Is that clear?'

'Presumably there's a *but*?' John said.

'No, there isn't.'

'Nothing about this makes any sense,' Naomi said. 'We've been living a nightmare since Friday morning.'

Dettore looked at her for some moments before replying. 'Only since *Friday*, Naomi? Are you sure it's only since then?'

She stared, bleakly, back at him. 'What's that supposed to mean?'

'I think you understand.'

123

They travelled two stops on the monorail.

'What is this place?' John asked Dettore. 'Is it some kind of government research campus? And this tube train thing? You don't exactly seem to have traffic congestion above ground.'

'I'll explain it all later on,' he replied.

They stepped onto a platform, then walked over to an elevator. A boy and a girl, who looked to be in their late teens, both tall and beautiful, dressed in dark blue jump-suits, exited.

'Good morning, Brandon, morning, Courtney.'

'Good morning, Dr Dettore,' each of them said warmly, as if they were greeting a good friend. They spoke in American accents, like everyone else here, so far.

'I have Parent People visiting today,' Dettore said, smiling at John and Naomi.

'Welcome, Parent People!' Brandon said,

'We hope you have a great visit, Parent People!' Courtney said.

In the elevator, Naomi quizzed Dettore. '*Parent People?*'

'Folks like you and John,' he replied.

The doors opened and they followed Dettore out into a wide corridor with a dark grey carpet and pale grey paint. Along one wall were glass observation windows, and along the opposite one were flat-screen televisions, the displays of which changed every few seconds with differing mathematical formulae.

Several children walked past them, their ages ranging from around three, he guessed, to their late teens. They were all in pairs, always a boy and a girl, all dressed in jumpsuits and plimsolls. All beautiful-looking. All were chatting animatedly to each other as they walked, each of them greeting Dr Dettore cheerily, and it was clear he knew all their names.

Naomi looked at each of them in turn as they came into the corridor, her heart jumping every time in the desperate hope that it would be Luke and Phoebe. She wondered, darkly, whether the appearance of these children had been stage-managed by Dettore and they had been ordered to look cheery. But despite her anger at the man, she could not convince herself of this. They all looked natural, healthy and happy. It was a strange sensation; there seemed no tension between any of the children, no ragging, no teasing. A surreal harmony.

Dettore stopped by an observation window. Naomi and John joined him and found themselves looking down at a basketball game. Kids playing energetically, a hard but good-natured game.

They moved on, past another window that looked down into a huge indoor swimming-pool complex. In one pool, teenage kids were swimming lengths. In another, they were practising diving. In a third, a game of water polo was in progress.

Then a hundred yards or so on, at the next window, Naomi shot out her hand and gripped John's.

It was a classroom. Twenty children sat in pairs at double desks, each with their own computer workstation in front of them.

In the third row, seated together, were Luke and Phoebe.

Naomi felt her heart heave, and tears welled in her eyes. They were here! They were alive! Sitting, looking so beautiful in their white jumpsuits, their hair neat, their faces scrubbed, typing, their tiny faces scrunched in concentration one moment, then looking up at their teacher in anticipation the next.

The teacher, a handsome man in his thirties, was on a raised dais, just like any school teacher, but instead of a white board he had a huge electronic screen, on which was a complex-looking algorithm. As they watched, he tapped the screen with a long pointer and the algorithm changed.

Luke raised his hand.

He was asking a question!

Naomi watched, feeling a thrill she just could not explain, and sensed John was experiencing the same.

The teacher said something and the whole class erupted into good-natured laughter, led by Luke. The teacher nodded, turned to the screen. And, to Naomi's astonishment, *made an adjustment to the algorithm with his pointer.*

'You've got smart kids,' Dettore said. 'We have a lot of very bright kids here, and Luke and Phoebe are right up there towards the top of the scale.'

'Can we please go down to the classroom, I want to see them *now*,' Naomi said.

Dettore looked at his watch. 'Coming up to break, just a couple of minutes.'

He led them on down the corridor.

'What is this place?' John asked again. 'Who are all these kids? What are you doing here with them, Dr Dettore?'

Without answering, Dettore led them down a flight of

stairs and they came out into a huge, bustling, open-plan self-service dining area. Again it was filled with kids all sitting in pairs, beautiful, friendly little people, chatting away.

They followed Dettore out again, along a corridor similar to the one upstairs, then they stopped outside a door. 'Grade Two classroom,' he said to John and Naomi.

Moments later the door opened. A boy and a girl walked out, then another, turning right towards the cafeteria, followed a moment later by Luke and Phoebe, all smiles, sharing a joke.

Then they saw their parents and stopped in their tracks.

The laughter vanished instantly from their faces. It was replaced by faint smiles.

Naomi took a step towards them, with her arms out. 'Darlings! Luke! Phoebe! My darlings!'

They allowed each of their parents to lift them up and cuddle and kiss them, and showed some embarrassed reciprocation. When John and Naomi put them back down, they stood, motionless as waxworks.

The last of the children came out of the classroom, followed by the teacher.

Dettore introduced them. 'This is Adam Gardner, our senior computing sciences teacher. This is Dr Klaesson and Mrs Klaesson.'

'Great to meet you!' He held out his hand. 'You have awesome children! I've had Luke and Phoebe in my class for just one hour, and already they're teaching me things I don't know.' He looked down at the twins and their faces lit up at him in response. Lit up with such passion, John and Naomi were taken aback.

The teacher excused himself and headed off towards

the cafeteria. Dettore said, 'OK, I guess you guys would like some privacy. You're going into a private room with your parents and you'll discuss whatever they want to discuss with you. And if at the end of their visit here they decide you are going to go back with them to England, you will go. You hear what I'm saying?'

Neither child responded.

124

They sat on comfortable sofas in an air-conditioned room with a view out across the campus, chromium shutters partially closed against the sunlight; John and Naomi on one side of the coffee table, Luke and Phoebe on the other, each child sipping a bottle of mineral water through a straw.

John glanced at the clock on the wall and suddenly asked if there was a men's room and Naomi said she needed a loo, too. Luke and Phoebe led them out into the corridor and directed each of them.

John went through into an immaculately clean toilet. He urinated, then went to the washbasin, and ran the taps to muffle sound. He went over to the window, cracked it open, looked at the sun in the sky and glanced at his watch, which was still on UK time. John had intentionally excused himself at noon and yet his watch said it was 2 a.m. That meant they had travelled ten time zones ahead. He squinted as he stared at the sun and tried to judge its elevation in the sky. The sun was nearly at the zenith. It was not quite a month after the winter solstice, the date when the sun would be at the zenith over the Tropic of Capricorn, twenty-three degrees below the equator. The fact that sun was perfectly poised above him at the highest point in the sky showed they were probably just north of the Tropic of Capricorn. Based on the time of his watch and the position of the sun at noon, this placed them just a bit north of the Tropic of Capricorn in the South Pacific.

This was not a definitive experiment; they could still be over one thousand miles from the nearest population centre, but it was a start.

Back in the room with their children, Naomi leaned forward and poured milk into her cup on the coffee table. This could not be happening, she thought. John and I can't be sitting here, having a formal meeting with our children, as if we're discussing some property deal, or a used car, or a bank loan or something.

Luke, cradling his mineral water between his tiny hands, said, 'I am really not clear why you are so anxious for us to return to England with you.'

'Because we're your *parents*!' Naomi said. 'Children grow up at home with their parents. That's how life works!'

'It doesn't work like that here,' Phoebe retorted. 'Only very few kids here have Parent People. Mostly they are original *New People*.'

'What's the difference?' John asked.

'Really, Parents, isn't it obvious?' Luke said. 'They're the kids who aren't saddled with baggage.'

'They didn't have to develop the way we did inside a woman's womb,' Phoebe clarified.

Naomi shot a glance at John and saw the shock on his face. After a moment she asked, only partially tongue in cheek, 'You found that a hardship, did you, darling?'

But there was no hint of humour in Phoebe's response. 'It's a totally archaic and pointless method of reproduction, which subjects children to unacceptable risks. Parent birthing is no way to protect the long-term future of a species.'

John and Naomi were momentarily stunned into silence.

Then Luke's expression softened a little. 'Phoebe and I

don't want you to think we aren't grateful for all you both did. We feel very privileged.'

Sensing a thaw, Naomi said, 'And we're very proud of you both, enormously proud.' Turning to John, she said, 'Aren't we, darling?'

'Hugely!' John said. 'Look, I think you both understand that you are way smarter than other kids back home, but you've kept it concealed from us. Now that we know, we can help you realize your potential. There are some terrific specialist schools you can go to – we have a list—'

Phoebe, eyes raised, interrupted him. 'This is what everyone here who's descended from Parent People has to deal with.'

'Your expectations of us may be high, Parents,' Luke said. 'But I'm not here to serve your expectations, nor is my sister.'

John and Naomi stared back, trying to absorb what they were saying.

Then Luke continued. 'I've been assessing the world, and frankly, it doesn't work very well. There need to be a lot of changes, totally new mindsets applied to the problems, and a new paradigm for the future worked out, otherwise there isn't going to be any future.'

'Any future?' John echoed. 'What do you mean by that?'

'You couldn't even protect us from the Disciples – we had to ask for help externally.'

'Can you explain that, darlings?' Naomi said, her voice sounding brittle. 'Can you tell us what happened?'

'I think there are more important issues we should be discussing,' Phoebe said, imperiously. 'You need to understand the fundamentals of where we are coming from.'

Naomi glanced at John. They seemed to have matured

years, mentally, in the past few days. She was finding it very hard to accept that her children were capable of talking in such a very adult way. To accept anything here. She felt she was in the middle of a bad dream.

'Tell us what you believe those fundamentals are?' John asked.

'Well,' Phoebe said, 'to start with, we know you made genetic choices about us, because you wanted us to be better than other kids. You wanted us to become perfect people.' She gave her parents a challenging stare.

'Your mother and I—' John started, but Naomi interrupted him.

'Listen, you two,' she said. 'You need to understand our reasons. After we lost your brother, Halley, your father and I wanted to ensure nothing like that was ever going to happen to you. We wanted you to be as healthy and as free from the spectre of diseases as possible. Was that so wrong?'

'No, quite reasonable,' Luke said. 'So what's your problem?'

'Our problem?' Naomi said after some moments. 'Our problem is that we want you to come home with us.'

'Why exactly do you want us to come home with you?' Phoebe asked.

'Because—' Naomi floundered for a second. 'Because we love you.'

'Although you have very advanced intellects,' John interjected, 'you are still small children. You need the love and guidance that parents can give you – that we – your mother and I – really want to give you.'

'You know what you Parent People are?' Luke said. 'You're just one more generation in an unbroken chain going back thousands of years, of humans who have made a muck of the world. *Homo sapiens!*' he sneered. '*Sapiens* means *wise*. Your species isn't wise, under your stewardship the world is out of control. You've created nuclear and chemical weapons of mass destruction that any no-brainer with a gripe can go and buy, somewhere in the world. Your scientists claimed to have proven that God does not exist, but you allow your planet to be ravaged by religious fanatics. You are destroying the ecosystem because you cannot agree on a united ecology plan. You print more information every week than any human being can read in a lifetime. And you want to give *us* guidance? I think that's pretty damned breathtakingly arrogant.'

'Other animals don't cling on to their young,' Phoebe said. 'They let their offspring go as soon as they can fly, or swim, or hunt for food. Why are you so desperate to cling to us and hold us back? You've had a big chunk of your lives, but Luke and I have barely started. Unless we can make fast and dramatic changes, there is no future on this planet for anyone. Go home. Go back to your obsolete ways and leave us New People to sort out the future.'

John tried hard to keep calm, to show them they were capable of understanding. 'And how do you plan to sort out the future? What exactly will you do?'

Phoebe's tone suddenly became more pleasant. She smiled at her parents. 'There really isn't any point in trying to explain it to you. This is not something you or any Parent People could understand. I'm not trying to sound patronizing or anything like that. It's just a fact.'

'Kids,' John said, 'the people who were trying to kill you have all been arrested by the authorities. It's safe to come home now. We can keep you safe. If you want to make a difference to the world, which you have clearly shown you are capable of doing, you should come out of isolation. We'll give you all the support you need to achieve this.'

Phoebe replied, 'Luke and I need to talk about this. Please leave us alone for a while.'

Dettore, who had quietly entered the room without them noticing, said, 'John and Naomi, let's go take a walk.'

125

Outside, in the blinding sunlight and searing midday heat, in air perfumed by hibiscus and bougainvillea, John and Naomi followed Dr Dettore along a green-painted path through the vast, silent campus. Dettore pointed out and named each of the buildings they passed, but they barely took anything in.

Both of them were traumatized from their meeting with Luke and Phoebe. John squinted at his surroundings, wishing he had his sunglasses and lighter clothes. He felt sticky, grungy and unwashed, and his growth of stubble itched. But right now none of this was important. Nothing mattered except answers to all the questions he and Naomi wanted to put to Dettore. Answers that until today they had both despaired of ever getting.

And, even more importantly, finding some way to reach into their children's hearts and persuade them to come home. Which would involve putting Dettore's word to the test, to see if he really would allow them to do this.

The silence was spooky. It was like being in a ghost city. Or being back on the cruise ship, he thought. 'Why do you have all this camouflage on the buildings – and this green paint on the runway and the paths, Dr Dettore?' he asked. 'Why do you want to be invisible?'

'What are you scared of, Dr Dettore?' Naomi asked.

Dettore strode on, taking easy, confident strides, like a lion who knows he has no predator. The king of the jungle, king of this island, invincible. John loathed him more with every passing second. He loathed the man's conceit, loathed him for the way he had deceived Naomi and himself, for destroying their lives, for taking their children. And yet despite all this, the scientist in John could not help being awed by aspects of the man.

Dettore stopped and opened his arms expansively at their surroundings. 'Let me tell you the point. Do you remember the Inquisitions in France, Italy and Spain, which terrorized free-thinking people for five centuries in the Middle Ages? Do you remember an Italian scientist called Galileo – a professor of mathematics at Pisa? He improved the telescope to the point where he was the first human to see the moons of Jupiter? In 1632, he published a book backing up Copernicus's theory that the earth rotated around the sun, rather than the reverse. The Inquisition made him recant this absurd theory – or be put to death.'

Neither John nor Naomi said anything.

'Just like Hitler and Stalin, the Inquisition was indiscriminate. It put to death the intelligentsia along with the proletariat. Yet somehow, the Inquisition got away with it, because it was all done in the name of God. Religion gave it a cachet, and a legitimacy.' Dettore paused, looking hard at John and Naomi for some moments. 'You wonder why we need to be in hiding here – the reason is simple. Sooner or later a bunch of religious crazies with ideas that have not moved on since the dark ages would have hunted me down and killed me. If not the Disciples of the Third Millennium, then another group.'

'And you wonder why?' John said. 'You're using child labour and genetic engineering and it surprises you that people are against you?'

Dettore pointed up at the sky. 'There are satellites up

there, photographing every inch of our planet, every hour, John and Naomi. American, Russian, Chinese and other nations, also. They're looking for anything out of the norm, new structures, people in places that were once unoccupied. Everything gets logged, examined, questioned.'

'Is that why your entire transportation system is underground?' John asked.

'Of course. We're invisible here and we intend to remain that way until it is no longer necessary.'

'Which will be when?' said Naomi.

'When the world is ready.'

'For what?' she demanded.

'For the kind of wisdom and humanity we're developing here. None of the kids here will grow up to be the kind of man who will put a bomb full of nails in a crowded London pub. Or Semtex in a car in a street market full of women and children. Do you both want to allow this mayhem of so-called *civilization* to go on and on and on, for ever? The world has lurched from the clutches of one fanatic or despot to another. Nero, Attila the Hun, Napoleon, Stalin, Hitler, Hirohito, Mao Tse Tung, Pol Pot, Saddam Hussein, Milosevic, Bin Laden, Mugabe. Where is it going to end? In some big party with balloons and crackers and everyone shaking hands and saying, *Look, OK, guys, sorry, we've had a lousy few thousand years, let's all be friends now so our kids can have a nice future?* I don't think so.'

'Who's financing all this, Dr Dettore?' John asked, unmoved.

Without slowing his pace, he answered, 'Concerned people. Philanthropists around the globe who don't want to see civilization fall back into the hands of religious fanaticism and despots, the way it was in the dark ages.

Who want to secure a future for humankind based on solid science.'

'I want to know something,' Naomi said. 'Why, when we came to you wanting a boy, did you deceive us and give us twins?'

Dettore stopped and faced them. 'Because you would never have understood. Simple as that.'

'Understood what?' John said.

He looked at each of them in turn. 'Your child would have been lonely without someone to share his superior intellect with. He would have felt like a freak among other kids. By having two, they were able to bond and see the world clearly, in perspective.'

'Don't you think that should have been our decision?' Naomi said.

'I didn't feel you were ready to understand,' he replied.

John felt his anger rising. 'That is an incredibly arrogant thing to say.'

Dettore shrugged. 'The truth is often hard to accept.'

'I can't believe what I'm hearing. We agreed – you, Naomi and I – a list of enhancements for our child. How much more did you add that you never told us about?'

'Important things that I felt you were overlooking.'

'And what the hell gave you the right to do that?' Naomi said, her voice rising.

'Let's go back to my office,' Dettore said. 'You look hot and uncomfortable. You guys need a shower and a change of clothes, and some food and some rest. You've had a long journey and you're tired. Let's get you freshened up and rested, and we'll talk more.'

'I don't need to freshen up,' Naomi said. 'I don't want to rest. I want to get on a plane back home with my children. That's all I need. Don't *tell* me what I need.'

Dettore's expression hardened. 'There are a load of smart people here, Naomi. All of us with one common interest: the future of the human species.' He turned to John, then Naomi again, to include both of them. 'We have three Nobel Prize-winning scientists and eight McArthur Award-winners here. And twenty-eight scientists who have been put forward for Nobel Prizes. I'm telling you this because I don't want you to think I'm just a lone charlatan working in the dark here, or some kind of lone crazy voice in the scientific wilderness.'

'You're entitled to whatever vision you want, Dr Dettore,' Naomi said. 'But you are not entitled to abduct children and turn them against their parents.'

'Then, for the moment, we'll have to agree to disagree.' He smiled, and walked on.

John followed him, angry at Dettore, angry at himself for feeling so damned helpless and useless here, his brain churning. Then he heard a thud.

He looked up. For an instant he thought part of the back of Dettore's head had been blown off; something fell away from it, taking a chunk of hair and skin with it. A lump of rock, he realized, turning for an instant in horror to Naomi, who was standing, her arms outstretched, with an expression of grim satisfaction on her face.

Then he turned back to Dettore, who sagged onto his knees, almost in slow motion, then fell headlong forward and lay still. For an instant the exposed patch on his head looked pale grey, like cracked slate, then blood rapidly began covering it over and spreading into the hair beyond.

126

Naomi bolted, sprinting back down the path. The fading slap of her shoes, the drumming of his own heart and the roar of panic in John's ears were the only sounds.

John ran over to Dettore and knelt beside him. He stared at the blood spreading across the collar and shoulders of Dettore's jumpsuit. Panic spread deeper through him.

He scrambled to his feet and ran after her. When he was a few steps behind, he called out, 'Naomi! Stop! Stop! Where are you going?'

'To get my children,' she said without turning her head.

He grabbed her arm and jerked her to a halt. 'Naomi! Hon!'

She stared at him with eyes that were barely focusing. She was shaking, hysterical. 'Let me go!'

'You might have killed him.'

'I'll kill you, too,' she said. 'I'll kill anyone who tries to stop me taking my children home.'

John looked over his shoulder at the distant, motionless figure. Then up at the windows of the buildings all around. Any moment doors would open and people would be running towards them. They had to get out of sight, that was their first priority. Beyond that, he had no thoughts, no ideas, no plan. All his instincts told him that Dettore had been their one lifeline here. This wasn't about taking their children home any more. It was about trying to survive.

Frantically, he looked around, trying to get his bearings. He stared at the red-brick structure that he thought Dettore had said, just a few minutes before, housed the Department of Astrophysics. Then at another housing the Library and General Research Facility. As his eyes roamed from building to building, he simply had no idea which was the one they'd seen Luke and Phoebe in – it could have been any of two dozen different ones. A voice inside his head screamed:

Get inside! Got to get inside! Out of the open! Under cover!

Shelter!

Hide!

The Department of Astrophysics was the nearest. Holding Naomi's hand, he dragged her, half running, half stumbling towards it.

Where the hell's the door?

They ran along the front of the building, past huge darkened-glass windows, past flower beds and a pond, and around the side. A small glass door in front of them was marked FIRE EXIT ONLY. He tried to pull it open, but could get no purchase; there was no handle on the outside, no gap big enough to get his fingers inside.

'Are they in here?' Naomi said. 'Is this where Luke and Phoebe are?'

'Maybe. We'll start here.'

She was sobbing. 'John, I want my children. I want Luke and Phoebe.'

'We'll find them.' He dragged her further along and round to the far side, and realized this must be the main entrance. Ahead of them two children, a boy and a girl of about six, walking hand-in-hand in their white outfits, skipped up some steps then carried on straight towards a window in the centre of the building. When they were a couple of yards from it, a section of the glass rose, then dropped seamlessly behind them after they had entered.

John led Naomi towards the window, and the section rose up for them as they approached. They went through into the air-conditioned chill of a huge, deserted atrium with a marble floor, and a massive Foucault pendulum suspended from the ceiling. It felt like the lobby of a grand hotel, except there was no front desk, no staff. Just twin elevator doors on the far side. The children had disappeared.

Where?

The elevators? It was the only possible place they could have gone, John thought, and, still holding Naomi's hand, dragged her over. He couldn't see any buttons. He looked up and down. Nothing, no apparent means of summoning the damned thing. *There must be!* He turned and looked behind them. The place was still deserted. There must be a staircase, a fire exit route. Moments later there was a chime, and a light went on above the right-hand elevator door.

John tightened his grip on Naomi's hand. The door opened.

The car was empty. They went in; John looked at the panel and pressed the bottom button.

Then from across the atrium he heard a shout. Two figures in white jumpsuits, teenagers, were running across the floor towards them. More were coming in through the glass door.

Panicking, John stabbed the button again, then again. The first two were getting nearer, yards away. Then the doors closed.

Furious banging on them.

Naomi was staring at him like a zombie. The car started sinking. John pulled out his phone, stared futilely at the display. As before, it said, NO SIGNAL.

There had to be some means of getting through to the outside world. There had been a phone in Dettore's office, must be satellite phones around. There must be supplies coming in by plane or boat, or both; there had to be some way of getting word out, or getting away from here.

How?

The doors opened onto a deserted monorail platform. He pulled Naomi out, looked right and left. Two dark tunnels. A narrow gridded inspection sidewalk went into the tunnel in both directions. He pulled her to the left, into the tunnel, running as fast as he could into the darkness.

They covered a few hundred yards, then heard shouting behind them. He turned and saw several flashlight beams following them. Naomi stumbled, recovered. There was light ahead of them, a long way in the distance. The flashlights behind them were getting closer. His lungs were aching, Naomi was silent, following him, clinging to his hand. He ran even faster now.

The light ahead was getting closer. The voices behind them getting closer, too. Gaining on them. They burst out of the darkness onto another platform. An elevator door, and beside it, an emergency exit door. He pulled it and led her through into a dimly lit concrete stairwell that only went up.

He pounded up the stairs, two, sometimes three at a time; Naomi, close to collapse, tripped repeatedly so that he was almost dragging her up by her hand. He could hear voices at the bottom. Then they reached the top and a door with a push-bar. He jerked the bar and shoved the door, and they both stumbled forward into a long, brightly lit corridor with a tiled floor and walls that looked like they were made of brushed aluminium. There was a double door with two glass portholes, like a hospital ER entrance, at the far end.

They raced down towards it, but a few yards before they reached it, two figures came through.

Luke and Phoebe.

More small figures began crowding in behind them.

127

Luke spoke sharply. 'You have done a terrible thing, Parent People. You have brought your old ways to this place. You have shamed us. You have only been here a few hours and already you have sullied the place. No one has ever been violent on this island. The New People here didn't even know what violence is. Now you've shown them. Are you proud of that?'

'We . . .' John started to reply, not sure what he was going to say, then his voice trailed away.

Naomi was trembling in shock at what she had done. 'Where are we?' she asked in a faltering voice. 'What is this place? What is going on?'

'You are not capable of understanding even if we were to explain it to you.'

'You brought us into the world,' Luke said. 'Would you like to tell us why you did that?'

'Yes, what exactly was your agenda?' Phoebe added.

'We wanted to have a healthy child, one that did not have the disease genes your mother and I were both carrying – that was our agenda, nothing else,' John said, scarcely believing he was having this conversation.

'Fine, here we are, you succeeded. We are healthy,' Luke said. 'Would you like to see our medical records? They are really quite exemplary. We are very much healthier than the world you have brought us into.'

Then Phoebe said, 'Everyone seems to be afraid of genetics. We read that people are saying that Mother

Nature isn't great, but she's better than the alternatives. Oh yes, hallo, what planet are you on? Mother Nature has dominated *Homo sapiens* since the species first appeared five hundred thousand years ago. And what a screw up! If Mother Nature was a political leader, she should have been executed for genocide! If she was chief executive officer of a multinational company, she'd have been fired for incompetence. Why not give science a chance at the helm? Is science, in the right hands, going to make an even bigger mess?'

'What do you call *the right hands*?' John replied.

'The man you have just tried to murder,' Luke said, staring at Naomi. 'Dr Dettore. The biggest visionary this planet has ever seen. The man you just tried to kill.'

'You need to leave now, Parent People,' Phoebe said darkly. 'Before too many people here find out what you have done. We will take you to your plane. You need to know that everything on this island is recorded. If you go now, we'll erase the tape showing you trying to commit murder, Mother, which is more than you deserve, but you are our parents . . .'

'We don't really want to kill you,' Luke said. 'That would just bring us down to your level. We want you to leave. Forget you were ever here. Forget all about us and everything you saw.'

'I can never forget you both,' Naomi said.

'Why not?' Luke replied.

Naomi blinked tears from her eyes. 'You are our children and you always will be. Our home will always be your home. Maybe, one day, when you are older you might come and visit us.' Her voice faltered. 'Perhaps you have things you'll be able to teach us.'

John nodded, then added, 'Our doors will always be

open. I just want you to understand that there will always be a home for you with us, if you ever want or need it. Always.'

'We understand you very clearly,' Phoebe said.

128

Once upon a time I nearly killed a man.

I write it this way because it makes it feel less real to me. That's one good thing about the human brain, it constantly revises the past, cutting bits here, adding bits there, presenting it in an ever more palatable way – the way we would have liked things to have been, rather than the way they really were.

Sören Kierkegaard wrote that life must be lived forwards but that it can only be understood backwards. I wind back the tape inside my head all the time. Returning to Halley's death. Returning to that decision John and I made to go to Dr Dettore's Clinic. Returning to that moment – incredible that it was eight years ago – when I was following John and Dr Dettore up the path, in the bright sunlight. That moment I knelt and picked up the rock and threw it.

I wind that tape, trying to analyse what I had intended. Did I want to kill him? Or did I just want to throw the rock for no other purpose than to vent something out of me?

There's a part of me that hopes that the latter is the truth, but my conscience tells me differently. This, as Luke and Phoebe told us, is one of the flaws of us Parent People. A flaw that defines our species. They told us that we have failed emotionally to keep pace with our advances in technology. We're a species that is on the verge of being able to travel faster than the speed of light and so much else our ancestors could never even imagine, yet hasn't learned how to deal with the hatred in our hearts. A species that can still only resolve problems by throwing rocks at each other. How can I argue against that? How can I download copies of the morning newspapers and read all the terrible stuff going on in so many places in the world and persuade my kids that no, they are wrong, we have learned to do things differently now?

This is my first diary entry in a long, long time. I just lost enthusiasm for writing it. I lost enthusiasm for everything. After years of therapy, I feel a little stronger now. Perhaps I'm slowly getting better. John and I rarely talk about it any more, as if we've made an unspoken decision to put the past behind us and concentrate only on the future.

You are taught as a child that your parents are right, that you must learn from them, and pass on that stuff, in turn, to your own children. It's a strange moment when you realize that the world is no longer as you understood it.

None of us knows what the future holds. Perhaps we'd go mad if we did. We have dreams into which we escape. Dreams that we hold in our hearts. In my dreams Halley is alive and well and growing up, and John and Halley and I do things together and are happy. We go on holidays and we visit theme parks and museums and we play in soft white sand by the ocean and we fool around and laugh a lot. And then I wake.

Sometimes when my memory is being kind to me, the rock I threw at Dr Dettore feels like a dream. But mostly I live it, every hour of every day. I take pills at night and sometimes they're my friends and they let me sleep, and if they are being really good friends to me, they let me sleep all through the night without dreaming.

Those are the rare days when I wake refreshed. When I feel there is something to look forward to. I'm sure that's when you really know you are happy – when you wake up wanting to embrace your future, rather than trying to squirm away from your past.

From time to time I Google Dr Dettore, and the names of Luke and Phoebe Klaesson. But nothing new ever comes up. To the outside world, Dr Dettore died in a helicopter crash, end of story. The mystery place that we went to remains a secret. After we returned, John spent months at his computer, on Google Earth, trying to find the island, but he never did.

The police tried, too, but they had no success either. Not that we gave them much help. We never told them Dettore was still alive. We felt that if that got out, sooner or later some fanatic group would track him down – and the lives of everyone on the island would be in danger. Despite everything, John and I do love our children. We're their parents, we always will love them. I worry about them all the time. About how they are getting on, their health, and I have this constant fear, which never goes away, that if anything were to happen to them, we would probably never know.

We made a decision not to have more children. John immersed himself in his work. I've become involved in a number of local children's charities. We have two dogs, black Labradors called Brutus and Nero. They're adorable, and good guard dogs, too. We don't feel in danger any longer, but we are still careful over security. I expect we always will be.

It is one of those rare days today, when I feel happy. Not for any reason I can define except, perhaps, because of how far the past has now receded. I came across a quotation from a book of the wisdom of American Indians, which in so many ways now sums up where John and I are, regarding Luke and Phoebe.

'Although we are in different vessels, you in your boat and we in our canoe, we share the same river of life.'

129

Mixing his drink had become John's ritual every evening when he arrived home from work. Alcohol helped him numb the pain. The heartache of the loss of his children was constantly with him, but so was another loss of something else, almost equally important to him: the passion he had once held for his work. The truth was that since leaving Dettore's island he felt, in ways he could not define, a changed man.

He kissed Naomi, poured himself a large whisky on the rocks, then went into his den and logged on to check his emails. Outside he could hear the bleating of sheep in the fields around them. Spring. New life starting over. The air was warm this evening, and the forecast was fine for the weekend. He would get the barbecue and the garden chairs and table out of the garage. Maybe this year, for a change, they would have a good summer.

Then he froze. He read the first of the new emails that had just downloaded in disbelief. Then he read it over again, before running to the door and yelling for Naomi to come in and see this.

She stood with her hands on his shoulders as he sat down in front of his computer, and they both stared silently at the words on the screen:

Arriving 15.30 tomorrow, Saturday, Gatwick Airport, North Terminal, British Airways Flt 225 from Rome. Please meet us. Your children, Luke and Phoebe.

130

Naomi clutched John. Her eyes danced with happiness, but also with a thousand questions. 'Is this real, darling? It's not a hoax?'

'It's a real email,' he replied. 'But I can't tell who sent it.'

'Can't you find out where it's from? Its source or something?'

'It's a Hotmail account. You can set one up in a couple of minutes from any internet café in the world. It won't be traceable.' He shrugged. 'Who knows if it is real – but it would be a pretty sick practical joke.'

'Do you think they're coming home? Permanently?' she asked.

'I've no idea.' He stared at the email again, reading the short message carefully. 'They'll be coming up to their twelfth birthdays. Who knows what their mindsets will be. Maybe they've outgrown the island, or perhaps they want to go to university here. Perhaps they're just curious to see us. Or maybe they've been sent to teach us some lessons about how we should be shaping the world.'

'I'll have to make the spare beds up – they'll have way outgrown their original little beds. What about food? What shall we get them?'

'We could ask them when we see them. Maybe they'd like a treat, something different to the wholesome food they'd be getting on the island. McDonald's or something?'

She kissed him on the cheek and put her arms around

him and clung to him tightly. 'God, oh God! I sooooo hope they are coming back to live with us. That we can be a family again. Wouldn't that be incredible?'

John squeezed her arm. 'Don't get your hopes up too high, we have no idea what they will be like nor what their agenda is. It's a pretty cold email. No love or kisses.'

'We never have had love of that kind, from them.'

'Exactly.'

'But I think they do love us, in their own weird way.'

John said nothing.

'Please don't let this be a hoax, John. I couldn't bear it. I'm so excited. I just can't believe it, I really can't!

'Let's see.'

She stroked his forehead. 'Aren't you just a teeny bit excited?'

'Of course I am! I guess I'm in shock. And at the same time, you know, I—'

He hesitated.

'You what?' she asked.

'I'm nervous. I don't know what to expect. Maybe they need money – isn't that why kids go and see their parents most of the time? They're getting to an age now where they probably want to start buying stuff. You know, music, clothes.'

'They're not teenagers yet,' Naomi replied.

'Dettore said they would have accelerated growth and maturity. They may still only be eleven, but my guess is they're going to look like advanced teenagers.'

Naomi stared at the bald wording of the email. 'That reads like – like we just haven't seen them for a few days. As if they've been away on holiday – it's so strange to send that and no more after eight years.'

John smiled wistfully. 'The sad thing is, I don't find it

strange at all. That's how they always were. Clearly nothing's changed in the manners department.'

'Are we even going to recognize them?'

'Of course. And, if for any reason we don't, Luke and Phoebe are sure as hell going to recognize us.'

131

Naomi gripped John's hand tightly as they crossed the walkway from the short-term car park and entered the Arrivals hall. They were thirty minutes early – as a Swede, John was always strictly punctual, and they were taking no chances today.

They were both as nervous as hell. John felt a lump in his throat and his mouth was dry. Naomi scanned the hall as they entered, just in case, by any chance, the twins had already arrived, perhaps on an earlier flight. Although of course she knew that was unlikely. She looked at the people seated in the Costa café, in the WH Smith bookstore, then all around her. Then she checked her watch: 3.02 p.m. The flight was due on time at 3.30, and they had been monitoring its progress on the Saab's computer screen. It would be a further half hour, at least, she knew from experience, before they came through – and longer if they had checked baggage.

Both of them wondered whether the children would be travelling alone or accompanied by an adult – perhaps Dettore himself?

They stopped a few yards away from the people waiting in front of the barrier that delineated the walkway out from the Arrivals doorway. Naomi was feeling almost sick with nerves and anticipation. So many questions were going through her mind. All around them stood men in suits holding placards up with names on them. Limousine and taxi drivers waiting to do pickups. She glanced at a few of the names, just in case. In case what? In case there was one for Dettore? STANNARD. MR FAISAL. FRANK NEWTON. MRS APPLETON. OSTERMANN PLC

She was shaking. Excited but scared at the same time. And impatient. Willing each slow minute to tick away. John kept looking at his watch, and whenever he did so, she looked again at hers. But mostly she kept her eyes on that exit doorway. Anxiously watching the people coming through. An efficient-looking businessman pulling a small black holdall strode past. Then an elderly Indian couple pushing a precariously loaded baggage trolley. Then a woman with twin girls, followed closely by a man who was talking to her, also pushing a trolley.

Still twenty minutes to go before they could realistically expect the children to come through.

The twenty minutes passed, followed by another ten. There was a constant stream of people coming out now, as if several flights had all come in around the same time. Another ten minutes.

'I hope to God they're coming, John.'

He nodded. Then they saw two tall figures emerge and their hopes rose. A youth in his late teens and a girl the same age. The boy was handsome, with mussed-up blond hair, the girl was slender and attractive. They were pushing a trolley stacked with expensive luggage. Both Naomi and John took a step forward. The boy put his arm around the girl and kissed her on the lips. Then the next moment the boy waved at someone in the line of waiting people and the two of them hurried over eagerly. Not their twins.

An airport worker pushed a wheelchair containing a young woman in an anorak, with her leg in a plaster cast, accompanied by another woman pushing a trolley with suitcases and skis on it. They were followed by a small

Middle-Eastern group, the women in burkas. Then, following behind them, two elderly people were being pushed in wheelchairs by airport workers. John and Naomi barely noticed them; they were intently concentrating on who would be coming next through the doorway.

The airport workers halted the wheelchairs. Each contained a small, elderly person. Both had a tiny holdall on their lap. John glanced at them. Two old men, he thought at first glance. Except then he noticed one was wearing an orange T-shirt, blue shorts and sneakers, and the other was wearing a white blouse, denim skirt and sparkly trainers. Male and female, he realized, with a sudden, sharp tug of nerves in his throat.

Their heads were disproportionately large to their tiny bodies, their craniums swollen like misshapen walnuts, the bones clearly delineated beneath the tight, uneven skin. Their eyes were all that John and Naomi could recognize. Blue protruding eyes, wide, round and staring. Both of them had half their crumbling teeth missing.

The female one was pointing at them. The two airport workers nodded and began to wheel them over to John and Naomi. Then they stopped right in front of them.

John and Naomi stared down, unsure for some moments quite what was going on. Naomi looked in horror at their pitiful faces. The faces of people in their late eighties, perhaps even older. The male had a few white wisps of hair either side of his skull. The female was completely bald.

The female looked up and gave a pitiful smile that almost broke Naomi's heart. Then the male did the same.

'Hello, Mummy. Hello, Daddy,' Luke said. His voice was thin and young, like the voice of the child he still was.

Phoebe smiled, a little sheepishly. She looked at each

of her parents in turn. 'You said we could come home, any time, that we would always be welcome.'

Naomi knelt, weeping. She hugged Phoebe, then Luke. 'Of course, my darlings. There's nothing your daddy and I would love more. Of course it's still true. Welcome home!'

John looked at the two men who were standing behind the wheelchairs. 'Do they have any luggage?'

One shook his head. 'No, no luggage. Just those little bags.'

'We don't need much,' Phoebe said. 'We won't be staying for long.'

'Why? Where are you going?' Naomi asked, faltering, through her tears.

She glimpsed John's tight, ashen face. And in the stark silence that followed, fighting back more tears, she understood.

ACKNOWLEDGEMENTS

When I began researching for this novel, a decade ago, people told me that 'designer babies' were the stuff of science fiction. Not any more . . . A decade ago a leading genetics scientist really did tell me that parents in the near future would be able to choose the level of empathy their child could experience. Do they want a sweet, gentle child, who may be trampled on by others in life? Or a tough kid, who could end up being a sociopath? Such choices are almost impossible for us to make. But that future is almost upon us.

As ever I owe a thank you to very many people, but none more so than to those who have believed in and championed this book through its very long and at times despairing journey from inception to publication. My wonderful agent, Carole Blake, who has had faith from when it was just an idea bubbling in my head. My super-star editor, Wayne Brookes, who was passionate about it long before anyone else. All those who gave me utterly invaluable critical input and editorial help, especially Anna-Lisa Davies, Susan Ansell, Susan Opie, Martin and Jane Diplock, Nicky Mitchell and my brilliant assistant, Linda Buckley.

One person, who I met by one of life's happiest chances years back when he was a Detective Inspector, Dave Gaylor – the career role-model for my Roy Grace character – has been an incredible help to me in so many ways with this book, and I owe massive thanks to him.

Very big thanks also to Steven D. Goodman, PhD, Associate Professor, Division of Biomedical Sciences, University of Southern California for so rigorously checking every biological fact, and to David J. Anderson, Seymour Benzer Professor of Biology; Investigator, Howard Hughes Medical Institute, PhD, 1983, Rockefeller University, Genetic dissection of neural circuits controlling emotional behaviours, who gave me so much material. Also a huge thank you to Dr Penelope Leach, and her definitive work *Your Baby And Child*, Robert Beard, FRCS, Anthony Kenney, FRCS, FRCOG; Paul Tanner; Raymond Kurzweil, the Cognitive Sciences Department of Sussex University, and the Rutherford Appleton Laboratory, Dave Chidley of Royal Caribbean Cruise Line, and Leif Karlsson, Master of MV Azamara Quest.

Very special thanks are due to Geoff Duffield, whose vision and passion for this book have been so instrumental in making it happen, and to the entire Macmillan team.

A huge debt as ever to Chris Webb of MacService, whose genius at fixing problems with my computer makes me wonder if he himself is a 'designer baby' instilled with technology genes!

I'm incredibly lucky to have Midas as my publicists, and no author could have a greater dream publicity team than Claire Richman, Sophie Ransom, Steven Williams and Tony Mulliken.

There were times when I thought that writing this novel was going to be too hard a task because I was tackling too complex a subject, and Helen has been tirelessly supportive, encouraging me through some of my darkest hours.

And the last words as always to the ever-cheerful Coco, lovely Phoebe and totally laid-back Oscar. They never let me put in too many hours without reminding me that there is a world out there beyond my laptop, and that we should go and take a walk in it . . .

Peter James
Sussex, England
scary@pavilion.co.uk
www.peterjames.com
Find and follow me on http://twitter.com/peterjamesuk

NOT DEAD YET

OUT NOW

Read the opening chapters of the new Roy Grace novel

from the number one bestseller PETER JAMES

1

I am warning you, and I won't repeat this warning.
Don't take the part. You'd better believe me. Take
the part and you are dead. Bitch.

2

Gaia Lafayette was unaware of the man out in the dark, in the station wagon, who had come to kill her. And she was unaware of the email he had sent. She got hate mail all the time, mostly from religious nutters or folk upset by her swearing or her provocative costumes in some of her stage acts and music videos. Those emails were screened and kept from bothering her by her trusted head of security, Detroit-born Andrew Gulli, a tough ex-cop who'd spent most of his career on close protection work for vulnerable political figures.

He knew when to be worried enough to tell his boss, and this piece of trash that had come in, on an anonymous Hotmail account, was not something he figured had any substance. His employer got a dozen like this every week.

It was 10 p.m. and Gaia was trying to focus on the script she was reading, but she couldn't concentrate. She was focused even more on the fact that she had run out of cigarettes. The sweet, but oh so dim-witted Pratap, who did all her shopping, and who she hadn't the heart to fire because his wife had a brain tumour, had bought the wrong brand. She had her limit of four cigarettes a day, and didn't actually *need* any more, but old habits die hard. She used to mainline the damned things, claiming they were essential for her famed gravelly voice. Not so many years back she'd have one before she got out of bed, followed by one burning in the ashtray while she showered. Every action accompanied by a cigarette. Now she was kicking free, but she *had* to know they were in the house. Just in case she needed them.

Like so much else she needed in life. Starting with her adoring public. Checking the count of Twitter followers and Facebook *likes*. Both were substantially up again today, each nearly a million up in the past month alone, still keeping her well ahead of both the performers she viewed as her rivals, Madonna and Lady Gaga. And she now had nearly ten million subscribers to her monthly e-newsletter. And then there were her seven homes, of which this copy of a Tuscan palazzo, built five years ago to her specification on a three-acre lot, was the largest.

The walls, mirrored full length floor-to-ceiling to create the illusion of infinite space, were decorated with Aztec art interspersed with larger-than-life posters of herself. The house, like all her others, was a catalogue of her different incarnations. Gaia had reinvented herself con-stantly throughout her career as a rock star, and more recently, two years ago at thirty-five, had started reinvent-ing herself again, this time as a movie actor.

Above her head was a huge, framed monochrome signed photo of herself in a black negligee, titled WORLD TOUR GAIA SAVING THE PLANET. Another, with her wear-ing a tank top and leather jeans, was captioned, GAIA REVELATIONS TOUR. Above the fireplace, in dramatic green was a close-up of her lips, nose and eyes – GAIA UP CLOSE AND PERSONAL.

Her agent and her manager phoned her daily, both men reassuring her just how much the world needed her. Just the way that her growing social networking base – all outsourced by her management company – reassured her, too. And at this moment, the one person in the world she cared about most – Roan, her six-year-old son – needed her just as much. He padded barefoot across the marble floor, in his Armani Junior pyjamas, his brown hair all mussed up, his face scrunched in a frown, and tapped her on the arm as she lay on the white sofa, propped against the purple velvet cushions. 'Mama, you didn't come and read me a story.'

She stretched out a hand and mussed up his hair some more. Then she put down the script and took him in her arms, hugging him. 'I'm sorry, sweetie. It's late, way past your bedtime, and Mama's really busy tonight, learning her lines. She has a really big part – see? Mama's playing Maria Fitzherbert, the mistress of an English king! King George the Fourth.'

Maria Fitzherbert was the diva of her day, in Regency England. Just like she herself was the diva of her day now, and they had something profound in common. Maria Fitzherbert spent most of her life in Brighton, in England. And she, Gaia, had been born in Brighton! She felt a connection to this woman, across time. She was born to play this role!

Her agent said this was the new *King's Speech*. An Oscar role, no question. And she wanted an Oscar oh so badly. The first two movies she had made were okay, but had not set the world on fire. In hindsight, she realized, it was because she hadn't chosen well and the scripts were – frankly – weak. This movie now could give her the critical acclaim she craved. She'd fought hard for this role. And she'd succeeded.

Hell, you had to fight in life. Fortune favoured the brave. Some people were born with silver spoons so far up their assholes they stuck in their gullets, and some, like herself, were born on the wrong side of the tracks. It had been a long journey to here, through her early days of waiting tables, and two husbands, to the place she was now at, and where she felt comfortable. Just herself, Roan and Todd, the fitness instructor who gave her great sex when she needed it and kept out of her face when she didn't, and her trusted entourage, Team Gaia.

She picked up the script and showed him the white and the blue pages. 'Mama has to learn all this before she flies to England.'

'You promised.'

'Didn't Steffie read to you tonight?' Steffie was the nanny.

He looked forlorn. 'You read better. I like it when you read.'

She looked at her watch. 'It's after ten o'clock. Way past your bedtime!'

'I can't sleep. I can't sleep unless you read to me, Mama.'

She tossed the script on to the glass coffee table, lifted him down and stood up. 'Okay, one quick story. Okay?'

His face brightened. He nodded vigorously.

'Marla!' she shouted. 'Marla!'

Her assistant came into the room, cellphone pressed to her ear, arguing furiously with someone about what sounded like the seating arrangements on a plane. The one extravagance Gaia refused to have was a private jet, because of her concerns over her carbon footprint.

Marla was shouting. Didn't the fuckwit airline know who Gaia was? That she could fucking make or break them? She was wearing glittery Versace jeans tucked into black alligator boots, a thin black roll-neck and a gold neck chain carrying the flat gold globe engraved *Planet Gaia*. It was exactly the same way her boss was dressed tonight. Her hair mirrored her boss's, too: blonde, shoulder length, layered in a sharp razor cut with a care-fully spaced and waxed fringe.

Gaia Lafayette insisted that all her staff had to dress the same way – following the daily emailed instructions of what she would be wearing, how her hair would be. They had, at all times, to be an inferior copy of herself.

Marla ended the call. 'Sorted!' she said. 'They've agreed to bump some people off the flight.' She gave Gaia an angelic smile. 'Because it's *you*!'

'I need cigarettes,' Gaia said. 'Wanna be an angel and go get me some?'

Marla shot a surreptitious glance at her watch. She had a date tonight and was already two hours late for him, thanks to Gaia's demands – nothing unusual. No previous personal assistant had lasted more than eighteen months before being fired, yet, amazingly, she was entering her third year. It was hard work and long hours, and the pay wasn't great, but the work experience was to die for, and although her boss was tough, she was kind. One day she'd be free of the chains, but not yet. 'Sure, no problem,' she said.

'Take the Merc.'

It was a balmy hot night. Gaia was smart enough to understand the small perks that went a long way.

'Cool! I'll be right back. Anything else?'

Gaia shook her head. 'You can keep the car for the night.'

'I can?'

'Sure, I'm not going anywhere.'

Marla coveted the silver SL55 AMG. She looked for-ward to driving the fast bends along Sunset to the con-venience store. Then to picking up Jay in it afterwards. Who knew how the night might turn out? Every day working for Gaia was an adventure. Just as every night recently, since she had met Jay, was too! He was a budding actor, and she was determined to find a way, through her connection with Gaia, to help him get a break.

She did not know it, but as she walked out to the Mercedes, she was making a grave mistake.

3

Thirty minutes earlier, the valium had started kicking in as he set off from Santa Monica, calming him. The coke he had snorted in a brief pit stop in the grounds of UCLA in Brentwood, fifteen minutes ago, was giving him energy, and the swig of tequila he took now, from the bottle on the passenger seat beside him, gave him an extra boost of courage.

The '97 Chevy was a rust bucket, and he drove slowly because the muffler, which he couldn't afford to fix, was shot, and he didn't want to draw attention to himself with its rumbling blatter. In the darkness, with its freshly sprayed coat of paint, which he had applied last night in the lot of the deserted auto wash where he worked, no one would see quite how much of a wreck the car was, he figured.

The tyres were totally bald in parts, and he could barely afford the gas to get across town. Not that the rich folk around here, in Bel Air, would have any concept of what it meant or felt like to be poor. Behind the high hedges and electric gates were huge mansions, sitting way back, surrounded by manicured lawns and all the garden toys of the rich and successful. The *haves* of LA. Some contrast with the *have-nots*, like the decrepit rented bungalow in the skanky part of Santa Monica he shared with Dana. But that was about to change. Soon she was going to get the recognition she had long deserved. Then they might be rich enough to buy a place like the ones around here.

The occupants of half the homes he passed by were named on the copy of the *Star Maps*, so it was easy to figure out who was who. It sat, crumpled and well-thumbed, beside him, beneath the half-empty tequila bottle. And there was one sure way to cruise the streets of Bel Air without drawing attention to yourself from the infestation of police and private security patrols. Hey, he was an actor, and actors were chameleons, blending into their roles. Which was why he was dressed in a security guard uniform, driving right along the outside perimeter of Gaia Lafayette's estate, passing the dark, fortress-like gates in a gleaming Chevy station-wagon emblazoned with large blue and red letters: BEL-AIR-BEVERLY PRIVATE SECURITY SERVICES – ARMED RESPONSE. He had applied the wording, from decals, himself.

The arrogant bitch had totally ignored his email. It had been announced in all the Hollywood trade papers last week that she had boarded the project. She was going to be playing Maria Fitzherbert – or *Mrs* Fitzherbert as the woman had been known to the world – mistress of the Prince of Wales of England and secretly married to him. The marriage was never formally approved because she was a Catholic, and had the marriage been ratified, then her husband could never have become King George IV.

It was one of the greatest love stories in the British monarchy. And in the opinion of the showbiz gossip websites, one of the greatest screen roles ever to have been offered.

Every actress in the world, of the right age, was after it. It had *Oscar potential* written all over it. And Gaia was so not suitable, she would make a total screw-up. She was just a rock star, for God's sake! She wasn't an actress. She hadn't been to drama school. She hadn't struggled for years to get an agent, to get noticed by the players in this city who mattered. All she had done was sing second-rate songs, peel off her clothes, flaunt her body, and sleep with the right people. Suddenly she decides she's an actress!

In taking this part, she had screwed a lot of genuinely talented actresses out of one of the best roles of the past decade.

Like Dana Lonsdale.

And she just did not have any right to do that. Gaia didn't need the money. She didn't need to be any more famous than she already was. All she was doing now was feeding her greed and vanity. Taking bread out of everyone else's mouth to do that. Someone had to stop her.

He patted the pistol jammed in his pocket, uneasily. He'd never fired a gun in his life. The goddamn things made him nervous. But sometimes you had to do what you believed was right.

It was his pop's gun. He'd found it beneath the bed in the old man's trailer, after he had died. A Glock. He didn't even know the calibre, but had managed to identify it, from comparisons on the internet, as a .38. It had a loaded magazine of eight bullets, and on the floor beside the gun he had found a small carton containing more.

At first, he had planned to try to sell the thing, or even just throw it away. And right now he wished he had binned it. But he couldn't. It was there, in his home, like an ever-present reminder from his father. That the only way to stop injustices was to do something about them.

And tonight the time had come. He was intending to stop a big injustice.

Oh yes.

4

Like many farmers, early morning was Keith Winter's favourite time of the day. He liked to be up before the rest of the world, and he particularly loved this time of year, early June, when the sun rose before 5 a.m.

Although, on this particular day, he walked out of his house with a heavy heart, and crossed the short distance to the chicken shed with leaden steps.

He considered Lohmann Browns to be the best layers, which was the reason he had 32,000 of this particular breed of hens. By looking after them and nurturing them carefully, free range, during their short lives, the way he did here at Stonery Farm, he could get their eggs to taste consistently better than any of his rivals.

He kept the birds in humane, healthy surroundings, gave them all the space they needed, and fed them on his secret diet of wheat, oil, soya, calcium, sodium and a programme of vitamins. Despite the fact that his hens were aggressive in nature, and cannibals if given the chance, he was fond of them in the way that all good farmers cared for the animals that gave them their livelihood.

He housed them in a dry, clean, modern single-storey building, with a large outdoor run, that stretched out for over one hundred yards across the remote East Sussex hilltop property. Alongside were shiny steel silos containing the grain feed. At the far end were two lorries that had arrived a short while ago, at this early hour. A tractor was parked near by and sundry agricultural equipment, a rusting shipping container, pallets and sections of railing lay haphazardly around. His Jack Russell bounded around in search of an early rabbit.

Despite the strong breeze coming in off the English Channel, five miles to the south, Keith could feel the approach of summer in the air. He could smell it in the dry grass and dusty soil and the pollen that gave him hay fever. But although he loved the summer months, the advent of June was always a time of mixed emotions for him, because all his cherished hens would be gone, to end up in markets, with their final destinations being as nuggets, or soup, or ready-to-eat chicken dishes.

Most farmer acquaintances he talked to considered their hens to be nothing more than egg-laying machines, and in truth his wife Linda thought he was a little nuts the way he became so fond of these dumb creatures. But he couldn't help it; he was a perfectionist, obsessive about the quality of his eggs and his birds, constantly experimenting with their diet and supplements, and forever working on their accommodation to make it as conducive as possible for laying. Some eggs were trundling out of the conveyor belt into the grading machine, as he entered. He picked one large sample up, checked it for blemishes and colour consistency, tapped the shell for thickness and set it down again, satisfied. It trundled on past a stack of empty egg-cartons and out of sight.

A tall, solidly built sixty-three-year-old, with the youthful face of a man who has retained all his enthusiasm for life, Keith Winter was dressed in an old white T-shirt, blue shorts, and stout shoes with grey socks. The airy interior of the shed was partitioned into two sections. He entered the right-hand section now, into an echoing cacophony of noise, like the incoherent babble of a thousand simultaneous cocktail parties. He had long got used to, and barely even noticed, the almost overpowering reek of ammonia from the hen droppings, which fell through slats in the gridded metal floor into the deep sump below.

As one particularly aggressive hen pecked, painfully, at the hairs on his leg, he stared along the length of the shed, at the sea of brown and white creatures with their red crests, all strutting around in a busy manner, as if they had important engagements awaiting them. The shed was already starting to thin out, and large areas of the gridding were visible. The catchers had started early this morning, nine workers from Eastern Europe, mostly Latvian and Lithuanian, in their protective clothing and face masks, grabbing the hens, carrying them out through the doors at the far end and placing them in specially designed cages in the lorries.

The process would take all day, at the end of which the shed would be empty, leaving just the bare grid. A team from a specialist company would then come in to lift up the grid slats and remove the year's four-foot-deep collection of droppings with a mechanical bobcat.

Suddenly, he heard a shout from the far end, and saw one of the workers running towards him, dodging through the hens, his face mask removed. 'Mr Boss!' he shouted urgently at Keith, in broken English, with a look of panic on his face. 'Mr Boss, sir! Something not right. Not good. Please you come have look!'

5

The electric gates were opening!

Shit!

He was so not expecting this. He was jumpy, his thoughts all over the place. And he remembered he had forgotten to take his medication today; the one that kept the insides of his head all cohesive. Who was coming out? Probably a change of security guards, he thought, but this was too good an opportunity to miss. Just in case it was the bitch herself! She was known to like going out on her own. Although most of the time when she went jogging, according to the press, she had more security guards around her than the President of the USA.

He braked hard, switched off the Chevy's engine and pulled the gun out of the front pocket of his pants. He stared at the gates. At the blazing headlights of a car at the bottom of a winding drive, waiting for the gap to be big enough to drive through and out into the street.

He sprinted across the road and in through the gates. He saw the Mercedes halted, waiting. Smelled its exhaust mingled with the scent of freshly mown grass. Music pounded from its stereo, a Gaia song!

How sweet was that! Listening to her own music in her last few moments of life! She would die listening to it! How poetic was that?

The roof was down. Gaia was driving! She was alone!

I warned you, bitch.

The big Mercedes engine rumbled away, a steady,

584

musical boom-boom-boom. A gleaming metal beast waiting for the driver to press the pedal and thunder forward into the night. The gates continued opening, jerkily, the right-hand one faster than the left.

In a clumsy, fumbling movement, despite all his rehearsals, he flipped off the safety catch of the Glock. Then he stepped forward. 'I warned you, bitch!' he said. He said it loud, so she could hear. He saw her stare at him out of the shadows of the cockpit, like she was full of questions.

He had the answer in his shaking hand.

He saw the expression of fear on her face as he came closer.

But this was not right, he knew. He should turn away, forget it, run. Run home? Run home a failure?

He pulled the trigger and there was a much louder explosion than he had imagined. The gun jerked as if trying to break free of his hand, and he heard a thud, as if the bullet had hit something in the distance. She was staring at him wide-eyed in terror. Not a scratch on her. He had missed.

He aimed again, pointing the gun closer at her. She raised her hands in front of her face as he fired again. This time a piece of something flew off the back of her head and some of her hair stood up, in a row of spikes. He fired again, straight into her forehead and a small, dark hole appeared in the centre. She slumped back, quivering like a landed fish that had been hit several times with a hammer, her eyes still staring at him. Dark liquid leaked from the hole and ran down and along the bridge of her nose. 'You should have listened,' he said. 'You should have obeyed me.'

Then he turned and ran away, back to his car, in a daze.

6

Gaia was coming to Brighton! The icon coming back to the city where she was born. Brighton's most famous living star was returning home to play Brighton's most famous historical female. It was a match made in heaven. A dream for Gaia.

And an even bigger dream for Anna Galicia. Her biggest fan.

Her number one fan!

Only Anna knew the real reason why Gaia was coming here. It was to be with her! The signals had all been very clear.

Unequivocal.

'She's arriving next week, Diva, what do you think of that?'

The cat stared at her without any expression she could read.

The star of stars was arriving next week. Anna would be there at the hotel to greet her in person. Finally, after years of adoring her, and of communicating with each other from afar, she would have the chance to meet her. Perhaps touch her hand. Even, if things went really well, she might be invited into her suite, to drink cocktails with her – and then?

Of course you could never tell whether Gaia was into men or women at any given time. She flaunted each new relationship openly. Going through lover after lover, in search of – *the one*! She had been married twice, to men, but that was a long time ago. Anna followed her life online, on television, in newspapers and magazines. And she and Gaia had been flirting secretly with each other for years in code. Their own secret code that Gaia used as her emblem on all her merchandise. A tiny, furtive fox.

Secret fox!

Gaia had been sending more and more signals to her in recent weeks. Anna had the evidence stacked in neat piles of newspapers and magazines neatly laid out, each individually protected in a cellophane folder, on the table in front of her.

She had rehearsed that moment when they would finally meet a million times over, in her mind. Struggled with her doubts. Maybe start with asking for her autograph to break the ice? This wouldn't be too much to ask for her number one fan, would it?

Of course not.

Secret fox!

Gaia was famed for adoring her fans. And none was as devoted as herself. She had spent her entire inheritance of her late mother's house, and on top of that, almost every penny she had ever earned collecting her memorabilia.

Anna had always bought the best seats at Gaia's concerts when she had performed in England. She had made sure she was first in line, either in person, or on the internet. She had secured a front row ticket for every single night Gaia had performed in her smash hit West End musical, *Sainted!* – the life of Mother Teresa.

And of course she always sent Gaia an apologetic email if she was going to be unable to attend because she had not been able to secure tickets. Wishing her well. Hoping the evening would be fine without her. And of course, the sign.

Secret fox!

Anna sat, dreamily, in the upstairs room of her little house in Peacehaven, close to Brighton. In her *shrine*. The *Gaia Museum*! If she breathed deeply – really deeply – ignoring the smells of dried-out cardboard and paper and plastic and polish, she believed she could still detect Gaia's perspiration and perfume from the costumes her idol had worn at concerts, which she had bought at charity auctions.

Every inch of wall space was covered in images and souvenirs of Gaia. Autographed posters, glass cabinets, shelving stacked with her CDs, a silver balloon which she kept continually inflated, printed with the words GAIA INNER SECRETS TOUR which she had bought two months ago when the singer had last been in the UK. Framed tickets of every Gaia concert around the world she had ever attended, concert tour schedules, bottles of her health-giving mineral water, and a treasured collection of her personalized monogrammed coat hangers.

Several headless mannequins stood around the room, each wearing a Gaia dress she had bought at online auctions, and encased in transparent covers to protect them – and above all, to preserve the scent and bodily smells of the icon, who had once worn them on stage. More items of Gaia's clothing lay, in labelled boxes, wrapped in acid-free tissue paper.

There was also a treasured fly-fishing rod that Gaia had been photographed using for one of her GREAT OUTDOORS GAL posters, that Anna had lovingly framed, with the rod beside it. The rod reminded Anna of her father, who used to take her fishing when she was very young. Before he'd abandoned her and her mother.

She sat, sipping from a Martini glass the Gaia special cocktail she had lovingly mixed from the recipe Gaia had published – a mojito, with loganberries added for health-giving properties and guarana for energy – while listening to her idol's greatest hit playing at full blast, 'Here To Save The Planet Together!'

She raised the glass in a toast to one of her favourite images of all, the close-up of the icon's lips, nose and eyes, titled GAIA UP CLOSE AND PERSONAL.

Diva, her small Burmese cat, walked away from her, back arched as if in anger. Sometimes Anna wondered if she was jealous of Gaia. Then she turned back to the cuttings on the table and stared at one, the Spotted section of *Heat* magazine. It was a photo of Gaia, in black jeans and top, shopping in Beverly Hills, in Rodeo Drive. Beneath was the caption:

Gaia shopping for new movie role?

She smiled excitedly. Black! Gaia had put that colour on just for her!

I love you, Gaia, she thought. I love you so much. I know you already know that! And of course, soon I will tell you in person, face to face here in Brighton. Next week. Just five days' time.

Please be wearing black then, too.

Secret fox!

7

The partially complete skeleton lay on the steel table, bathed in the glare of the overhead lights of the post-mortem room. Detective Superintendent Roy Grace stared down at the skull, its creepy rictus grin like a final Parthian shot of mockery. *Goodbye cruel world, you can't hurt me any more! I'm gone! I'm out of here!*

Grace was eight weeks shy of his fortieth birthday, and in his twenty-first year with Sussex Police. Just under five feet eleven inches tall, he kept his figure in shape by relentless exercise. His fair hair was cut short and gelled, thanks to his styling guru, Glenn Branson, and his nose, squashed and kinked after being broken in a scrap when he'd been a beat copper, gave him the air, on first acquaintance, of a retired prize fighter. His wife, Sandy, now missing for almost a decade, once told him he had eyes like Paul Newman. He'd liked that a lot, but had never quite believed it. He just considered himself a regular guy, unexceptional, doing a job he loved. Although, despite his years working on homicides, human skulls always spooked him.

Most police officers claimed they got used to dead bodies, in any form, and that nothing bothered them, except for children. But every body he encountered still bothered Grace, even after all his years in this job. Because every corpse was once a person loved by their family, their friends, their lover, however fleetingly for some tragic people that might have been.

At the start of his career he had promised himself that

he would never turn cynical. Yet for some of his colleagues, becoming a cynic, alongside gallows humour, was their emotional carapace. Their way of staying sane in this job.

All the dead man's component parts that they'd recovered so far had been neatly and precisely laid out by the forensic archaeologist, Joan Major. It was like a flat-packed piece of furniture that had arrived from a DIY store with some key bits missing, he thought, suddenly and irreverently.

Operation Violin, on which he was the Senior Investigating Officer, was winding down. It was the investigation into two revenge murders and an abduction. Their prime suspect, who had been identified by New York detectives as a known Mafia contract killer, had disappeared. It was possible he had drowned attempting to avoid arrest, but equally likely, in Grace's view, he had left the country and could now be anywhere in the world, under one of the host of aliases he was known to use – or, more probably, a new one.

Nearly four weeks on from the suspect's disappearance, *Operation Violin* had moved into *slow time*. Back on the roster as Duty SIO for this week, Roy Grace had stood down most of his team, retaining just a small workforce to liaise with the US. But there was one more element to the operation that remained – and lay in front of him now. And time didn't get much slower than for fully decomposed, and picked clean, skeletal remains. It had taken the best part of a week for the Specialist Search Unit's team to cover every inch of the massive tunnel and surrounding inspection shafts, and to recover the remains, some of which had been scattered over a wide area by rodents.

The Home Office pathologist, Dr Frazer Theobald, had done much of his painstaking post-mortem in situ, before the remains were brought here last night, without being able to come to any conclusions as to the cause of death. He had departed a few minutes ago. Without any flesh or body fluids, with the absence of any signs of damage to either the skull or the bones, such as from a heavy instrument or a knife or a bullet, the chances of finding the cause of death were slim.

Several members of the investigating team remained in the room, gowned up like himself in green pyjamas. Cleo Morey, Grace's fiancée, thirty-two weeks pregnant, was the Senior Anatomical Pathology Technician, as the Chief Mortician was officially termed. Her green PVC apron lay draped over the bulge of their baby, as she slid a body wrapped in white plastic sheeting out of a door in the floor-to-ceiling bank of refrigerators, eased it on to a trolley and wheeled it through into another section of the room, to prepare it for a post-mortem.

Philip Keay, the Coroner's Officer, a tall, lean man, with swarthy good looks beneath short dark hair and bushy eyebrows, remained dutifully present, although engrossed at this moment with his BlackBerry.

This stage of the investigation, which was focused on trying to establish the identity of the dead man, was being led by Joan Major, a pleasant-looking woman, with long brown hair and fashionably modern glasses, who had a quietly efficient manner. Grace had worked with her several times in the past, and he was always impressed by her skills. Even to his experienced eye, all skeletons looked much the same. But to Joan Major, each was as individual as a fingerprint.

She dictated into her machine, quietly but clearly enough so that anyone who wanted to listen, could. She began with the skull.

'Prominent brow ridges. Sloping forehead. Rounded superior orbit. Large mastoid process. Extended posterior zygomatic arch. Prominent nuchal crest.'

Then she moved on to the pelvis. 'Narrow sciatic notch. Oval obturator foramen. Pubic bone shorter. Narrow sub-pubic angle. Subpubic concavity absent. Sacrum curved.'

Roy Grace listened intently, although much of what she said was too technical for him to grasp. He was tired and stifled a yawn, glancing at his watch. It was 11.45 a.m., and he could do with another coffee. He'd been up late last night, playing in his weekly boys' poker game – where he'd ended forty pounds up. It had been an exhausting few weeks, and he was looking forward to having a curry with Cleo tonight, and kicking back, watching some Friday night junk television, ending, as they usually did, falling asleep watching their favourite talk show host, Graham Norton. And, glorious thought, they had no plans for the weekend. He was particularly looking forward to some time alone with Cleo, enjoying those precious last few weeks before, as he had been warned by his colleague Nick Nicholl who had recently become a father, their lives changed for ever. Originally, they had hoped to have their wedding before the baby was born, but the process for having Sandy declared legally dead, and work, had got in the way of that. Now they had to make new plans.

He also needed the breathing space, after the past hectic weeks, to focus on the vast bundle of trial documents of a snuff movie murder case involving a particularly nasty specimen of humanity he'd arrested, Carl Venner, whose trial was listed to come up at the Old Bailey in the next couple of weeks.

He turned his focus back to the forensic archaeologist. But within a few minutes, although he tried not to be, inevitably he was distracted by Cleo. A few weeks ago she'd been in hospital with internal bleeding. She had been warned not to do any heavy lifting, and it worried him to see her now, removing the body and rolling it on the trolley. Working in a mortuary, it was inevitable you would have to lift things. He was scared for her, because he loved her so much. Scared, because as the consultant had warned, with a second bleed her life could be in jeopardy as much as their baby's.

He watched her stop the trolley alongside the naked cadaver of an elderly woman she had just finished preparing. The skull cap had been removed, and her brain lay on a Formica tray above her chest. On the white wall chart above there were blank spaces for the dimensions and weight of the dead woman's internal organs. At the top, the name Claire Elford was handwritten in black marker pen.

It was a grim place to work and the job was tough. He could never fully understand its appeal to Cleo. She was a statuesque beauty, her long blonde hair clipped up, hygienically; she would have looked more at home in a smart London advertising agency or art gallery or magazine publisher – but she truly loved her job. He still could not believe his luck, that after almost ten years of hell, following Sandy's disappearance, he had found love again. And with someone so gorgeous and such fun to be with.

He used to consider that Sandy was his soulmate, despite their constant arguments. But since beginning his relationship with Cleo, the word *soulmate* had taken on a whole new meaning. He would die for Cleo, he truly would.

Then turning his focus back to the forensic archaeologist, he asked, 'Joan, can you give us any indication of his age?'

'I can't be too precise yet, Roy,' she said, moving back

to the skull and pointing. 'The presence of a third molar suggests adult. The medial clavicle fused suggests he is older than thirty.' Then she pointed at the pelvis. 'The auricual surface is phase six, which would put him between forty-five and forty-nine. The pubic symphysis is phase five – less precise, I'm afraid – which could put him anywhere from twenty-seven to sixty-six. The wear in his teeth indicates towards the upper end of this age spectrum.'

She pointed at parts of the spine. 'There are some osteophytic growths which again are suggestive of an older individual. In terms of race, the skull measurements suggest Caucasian, European – or European region – origin, but it's difficult to be more precise. As a general observation, pronounced muscle attachments, particularly noticeable in the humerus, suggest a strong, active individual.'

Grace nodded. The skeletal remains, along with a pair of partially gnawed sea boots, UK size nine, had been discovered by chance in a disused tunnel deep beneath the city's principal harbour, Shoreham. He already had a pretty good idea who this man was, and all that Joan Major had said was helping confirm this.

Six years earlier, an Estonian Merchant Navy sea captain called Andrus Kangur had disappeared after berthing his container ship loaded with timber. Kangur had been under observation by Europol for some years on suspicion of drugs trafficking. The man wasn't necessarily a great loss to the world, but that wasn't for Roy Grace to judge. He did know there was a probable motive. According to information from the Divisional Intelligence Unit, which, following a tip-off, had had the ship under surveillance from the time it entered the port, Kangur had tried to double-cross whoever was behind this cargo, and had not been too smart in his choice of whom he had screwed: a high-profile New York crime family.

From the evidence so far gathered, and from what Grace knew about the likely assailant, the unfortunate captain had been chained up in what amounted to an underground dungeon, and left to starve to death or be eaten by rats. When they had found him, all of his flesh and almost all of the sinews and his hair had gone. Most of his bones had fallen in on each other, or on to the floor, except for one set of arm bones and an intact skeletal hand, which hung from a metal pipe above him, held in place by a padlocked chain.

Suddenly, Roy's phone rang.

It was a cheery and very efficient Detective Sergeant from Eastbourne CID, Simon Bates. 'Roy, you're the Duty SIO?'

Immediately Grace's heart sank. Calls like this were never good news.

There were four Senior Investigating Officers in the Sussex CID Major Crime Branch, taking it in turns to be the Duty SIO, one week on, three weeks off. His shift was due to end at 6 a.m. on Monday. *Shit.*

'Yes I am, Simon,' he said, about as enthusiastically as a dental patient agreeing to root canal work. He suddenly heard a strange clicking sound, which lasted for a few seconds; interference from somewhere.

'We have a suspicious death at a farm in East Sussex.'

'What information can you give me?'

The clicking stopped. He listened to Bates, his heart sinking, his weekend down the khazi hours before it even begun. He exchanged a glance with Cleo, and could see, instantly, that she understood what was going on. She gave him a wan smile.

'I'm on my way,' he said.

He hung up and immediately dialled the Chief Constable's Staff Officer, Trevor Bowles, informing him that it sounded like there was another murder in the county, and that he would report back with more details later. It was important to keep the CC informed of a potential major incident, as well as the Deputy Chief Constable and the Assistant Chief Constables, to avoid the risk of their being in the embarrassing position of hearing the news third hand from the media.

Next he dialled his colleague and friend, Detective Sergeant Glenn Branson.

'Yo, old timer, what's popping?' Branson answered.

Grace grinned at his use of rap language, a recent affectation that he had picked up from a movie. 'I'll tell you what's about to be popping – your ears. We're going up a hill.'

8

I made a mistake, bitch. You were lucky. But that changes nothing. Next time I'll be the lucky one. I will get you anywhere in the world that you go.

extracts reading groups
competitions books new
discounts extracts
competitions
books new
reading groups events
events books
extracts
new reading groups
interviews
events extracts
discounts
new books events
events new
discounts extracts discounts

www.panmacmillan.com

extracts events reading groups
competitions books extracts new